Praise for the Novels of John Hands

BRUTAL FANTASIES

"One of the year's best espionage novels."
—*Daily Telegraph* (London)

"Hands builds and holds a palpable sense of tension that has all the drama and intimacy of good theater."
—*The Times* (of London)

DARKNESS AT DAWN

"Explosive."
—*The European*

"A rip-roaring read."
—*The Independent*

PERESTROIKA CHRISTI

"I could not put it down. . . . an elaborately crafted plot leads to a surprise outcome."
—*Guardian* Books of the Year

Books by John Hands

Brutal Fantasies
Perestroika Christi
Darkness at Dawn

Published by HarperPaperbacks

BRUTAL
✤-FANTASIES-✤

John Hands

HarperPaperbacks
A Division of HarperCollins*Publishers*

HarperPaperbacks
A Division of HarperCollins*Publishers*
10 East 53rd Street, New York, N.Y. 10022-5299

This is a work of fiction. The characters, incidents, and dialogues are products of the author's imagination and are not to be construed as real. Any resemblance to actual events or persons, living or dead, is entirely coincidental.

ISBN 0-06-101125-8

HarperCollins®, 🔥®, and HarperPaperbacks™
are trademarks of HarperCollins*Publishers*, Inc.

Cover illustration by Danilo Ducak

A paperback edition of this book was published in 1996 in
Great Britain by HarperCollins*Publishers*

First HarperPaperbacks printing: March 1997

Printed in the United States of America

Visit HarperPaperbacks on the World Wide Web at
http://www.harpercollins.com/paperbacks

10 9 8 7 6 5 4 3 2 1

For Paddy

We had fed the heart on fantasies
The heart's grown brutal from the fare
W. B. YEATS

Chapter ✛ One

IN MY BONES I knew this London assignment was fated.

When I walk the streets of this city memories reach out across the years and draw me to places we shared. At the Tate Gallery I don't see the Turner collection but the wonder in her eyes. At the Wigmore Hall I don't hear the Handel organ concerto but sense her stillness. On the untamed spaces of Hampstead Heath I feel her vitality. Up the lane to Hampstead village, and I peer through the window of our favorite Italian restaurant to see her waiting for me. My heart quickens. The redhead turns round, but it's a girl in her twenties. The memories, so vivid and so powerful, taunt me with what might have been and mock the emptiness of what remains. Part of me wants to seek her out, but the part of me that knows she is still married is consumed by anger at her betrayal. And this time I can't find refuge in my work.

CIA management has ended my operational career as effectively as though it had put me in mothballs. When I first came to London station we were fighting the cold war at its cutting edge, and that kept the adrenaline pumping. Today only air conditioning pumps through CIA's secure floor in the embassy's north wing. Most of the officers are following the motions of liaising with their opposite numbers in Britain's MI6, compiling reports which are processed by the senior reports officer, endorsed by the senior analyst or myself, given all possible cross references, and sent encrypted into the electronic ether to disappear without trace. Well, not quite without trace. The originating officer has added one more notch to his electronic record, one more step toward those magic numbers of fifty years of age plus twenty years of employment when he can claim the jackpot of the clandestine service's early retirement pension. And after that? A comfortable job with Fairways Corporation or one of the company's many other proprietaries, or perhaps just a log cabin by the Great Lakes or a condo in Florida. I can't believe I'm looking at a reflection of myself when I see their eyes bereft of passion. Is this all that I can look forward to for the rest of my life?

The phone rings. "Yes?"

"Hi, it's Lorna. Would it be convenient for the chief to pop in?"

Popping into my office is Lawrence Palmer's way of showing that he doesn't feel threatened by a deputy who merits his own station. But, although he's only ten yards away, his secretary has to arrange this informal meeting.

Palmer has the kind of beard which is popular with CIA officers of his generation: white, short, and all over, as though he hasn't bothered to shave for a couple of weeks. I suppose he must trim the beard to keep it that length, but there are no telltale signs, no borders with cleanly shaven upper cheeks or neck. That must take a lot of care. I wonder if it's done to camouflage a double chin. As I'm thinking about Palmer's beard I find myself feeling the flesh under my own chin, loose where once it was firm. Christ, I'm not destined for the elephant's graveyard just yet.

Palmer opens the door, smiles, and perches on the

window ledge. Following company policy of Friday dress-down to bolster flagging morale, he's wearing a brown cord suit and a bottle-green turtleneck. "I've just had an eyes only from Dave," he says. "He wants to know when you'll input your contribution to Jack's paper for Congress. Jack's desperate to head off the Bureau's attempts to take over counterterrorism overseas."

I take a file from my Pending tray, drop it on the desk, and lean back in the leather executive chair. "You're the analyst, Lawrence, so you tell me. The number of US citizens killed each year by terrorism outside the States has averaged eight in the last five years, compared with twenty two thousand five hundred regular homicides in the USA and double that number of deaths on the road. How do you massage the figures to claim a budget of three and a quarter billion dollars?"

He smiles weakly. "The terrorist is a powerful enemy. He fits deep into the American psyche: cowboys versus Indians, good guys versus bad guys. I'm sure you'll find a way."

"For Christ's sake, Lawrence, the US taxpayer is safer in Cairo or Belfast than he is walking the streets of our cities, driving on the Interstates, or visiting a Federal building in Oklahoma."

Palmer shrugs. "If you want a good angle on terrorism consult MI5. The person you need to talk to is called Maitland, Edward Maitland. He's the Brits' most experienced terrorism man, and a shrewd operator."

"Thanks," I say. For nothing. Maitland helped inflict those wounds twenty years ago. That's why I've avoided him. I'll have to see him soon, I know. But not now. Not Friday afternoon.

One benefit of this assignment, which CIA management was eager to point out, is an immaculately restored and modernized fifteen-room Georgian house, a housekeeper/cook with her own basement apartment, and a view over one of London's most exclusive garden squares. I guess it does beat living in a two-bedroom house in King's Manor, buying groceries Saturday morning from Giant Food at the McLean shopping mall, and having basket chicken and a beer in Charley's Place at Route 123 and Old Dominion Drive.

A phone rings in the drawing room. I put down the glass of Jim Beam on a Chippendale side table and pick up the handset of the internal phone. "Yes?"

"It's Dover sole this evening, Mr. Darcy. Which wine do you want?"

"There's a Chablis in the refrigerator, Imelda."

"What time do you want dinner?"

"You might as well start cooking now." Why not? There's no one else in the other fourteen rooms.

I finish the bourbon and go downstairs to draw the dining room drapes. Across the fenced-off gardens, lights shine from windows in all five stories of the white stuccoed row houses on the other side of Chester Square. The Volvo Estate with a Clinton/Gore fender sticker is parked in front of the house directly opposite. So that's where they live. The counselor for administrative affairs brought his wife and three daughters to the embassy's Veterans' Day reception. In the course of recruiting me to the Americans Abroad for Clinton Club the wife mentioned that we were neighbors. My attention, however, was distracted by her eldest daughter, who was in her final year at the American School. With her fresh face, long tousled hair, and short woollen dress hugging a slender figure, she could walk straight onto a Calvin Klein catwalk. It's when you stop looking at your colleagues' wives and start looking at their daughters that you have to admit to middle age.

Lights in the house go off. The counselor and his family load suitcases into the Volvo. I wonder what outing the five of them are embarking on this weekend. A buzzer sounds. I draw the velvet drapes, take the dinner out of the electric service lift, and put it in front of the one place setting on the polished antique oak table designed for ten.

The white plastic portable television set at the opposite end of the table clashes horribly with the Georgian decor, but it provides company over dinner. The anchorman for Channel 4's seven o'clock news cuts short yet another item about the government's unpopularity, hesitates, looks at his video cue, and says to camera, "While we've been on the air we've received reports of a large explosion in a public house just outside Cheltenham. Our correspondent Gita Sharma is on the line." He picks up a telephone while a still of an attractive Indian woman's head appears in the upper right-hand quarter of the screen. "Gita, can you hear me?"

"Yes, Peter," a disembodied voice replies. "About twenty minutes ago there was a large explosion at a pub called The Albion, less than two miles from the center of Cheltenham. There's absolute chaos. The street's now cordoned off, but I counted at least ten ambulances and half a dozen fire engines there."

"Thanks, Gita." He turns back to face the camera. "We hope to get a full report on this before the end of the program. Meanwhile, in Westminster, MPs were speculating about the effects of the latest trade figures on . . ."

One Dover sole and half a bottle of Chablis later the anchorman interrupts an interview to say, "And now, back to the story that broke while we were on the air. We have a special report from Gita Sharma in Cheltenham."

The picture cuts to the animated head of the Indian woman. Behind her, mesmerising stroboscopic blue lights and wailing two-tone sirens punctuate a scene of fire engines, ambulances, and police cars bathed in night lens infrared. The camera pulls back. Beyond a blue and white banded ribbon, shirt-sleeved ambulance-men carry stretchers, yellow-helmeted firemen maneuver ladders and hosepipes, and reflective-bibbed policemen shepherd walking wounded up a broad village street.

"At approximately seven o'clock this evening," says Gita Sharma to camera, "an explosion ripped apart an annex at the rear of the seventeenth century Albion public house here in the village of Prestbury, less than two miles from the center of Cheltenham. The annex was known as the skittle alley, and it is believed a party was taking place there at the time. At least nine people are feared dead and many more injured. The area is being cleared in case there is a second explosion. The police are saying nothing at the moment, but bomb disposal experts with sniffer dogs have arrived from Hereford. This is Gita Sharma, Channel 4 News, Cheltenham."

In the studio the anchorman reads from a sheet of paper. "ITN has received a telephone call from the IRA claiming responsibility. The message said that the bombing of spies from GCHQ, Britain's electronic eavesdropping center, was a reprisal for attempts by the British intelligence services to undermine the peace process in Northern Ireland." The anchorman looks straight at me. "If confirmed, this breaking of the IRA ceasefire will have shattering implications for peace in Northern Ireland. Further developments will be given in ITN's News at Ten. In the meantime, on the night in which at least nine people are feared dead in the bombing of a Cheltenham pub, this is Peter Frost of Channel 4 News. Good evening."

It is only when the signature tune begins that I realize the phone has been ringing.

"Yes?"

"You need to come to the office."

Within ten minutes the headlights of my car flash at the woman police constable in the glazed booth at the rear of the embassy. She checks my identity, raises the barrier, and I drive down the ramp to the basement parking lot.

The elevator from the basement opens on a dimly lit fourth floor lobby. A bright light shines from underneath the closed door to the north wing. After inserting my card in the lock and punching a code in the panel, I open the door and head for the communications center. Cheryl Pickering, our signals duty officer, and a man I don't recognize are waiting in the room filled with flickering computer terminals and television monitors.

"John, this is Ron Phillips from SUSLO London," she says. "Ron, John Darcy is our deputy chief."

I begin to fear the worst.

The freckle-faced Phillips from the Senior United States Liaison Office at the embassy looks uncomfortable in civilian clothes. He speaks as though reading from an army manual. "At 19.42 local time I received a flash from SUSLO Cheltenham advising of an explosion in a public house at which an NSA officer was giving a party."

"Christ Almighty." I turn to Cheryl. "Have you gotten hold of Lawrence?"

"Lawrence and his wife are attending a gala concert at the Barbican hosted by the Duchess of Kent to raise money for . . ."

"Volume," I say, pointing at the television set permanently tuned to CNN.

Cheryl presses a button and the female newscaster's mime becomes audible tragedy. ". . . the death toll in the terrorist bombing of a public house in Cheltenham, England, has risen to twelve. At least five of those killed are Americans. The youngest victim is four-year-old Lucy Ford."

The picture cuts to the distraught face of a woman in her late twenties over the caption "Madeleine Ford, mother of victim." The woman is grasping a battered teddy bear. Tears stream down her cheeks. She begins to speak in a Texan drawl, but sobs rack her body and I have to strain to catch what she is saying.

"It was . . . it was a massacre . . . We couldn't see . . . Lucy . . . We found her . . . underneath the wreckage . . . I just can't get over it . . . We didn't find her . . . her legs . . . I know people say . . . say you should forgive. I can't . . . I can't! . . . I hate them for what they've done . . . They've destroyed my child's life . . . My Lucy, who never did any harm . . . I hate them."

"Tell Lawrence," I say to Cheryl, "that there's a meeting in his office at nine o'clock tomorrow morning and . . ."

"Lawrence and Bea are scheduled to go straight from the concert to Norfolk for a weekend house party at . . ."

"I don't care if you have to tell the Queen to tell the Duchess to tell Lawrence to haul his ass over here, but tomorrow morning he has a meeting with Todd Fraser, Stan Brooks, the SUSLO chief, the Bureau rep, and me. Next, have the staff aide to the ambassador set up a meeting at ten for Lawrence to brief the ambassador and his senior staff. When you've done that, come to my office. I'll have a signal for you to send to European Division copy to Counterterrorism Center." I turn to Phillips. "Have an update on my desk at zero eight-hundred hours tomorrow."

"Yes, sir."

Adrenaline pumps through my system once more: we'll soon see who's in mothballs. Yet after I've drafted the signal, my hand hesitates over the secure phone. But I can't postpone this any longer. I pick up the phone, dial the MI5 duty officer, and say in as steady a voice as I can manage, "I need to speak with Edward Maitland."

Chapter ❖ Two

I DON'T KNOW whether I hate Edward Maitland more than I feel guilty about him.

When we first met he provoked a mixture of resentment and envy. It was June 1973 and I was filled with enthusiasm and, I have to admit, self-importance. In those days London was the stopping-off point for most official American delegations traveling to Europe, the Middle East, Africa, and beyond the Iron Curtain. London was where you established personal relationships with comers in Reuters and other news media, in political parties, and in Britain's intelligence services. In short, it was a place which could help make your career. Not only had I been assigned to London for my first overseas tour, but I had been tasked with a special mission. Nobody but the chief of station knew of it, and I was to bypass the senior reports officer and cable direct to Counter Intelligence Staff at Langley.

Within twenty-four hours of landing at Heathrow I dialed Edward Maitland's home number and repeated the coded message which the chief of CI Staff had given me.

"Our mutual friend, Jim, has given me some flies to help you catch a big trout."

"Splendid," the voice at the other end of the phone replied. "Where are you billeted?"

"Boydell Court, in a street called St. John's Wood Park."

"Even better. Be outside at ten-thirty prompt on Saturday and I'll collect you."

"But . . ."

"Yes?"

"How will I recognize you?"

"I'll be wearing an MCC tie."

I had no idea what an MCC tie was, but there was no mistaking Edward Maitland. Instead of the discreet meeting I'd expected, a red convertible two-seater sports car squealed to a halt outside my apartment house, and out jumped a man wearing a maroon and white striped blazer, white pants, and a ketchup and mustard striped necktie.

"Welcome to Blighty," he said. Hazel eyes examined me. "The name is Maitland, Edward Maitland, but you can call me Edward."

You would never think of calling him Ed or Eddie or Ted. His chestnut hair was sharply parted on the right and neatly combed back and to the side. I discovered later that he was only two years my senior, but he seemed older. He possessed lean good looks plus the casual athleticism and air of effortless superiority which are bred in the English Home Counties, nurtured by English private schools, and honed in the best British regiments. "Jump in," he commanded. "Afraid it's a bit of a squash in the back, but we're not going far."

I was bursting with vital and ultrasecret information to give Maitland, and yet here was a straw-haired man of about my own age sitting in the passenger seat. "John Darcy, an old friend," Maitland announced. "And this is Tim Ralston of New Zealand's security service."

My God, here was I, undeclared to the British authorities, and Maitland was introducing me to a foreign intelligence agent!

"Pleased to meet you," said Ralston, extending his arm. "How long have you known Edward?"

"Not long," I said as I clambered into the tiny space behind the two bucket seats. "Where are we going?"

"Mecca," said Maitland. "The Arabs may be taking over St. John's Wood, but they'll never take over the mecca of all true Englishmen."

The roar of the MGB's engine drowned further conversation. Maitland executed a deft three-point turn and accelerated down the street. I clung on as he raced through traffic and finally swerved to a halt on the main road outside a large stadium. He stuck a police pass to the windshield and said, "Supplies in the boot, Tim."

Ralston opened the trunk, removed a wicker hamper, and we both followed Maitland across the road to the stadium. Instead of joining the queue for the turnstiles, Maitland led us to a pair of opened black wrought iron gates, on one of which hung a notice, "Members and Guests Only." He gave a steward two tickets and flourished a small red book. Ralston struggled to keep abreast of Maitland as he swept through the crowd and headed up the steps of a stand next to a large and ancient multistoryed red-brick clubhouse he called the pavillion.

The sun blazed down on a vast oval lawn. Shirt-sleeved men buzzing with reverential expectation, as though they were about to witness a papal mass, began to fill the double tiers of wooden benches in the bleachers and old double-decker covered stands that bordered the lawn. In our stand and on the pavillion terrace and balconies—where they were sipping gin and tonics—the spectators wore fawn suits or crumpled white linen jackets or navy blue or vulgarly striped blazers like Maitland's; many wore that ketchup-and-mustard necktie and many wore panama hats. I could see no women in the pavillion; the few in our stand displayed fashionable cotton frocks and straw hats and waved to each other.

"This is what I call heaven," sighed Maitland as he stretched out his long legs in front of him.

"Good on you for the invitation, Edward," Ralston said as he surveyed the scene. "The Saturday of a Lord's Test against the old country is something to tell my grandchildren about."

By now I was sweating profusely, but I didn't know how people in Maitland's sector of Britain's class-ridden society would respond if I took off my suit jacket, unbuttoned my vest, and loosened my tie.

"What *is* that tie, Edward?" I asked.

"MCC. Marylebone Cricket Club."

"You've sure pulled one hell of a crowd for a club game," I said, "even if a lord's team is playing."

Ralston burst out laughing while Maitland merely smiled.

"John," said Ralston, "this is an international match between England and New Zealand. The ground is called Lord's and it belongs to the MCC. It's the home of cricket."

"I see," I said uncertainly. "When does the game begin?"

"Two days ago," said Maitland. "New Zealand are about to resume their first innings."

At lunchtime Maitland opened the wicker hamper and offered smoked salmon sandwiches and champagne. I was parched and resentful, and drank more than I should. Maitland stood up and waved his glass to a group of spectators at a bar below a stand on the other side of the pavillion. "Colleagues," he said to me. "They always congregate by the

Tavern. If the Russians ever discovered that the office closes down for the five days of the Lord's Test every year, the buggers would know when to strike." He put his fingers to his lips. "State secret. Not to be passed on."

I could think only of the infinitely more important secret that I had been entrusted to pass on to him. Fortunately, Ralston spotted some fellow New Zealanders and excused himself at the end of the day's play.

"Edward," I said, trying to control my anger at his patronizing attitude, "there is a very important matter we must talk about."

"Indeed, but first a good meal."

He threaded the MGB through the departing crowds and parked outside a baroque apartment house less than half a mile from the stadium. Now I was assigned the role of porter, carrying the wicker basket while he pushed back the black wrought iron concertina door of the elevator.

On the third floor he unlocked an apartment door and called out, "We're back. Mine's a Scotch and I don't know what John will have." He turned to me. "Afraid we don't stock bourbon or rye."

The woman who brought Maitland his Scotch stopped me in my tracks. Red hair, the color of a fox but shiny, fell in gentle waves to the top of her breasts. Her large gold-flecked green eyes were those of a wild cat, by turns nervous, by turns glinting with the promise of danger. That evening it was only the nervous eyes I saw. "Hello, my name's Jill. May I get you a drink?"

"Yes, er, thank you," I stammered. "The same as Edward, please."

"How was the game?" Jill asked when she handed me the glass.

I shrugged helplessly.

"Absolute bloody disgrace," Maitland said. "Illingworth tried to bore them out. Bowled tight as a fish's arse, with as

much hope of penetration. You didn't miss much." He
turned to me. "It was Jill's ticket you had."

"I do apologize," I said to her. "I didn't realize. If I'd
known . . ."

Her gentle laugh cut me short. She put her hand on my
arm. "There's no need to apologize. I found plenty of things
to do."

"Like preparing dinner," Maitland said. "I'm starving."

I couldn't, of course, discuss the top secret material over
dinner—which was superb—nor did I much feel like it, especially after the second bottle of claret. I found myself
glancing at Jill and wondering why such an exquisite creature had married Edward Maitland. Suddenly I became
aware that Maitland was watching my covetous eyes follow
Jill as she took the empty plates through to the kitchen.

"I see you approve," he said to my blushes. "There's
plenty more where that came from. I'll show you what the
registry has to offer when you call in the office. But after
Tuesday, when the cricket's finished."

In those days MI5 was based at Leconfield House, a building of teak-inlaid corridors and corniced offices not far from
the embassy in Mayfair. On the following Thursday Maitland showed me the registry. It occupied the whole of the
first floor—which he called the ground floor. Compared
with the computerized efficiency of Langley this place came
out of the stone age. Everything was done by hand, from
sorting, checking, and filing incoming material, through lo-
cating files by card indexes, retrieving them from innumer-
able stacks, putting them in trolleys, and wheeling the
trolleys to elevators up to the floors above where the officers worked.

"Much prettier than computers, don't you think?" Maitland asked afterwards in the Pig and Eye Club, the staff bar

on the top floor. "Our registry queens come in two types: nuns or showgirls. The nuns . . . well, you saw for yourself. They're here for a lifetime. The showgirls, on the other hand, the best selection of debs you'll find in any office in London, tend to last nine months. Anyone take your fancy?"

I was too embarrassed to answer.

He laughed and stubbed out his cheroot. "Drink up, and we'll go through to the canteen. Most of them will be there for lunch, so you can have another shufti. Don't look so shocked. All part of the special relationship."

What struck me most about the people we met in the staff restaurant were the men: former colonial police, former soldiers, former journalists, former teachers—former everythings distinguished by boring mediocrity and dowdy chain-store suits, apart from the ex-colonials who sported navy blue blazers with badges on their breast pockets. Edward Maitland was an exception. Little wonder that this dashing former military intelligence officer had captured the queen of the registry queens, for Jill Maitland wasn't merely a stunningly attractive woman from a wealthy family, she had, I learned, a good honors degree in English from Oxford University.

My work with Maitland kept me apart from State and company people at the embassy. But social isolation and Maitland's arrogance were prices I willingly paid to be at the heart of an ultrasecret mission—and to be in Jill's presence: to have her gold-flecked green eyes look into mine, to have her cool hand touch my arm. I was an innocent abroad, inspired by patriotism and intoxicated by infatuation. As Graham Greene wrote in *The Quiet American,* "innocence is a form of insanity." I shed my innocence, however, and developed another form of insanity after Edward Maitland was assigned to Northern Ireland.

Chapter ✦ Three

IN THE TWENTY or so years since Maitland was first assigned there, Northern Ireland has not been of much concern to the company. CIA benefited from MI5 and MI6 experience of combating urban terrorism, but Northern Ireland was a local problem we were well out of. The Cheltenham bombing of US intelligence personnel and their families changes all that, disrupting the usual weekend quiescence of London station.

Normally on a Saturday morning our secure floor is like a *Mary Celeste:* not a piece of paper to be seen on the top of locked metal desks or in the trash cans or on the walls, where locked canvas roller blinds cover maps and charts, and only the silent glow of computer and television monitors in the communications room manned by a signals officer reading a paperback novel belies the impression of total abandonment. This Saturday morning, however, I've sent and received a stack of signals by the time Lorna rings to say, "It's nine o'clock. The chief's ready to start the meeting you asked for."

I can guess the line Lawrence Palmer will take. Like most Ivy League company men, Palmer prides himself on being an Anglophile; he disapproves of a President who has upset the Brits by supporting Dublin's line in the Northern Ireland peace process.

The first thing I notice when I walk into Palmer's large office is that one person is missing. The second is the levels in the glasses and bottles of mineral water in front of the four people seated round the conference table. I estimate these four have been here at least half an hour.

"Now you've arrived, John, we can begin," says Palmer. Our chief of station is wearing a very British tweed jacket over a white shirt opened at the neck to show a red silk cravat, which he will have chosen to complement his white beard. Palmer sees himself as an intellectual. He can afford to. With a career in the intelligence side of the company he's never had to dirty his own hands with clandestine work, with bribing, blackmailing, burgling, subverting, destroying reputations and, where necessary, destroying people.

Before I can brief them on the latest casualty figures from the Cheltenham bombing, Todd Fraser starts speaking. The station's counterterrorism officer stands out from the pre-retirees who occupy most of the liaison slots. He comes from the Mormon generation which followed my own Irish-American intake, instantly recognizable by his sincerely intense face, short hair, and three-piece gray vested suit: wind him up, point him at any target, and he'll arrive there by the optimal route, untroubled by doubt, danger, or legal restraint. Yet in despising Fraser am I not despising the person I was twenty years ago? "The latest casualty figures from the terrorist bombing in Cheltenham," he says, "are fifteen dead and thirty-seven injured. Eight of the dead and sixteen of the injured are US citizens."

The one person I haven't met before is Bruce Davis, the Senior United States Liaison Officer, who coordinates the work of the National Security Agency in Britain. A hand-some man, whose short black Afro-Caribbean hair and moustache contrast with his coffee-colored skin, he looks as though he maintains his military fitness program. "Of the eight US fatalities," he says, "three are NSA, two are wives, and three are children. All sixteen US injured are NSA or family." From the suppressed emotion with which he makes the announcement I'm sure that he too has a wife and children over here.

"Meade has signaled that our number one priority is to prevent disclosure that the American dead and wounded are NSA," Davis continues. "Our security people at GCHQ have arranged for the hospitalised to be isolated from the media. Meantime we're preparing a cover story. Stan will ensure that MI5 cooperate in selling the cover to the British authorities and the media."

Stan Brooks, the station's MI5 liaison officer, nods. In his stone-colored safari suit he already looks like an American retiree doing London.

"I would have thought our number one priority was to catch the bombers," I say. "Where's Litynska? We need to bring in the Bureau."

Palmer raises his eyebrows. "With DIA squeezing us out of nuclear proliferation and DEA cutting us out of drugs, Jack will not be pleased if we let the Bureau into counter-terrorism overseas."

"With respect, Lawrence," I say, "this is operations, not intelligence. We need to harness all available resources to track down these terrorists."

"Indeed," Palmer replies. "Todd's task will be to place the Agency's resources at the disposal of Edward Maitland and his people at Five."

Fraser is as near as he ever will be to a smile.

"I'm handling this myself, Lawrence," I say quietly.

In the silence that follows Davis looks straight ahead,

Brooks studies his papers, and Fraser studies me. So this is what they were discussing in the half hour before my arrival. Davis won't take sides, provided NSA are kept out of it; Brooks wants an easy life; and Fraser wants this job to prove himself.

"I think you and I should leave all the running around to the young men," says Palmer at his most conciliatory.

"When I can't make five miles in under thirty-five minutes," I say, "then I'll let the youngsters do the running. Meantime, this job needs experience."

"I agree," Palmer says. "That's what Todd can provide, recent experience. After all, it's a long time since you were in London station. Todd has been here over a year and he's acquired assets in counterterrorism."

Fraser is like a spring ready to uncoil. I can't say that I blame him, but no rookie is going to stop me from taking on this operation. "Who are your assets, Todd?" I ask.

"Apart from my liaison at Six, I have journalists at the *Sunday Times,* the *Daily Telegraph,* and the *Sunday Express,*" he answers promptly. "People who have a direct line to Sinn Féin and the IRA."

I give him a cold smile. "Their direct line is to Five, who plant stories to validate their own policies in a game of Chinese whispers. That's where experience comes in. Neither am I jumping to conclusions about who planted the Cheltenham bomb. The IRA has now denied it was responsible."

The silence this time is even longer. Finally Palmer steels himself. "John, there's a distinct benefit to you in Todd taking this particular case."

"Spit it out, Lawrence," I say, trying to control my temper.

Palmer can't, so Fraser steps in. "Let's face it, John, I don't have an Irish–American background, and so nobody will even think of questioning my impartiality. First thing

Monday Stan here will see his opposite number in Five, and
I'll . . ."

"I'll leave you to brief the ambassador, Lawrence," I
snap. "I'm having lunch with Edward Maitland tomorrow."
I stand up and walk to the door. As an afterthought I add,
"I'll let you know Monday if I need any assistance from
Todd or Stan."

Chapter ❖ Four

I'VE SEEN MAITLAND only once since I left London nearly twenty years ago. On that occasion I held all the aces and he was forced to play my game. This time it is I who need him, and he's chosen a meeting ground on which I'll feel least comfortable. From the outside the Garrick Club is a soot-blackened palazzo, standing incongruously among the fashionable restaurants, cafés, wine bars, hairdressers, designer clothes shops, and booksellers between Leicester Square and Covent Garden in London's theater district, a world away from the traditional clubland of Pall Mall and St. James's Street of imperial London. Once inside the tall, glazed inner doors, however, it is as though the British have never lost their empire.

A red-liveried porter directs you up an imposing oak staircase beneath a glass dome. Huge Victorian oil paintings hang from the cream walls, and plinthed busts and yet more portraits face you on the landing. To the right, past a red screen filled with nineteenth-century costume sketches studded with sequins, is the drawing room, where members greet their guests. No danger of meeting your butcher, or even your doctor, still less a black face, in this grand Victorian room of ornamented ceiling, gilt-framed portraits, claret walls, burgundy carpet, port leather armchairs, and conversations which exude the confidence of an alumni reunion at an exclusive boarding school.

Edward Maitland has changed. His face is even leaner and the sardonic expression more pronounced. His chestnut hair has turned gray, but is longer, with sideburns. His flamboyance is now that of the British establishment: a dark blue and white pinstriped suit tailored in Savile Row, with four buttons on the cuffs of his jacket and a white silk handkerchief flopping from his breast pocket, shining handmade black shoes, the whitest cotton shirt I've ever seen, gold cufflinks, and a necktie of cucumber and salmon stripes. Do the British ruling class choose their neckties to camouflage food stains?

He sits in an armchair, chatting with a man in his late thirties who is wearing an identical tie but, I'm thankful to see, an Italian designer sportcoat and slacks. At least I'm not the only one in casual dress.

"John, long time no see," Maitland says. He stands, but doesn't offer his hand. "You haven't changed at all."

"It's been twelve years, Edward."

"Really? Permit me to introduce Jeffrey. Jeffrey, this is the American I was telling you about."

I try to figure out from Jeffrey's glint of amusement just what Maitland has been telling him.

"Let's have a drink," Maitland says. He sweeps off across the landing to a bar in which oil portraits fill almost every square inch of the eau-de-Nil walls. There are few bars where I can go these days and bring down the average age, but this is one. Or perhaps British club members simply look old. Several share Maitland's dandified style and his taste in neckties. They include one member of the British cabinet, who nods discreetly to Maitland. Satisfied that I've noticed, Maitland asks, "What's your poison, John?"

"Mineral water, please, Edward."

"Then you have changed. Has eliminating alcohol been the secret of retaining your youthful looks?" Without waiting for a reply he turns his back on me and says, "Rodney, two G and Ts and some of that fizzy water in green bottles."

Maitland hands me the mineral water, lights a cigar, and says to Jeffrey, "And how is young Timothy?"

"Only twelve," Jeffrey replies, "but already showing plenty of promise. A good right hand bat who can turn his arm over and produce some nifty offbreaks. Top of the school batting averages, so we're eager to see what Marlborough will do for him. And your girl?"

"Emma's doing splendidly at Roedean. Interviews for Oxford next month. High hopes there."

Feeling like a spare dick at a wedding I fume quietly and examine the paintings. Most are Victorians in absurd costumes, but some portraits are modern. I recognize Laurence Olivier. He's wearing that same damned tie.

"Never been here before, then?" It's Maitland.

"I've never needed to," I say with studied politeness.

"You see some of Britain's finest thespians on the walls. This place was founded as a club where members of the aristocracy could meet actors—and obtain the addresses of showgirls," he adds with a smirk.

"That isn't the purpose of my visit."

"What a splendid sense of humor," Maitland says to Jeffrey. "I fear that John, like all Americans, is impatient. Will you forgive us?"

"Certainly," Jeffrey replies. He finishes his gin and tonic, smiles at me, and leaves.

"The fellow's a television presenter," Maitland says when Jeffrey has gone. "Our standards are slipping."

"About the Cheltenham bomb," I begin.

Maitland puts his fingers to his lips. "Not done to talk business here. Against club rules."

"Then why are we meeting here?" I ask before I can stop myself.

He gives me a curious look, but desists from asking why I refused his invitation to lunch at his home. "There's no danger of bumping into people from the office. I doubt that any of them would be accepted even at the In and Out. Let's go down to the coffee room."

"I'd rather have lunch first."

His patronizing smile hasn't changed. "My dear John, that is where one does have lunch."

I follow Maitland down the staircase and into a lofty chandeliered room whose crimson walls are hung with yet more dead actors painted in their roles. The layout recreates in part what I guess is the dining room of a British private school: a long table seating thirty or more occupies the center of the room. Those members who wish to dine less sociably occupy small tables by the walls.

I'm relieved that Maitland avoids the superannuated schoolboys' table and leads me to one by a screen in the far corner. No doubt he is relieved that this club is a refuge from the transatlantic fashion of waiters treating you as their equal. The French waiter proffers two menus. Mine has no prices on it.

"Afraid there's only a limited choice on Sundays," says Maitland, "but that hardly matters. Roast beef with Yorkshire pudding, potatoes, and sprouts is always available. I recommend the soup for starters."

I choose smoked eel followed by roast chicken.

"I assume you want the NSA connection kept out of it?" Maitland asks after he pushes his empty soup plate to one side.

Before I reply another waiter approaches and pours a little of a Chateau Siran '82 for Maitland to taste. He tips the glass toward the white tablecloth to examine the color, and then brings the brick-red wine near his nose, swirls the glass, sniffs, and nods. The waiter half-fills my glass and then Maitland's.

"The press, unfortunately, aren't as cooperative as when you were last in London," Maitland says as he tucks into his traditional English Sunday lunch. "Time was when you'd have a quiet word here with the editors and that would be that. I'll speak to Jennifer Ackroyd, the officer I've assigned for this business. I'm sure she'll do her best."

Maitland taught me most of what I know about wine. I must admit that this one is superb and more than compensates for the undistinguished chicken and overcooked broccoli and carrots. "A woman case officer?"

He smiles with satisfaction that I appreciate his choice of wine. "Half our operatives now are female."

"I'm pleased to see that you've come round to appreciating women's talents."

For a moment the smile freezes, and then he continues smoothly, "Women are well skilled at concentration and analysis, they have a good head for keeping their eye on the ball, and they are psychologically better adjusted for coping with the pressures of working under cover. That's the line we feed to our tame journalists. The fact is we can't recruit enough men. They go into the City or private companies or even the regular civil service, where at least they can be involved in policy making. When we do manage to recruit men with a double digit IQ, after a few months of listening to tedious telephone taps, reading boring mail intercepts, entering hundreds of cross references into the computer, and writing endless reports with nothing to show for it, they leave. Let's face it, they may as well be working in a life assurance office for all the fun it is these days."

"I don't call Cheltenham fun."

He looks at my plate with its uneaten vegetables. "I promise you the cheeses are top quality."

"A spokesman denied that the IRA was responsible."

Maitland's thin lips curl in a sardonic smile. "As the whore said of the bishop, he would say that, wouldn't he?"

Another waiter wheels up a battered trolley. Maitland selects Cheddar and Stilton. I pick Brie and Edam.

After the waiter has gone, I ask, "When do we go?"

"Do try one of these," he says, offering what looks like a black communion wafer. "Charcoal biscuits. Time was when you could drink as much as you liked, eat a few of these, and when you blew into a police Breathalyser it registered sober. Sadly, they don't fool the new generation of Breathalysers."

"You haven't answered my question, Edward."

"We don't. Port?"

"Edward, eight of the dead and nearly half of the injured were US citizens. What's more, they were NSA and their families. This is a matter of US national security."

He beckons the wine waiter. "You must understand, John, that the Gloucestershire Constabulary are in charge. They don't want us around, and they certainly don't want you and your American methods."

"Five are in charge of combating Irish terrorism in Britain," I state after I wave away the port.

"We're not the FBI. While we take the lead in intelligence-gathering operations against the IRA, when it comes to a police investigation of a specific incident, the local plods are in charge—and they don't want us on their turf."

"I repeat. This is not some domestic little incident. US national security is involved."

Maitland samples his port. "I've already set up a crisis unit on the intelligence side, with input from GCHQ, NSA, the RUC, RUC Special Branch, the Garda and the Garda

Special Branch, plus the FBI for possible US connections. What more can I do?"

"I want direct input—and output."

Maitland puts down his glass with a sigh. "My dear John, there are established channels for such matters. Any relevant intelligence that the CIA Counterterrorism Center has is passed on to the liaison officer in Washington, who passes it on to our friends across the river, who pass it on to us. If anything we find has a bearing on US national security, our CIA liaison officer will pass it on to Stan Brooks in your office."

"Edward, I am going to Cheltenham—with or without your cooperation."

Maitland stares at me and then shakes his head. "How typical. I should have remembered how headstrong you are. If nothing will persuade you otherwise, then I had better guide you as usual, to prevent you crashing around like a bull in a china shop. Be outside Thames House tomorrow at ten prompt and I'll collect you."

I have the weapon to puncture Maitland's patronizing. Can I trust myself to spend a full day with him tomorrow without using it? But if I do succumb to the urge to tell him what really happened after he was transferred to Northern Ireland over twenty years ago, will it ruin my chances of finding the Cheltenham bomber?

Chapter ✛ Five

It wasn't just that Mom and Pop went to mass at least twice a week, or that Woodside was solidly Catholic. Classmates from St. Sebastian's grade school, from Regis High, and from Fordham lost their faith, usually when they found their manhood. But I never did. Catholicism was not a matter of bog-Irish blind belief. It was inspirational and it was reasonable. There could only be one truth, and it was entirely logical for God to provide mankind with an infallible guide to that truth. The Church was the rock of certainty in the shifting sands of the sixties, and a source of reassurance when my world seemed to fall apart in the early seventies after Jill and Edward Maitland left for his first Northern Ireland assignment.

Each day brought a new sensation from the Watergate hearings; rumors circulated that Nixon had sacked CIA director Dick Helms because Helms had refused to assist in the cover-up; other rumors alleged that our current director, William Colby, had involved the company in the cover-up. Nobody knew what to believe: working in such a secretive and tightly compartmented organization we had no more information than any other *Washington Post* readers. After Nixon resigned I didn't know what bomb-shells would explode next. They came in the form of a se-ries of *New York Times* articles alleging that CIA had undertaken a massive covert operation against Chile's de-mocratically elected President Allende, who had been killed the previous fall in a military coup, and that CIA had mounted large scale illegal covert operations against anti-war and other dissident movements in the USA.

London station responded to the attacks on the company by closing ranks in a fervor of organizational loyalty, but I was left on the outside. My colleagues' resentment of a ju-nior officer who bypassed normal procedures and reported direct to Counter Intelligence Chief Angleton at Langley culminated on Christmas Eve when the deputy chief of sta-tion summoned me to his office. "Mr. Darcy, it is my great sadness," he said with a smile, "to have to tell you that your patron and protector, James Jesus Angleton, has just been fired. Have a happy Christmas."

I was in no mood for parties, even if I'd been invited, when I left the concrete-and-glass monstrosity of the em-bassy which squats beneath a giant golden eagle and dom-inates what is otherwise one of London's most elegant squares. Putting up the collar of my overcoat against the cold wind which blew across the tree-lined central garden, I turned right as though on automatic pilot. Five minutes' walk past graceful redbrick buildings whose street-level shops offered gold sinks and faucets, gilt-framed paintings, and gold inlaid dinner services brought me to the refuge that I had come to regard as my private chapel. I kneeled next to one of the shiny black and brown speckled pillars of the Jesuits' Farm Street church. The gothic pointed arches and sweeping spaces drew my eye unwaveringly to the intricately sculpted white stone and gilt high altar with

its central tabernacle and the red flickering votive lamp
which signaled the Real Presence.

Gradually the church filled with men in cashmere over-
coats and women in furs and jewelery—people I never saw
at Sunday mass, still less at the early morning daily mass. The
mass of Christ's Nativity seemed for them to be another
Christmas party. Enthusiastically they joined in the carols.
I remained silent. I had lost the capacity to *feel* the truth.

When mass ended I set off alone to my apartment in St.
John's Wood, swallowed a large Jim Beam, and went to bed
depressed.

Six hours later the phone woke me.

"Happy Christmas, John."

I sat up in bed. "Jill! Happy Christmas! Where are you?"

"London. Look, if you're not doing anything else, would
you like to come round to the flat for Christmas dinner, say
seven or seven-thirty?"

"Try stopping me."

I spent most of the day searching for Christmas presents,
but the shops were closed. Finally a pub in Swiss Cottage
came up with a box of Edward Maitland's favorite cheroots,
and the flower stall outside University College Hospital produced a bunch of red roses for Jill.

Jill opened the door of the Maida Vale apartment. She
wore a simple green silk dress with a low-cut neck. The
color and the material complemented her long shiny red
hair. While she stood still the dress looked demure. When
she moved it showed the curves of her lithe figure. I was
even more smitten than when I first saw her—if that were
possible.

"Happy Christmas, Jill," I said, and thrust the roses in
her direction as nonchalantly as I could. "Where's the old
son of a gun?"

She bit her lip. "I'm afraid Edward's still in Northern Ireland." She gave me a sidelong glance. "I hope you don't mind."

"Of course not . . . I mean, er, I'm sorry, of course . . ."

She touched my arm. "The roses are wonderful. What a lovely Christmas present. Thank you, John."

She led me through to the drawing room. I had once remarked that the baroque cornices and ceiling rose didn't suit the dimensions of the room. Since my last visit nine months before, their obtrusiveness had been softened by a new color scheme of white and greens, with wallpaper in Regency stripes.

"I hope you approve of the decor," Jill said.

"It's terrific."

"I'm sorry about the short notice. I hope it didn't inconvenience you."

"Any excuse to avoid the embassy Christmas dinner." What a dumb thing to say!

"Edward didn't give much warning that he wasn't coming, and I couldn't face going to my parents'." She pushed her hair back behind one ear. "I wanted to be with friends."

"Who else are you expecting?"

She ran her fingers along the top of the avocado-colored velvet Regency sofa between the matching high-back armchairs. "You're the friend."

I blushed. If only Jill weren't married. But this was fantasy land. She was married—just think yourself lucky that she counts you a friend, I told myself.

"Do sit down, John. Would you like a bourbon?"

"Yes, please." I sat on one of the armchairs.

She produced a new bottle of Jim Beam from a walnut corner cabinet.

"When do you go back?" I asked, and then kicked myself in case she thought that I couldn't wait to be rid of her because Edward wasn't here.

She poured herself a sherry. "I don't." She turned, and the wild cat's nervous green eyes sought my reaction. "Have you ever been to Belfast, John?"

"I've been to the South, but never to Belfast."

She sat down in the armchair opposite me and smoothed her skirt as far as it would go down her thighs. "It's not exactly London, or Dublin." She sipped her sherry. "I tried. I visited Edward's aunt but, to be honest, we had nothing in common."

"He has an aunt in Belfast?"

"His father was born and raised in Belfast's Cherry-valley." A conspiratorial smile lit her face. "Despite the impression he likes to give, Edward is not Home Counties." She bit her lip. "I'm sorry, that sounds disloyal. I think the turkey's ready."

At her request I selected one of Edward's clarets and decanted it into a Waterford crystal decanter. I carved the turkey in the dimly lit dining room while she brought the vegetables through from the kitchen.

For a while we ate in silence, separated by a red candle which stood in a circle of mistletoe, the apartment's token concession to Christmas. The flickering candlelight played on the rise of her breasts and the valley between, which led down below the neckline of her dress. I forced myself to look away. I kept telling myself that Jill Maitland was a married woman, the wife of an absent colleague, and that I must resist temptations of the flesh.

"I was lonely," she said. "I came back in August."

"August! Why didn't you tell me?"

"I thought of doing so. Several times." She looked down at her plate. Her red hair, burnished by the candlelight, fell over the top of her breasts.

"I assume Edward flies over for weekends," I said.

"Not many." She emptied her glass.

I couldn't resist the barb. "Not even for his cricket? That NCC or whatever club it is."

She failed to stifle a giggle. "That's another impression he likes to give. It's my father who's a member and gets the guest tickets. Edward had A Branch forge him an MCC membership card." She put her hand to her mouth. "I shouldn't have said that."

Maitland's patronizing angered me; to know that it was based on deception added insult to injury.

I refilled both glasses. "Was Belfast that bad?"

"Belfast was bad enough, but Edward was never home."

The recollection of his remark about Jill, *there's plenty more where that came from,* rekindled my resentment. Emboldened by the wine I said, "Has he got another woman there?"

"No. I'm sure he hasn't." I loved the way she pushed her hair back behind one ear when she was nervous.

"Then why?" I couldn't imagine any sane man leaving Jill on her own.

She emptied her glass. "Will you pour me another, please, John?"

She sipped her wine and said nothing.

"There is another woman," I prompted.

She shook her head. "Edward spends most of his time with military intelligence, at Lisburn and at some highly secret place in Castledillon in County Armagh."

"What on earth does he do there?"

"Smooth ruffled feathers, I imagine."

I could only imagine Maitland ruffling smooth feathers. Jill read my thoughts. "Military intelligence resented Five taking over the lead in Northern Ireland. Since the office recruited Edward from military intelligence, it thought he would be the ideal liaison."

"Liaison duties won't keep him away from home," I insisted.

She shrugged. "You know Edward. He loves undercover operations. Northern Ireland is where the action is these days."

I think she felt that she'd said too much, for she ate in silence till the meal was ended. I was too torn to know what to say.

I cleared the plates and took them through to the kitchen. Blue smoke and an acrid smell met me.

"Oh no!" Jill cried. "The Christmas pudding!"

She ran toward the stove, picked up the smoking pan, yelped, dropped it, and the Christmas pudding splattered over the floor.

"Jill! Are you OK?" I took her wrists and looked for burn marks on her hands.

Tears rolled down her cheeks.

I put my arm round her and she buried her face in my shoulder. She sobbed and I stroked her back to comfort her. The velvet skin caressed my fingers; her hair smelled of rose petals. She held me tight, with her breasts warm and firm against my chest. I felt her groin against my right thigh. The pressure on my thigh relaxed, and then it began again. The alternating pressure and relaxation coincided with her sobs, and then took on a rhythm of their own. I tried to move so that she wouldn't feel my arousal, but this only increased the wantonness of her rubbing against me. She raised her head and pressed her cheek to mine. The sobbing became a labored breathing, and she turned her head to seek my mouth. That's when I saw the dangerous glint in the wild cat's eyes. She kissed with an intensity which shocked and thrilled, and ended my struggle to keep the relationship platonic. She led me through to the bedroom and kissed me again. My hand grappled with the zipper of her dress. Impatiently she helped me and, as though possessed by a demon, undressed me. In bed she climbed on top and made love with an urgency that almost unmanned me. Afterwards she rolled off and fell into a deep sleep. She hadn't spoken a word. I lay there, feeling guilty and used, wondering whether to get up and leave. I must have drifted off into a restless sleep, because I next remembered gentle kisses on my cheek. I tried to speak, but she put a finger on my lips and kissed each eye in turn. The dervish had been replaced by an angel. All thoughts of leaving melted in her caresses, and when we made love again it was with a mutual tenderness that banished all my guilt and anger, and left me longing to be with her all my waking hours. That longing has never left me.

On Friday she came for dinner at my apartment and stayed the weekend. We spent most of the time in bed. On Saturday morning I brought her coffee and toast. She was still asleep, and I was pleased with myself for buying the black silk pillow cases and sheets, which formed the perfect background for her long red hair.

On Sunday morning she propped herself on an elbow and traced a finger down my brow to the end of my nose. "What's wrong, John?"

"Nothing."

"You can't fool me, John Darcy."

I turned to look at eyes which could see into my mind. "This will be the first Sunday I've missed mass for . . . for as long as I can remember."

"Then don't! Come on, get up. I'll come with you, if you want."

"I can't. I'm . . . I'm in a state of mortal sin." It must have sounded terribly pompous.

"Go to confession. That's what Catholics do, isn't it?"

I sank back in the soft warm sheets that smelled of scent and sweat and semen. How could I explain that, unlike her Anglicanism, Catholicism wasn't a pic'n'mix faith? It offered absolute certainty, but the price was absolute obedience. How could I go to confession and promise never to see Jill again?

She brushed my forehead with her lips. "I'm sorry, John. That was insensitive of me. I should have known better from Elizabeth."

I stroked away the long red hair that fell on my face like caresses. "Your sister's a Catholic?"

She nodded. "She converted in order to marry her dishy American banker, and now she's more Catholic than the Pope." She lay back and studied the ceiling. "John, I'm asking too high a price of you. I won't come here again. We can still be good friends."

"No!" I pulled her round toward me. "You must stay!" But was this her kind way of rejecting me? "Only if you want to," I added lamely.

She took my face in her hands and kissed me. "Yes, John Darcy, I do want to."

She couldn't stay all week. If the station chief found out that I was having an affair with the wife of a foreign intelligence officer, he would put me on the next plane to Washington. However, we were both familiar with clandestine tradecraft and it didn't prove difficult to conduct a secret liaison.

During the week she stayed at the Maida Vale apartment, but Fridays she came over to my apartment and had dinner ready for me when I returned from work. Several other junior company officers lived in Boydell Court, and so Jill avoided the public areas at the times they left for and returned from the embassy. Whenever we slipped out to catch a movie at the local Odeon or have a drink at Ye Olde Swiss Cottage pub, she wore dark glasses and a large headscarf or a wig.

Emboldened by our success we spread our wings. Jill introduced me to Turner at the Tate Gallery, to Handel at the Wigmore Hall, to Georgian architecture at its finest in Bath and Regency at its most extravagant in Brighton, to the bleak magnificence of the Yorkshire moors and the rolling softness of the Sussex downs, and to so much else that my Irish-American suspicion of all things British vanished under her bewitching spell.

We hardly ever talked of Edward, and then only on the rare occasions when Jill rang to say that she couldn't see me because he was coming home for the weekend or for meetings at the office. On a couple of those weekends he invited me round for a drink, but I always found an excuse. The guilty part of me wanted to ignore his very existence, the besotted part wanted to ask Jill to leave him, but I held back for fear that forcing the issue would destroy what had become the most precious thing in my life.

Jill was disarmingly honest. She never conspired in those lies that lovers love to hear: the adulations of eyes and lips and mind, and the assurances of everlasting love. And so joy overwhelmed me when she broke off from washing the dishes at my apartment one Friday evening and said, unprompted, "You know, John, I haven't loved anyone as much as I love you, and I'm sure I never will."

Those words banished the doubts and fears that haunted me after I had abandoned the anchor of God and his Church. Certainty flooded once more into every interstice of my being. This was a love that would never die.

Chapter ✣ Six

"BODY NUMBER FOUR. White female aged between twenty-five and forty-five wearing light green top, dark green trousers, white string underpants and white bra, with yellow metal Seiko watch on left wrist, gold ring on left wedding finger, and right arm missing." The words are pronounced in clipped tones by the Cheltenham coroner's officer, a small man with a pencil moustache, a sharp face, and the abrupt bearing of a man used to reading statements aloud in court.

No one moves among the knot of relatives, whose faces are rendered ghoul-like by the harsh light of neon tubes reflecting off large white refrigerated cabinets lined against shiny institutional green walls. Bruce Davis, soberly dressed in a two-piece dark-gray suit, edges forward. Suppressing a shiver in the bitterly cold mortuary, I leave Maitland's side and follow him.

The unmarked face is beautiful. Little remains of the charred bra and the G-string underpants. Blisters crisscross the leathery skin of the burnt torso, and shreds of flesh hang from the right shoulder. The fingernails of the left hand glisten with green nail varnish. The sour smell of charred human flesh invades my nostrils and the back of my throat, and I turn away to avoid retching.

"This is Mrs. Thomson," Davis says in a low voice which is drowned by the drone of huge air conditioning units.

"Speak up," says the coroner's officer.

"This is Mrs. Thomson," Davis repeats.

"Full name?"

"Georgina."

"Date of birth?"

"Look," says Davis, "I'll file full details later, OK?"

The coroner's officer turns to a middle aged woman waiting with a shorthand notebook. "Body number four. Thomson, Georgina, presumed citizen of the United States of America. Full details to be forwarded by American representative."

A mortician, anonymous in white face mask and soiled white laboratory coat, reaches forward with his fleshcolored latex gloves, pulls the loose white sheet back over the body, zips up the white plastic bag, slides the bag from the trolley onto the bottom of the four shelves inside the refrigerated compartment, and closes the large white door.

The score or so of us move to the second door. The mortician opens it, pumps up the trolley to the height of the top shelf, slides the tray onto the trolley, and lowers the trolley to waist height. The large white bag appears almost empty.

"Body number five. White female aged between three and six with blonde hair wearing a white dress with rose patterns. Both legs missing."

A strangulated cry pierces the drone of the air conditioning units. Two friends support Madeleine Ford, the Texan woman I saw interviewed on CNN. She recovers, pushes the mortician aside as soon as he has unzipped the bag, and pulls back the white sheet. "Lucy," she wails. "Lucy. I want my daughter!"

"I'm very sorry, madam," the coroner's officer says. "No bodies may be released until our inventory is complete."

"You haven't cleaned her face," Madeleine Ford sobs.

"Bodies must remain untouched until Forensic have completed their work. If you will bear with us, madam, unidentified appendages are in cabinet six."

I've seen many mortuaries and many bodies. I've never seen such carnage. I put my arm around Madeleine Ford and coax her away from the cabinet.

"Body number six," the coroner's officer continues. "Black female aged between fifteen and twenty with no head, wearing black ski pants, gray sweatshirt, red T-shirt, white bra, and white underpants."

This is the best argument for the death penalty: whoever ordered this coldblooded slaughter deserves no less.

"Have you seen enough?" Maitland asks. "Time for a spot of lunch before meeting the plods."

Maitland has graduated from the bright red convertible MGB of twenty years ago to a gleaming silver Jaguar Sovereign. I sink into the brown passenger seat of this opulent car that smells of leather and polish and stale cigar smoke. Above the gear shift the walnut dashboard displays old-fashioned dials and large switches. It's like a gentleman's club on wheels. Maitland tells me that it's ten years old, though you would never guess from the condition. I wonder if he can afford it on his salary, or if Jill's father continues to support his pretensions.

Maitland turns the key in the ignition. The engine makes almost no noise. "Much more faithful," Maitland says, "than the electronic versions made after Ford took over Jaguar."

The car leaves the modern extension at the rear of the

Cheltenham General Hospital. Opposite the abbey-like buildings of Cheltenham College we turn into a main road. "Have you ever been to Cheltenham before?" Maitland asks.

"No," I reply.

He drives down Montpellier Terrace, making a right round the traffic circle by the dome of the Montpellier Rotunda above its colonnaded first floor, past shop fronts divided by caryatids, and turns right to pull up outside the neoclassical pillared façade of the Queen's Hotel, modeled on the St. Petersburg Winter Palace according to Jill when she showed me round Cheltenham twenty years ago.

"If you've never been to Cheltenham, then you have never experienced the exquisite cuisine and service of the Regency Restaurant," Maitland says. "We must put that right." He leads me into the hotel's restaurant in which Jill and I, impatient with the leisurely waiters, hurried through dinner before scampering upstairs to our bedroom. The morning after we gazed out of the tall sash window across islands of rippling daffodils and tulips rising from a long stretch of lawn to the most elegant terrace I'd ever seen, a classical Regency design in pale golden Cotswold limestone.

The Cotswold stone frontage of the modern four-story Gloucestershire Constabulary Headquarters on Lansdown Road suggests some continuity with the Regency heart of Cheltenham. The suggestion is deceptive. Inside, pale green corridor walls littered with untidy noticeboards and civic posters, scuffed rubber floor tiles, and hollow doors leading to anonymous rooms with utilitarian office furniture might be those of any modern police station.

The conference room, which overlooks the busy main road, at least has brown and white wallpaper. Ranged along the wall opposite the windows are glass cabinets displaying silverware and sports trophies, and above these hang portraits of previous chief constables, from a stern Victorian gentleman through a sideburned admiral and a succession of moustached colonels in service dress uniform to the genial smiles of modern police officers in their black uniforms with silver symbols of office splashed on collar and shoulders.

Assistant Chief Constable Williams sits at the head of a large mahogany table. He is the only one in the room wearing a uniform. Four men and a young woman who, I presume, is a clerk are seated along the sides of the table.

"So sorry we're late," Maitland says. "Mr. Darcy is a political liaison officer at the American embassy, and he wanted to assist the relatives at the identification of bodies."

Williams, a confident man in his mid-forties with steel-gray tightly curled hair, rises to greet us. "Chris Williams," he says. "Pleased to meet you, Mr. Darcy." He indicates we should sit opposite him at the other end of the table. "I've often wondered what political liaison officers do," he adds.

Maitland steps in to field this one. "Mr. Darcy is here to facilitate arrangements for the treatment of US citizens and the return of bodies to America."

This clearly doesn't fool the assistant chief constable who, Maitland has warned me, is ambitious. "Detective Superintendent Forester," he says, "heads our inquiry team for this incident and was in the process of updating us."

The ruddy-faced Forester, also in his mid-forties, is well-built and, I estimate, over six feet tall. Just like Pop in his Sunday best, Forester in his slate-blue suit and flowered tie still looks, moves, and talks like a cop. "The identification process was completed nearly two hours ago," he says pointedly. "It's raised yet another problem."

"Perhaps I should explain, Mr. Darcy," Williams says, "that I called this meeting to resolve several problems which Superintendent Forester's team are facing."

"As I was saying, sir," Forester continues, "at the identification it appears that a black American gentleman, presumably from GCHQ, acted as a minder to the US relatives. The coroner's office, and consequently ourselves, have been unable to obtain the names, addresses, occupations, and lengths of residence in the UK of the non-UK citizens deceased."

"I'm sure that Mr. Darcy can supply the details," Williams says smoothly.

Again Maitland fields the question. "I'm sure you appreciate that such details are covered by the Official Secrets Act."

Williams raises his eyebrows. "And I'm sure Mr. Darcy appreciates that our press officer is under constant pressure from the media for information. If he recycles the answers you're giving to Superintendent Forester, the media will assume that all those killed were spies, as the IRA statement claimed. This will prompt them to ask what American spies are doing in Cheltenham. Is this what Mr. Darcy really wants?"

Williams is not only ambitious, he's smart. I let him have Bruce Davis's cover story about off-duty United States Air Force officers attending a birthday party.

Williams looks at me. "I suppose that sounds plausible."

Forester looks unhappy. "In addition, sir, I have been denied cooperation in interviewing and obtaining statements from the American survivors of the bombing."

"Let me have your questions," I say, "and I'll obtain the statements you need subject to considerations of national security."

"My officers need to be there for follow up questions," Forester states.

"I'll arrange for a team of counterterrorist officers to assist the investigation," I say.

"I'm sure the chief constable would wish me to thank

you for your kind offer," Williams says, "as he also thanked the Metropolitan Police Antiterrorist Squad for their equally kind offer. But he would also wish me to point out that the crime took place within his constabulary. A knowledge of local witnesses, informants, unusual occurrences or movements in the district, suspicious activities by anyone with Irish connections either working here permanently in the stables or visiting for the races, and a thorough check of the boarding houses can only realistically be undertaken by the local police force under Superintendent Forester's able direction."

"I was referring to the security and international aspects," I say.

"Inspector Bew of our Special Branch has this all under control," Williams replies.

"I'm in the process of setting up a joint intelligence group," says Bew, a man in his late thirties who has parted his hair just above his left ear with long strands combed across to his right ear in a futile attempt to camouflage the balding patch on top of his head. "The JIG will liaise with the Security Service and with the Secret Intelligence Service and through them, if necessary, with any foreign intelligence services." He nods to the young woman on his left. "Ms. Ackroyd heads the Security Service's crisis unit for this incident and is working with me to establish the appropriate systems and channels."

Jesus Christ! So this woman in her mid-twenties, who has been writing furiously in a student's foolscap pad and whom I've assumed to be a clerk, is the officer that Maitland has put in charge of the case for MI5. This investigation is going to get nowhere very slowly.

"I appreciate your lead role and the importance of local knowledge," I say to Williams, "but I'm sure your chief constable will appreciate that the United States government wants to do all within its power to assist him apprehend the murderers of US citizens. It will place at his disposal operatives experienced in investigating international terrorist acts."

Williams stares at me. "Mr. Darcy, you may inform whoever represents the Central Intelligence Agency at your embassy that the chief constable of Gloucestershire does not intend to follow the Lockerbie example."

"I'm sure the Agency representative appreciates that the bombing of an American aircraft over British territory is different from the bombing of a British pub on British soil, but if your chief constable means . . ."

"What my chief constable means, Mr. Darcy, is that he does not intend to allow his investigation to be hijacked by the CIA, enabling the American government to decide it is politically expedient to prosecute only those who plant the bomb and not those who commission and plan the atrocity. Is his meaning clear?"

Chapter ✛ Seven

IN THE INTELLIGENCE community, as in Humpty Dumpty's world through Alice's looking glass, words mean just what we choose them to mean, neither more nor less. The white letters on the brown noticeboard say OAKLEY: JOINT TECHNICAL LANGUAGE SERVICE.

These words mean the larger of the two Cheltenham sites of Britain's worldwide electronic eavesdropping headquarters.

Maitland drives through the opened wire-mesh gate, passes a departing gray British Telecommunications van, and halts in front of a raised yellow pole which ought to be blocking the road. He makes no effort to lean out of the Jaguar's window into the rain, and so one of the security guards has to leave the shelter of his cabin in order to peer at Maitland's identification. With their black flat hats and their heavy black raincoats beneath reflective bibs, these unarmed guards look as threatening as ticket inspectors on London buses. They prove just as ineffective. The guard goes back to his cabin and returns with two green visitor badges for us to wear on chains round our necks. "Would you like to leave your vehicle in the visitors' car-park to the left, sir, please?" he asks.

"Certainly not," Maitland replies and drives straight on.

He is halted after twenty-five yards by raised floor barriers between four booths spaced across the road like a turnpike toll stop. Maitland impatiently waves his identification at the guard in the nearest booth, who lowers the barrier without examining our visitor badges.

The road bears left between a clutch of Second World War white Quonset huts and proceeds uphill toward buildings which can't be seen from the narrow perimeter fence to the road outside. To our left, rolls of razor wire fill the gap between a four-foot-high chain-link inner fence and a ten-foot-high chain-link outer fence which is also topped by a roll of razor wire. Trees and bushes outside the fence mask the site from the adjacent meadow. Three-hundred yards after the entrance we pass through an inner gate and then take the right hand fork in the road, still climbing. At least the physical security measures we insisted upon are functional even if the British guards are not.

Maitland drives half the length of a nondescript sand-colored brick building and parks in the turning circle outside its main entrance. Opposite, the tops of white sails move eerily across the flat crest of a hill which separates this side of the site from a reservoir. Ahead, a huge modernistic octagonal green-panel and glass construction, buttressed by four large brick towers, looks down on us. "M Block," Maitland says as he locks the Jaguar's doors. "Our magic block." I know. We paid for it.

I follow Maitland through the double glass doors into the spacious entrance hall of C Block. After telephoning, the guard says, "Somebody is coming to let you in to the SUSLO corridor."

Maitland accompanies me to the elevator just outside

the door to the Senior United States Liaison Office to the right. "I'll pop upstairs to the director's suite. Give a bell if you need me."

Large pink-framed spectacles dominate the face of the short woman who opens the door to the SUSLO corridor. The pink matches the color of large earrings, which take over where her dyed blonde hair comes to an abrupt end.

"Hi," she says, "I'm Ellen Rochberg, senior personnel officer."

I follow the black and white houndstooth tweed suit and its swaying hips down the corridor to Bruce Davis's large office, which has a view uphill to M Block. Davis unwinds himself from the seat behind the conference table to greet me. He's taken off the jacket of the dark suit he was wearing this morning, loosened his tie, and undone the top button of his white shirt. "John, glad you could make it. How were the cops?"

"Determined to stay in control. The detective heading the investigation complained that you prevented him from getting the facts about the American dead and injured."

"Did the cover hold?"

"The assistant chief constable saw through it. It would help to know exactly what it is I'm covering."

"Sure." Davis resumes his seat in front of the rain spattered window. "Ellen?"

Rochberg pushes across Clarence Thomson's personnel file. I look at the photograph of the man who gave Georgina Thomson the "yellow metal Seiko watch on left wrist and gold ring on left wedding finger." Even on this formal Polaroid Thomson shows a gleam of ivory teeth below his Zapata moustache. The whole of his face is relaxed in a smile, but most of all I see the man in his laughing liquid brown eyes. He and Georgina would have been fun to be with.

Rochberg takes off her large pink-framed spectacles and holds them in a reflective pose. "Clarence Thomson was one of the few NSA staff to go native. He asked for an extension to his three-year tour, sent his daughter to Cheltenham Ladies' College, and moved out of a modern house with its own garage in order to buy a Regency house which he was restoring."

"Social life?"

"While guys here travel out to the US Navy base at High Wycombe to find cold beer and a game of bowls, Clarence and Georgina Thomson drank in the local pubs and played skittles. He hired the skittle alley at The Albion for his birthday party."

"Why?"

Rochberg looks across the conference table to a mournful man with rheumy eyes and a squashed nose. Mario Falcone, the senior US security officer at GCHQ, blows his nose noisily into a large handkerchief before saying, "Skittles is popular round these parts with the Brits. Clarence was into it in a big way. He formed his own team, the Prestbury Pilgrims, who played league games Wednesdays." He shakes his head. "He persuaded me to join. I was supposed to go to the party, 'cept I came down bad with a cold."

"Whom did he invite to the party?" I ask.

"Just friends," says Falcone. "Clarence had a lot of English friends. Most of them work here, most of them were Prestbury Pilgrims. The Americans he invited were old buddies from USAF days, plus the other American on his combined party."

"And you?"

Falcone looks even more morose. "I thought he was mixing too much with the Brits, especially out of hours, not good for security, so I had him into my office for a long talk." He turns his head away and sneezes. "Clarence was the type of guy it was impossible not to like. Instead of me persuading him to stick to his own crowd, he has me down at The Albion, warm beer and all."

"How many at the party were working on intercepts of IRA communications?" I ask.

"None," Davis replies. "What's troubling you, John?"

I stand up and walk to the window for some inspiration. Puffs of white smoke escape from the chimney of the incinerator behind the green octagonal of M Block; beyond, a meadow rises into angry black clouds as night closes around us. "It doesn't make sense."

"What doesn't?" Davis asks.

I turn to face them. "The IRA. Look at it from their point of view. The IRA ceasefire has enabled its political wing to forge a common front with the main nationalist party in Northern Ireland, with the Irish government, and with the Irish American political lobby. They're in the middle of negotiations with Britain over the constitutional future of Northern Ireland. The White House is pushing the British government to go the extra mile for an agreed solution. It's even offering economic help as an incentive for the Ulster loyalists to come on board." I shake my head. "The IRA is heading toward what it's fought for since 1916, an independent and united Ireland. And now? This bombing will wreck the negotiations and destroy its support in the US."

"But if not the IRA, who?" Davis says.

I walk to the table. "Let's go through the possibilities. Who was Clarence Thomson? Did he have any enemies, any problems?"

"Lieutenant Colonel Clarence Thomson joined NSA from US Air Force Intelligence," Davis says. "You heard Mario. Everyone liked him."

"Problems? Financial? Women? Drink? Drugs?"

The other person at the table, Harlow Duffin, the Alcohol Misuse Officer, scratches his shining pink skull and says in a Southern drawl, "We sure do have drink problems round here, but them's from the guys who buy their hooch cheap at the PX and drink the stuff at home. As for Clarence, I don't know nobody with fewer problems."

"The fees at Cheltenham Ladies' College are high," says Rochberg. "And he was paying off a mortgage on his house."

"Can we run a check on his bank, find out if he was borrowing money and from whom?" I ask.

"John," says Davis, "nobody's going to waste fifteen people and cripple another thirty-seven because of some unpaid school fees. This is Cheltenham, England, not Moscow."

"Sure," I say, "but if he needed more than a lieutenant colonel's salary, then he was vulnerable. If the Russians can bribe the head of our Soviet Bloc counterintelligence staff at Langley, they can get to an NSA officer here. And if things go wrong, say he decides to quit and come clean with us on what he's told them, then taking him out along with a bunch of others and claiming it was the IRA distracts attention away from him and from them."

"Don't let Aldrich Ames get to you, John," says Davis.

"It's just an hypothesis, Bruce. We'd be wrong to jump to conclusions about this. We have to explore all the possibilities. Precisely what was Clarence Thomson doing here?"

Davis gets up, pulls the blinds down over the window, and turns on the lights. "Clarence worked in K Division, in a section that analyzed the intercepts of Iraqi Air Force communications."

At last, we're getting somewhere. "Who else was in the section?"

"It was a combined party. In theory, because this is a British establishment, a Brit is section head and our people are advisers and consultants. In practice Clarence ran this three-man section. The notional head was Mike Nesbitt, a fluent Arabic speaker, and the third man was a Texan, Gary Ford, who has a Harvard PhD in math and is a genius at breaking Iraqi codes."

"Is he the father of Lucy Ford, the four years old . . . ?"

Rochberg nods. "His wife Madeleine was unharmed, but Gary is in hospital. Mike Nesbitt was killed."

"How important is this section?"

"Crucial," Davis says. "It takes the raw data from intercepts collected by satellite and other listening posts—voice communications, faxes, images on their computer screens—translates, deciphers and analyzes them, and produces reports we send priority to Fort Meade, who distribute the product to National Security Council, Pentagon, State, and Langley. It gives us the best intelligence we have on the Iraqi Air Force."

"And now?"

He holds out his hands in despair. "I've reassigned another codebreaker from the Egyptian section, but frankly he can't match Gary's brilliance. The Brits are trying to find someone as good at technical Arabic as Mike Nesbitt. I've asked Meade to supply us with a replacement for Clarence, but right now the West is blind to the Iraqi Air Force. It's going to take time to build up a team as effective as Clarence's."

"Right," I say, as I walk to Davis's whiteboard. I take a marker and start listing.

HYPOTHESIS	MOTIVE	OPPORTUNITY	OPERATIONAL SUCCESS
1. IRA targets British spies	None (counter-productive)	Unknown	Zero
2. Unknown intelligence service target their agent Thomson	To prevent him confessing his activities to US authorities	Handler knows Thomson's social habits	Total. And distracts from real motive

3. Iraqis target Thomson's section	To destroy West's current intelligence operations against Iraqi Air Force	Unknown	Total. And distracts from real motive

"Nobody believes that Clarence was a foreign agent," Falcone protests.

"For nine years nobody dreamt that the head of our Soviet counterintelligence staff was a KGB mole," I say. "My job is to establish facts, not beliefs. And whether Thomson was an agent or a victim, we start by checking out all his contacts. If I get Maitland to supply us with a list of all the telephone numbers that Thomson has called in the last year, can you put a tap on them, Bruce?"

"Sure. I'll have Menwith Hill do it electronically. That way we'll bypass all the British crap about warrants."

"Can we also tap the phones of all NSA people who work here?"

Davis screws up his face. "That's over two hundred and fifty." He shrugs. "Consider them tapped as from tomorrow."

"Next we need to check out all Thomson's contacts." I look at Falcone. "I'm sure you appreciate, Mario, that we got to prioritize all his friends who *weren't* there on Friday. We need to put them through the polygraph."

"If you say so. I'm the one who normally flutters people round here, so I guess you'll have to do me. But I warn you, we can't flutter the Brits."

"Can we tap their phones?"

"No problem," Davis says. "We can also activate their phones while they're on the hook and listen in to conversations in the same room as the phone."

"What about their security files? Will the director here cooperate?"

"John," Davis says, "this place costs over one and half billion dollars a year to run, and we pick up more than half the tab. The director knows which side his bread is buttered on."

"Let's call Maitland down and have him get the telephone numbers."

"Edward, make yourself at home," says Davis after Rochberg leads him into the room.

Maitland sits back from the table and gets out a cigar.

"Afraid SUSLO is a no smoke zone, Edward," Davis says. "Have some gum?"

"How terribly kind," Maitland says. "But no thank you." He scans the whiteboard while I brief him on what we want him to do.

"Happy to oblige," Maitland says, "but I fear it'll be a terrible waste of time and resources."

"How come?" Davis asks.

"You're barking up the wrong tree. In fact two wrong trees." He stands up and walks to the whiteboard. "You seem to be discounting the first hypothesis: the IRA. I'll give you two motives. One: the IRA still believes it can bomb its way to further concessions. The greater the killing, the greater the pressure on the British government to put an end to all the slaughter by coming to a deal with them. The IRA has been remarkably successful at employing that strategy in recent years."

"Come on," I say, "Sinn Féin is only at the negotiating table because the IRA declared a ceasefire."

Maitland smiles indulgently. "My dear John, there wouldn't be a negotiating table if IRA bombs over twenty-five years hadn't persuaded the British government that it can never defeat the IRA militarily."

"Why bomb now?" Davis asks.

"The negotiations are bogged down," Maitland says from

his lecturing position in front of the whiteboard. "Loyalists are blocking the IRA's goal of a united Ireland."

"I don't buy that theory," I say.

Maitland shrugs. "Then let me give you motive number two. It was Brendan Behan, I believe, who said that the first item on every IRA agenda is the split. We've seen it every time the IRA has called a ceasefire. The Provos split from the Officials, the Irish National Liberation Army split from the Officials, and so on. It's an equally plausible theory that the hardline group within the IRA who initially opposed the ceasefire believe now that the negotiations are leading nowhere. They're resuming the armed struggle."

"And opportunity?" Davis asks.

"May I ask how long you have been at GCHQ?" Maitland inquires.

"Just over a year," Davis replies.

"Then I must presume that you don't follow the gee gees. Most of the hurdlers and steeplechasers trained in Cheltenham are bred in Ireland. Just run a check on the trainers, stableboys, and stablegirls here and see how many Irish names you produce. Then look at the timing. The bomb went off six days after the Mackeson Gold Cup. The racetrack is less than fifteen minutes' walk from The Albion. A lot of Irish come over every year for that weekend of races. Especially now that the UK and Ireland are part of this absurd European Union, it would have been the easiest thing in the world for the IRA to join the punters and bring across explosives and detonators on the car ferry to Swansea or Pembroke."

"That's a strong case he's building, John," Davis says.

"But what about operational success?" I challenge Maitland. "No one spying on the IRA was at The Albion. Bombing Americans is totally self-defeating."

"Dear oh dear," Maitland says, "I see you're still firmly wedded to the conspiracy theory of history. I prefer the

cock up theory. And this was a classic cock up, like so many
IRA operations. How many people in Britain, John, even
know the number of Americans working at GCHQ, still less
what work they actually do here?"

Davis looks at me. I say nothing.

"I'll tell you," Maitland says. "From the prime minister
down, thirty people at most."

He pauses to let the number sink in. "The IRA's informants among the Irish community in Cheltenham simply told
them that The Albion was a pub popular with GCHQ staff,
and that one of them had booked the skittle alley for a party
six days after the Mackeson Gold Cup. Do you imagine that
the IRA would ever dream that an *American* would play skittles, a game that we English invented in Saxon times?"

Maitland leaves the whiteboard, sits down, and places
his right leg nonchalantly across his left knee. "As far as the
IRA is concerned, British spies booked the skittle alley for
a party. It was an ideal opportunity to do a spectacular
against what it regards as a legitimate target."

"The IRA denied it," I say.

Maitland gives a dismissive laugh. "Wouldn't you if you
discovered that you'd killed American women and children?
What you can't deny, my dear John, is that the telephone
calls made to ITN, the BBC, and Reuters which first
claimed responsibility all used the identifier 'P. O'Neill'.
That is a codeword for IRA communications about what it
terms its military operations."

Davis looks at me. "John, I guess you'd better wipe out
hypotheses two and three, otherwise certain people are
going to think you're letting your Irish-American background cloud your judgment."

The silver Jaguar slips out of GCHQ's Oakely site and makes
a right into a suburban road. Rain beats down on the

windshield and the wipers silently clear the glass. There is no air conditioning to clear the car of Maitland's cigar smoke.

The stone gates of a cemetery pass by on our right, and then we're through a mixture of detached houses with their own garages followed by redbrick municipal houses built in tandem. Less than five minutes after leaving GCHQ we exit a mini traffic circle—no more than white markings on the blacktop—and then make a right to find a road blocked off by a blue and white banded ribbon.

"You wanted to see it," Maitland says. "The Burgage was the main street of Prestbury village in Norman times. The Albion dates back to the early seventeenth century."

The road beyond the temporary police barrier is wide and dark. Halfway along, past an hotel and opposite a large white trailer serving as the police forward incident room, tall arc lamps focus on what appears to be a peaceful ancient pub in a quiet village street. But the light cast by the lamps is unreal. It's the kind of light they have at nighttime automobile pileups or big fires. The kind of light that means death.

"Excuse me, sir," says a drenched police constable with a dripping reflective bib over his black raincoat. "You'll be having to move on. The Burgage is closed."

Maitland says nothing but shows his police pass.

"Sorry, sir," the constable replies in his soft burr. "Would you be wanting to go through? With the rain we've suspended operations for the night."

Maitland turns to me. "Well?"

I can't deny that Maitland has proved helpful today. His patronizing snobbery infuriates me, but maybe it's all part of pretending to be grander than he really is. Is the poor bastard trying to live up to her expectations? It was cruel to think of puncturing his arrogance by telling him that I'd screwed his wife. "I guess there's nothing more to see tonight," I say.

"Then I think we should head back," Maitland says,

looking at his watch. He picks up his car phone. "I'll tell Jill to have dinner ready for nine-thirty."

Panic grips me. "No," I splutter. "I mean, thank you, it's very kind, but I think I'll stay up here. I promised Forester that I'd interview the American survivors. I want to make an early start."

Maitland turns his head and scrutinises me. His face is in shadow and I can't discern his expression. "As you wish."

It's not Edward, it's Jill that I fear. But why? What can she do to me after all this time?

"Yes, sir," the constable says, "the hotel is open, but it won't have much custom, seeing as how only those with a police pass can get to it."

"That suits me fine," I say, and hurry through the rain for fifty yards or so past the police barrier. A limp Union Jack hangs from the flagpole outside the Cotswold stone Georgian manor house called The Prestbury House Hotel.

I have no change of clothes, not even a toothbrush, and after checking in I head straight for the dining room. A group of twelve casually dressed men and women, mostly in their late twenties, are sitting either side of two tables placed together. Otherwise the place is deserted. I choose a table laid for two in the corner.

The dining room is Georgian at its simplest and most elegant, a beautifully proportioned extension that ends in a semicircular bay embracing three windows. A chandelier hangs from the corniced white ceiling and illuminates eggshell-blue walls and an Adam fireplace. The perfect place for a romantic weekend. I look down at the menu. Loneliness is trying to find a half bottle of decent wine.

"Are you a reporter too, sir?" The soft burr is similar to the policeman's. It comes from a waiter with a crumpled old face and a starched white linen jacket.

I nod.

"Won't you be wanting to join the others?"

American and Irish voices mingle with the English story-swapping from the long table: Sarajevo, Kigali, Grozny. And now Cheltenham? I suppose this is small beer by comparison. I shake my head at the waiter.

"Can't say as how I blame you, sir. The bomb at The Albion was no laughing matter. Bound to add to the ghosts hereabouts."

I stare past the flickering candle in the center of the table to the unoccupied chair opposite and remain silent. I have enough problems trying to exorcise the demon that haunts me.

Chapter ✤ Eight

THE CANDLE FLICKERED in the straw-covered Chianti flask on the red and white check tablecloth of our favorite restaurant. From the other side of the candle Jill reached out and touched my arm. "Thanks, John."

"I thought it would make a change from you cooking dinner every Friday." I hadn't yet summoned the courage to tell her the real reason for taking her out this Friday evening.

"Silly man," she said softly, keeping her right hand on my arm. "I'm not talking about dinner." In the candlelight her face seemed so pale, almost ghost-like, between the cascades of gleaming red hair. "I mean thanks for this last sixteen months. They've been the happiest of my life."

I wanted this moment to last for ever: her hand on my arm, the emotion-laden recording of "E Lucevan le Stelle" playing softly in the background, the smell of tomatoes and basil from the *pappa al pomodoro*, the grapy aftertaste of a young Chianti. We might almost be transported to Tuscany.

"What do you want to tell me, John?"

Jill could always read my mind. When she'd talked of

showing me Italy, she felt my pain at the mention of Rome, with its inextricable association with the faith I'd abandoned, and she subtly steered the planned vacation to Florence. Since Tuesday's announcement at the station, however, I feared that this, and all the other plans I'd dreamt of, would collapse.

I pushed my plate to one side. "I'm due for promotion to GS-11."

"That's wonderful." Her voice sounded strained. "I thought that . . ."

I placed my right hand over hers, gripping it to my arm. "When I return to the States in September."

"But you said . . ."

I released her hand. It was only when the waiter removed my untouched soup that I noticed Jill hadn't eaten hers. "*Red Weekly* has published the names and addresses of most of the station officers. The chief decided to cut short all our assignments. Ever since terrorists assassinated our Athens station chief, the company has been paranoid about our identities being exposed."

We both knew what I wanted to ask her, but Jill got in first. "There's something I've put off telling you, John. Edward's tour finishes next week."

"Next week!" For a moment I was speechless. Those gold-flecked green eyes glanced nervously in my direction and then looked down at the lamb stew which the waiter placed in front of her. "How long have you known?" I asked when he'd gone. "Why did you hide it from me?"

"Shush, John. The whole restaurant can hear."

"I don't care if the whole world can hear."

Tears formed in her eyes. "May we go, please?"

I paid the check. The waiter looked at two uneaten dinners and asked if anything was wrong. "Nothing," I said. "Everything's just dandy."

I waited for a cab on Heath Street, reflecting bitterly on

another dream: that we would live together in my favorite part of London, this village-within-a-city bordering the wild Hampstead Heath.

After a silent cab ride to Boydell Court we took the elevator to my apartment. I unlocked the door and said, "Are you keeping your coat on?"

Jill's eyes welled with tears, but her voice was quiet and measured. "I put off telling you, John, because I was afraid of what you'd ask me."

Her self-control shamed my petulance. "Forgive me, my love, that was vicious of me." I hugged her. "I . . . I'm just so afraid of losing you."

"Don't you think I feel the same?" she said into my shoulder.

"But I'm not married, like you," I said.

"But are you free?"

"What do you mean?"

"Nobody can just discard beliefs they've held all their life." She wiped away one tear that had escaped. "I'm not asking you to, John."

I didn't know what she meant, but I didn't care. We clung to each other. After making love that night we stayed locked together, as though fearing to let anything come between us.

When the sun found the gap in the drapes, I woke and looked at her. I couldn't imagine that long red hair on any other pillow but mine. She seemed scarcely to be breathing, but a smile of contentment wreathed her face. When she stirred I kissed her brow and asked, "Will you move in here and write to Edward to say that you're going to the States with me in September?"

Her small hand gripped the pillow case, and nervousness

returned to the wildcat green eyes. "I . . . I need time to think, John. Please."

"How much time do you need, for God's sake!"

She buried her face in the pillow.

Why had she thanked me for *sixteen* months' happiness last night? "Do you love me?" I demanded.

She turned to face me. "Haven't I shown it?"

"Then what is there to think about?"

She pulled up the sheet to cover her breasts. Her eyes looked down at the small fist gripping the sheet. "You see everything in black and white, John. Life isn't like that." When she looked up, her eyes pleaded. "Because I love you it doesn't mean I hate Edward. I hoped you'd see that."

"What *do* you feel for him?" I persisted.

"I feel I can't do a cowardly thing like leave a letter for him to find when he returns after two years in Northern Ireland. I should be there when he gets back. Please let me handle it in my own way."

After Edward returned I didn't hear from Jill for two weeks. It nearly drove me insane. I couldn't bear to be on my own in the apartment Friday evenings, yet I dared not leave in case she phoned or came round. Those hot May nights I couldn't sleep for thinking that she might be making love to him.

Finally she phoned to say that she could come round on Saturday afternoon. I resolved not to say a word, not to show my jealousy, lest it frighten her away.

On the hottest day so far of what had become a British heatwave, Jill stepped hesitantly into my apartment. She pushed her long red hair back behind one ear, and her anxious eyes sought mine. The short white Indian cotton dress I'd bought clung to her body with perspiration.

I said nothing, but held her to me. The wild cat in her

responded by wrapping herself round me. Desire over-whelmed me. We peeled off each other's clothes and sank to the floor, her red hair splayed over gray drawing room carpet, our bodies entwined in one long pulsating panting embrace until, sated at last, we rolled apart, held hands, and lay there in the heat. Only the sound of our breathing broke the silence.

After an eternity she spoke the first words since she'd entered the apartment. "Do you think I'm a whore?"

"No!" I sat up, but her eyes continued to stare at the ceiling. "Why do you say that?" I asked.

"Because you've thought a lot this past fortnight."

"Of course I have, but not . . ."

"Do you feel guilty?"

"No!" I said, as though vehemence could disguise doubt.

"I thought that's what consumed Catholics in the end. Guilt."

"Why bring all this up again?"

"I didn't want to face Edward on my own, so I asked Elizabeth to come and stay."

"The sister who's a convert? Did you tell her about us?" She nodded.

"What did she say?"

"She said you'd miss your faith."

How could I not miss what had been central to my life until a year and a half ago? At times during these last two weeks I'd dreamt of Jill obtaining an annulment, and of my brother Joe officiating at our marriage in the Jesuit church at Fordham University. The Vatican did grant annulments, though usually—or so it seemed—to Catholic royalty. What proof was needed to show that a marriage was not valid? I'd never asked Jill about her relationship with Edward. They had no children. There was an indefinable inner coldness about him. But I was straying into the realms of fantasy. "I've made my choice," I said. "Have you told Edward?"

"Not yet." She turned her head to face me. "Elizabeth invited me to visit her for six weeks, for your bicentennial celebrations. I want to see what America's like."

My heart leapt. "Where does she live?" I asked, trying to sound as casual as I could.

"Glenn was transferred to Citibank's head office. They're in New York now."

New York! New York! "Where in New York?"

"A place called Riverdale."

I was so happy I laughed.

She propped herself on her elbow and her hair fell over one half of her face. "What's so funny?"

I pushed her hair back. "Riverdale is in the Bronx, but those who live there never dream of calling it the Bronx. For them Riverdale is the place where Manhattan millionaires built summer palaces overlooking the Hudson at the beginning of the century."

"You know it?"

"It's less than three miles from where I went to college, and about the same distance from where my brother Joe has his parish."

I leant down and kissed the salty beads of sweat which were running from her brow into her eyes. "Washington isn't New York, and I'm no banker, but with a promotion to GS-11 I should be able to rent a place in Georgetown. You'll just love Georgetown. It's got beautiful row houses dating back to the eighteenth and nineteenth centuries, cobbled streets, terrific restaurants, and wonderful shops. Think of living in Hampstead next to the Potomac River with summers like this one every year."

The heatwave intensified. By the time Jill left, London was sweltering in ninety-five degrees Fahrenheit. Unlike New

York or Washington, this goddamned city had no air conditioning.

Tension in the office rose after the chief announced the detailed schedule of staff replacements. After the swinging cuts at headquarters made by our new director, the others fretted about what jobs they would be given—if any—back at Langley. I comforted myself with thoughts of life with Jill. Edward, fortunately, didn't return to MI5's K Branch, but was assigned to an enlarged and more powerful F Branch to tackle domestic subversion, and I was spared the embarrassment and guilt of meeting him.

Those six weeks dragged on for a lifetime. No phone calls, no letters, just memories and dreams.

At last the day arrived. I wanted to go to the airport, but Jill hadn't told me what time or what flight, and so I stayed at home waiting for the telephone. An agonizing two days later it rang.

She came on Saturday afternoon. It was far hotter than that Saturday in May, and I was dressed only in T-shirt and short pants as I went to open the door.

Her hair was swept back and tied in a ribbon. Despite the heat she wore a cotton jacket over a long dress. I went to take her in my arms. She said, "I must have a cold drink, John, please. Non-alcoholic."

I retreated to the kitchen to get two Cokes from the refrigerator. Perhaps she was shy and unsure of me after so long apart, or perhaps she didn't want me to think she was a whore.

She was sitting in an upright chair when I handed her one of the Cokes. I pulled up a chair to be close to her. "Welcome back, Jill," I said. "You look lovely."

She forced a smile. "Thanks, John."

"I've missed you," I said. "Like crazy."

"I'd be grateful for a glass, please, John."

"Sure." I went back to the kitchen.

When I returned she said, "How are things at the office?"

At the office! "Terrific. George Bush, our new director, has fired eleven of the top fourteen department heads at Langley. You probably read that the Senate's Church Committee called us unaccountable burglars, subverters, and assassins. At the embassy's bicentennial celebrations the regular diplomats treated us like pariahs. How was your trip?"

She poured her Coke into the glass and took a sip. "The visit gave me time and space to think." She put down her glass and entwined her fingers on her lap. "About the feelings we have for each other . . ."

"Have your feelings changed?"

She shook her head.

"Thank God for that. For a moment you had me worried." I stood up and moved toward her.

She picked up her glass, took another sip, and looked down into the black liquid. "Some things are more important than feelings . . ."

I stood in front of her. "Like what?"

"You know better than I do, John. There is a love even greater than . . ." She bit her lip. "I'm not expressing myself very well."

"What are you trying to say?" I demanded.

She put down her glass. For the first time she didn't avoid my gaze. "We mustn't see each other again."

I couldn't believe my ears. "But you promised . . ."

"No, John. I never promised anything."

"You said that you were going to the States to . . . to make sure it was OK for you to move there. Don't you like the States? Look, if that's the problem I'll quit the Agency and find a job here. I'll . . ."

"John, please. Don't make it any more difficult for me. I went to America to find some space . . . to . . . to try and sort out my life, away from the pressures here."

"And you decided to stay with Edward. Terrific. Now tell me why."

She looked down at her lap. Her fingers were intertwined so tightly that her knuckles were white.

"Does he have more money than I have? Is he a better screw?"

Her shoulders trembled. "I thought you'd understand."

"You've never loved me at all, have you? I was just a plaything, a substitute lay while Edward was in Northern Ireland. You make me sick, you and your British hypocrisy. What does dear darling Edward think about it all? Bit of a laugh, old sport, what?"

Her voice was barely more than a whisper. "I've never told Edward about us."

I shook my head. "Now I've heard it all! You really took me for a ride, didn't you?"

Those green eyes, like those of a trapped animal, pleaded for release, but her voice remained calm. "John, I will never ask you anything again, I promise. But if you ever felt anything for me, I beg you, please don't tell Edward about . . . about what we shared together."

I couldn't refuse her anything, even that. But I couldn't stay in the same city, the same country. The next day I booked my flight and told the office I was returning early because my mother was ill. Back at Langley I requested to transfer to Soviet Bloc Division. I resolved never to set foot in England again.

Chapter ✤ Nine

I STEP CAREFULLY through the wreckage at the rear of The Albion pub, still trying after all these years to rebuild my life. Jill Maitland may have destroyed my belief in God and in love, but she failed to extinguish the conviction that the values my country stands for are worth defending.

The downpour eased overnight, leaving one of those fine English drizzles which is more like mist than rainfall. They must have begun early. Policemen wearing blue overalls, blue safety helmets, and white masks which cover mouth and nose are systematically combing through the ruins. Like shattered megaliths bordering a desecrated long barrow, concrete slabs languish next to the blackened remains of a red carpet running parallel with a long narrow charred wooden floor. Only a part of one of the concrete walls—at the far end—remains standing. The rest of what was the skittle alley is reduced to concrete chunks, timber spars, tile shards, and glass splinters scattered over the lawn and over two uprooted yew trees. Part of the debris has smashed into the redbrick rear of The Albion, where half a

dozen yellow-helmeted people are checking for structural
stability. Even after a day of rain an acrid smell clings to the
devastation, like a spirit unwilling to depart the scene of
death.

Detective Superintendent Forester is still wary. I can't
blame him. He's a cop who wants to solve a crime, and he's
suspicious of "national security considerations" if they hin-
der his well-tried procedures. He hands me copies of the
questionnaire he's prepared for the American survivors. "I
reserve the right to follow up any answers if they indicate a
lead might be forthcoming."

"Sure," I say. "Tell me about the bomb."

"Dr. McKinnon is our forensic scientist." He leads me
to a man with a shaggy beard who is wearing a tweed overcoat. McKinnon breaks off from directing the policemen
from the Scenes of Crime Department and shakes my hand.

"As you can see from the cratering and the pattern of the
debris," McKinnon says in a broad Scots accent, "the bomb
was placed here, in the toilet, to the right after you enter the
skittle alley. My guess is that it was hidden in the cistern. The
whole place was a jerry-built addition, just after the Second
World War I'd say. Thin concrete walls, asbestos-tiled roof.
Almost complete destruction. The people standing at the
front of the skittle alley and those at the bar next to them
got the full force of the blast."

Forester returns to the trailer parked outside the front
of the pub.

"Do you know what caused the explosion?" I ask Mc-
Kinnon.

He nods. "I've little doubt. On Saturday afternoon we
unearthed part of the ballcock from the toilet cistern. It was
scorched and pitted, the sure sign of a high-detonating explosion. I took some swabs and sent the ballcock remains to
Fort Halstead."

"Any results?"

"Not from their forensic explosives lab, but I analyzed my swabs yesterday and found traces of pentaerythritol tetranitrate and cyclotrimethylene." He looks at me, and I pretend not to know what that means. "They're constituents of the highly explosive Semtex-H," he explains.

"Anything more?"

"You did say you were here to arrange medical treatment of the American injured?" The Scot's upward inflection at the end of the last word imparts a distinct skepticism to his question.

"And the return of bodies," I add.

"Is that right?"

"The relatives and the survivors are bound to ask me about the bomb, and I'd like to be able to tell them."

He raises his eyebrows. "If you really need to know, yesterday afternoon we found remnants of two AAA-sized batteries and pieces of an electrical blasting cap which served as the detonator. All we need to unearth now are enough bits to form part of an E-cell and that will confirm it's the IRA."

"That will prove it?"

"Let me put it this way. It'll be enough for the police to announce in that inimitable way of theirs that this incident has all the hallmarks of an IRA explosive device."

So Maitland was right after all.

"Look at it . . ." McKinnon waves his hand over the scene. "In all my twenty five years' work for the police I've never seen anything like this. The young constable who found one of the legs of a four years old girl had to be sedated and given sick leave. Can you imagine what it did to the girl's parents? If I had my way I'd take the leaders of Sinn Féin and the IRA, flog them to within an inch of their lives, then string them up from lampposts outside Belfast city hall."

If this sentiment is coming from a man who is educated, a professional hardened by a quarter century of examining murders, then what must the mass of tabloid newspaper readers be thinking?

"You look as if you've been working through the night yourself," he says.

I haven't. I've only tossed and turned with dreams of twenty years ago. But the stubble on my chin reminds me that I have no razor and I'm still wearing yesterday's underclothes.

Madeleine Ford runs her hand self-consciously through blond hair that hangs in unwashed straggles to her shoulders. Tears have reddened the rims of her eyes and run rivulets through hastily applied make-up. "Ah'm sorry," she says in her Texan drawl, "you haven't caught me at my best."

Refreshed by a shave and a shower, and wearing new underpants, socks, and shirt bought an hour ago from a smart shop in Cheltenham's Montpellier Street, I feel positively indecent amid this sleep-starved grief.

The Fords live in one of those modern detached houses on the road from GCHQ to Prestbury village, a house with every convenience and no character. Madeleine Ford sits down on a brown leather settee next to the battered teddy bear that I saw her holding when she was interviewed by CNN the night of the bombing. She is alert enough to notice my glance at the half empty bottle of rye from the PX next to an empty tumbler on the glass-topped coffee table in front of her.

"Would you like a drink?" she asks as she pours three fingers into the tumbler.

Eleven o'clock in the morning is far too early for me, but I say yes so she won't feel guilty.

"Help yourself to a glass from the cabinet," she says.

I take an identical tumbler from a glass-fronted cabinet,

sit down on a brown leather easy chair facing the settee, and reach across for her to pour in the rye.

She lights herself a menthol tipped cigarette. "Smoke?"

I draw the line at that.

"I haven't smoked since college," she says. Tears form and spill over before she can brush them away. "I never wanted Gary to take this lousy job. Two weeks after he submitted his PhD thesis, Harvard offered him an associate professorship. He would have been head of his own department by now." She drains her glass. "But no, those recruitment people, they appealed to his patriotism. Gary always was a sucker for that."

"I understand," I say. More than she realizes.

She stubs out the cigarette and lights another. "When can I have my Lucy back?"

"I'm seeing the coroner this afternoon. As soon as he agrees to release the bodies we'll make arrangements for Lucy to be flown home. In the meantime, I'll be most grateful if you can answer some routine questions that will help the police track down Lucy's killers."

"Shoot."

I place Forester's photocopied questionnaire on the coffee table and take out a pen. "What is Lucy's full name?"

She stands up, walks to the bureau that matches the drinks cabinet, takes a framed photograph, and hands it to me. "Isn't she beautiful?"

Surrounded by a halo of blonde curls the face of a young girl grins at me. If ever I'd been blessed with a daughter of my own, I couldn't have asked for anything more adorable than Lucy Ford. "Beautiful," I echo inadequately.

"Lucy Catherine Patricia Ford," Madeleine says as she resumes her seat.

"Age?"

"Four years, two months, and thirteen days."

The next question on the sheet marked "All questions

to be answered by interviewee" is: "Did the deceased have any lovers, friends, or associates who may be linked to terrorist groups?"

"That's all," I say.

She refills her glass. "That doesn't sound much for the British police to work on."

"Don't worry. Their forensic scientists are working flat out, and the police have launched a major investigation. I'll see they leave no stone unturned."

"I just hope they catch them, that's all. These people say they're fighting for the freedom of Ireland. They're fighting for nothing but themselves. There wasn't even a warning. They're psychopaths. Is there any chance they could be tried back home for the murder of American citizens? That way at least we could fry them."

"No. But if there's anything at all that the embassy can do, any counseling we can arrange . . ."

"Just get the bastards." She bursts into tears.

Looking out of windows that form a glass wall the length of the room, over silent deserted stands and an empty racetrack that curves out and round almost to the foot of the Cotswold Hills, it seems difficult to imagine that just over a week ago the Cheltenham Racecourse echoed to the pounding of hooves and the shouts of thousands of excited people—including, perhaps, two IRA bombers.

The chief constable of Gloucestershire takes his place at the center of a table bedecked with microphones, between Assistant Chief Constable Williams and an inspector who liaises with the media. Men and women carrying television cameras marked with the logos of CNN, NBC, ABC, CBS, BBC, ITN, RTE, and European and Japanese stations focus their lenses on the narrow, lined face of Chief Constable Alfred Quixall, the last of the genial faces I saw hanging on the wall of the Constabulary conference room. In the flesh he looks even older, as though he should have retired years ago. Between eighty and a hundred reporters sit on the rows of chairs in this grandstand banqueting suite requisitioned as a media center.

Unused to the bright glare of so many television lights, Quixall begins hesitantly, reading from the statement which I'm sure Williams has written.

He answers questions, echoing McKinnon's phrase about the bomb bearing all the hallmarks of an IRA explosive device. The inspector points to another journalist but, before she begins her question, one of the Americans in the party having dinner yesterday evening at the Prestbury House Hotel stands up and asks loudly, "How many of the Americans who died came over specially for this birthday party and how many were already here?"

Williams whispers into Quixall's ear. The chief constable says, "I understand that some were already in the United Kingdom."

"How many of them were working at GCHQ?" the American reporter demands.

"I'm afraid that information is not available," Quixall replies. "The lady in the brown suit, please."

Still on his feet the reporter turns to me. "Can the American gentleman at the back of the room, the one who is staying at the Prestbury House Hotel, please answer that question?"

"I'm afraid not," Williams intervenes. "Next question please."

"Will the chief constable at least tell us who the gentleman is, or has Britain become a police state?" the American reporter insists.

Williams again prompts his chief constable. "The gentleman is from the American embassy and is here to provide arrangements for United States citizens who have been injured or killed in this incident. I must insist we move on to the reporter whom Inspector Dempsey has indicated."

A young American woman jumps to her feet. "The embassy? Is he FBI or CIA?"

To shouts of "Answer! Answer!" which threaten to coalesce into one thunderous chant, the chief constable pales. "Mr. Darcy is part of the American support of this investigation," he stutters. "His role is that of liaison."

"FBI or CIA?" the American woman shouts. "Let's hear it from him!"

Rattled, the chief constable reverts to reading from his prepared statement. "I repeat: I appreciate that this investigation may develop into a criminal inquiry of international dimensions, and I have taken steps to ensure that the various elements comprising such an inquiry, both national and international, will channel their assistance and support through the mechanisms I have established. Thank you. That will be all, gentlemen."

Terrific. Even if these people put as much effort into pursuing the bombers as into protecting their turf, they'll still be way out of their depth.

Transparent plastic tubes go in and out of the prone body, electrodes are plastered to exposed skin and connected by cables to oscilloscopes flickering with irregular wavy green lines, and bandages swathe most of Gary Ford's head. Sights like this always make me queasy. I never could have become the jungle doctor I'd dreamt of back at St. Sebastian's grade school.

While I peer through the window of a private room in Cheltenham General Hospital, painted in the same institutional green as the mortuary, a bleary-eyed white-coated junior doctor warns me, "Five minutes at the most. Mr. Ford has severe head injuries. As soon as he's more stable, we'll transfer him to the specialist unit at Frenchay Hospital in Bristol."

"Does Mrs. Ford know?" I ask.

He looks uncomfortable and shakes his head. "The physician said she was suffering from shock over her daughter's death. The consultant here decided not to tell her of the extent of her husband's injuries until she was able to cope." He stifles a yawn.

"How long have you been working?"

"My shift was due to finish at eight o'clock on Saturday evening, but with over fifty people dead, dying, or injured I've had to stay on. Five minutes at the most, please."

The sound of the door opening prompts the body in the bed to stir. The bruised eyes open and struggle to focus on me. What comfort can I offer this man? I've brought him nothing but Forester's list of questions. The top of the bedside cabinet is bare, apart from a standard hospital water jug and beaker. No fruit or fruit juice or get well cards. Madeleine must have been so distracted by Lucy's death that she, too, forgot the needs of the living.

I sit on the edge of the chair next to the bed in this sterile room, put Forester's list of questions into my briefcase, and decide to invent answers later. "How are you feeling, Gary?"

"Fine," he manages to say. "Lucy . . ."

If he could sit up in bed and turn his head to the right toward the window, he would see a brick-built extension to the casualty department. If he could also see through the frosted glass windows set high in the first floor, next to large air conditioning vents, he would see the refrigerated cabinet containing the remains of his daughter. "Don't you worry," I say. "I've been with Mrs. Ford this morning."

He grasps my hand. Each word comes out after

considerable effort. "Good to hear American voice. They won't tell. Did they find my daughter?"

I squeeze his hand. "Yes," I say. "They found Lucy."

United States flags cover the first three in the line of eight caskets resting on trestle tables in a cavernous hangar at RAF Mildenhall. On the other side of the line of caskets, behind a white rope which corrals the crowd of black-garbed mourners, Madeleine Ford stares at the smallest of the five bare aluminum caskets.

The line of caskets points out of the hangar to a short ramp which leads up into the opening below the tail fin of a camouflage-green C-141. Starlifter. The rear of this four-engined transport aircraft with swept-back wings is framed by the rectangle of the hangar doors opened to a clear blue sky. The black clouds and rain of three days ago have vanished, dispelled by a bright autumn sun that mocks the somber mood inside the hangar.

A draft ruffles the white surplice of a US Air Force chaplain, but fails to disturb the heavy United States and United States Air Force flags next to him. Each is held vertically by a white-gloved US Air Force private in midnight blue service dress uniform, and flanked by a guard holding a Second World War M-1 rifle sloped against his right shoulder. The color guard is commanded by a master sergeant ramrod-straight behind the flags.

Madeleine Ford pays no heed; her grim face is fixed on that last casket. The chaplain's words draw me back to the requiem masses at St. Sebastian's. "Let us remember the words of Christ. 'I am the resurrection and the life. He who believes in me shall live, even though he dies; and no one who lives and believes in me shall ever die.'" But I have long since ceased to believe. The only certainty is death. "While we pause for a moment in silent prayer," the chaplain goes on, "let us beseech Our Savior to give us the strength to forgive, just as he forgave those who crucified him for our salvation." This God once asked too much of me, and now he asks too much of Madeleine Ford.

The chaplain's empty words die in the vastness of the hangar and are replaced by the slow slap of boot on concrete. An honor guard of one lieutenant bearing a saber followed by three pairs of privates in dress uniform march at funeral pace before stamping to a halt in front of the first casket covered by the Stars and Stripes. With precise, ordered steps, the pairs separate, move forward on either side of the casket, and turn to face each other. On command from the lieutenant the privates act as one to lift the casket onto their shoulders, turn, and march behind the lieutenant toward the hangar door.

When the lieutenant nears the color guard he raises his right hand to his chin, pointing the saber vertically upwards. "Present arms!" shouts the master sergeant. The riflemen, in three distinct movements, present their rifles vertically in front of them, and one of the flag bearers dips his gold-fringed flag by forty five degrees to show the gold and blue crest of an eagle on a shield against an ultramarine background.

"Order arms!" shouts the sergeant when the casket has passed. The rifles return to port arm and the Air Force flag to vertical.

In the sunlight now the lieutenant once more raises his saber. The guards either side of the ramp salute the flag-draped casket which follows the lieutenant into the dark bowels of the Starlifter.

"We've been discussing this at the National Security Council." The softly spoken words immediately to my left are barely audible above the marching boots and barked commands in the echoing hangar.

National Security Agency director Admiral George Ferguson, who has flown over to receive the bodies, continues to face the color guard. His lips barely move. "We want you to find whoever was responsible. And I don't mean those who planted the bomb, I mean the one who gave the orders."

I take his lead and stare straight ahead as a second honor guard process with the second casket. The first honor guard march back in tight formation from the C-141 and, with the same ceremony, pick up the third flag-draped casket.

"Are we seeking British permission?" I ask as Admiral Ferguson salutes this third casket on the call of "Present arms!" Under a longstanding agreement CIA and MI6 undertake not to operate in each other's countries without the prior approval and full knowledge of the host nation.

The second honor guard hoist the first of the undraped civilian caskets onto their shoulders.

"The UKUSA Treaty didn't prevent this."

"Is the National Security Council authorizing unilateral action?" I ask.

"If the Brits get him first, fine. But we don't want you hanging around until they get their act together."

"Will I get a signed directive?"

Admiral Ferguson turns his head to look at me. "Mr. Darcy, everyone wants this bastard nailed to the wall and hung out to dry. We don't care what means you use. We want action, not paper pushing. Do I make myself clear? If you have a problem with this, we'll get somebody else to do it."

The six pall bearers of the second honor march in step and line up either side of the one casket left in the hangar. For the first time they break rank. One guard steps forward, picks up the small aluminum casket of Lucy Ford, stands erect, turns, and begins a slow solitary march toward the aircraft. "I have no problems whatsoever," I reply.

Chapter ✦ Ten

PROBLEMS ARE SOLUTIONS in the making, according to Tony Petillo, one of my instructors at the Farm. Perhaps Stan Brooks believed this once, but it must have been a long time ago. Whatever energy our MI5 liaison officer possesses is directed toward the avoidance of problems, and in my proposed operation he sees far too many.

While I briefed the three of them, Brooks gazed out of my office window, as if wishing he could join the low-season tourists photographing the Roosevelt Memorial in the middle of Grosvenor Square. Now he is the first to respond, concerned to safeguard his risk-free passage to the condo in Florida or whatever else he's planned for retirement.

I say nothing, but stare into his tired eyes. They are set in a face drained by what he's had to do in his career and lined with the recognition that most of it has been pointless. A week ago I sympathized with Brooks, but after what I saw at Cheltenham I've no sympathy to spare. My silence forces him to spell out his objections.

"We can't undertake a unilateral operation here without

Five's approval," he states, "and they'll never agree to us tracking down whoever ordered the bombing."

"Nothing I saw at Cheltenham gives me any confidence that the Brits will find him," I say.

"Lawrence will never authorize it."

"Lawrence's job is to keep the Brits sweet, ours is to find the bomber."

"Will you take personal responsibility if the British do find out?"

"Your pension will be safe, Stan, provided: (a) you alert me to any suspicions the British may have about our operation; and (b) you copy me every scrap of intelligence the British have on the bombing."

He looks out of the window. I turn to Todd Fraser. "Now's your chance to show me how effective your assets really are." I wonder if he has only one gray vested suit and presses it every night so that it's always immaculate in the office, or whether he has a wardrobe full of identical suits to match hair that is always half an inch long and a face that is always determined and sincere. This time he's sincerely determined to prove me wrong about my dismissal of the British sources he's acquired. Good. The more he's out to show that I'm a has-been, the harder he'll work.

"I don't care what you do to track down the bomber," I add. "Operational funds are no problem. Any technical services you want, just ask and they're yours. There's only one law you mustn't break: the Brits must not find out that we're running our own operation."

"Will do," Fraser says.

"And please ensure that Counterterrorism Center copies us twenty-four hours before it replies to any MI5 information requests."

"No problem."

I turn to the other person seated at the conference table. "Can I count on your support?"

I know the answer Bruce Davis will give: Admiral Ferguson is his boss. But it's important to know how far he's prepared to go.

"What do you want, John?" Davis answers.

"Intercepts of any British or Irish phone, fax, or telex on request: no paperwork and no disclosure to the Brits."

"You got it."

Will he risk take-offs of GCHQ electronic surveillance made on behalf of MI5? "Plus covert monitoring of all British security intercepts that relate to the Cheltenham bombing."

His brow furrows. "Staff D?"

"Whenever you need them."

He nods. "You got it."

We're out of the starting gate. "I'm assigning the cryptonym GOLD CUP to this operation," I say.

"And if we do find the bomber?" Brooks asks.

I think of the child I've never had and of that small aluminum casket in the Mildenhall aircraft hangar. "Leave that to me."

"I can't possibly agree to an operation on British soil without the prior approval of the British authorities."

Lawrence Palmer takes refuge behind his large desk. I ignore the gesture for me to sit down on one of the two straight-backed chairs on the other side.

"I'm not asking for formal approval, Lawrence. No field project outlines and no operational progress reports to sign. You don't even know about it if you don't want to."

"Out of the question."

"Lawrence," I say patiently, "I've been asked to deal with whoever gave the order for the bombing."

"By whom?" Palmer explodes. "Why wasn't I informed?"

"By the NSC. I'm informing you now."

"Where's the signal?"

"There isn't one. They want plausible deniability."

He strokes his short white stubble of a beard. "We need a directive from the DCI," he says at last. "It's for your own good, John. You're at a critical point, career-wise. You'd be very exposed if anything went wrong."

It's not my career and my exposure he's thinking of. "We won't get one," I say. "You know that. I'll take full responsibility."

"That cannot override my responsibility as station chief to maintain good relations with our host nation."

"For Christ's sake, Lawrence, we're talking eight US citizens killed, including three intelligence operatives."

He stares hard at me. "Over the last fifty years the company has built up a close working relationship with British intelligence. We use them as proxies in their former empire where they have much better local knowledge. We rely on their support in Europe where the French resent us and the Germans are riddled with ex-Stasi. We've invested billions of dollars in NSA listening stations in Britain and British dependencies worldwide and in GCHQ. I'm not prepared to put all that at risk without a directive signed by the DCI."

"Have a good trip, John?" Dave Sutton asks after rising to greet me. "Sorry I can only squeeze in a social lunch." He resumes his seat with his back to the wall of the Kazan restaurant.

He's had me fly more than three and a half thousand miles for a social lunch? If he'd been that pressed for time he would have lunched me in Langley's seventh-floor executive dining room. The company's deputy director for operations never does anything without a purpose: the Kazan is five minutes' drive from Langley, but the only staff who can afford to eat here either use the seventh floor or go to

Maison Blanche in town if they want to impress. The message is clear: this meeting hasn't taken place.

Even as he hands me the menu his gimlet eyes focus past my head. His position in the end booth, combined with the mirrors spaced along the turquoise tiled walls, gives him a clear view of the other four turquoise booths and the parallel line of four tables dimly lit by ornate brass lanterns that hang below the swatches of turquoise fabric billowing from the ceiling. I glance at the brass-framed mirror behind Sutton's head to see what he's looking at. The other customers comprise two businessmen on an expense account lunch, four women executives networking, a middle-aged salesman planning adultery with a young secretary and, nearest to us, a birthday party of senior citizens quizzing the tuxedoed waiter about every dish on the menu. Satisfied that no one from the company is present, Sutton says, "I recommend the *tarama salatasi* to start. It consists of . . ."

"I know," I say. This Turkish version of red caviar is the nearest he gets these days to Russia.

He smiles. "Of course."

To show his gratitude after I'd covered for him in Moscow station after he was too drunk to act on a flash from Langley, Sutton had offered me half the beluga he'd bought with funds drawn for agent payments.

"You know you can trust me, John," he says after the waiter has brought the starter and refilled our glasses. "Tell me the problem."

He finishes off his first course and begins his main course and a second bottle of wine while I lay out the facts. "Does the NSC want me to find the Cheltenham bomber or not?" I conclude.

"Are you sure the British won't find him?" he asks between mouthfuls of lamb kebab.

"After the Gloucestershire police have spent the day

keeping everyone else off their turf, they have difficulty finding their way home in the dark."

"MI5?"

"The woman heading Five's team can't find her way to the bar without the bartender asking for her birth certificate."

He refills his glass. "Five's terrorism chief?"

"Edward Maitland."

He raises his eyebrows.

"He's closed me out."

His small, piercing eyes study me over the top of his glass of wine. "Are you willing to bypass MI5 and track down the bomber without an official directive?"

"If you'd seen what was left of the bodies, that four years old girl with no legs, you wouldn't need to ask."

He sips his wine. "I knew we could rely on you, John. CIA bringing the Cheltenham bomber to justice would be the best argument for keeping the Bureau out of counter-terrorism overseas."

I bite my tongue and say as calmly as I can, "Then get Palmer off my back."

He finishes off the glass. "I'll see what I can do."

Lawrence Palmer calls into my office. "I've had a priority from Dave Sutton," he says. "Training and Education want me to head up a three-week management course in January." He strokes his beard, always a sign that he's not at ease. "Bea is keen we go early, so we can spend Christmas with our daughter and son-in-law in Rhode Island, and see our son in Connecticut for New Year's. Would it be a terrible imposition if I asked you to mind the store for five weeks?"

I look pointedly at the pile of files on my desk, sigh, and then say, "Well, if it's to help Bea and you, Lawrence, I'll try and struggle through."

"Thank you so much, John. We won't forget this."

Trust Sutton. He's given me a clear run for five weeks without putting his own ass on the line. If Operation GOLD CUP goes wrong, I'm the fall guy who acted without authorization. On the other hand, acting chief of station gives me the opportunity to bypass the Brooks—Ackroyd liaison channel and go above Maitland's head to the power center of Britain's intelligence community.

Chapter ✢ Eleven

THE BROAD AVENUE connecting Parliament Square and
Trafalgar Square is lined with government offices. Adjoin-
ing Parliament Square is the grand Italianate palazzo of Her
Majesty's Treasury, built to extract money from the empire.
It is connected by a bridge over King Charles Street to the
even grander Italianate palazzo of Her Majesty's Foreign and
Commonwealth Office, built to rule over the empire. The
prime minister's residence in Downing Street is interposed
between the FCO and a deceptively unassuming neoclassical building used for spying on the empire. The large black
Rover stops outside. A woman with cropped auburn hair and
a power-shouldered primrose-yellow jacket emerges from
the rear door. The station's Jaguar pulls in behind the Rover
and I follow the director general of MI5 through the tall
black door and up a half dozen steps to where she is punching a code into a keypad next to one of three revolving doors.
A doorman directs me right to the security office.

"Good morning, John."

"Edward! I didn't expect to find you here."

Maitland gives me one of his sardonic looks. "When we found out what you'd put on the agenda, Bella thought I ought to attend to provide any detailed background required."

"Your first JIC?" he asks as we walk up a flight of stairs. I nod.

"When Thatcher put her own man in after the Falklands debacle, the Joint Intelligence Committee was a pain. Thankfully, the Foreign Office has regained control. You'll find that Peter is the ideal chairman. He's brisk, efficient, thinks on his feet, chairs meetings well, writes a good minute, and doesn't have the slightest understanding of intelligence matters."

Another flight of stairs and a left turn bring us to the room in which all of Britain's domestic and international intelligence requirements are decided and the resulting product evaluated.

Peter Derrick rises to greet me from behind a varnished light oak table at the window end of the room. He introduces me to the intelligence coordinator, the representatives of the Foreign Office, the Defense Ministry, and the Home Office, plus the heads of MI5, MI6, GCHQ, and the Defense Intelligence Staff who are seated behind a longer table to his right, and the JIC Assessments Staff seated behind a similar table to his left. I take the place indicated for me at the table opposite his, which completes the rectangular arrangement of the four tables. Soon I'm joined by the London representatives of the Canadian Security Intelligence Service and the Australian Security Intelligence Organization who, like the CIA station chief, attend for the international part of the Joint Intelligence Committee agenda.

It's mind blowing. Not a computer monitor, not a map, not a screen, not even a flip chart disturbs the featureless cream walls of this complacent room. The only items of technology are two telephones on a small table by the window shielded from outside view by antiblast gauze curtains. The British, of course, are clever enough to do without technological aids: a first class mind and a sound education always prove superior to American gadgetry. Even their education mustn't clutter their minds with specialist knowledge. Of all the people present, probably only Maitland and the chiefs of MI5, MI6, and DIS have actually run an intelligence operation. From their appearance the rest might be civil servants who left their suburban detached homes in leafy Esher or Wimbledon or Leatherhead and caught the 7.48 commuter train into Waterloo supremely confident of their ability to evaluate whatever is placed before them, whether it be a pension fund portfolio or an intelligence assessment of global dangers. Particularly the latter. Despite their loss of empire and their third-rate economy, these ranking British civil servants still assume they know what is best for the rest of the world.

"The first item on the agenda," says Derrick, "was requested by Mr. Darcy." He looks at me over the top of his spectacles. "It seems that while the cat's away the mice will play."

"Excuse me?" I say.

"I'm referring to Lawrence's absence." He smiles indulgently. "An assessment of future IRA intentions depends on whether or not they were responsible for the Cheltenham bombing, which is the question you are really asking, is it not, Mr. Darcy?"

"There is a view," says the florid man from the Home Office, to which in theory MI5 is accountable, "that this item should be taken in the domestic part of the agenda."

"The bombing of eight American citizens, including three intelligence operatives, makes this of concern to the United States," I state.

"Indeed," Derrick says. "And the United States has a vital role to play in this matter."

Derrick, at least, seems on the ball.

"As Assessment 1A shows," Derrick continues, "Sinn Féin is preparing to mount a publicity campaign in the States to try and persuade the American public that the IRA wasn't responsible for Cheltenham. Bella?"

"Correct," says Bella Edginton, MI5's director general. "We're about to move into the propaganda phase of this incident. It's vital that the British Information Service in New York has the ammunition to shoot down the Sinn Féin offensive. With your permission, the head of T Directorate will elaborate."

"Sending ministers over to exchange allegations with Sinn Féin leaders isn't enough," says Maitland. "We need to go for the emotional jugular. The CNN interview with the Texan woman whose daughter was killed proved extremely effective." He looks at me. "It would be helpful, chairman, if our American colleagues were to arrange for her and other relatives of the American victims to go on *The Larry King Show* and similar outlets to condemn Sinn Féin and the IRA."

Derrick looks over the top of his spectacles at me.

I try to restrain my anger. "In my humble view this 'incident' as you call it has somewhat more significance than material for prime time US television."

"I couldn't agree more," says Derrick. "The Cheltenham bomb has blown the peace process right off the rails."

"On the other hand," says the florid man from the Home Office, "the Prime Minister has had a much better press since he announced that the government has broken off all talks with Sinn Féin."

I grit my teeth. "If we can stick to hard intelligence, what has your secret line of communication produced?"

A silence falls, as though I'd asked the Queen for a copy of her tax returns.

Derrick feels obliged to break the silence. "The IRA did

contact us through the old channel established when Six was running operations in Northern Ireland," he admits. He looks to the MI6 chief.

"The intermediary gave us a written statement from the IRA denying they were responsible for Cheltenham," Donald Quickly says. "We replied by saying that it would help convince the government that their denial was genuine if the IRA fully account for the movements of their England Department in the two weeks leading up to Cheltenham."

"And?" I press.

"God knows how," says Derrick, "but an Ulster Unionist MP found out last night that we were still using the secret channel despite the PM's statement."

Is it my imagination or does Maitland look smugger than usual?

"He's going to demand in the House this afternoon," Derrick continues, "that the government sever absolutely all contacts with Sinn Féin and the IRA. The PM will have to agree. After Cheltenham he's come under a great deal of pressure from all sides, not just the unionists, to crush the IRA once and for all."

"About time too," says the Defense Intelligence chief.

"As usual," Derrick continues, "Dublin won't cooperate unless we can refute IRA denials that they were responsible. Until this is sorted out, I fear we're never going to be rid of Northern Ireland." He looks to the head of MI5. "Can you hold out any hope on this, Bella?"

She looks to Maitland.

"As Assessment 1B shows," says Maitland, "since 1986 the IRA has had about a dozen people permanently in Britain with the task of planning attacks. They remained in place after the IRA announced its ceasefire, but our surveillance records on four of them are incomplete."

"That doesn't answer the key question," I say. "Do you know who was responsible for Cheltenham?"

"We have a problem," Maitland replies. "The actual attacks are carried out by a pool of about twenty to thirty volunteers from the Republic of Ireland who are brought over as and when needed. The campaign is organized and funded from Dublin through a specialist and highly secretive England Department. That is why a joint operation with the Garda is essential if we're to destroy the IRA's organizational base." He glances at the chairman.

"We trust that Washington," Derrick says to me, "will now put pressure on the Dublin government."

Bruce Davis's copies of GCHQ intercepts show no communications between IRA General Headquarters in Dublin and Northern Command in Belfast which indicate anything contrary to their denials of responsibility for the bombing. "Edward," I say, "will you tell us precisely what evidence you have that proves the IRA ordered the Cheltenham bombing."

Maitland gazes at me as though he's guessed that I already know the answer. "Nothing that proves IRA General Headquarters is responsible," he says.

"Then why . . ."

"We're pursuing two lines of inquiry," Maitland says. "The first is that the Provisional Army Council covertly ordered the bombing in order that they could deny responsibility. That way they could use the bombing to pressure the British government into making further concessions in order to strengthen their hand against 'extremists' within their own movement."

"Typical Paddy cunning," mutters the Defense Intelligence chief.

"The second," Maitland continues, "is that the bombing was undertaken by a hardline splinter group who is receiving support from Irish republicans in the United States."

The United States! And Maitland is trying to freeze out

CIA as well as MI6. "Who are these hardliners?" I demand. "Precisely who are these republicans in the States?"

"The IRA men who opposed the ceasefire in the first place," Maitland replies smoothly. He glances to Edginton, who gives the slightest nod of the head to the JIC chairman. Derrick smiles and says, "I think it would be helpful at this stage to take advantage of your presence, Mr. Darcy, and seek an assurance that the CIA will not embark on its own investigation of this matter, but will work through the Security Service."

I look him in the eye and say, "You have my assurance that we do not intend to embark on our own investigation." Which is correct. We do not intend to embark because we have already embarked.

Chapter ✦ Twelve

A PALLID DAMP sky hangs like a shroud over Belfast, a city no longer certain of its future or even of its past. Victorian triumphalism is preserved in the pompous City Hall—an over-embellished domed Capitol-like building of grayed Portland stone in front of which a larger than life Queen Victoria surveys her domain—and in roads with names like Great Victoria Street, Royal Avenue, and Queen Street. I expected Queen's House to be similarly grandiose, but one block west of City Hall the original buildings of Queen Street have given way to modern offices for insurance companies who have flourished in the Troubles, and two blocks north my cab is stopped by yellow steel security gates and suspicious security officers.

"One bomb on the mainland an' it's back to the gates fer us," the cabbie grumbles to me. He shouts out of the window, "Another fer Queen's House."

An unarmed security officer dressed in a black uniform outer coat bends to look through the window. "I'll need to see your case, sir," he says to me.

"I haven't got one."

He looks at the cabbie, signals to his colleague, and waves us through the opened gate, past redbrick Victorian linen warehouses with upper floors abandoned and street floors converted to downmarket Kelly's Eye Bingo Club, Craft World Toyshop, and Leisure World.

In the middle of the block a brick bunker with blast-proof glass slits controls the gate in the chicken-wire fence that protects an old stone Royal Ulster Constabulary station. It peers across the road to Queen's House, a cheap medium-rise concrete construction flying the US flag. Sandwiched between a street-level Romano's Restaurant advertising Ulster fry, and three anonymous floors of the Post Office Northern Ireland Headquarters, the US consulate conveys an air of impermanence that contrasts with its imposing big brother in London's Grosvenor Square.

The door into the consulate leads through the frame of a metal detector and into a reception area of cream walls and gray carpet which resembles a small-town bank. Braving the challenging looks, I walk past the people standing in line and give my name to the receptionist. The overworked but cheerful blonde local recruit behind the glazed wall above the counter puts down the phone. She welcomes me in a clipped nasal accent which turns Northern Ireland into Norn Iron. A few minutes later an equally friendly brunette opens a security door and leads me into her office. "So sorry for the confusion," she says. "Since that bomb in Cheltenham we've been swamped by visa applications." She knocks at a door and gestures me into the inner sanctum of the consul general.

Paul Steinberg is a short, round man with a face that ought to be jolly. He frowns and reaches underneath his desk.

"Before you press the security button," I say, "you have got John Darcy." I toss my diplomatic passport onto his desk. "Everyone else gets Patrick Connor." I follow it with the US passport made out in that name, pleased that he hasn't recognized me in the brown wig and beard.

Steinberg glares. "I don't know what your game is . . ."

"I've just come to collect the package."

I remain standing. Steinberg remains seated behind the pictures of the President and the seal of office. Although the flag on the other side of his desk from the Stars and Stripes is the navy blue consular flag, Steinberg comes from the political section of the State Department. "Mr. Darcy, let me give it to you straight. Northern Ireland is a tinderbox right now. The administration's policy is to prevent the Cheltenham bomb sparking a resumption of the terrorist war."

"I appreciate that. The package, please."

"Hear me out. We've been pressurising the British to talk to Sinn Féin again, and we've been working our butts off to unfreeze American investment in order to keep the loyalists on board the peace process."

"Keep it up. The package, please."

"I do not want cowboys undermining our work here."

"Do I look like a cowboy? The package, please."

"I've protested . . ."

"I know. The package, please."

Steinberg glowers, gets up, and walks down the long cream and gray room, past framed posters of US landscapes, and out to the vault. He returns with a package wrapped in brown paper, puts it on his desk, and pushes across a receipt for me to sign. "I warn you, Darcy, you'll get no help from here if anything goes wrong in this operation."

"Who said anything about an operation? This is my lunch box."

On my way out the metal detector gives a loud bleep.

The Europa Hotel carries the reputation of being the second most bombed hotel in the world after the Commodore in Beirut. If I hadn't talked with the foreign correspondents in the lobby bar I'd never have guessed. Recently refurbished, the Europa's street-level plate-glass frontage and the lobby's kitsch cream imitation marble walls and fat columns suggest a confidence in the peace process which is not shared by the foreign correspondents from the perspective of their bar stools. After learning all I can I go to my room and unwrap the package that I'd sent, care of the US consul general, in the diplomatic bag.

The Browning 9mm semiautomatic is accurate, reliable, and old enough to be untraceable. If I do find the man who ordered the Cheltenham bombing, his death can be put down to feuding within the IRA or an IRA punishment shooting. The magazine slides into the butt with a satisfying click. I slip the gun back into the shoulder holster and tape it, the spare magazine, and two of my three passports to the underside of the bed.

The Divis Flats, a twenty-story concrete apartment house, used to give a sniper's view of the beginning of the Falls Road, one of the principal routes into West Belfast. It is now girdled by a British Army security platform and topped by communications antennae, cameras, and high-power directional microphones—which are countered by a story-high banner from the residents protesting DEMILITARIZE DIVIS TOWER. Since the ceasefire the British Army no longer patrol the streets, but a gray, enclosed, bulletproof RUC Jeep, with narrow peepholes at the rear and a freephone number for confidential information on terrorists stencilled on the side, passes me on a foray into this republican stronghold.

Since my arrival yesterday the sky has darkened and lowered, and now releases its burden as teeming rain. The old black cabs which ferry passengers between downtown

Belfast and the Catholic enclaves are full. On the glistening wet sidewalks women in garishly colored tracksuits push baby carriages, and men in denim jackets and jeans walk stoically on, their faces old before their time.

Belfast City Council has redeveloped the area, replacing most of the warren of Victorian slums either side of the Falls Road with new, high quality, redbrick row housing. The neat little streets to the north side are cut in two by a solid steel fence higher than the Berlin Wall, beyond which live the Protestant working class.

The redevelopment has left the Sinn Féin center in the Lower Falls Road as much an isolated relic of Victorian imperialism as is the ostentatious City Hall. Housed in a row of four dilapidated Victorian shops, with bricked up or steel-shuttered windows, security cameras, and large boulders on the sidewalk to prevent the parking of car bombs, this public face of physical-force republicanism proclaims its message in murals. A faded head and shoulders of the smiling long-haired Bobby Sands, the IRA's 1981 hunger strike martyr, exhorts greater patriotic effort from one gable wall. On the front façade bright new murals depict departing British troops amid slogans in English and Gaelic demanding FREE THE POLITICAL PRISONERS, DEMILITARIZE NOW! and DISBAND THE RUC.

I ease my way through the crowd of reporters in anoraks and photographers in multipocketed jackets, and press the entryphone button. "It's Patrick Connor," I say. "I have an appointment for ten thirty."

After a minute or so a buzzer sounds, the steel-reinforced door opens, and I walk into a steel mesh cage. The door closes behind, locking me in.

A grizzled man attired in blue denim jacket and jeans—the uniform of the Belfast unemployed—examines me through the mesh, presses a button to unlock the cage door,

and ushers me into a shrine to IRA volunteers killed in the
struggle since the early seventies. "We're running late,
Patrick," he says with the instant friendliness shown only by
the Irish and the Americans.

I join three others examining the plaques, photographs,
and posters in this dingy room with bricked up window and
television monitor showing other journalists still huddled
outside in the rain.

The doorman speaks on the internal phone, turns round,
and says, "Patrick, you're to go straight up."

Into the cage, out through another door, and I'm met
halfway up the dark, bare wooden stairs by a young man who
guides me to the "interview room," a stark, cramped place
with plaster spilling from tears in ancient yellow wallpaper
and a flowered red carpet which could have come straight
from a garbage can. I wait on the stool on one side of the
battered chipboard desk, by an old poster reproducing the
1916 Declaration of the Republic of Ireland and a new one
urging SEIZE THE OPPORTUNITY FOR PEACE—SINN FÉIN.

A man in a smart brown suit sweeps into the room,
shakes my hand, and says, "Sorry about the state of the
place, Patrick. As you can see, we aren't in it for the money."

Frank Gallagher, Sinn Féin's publicity director in Northern Ireland, has a wide face, sparse ginger hair, and a winning smile. He sits on the other side of the desk and offers
me a cigarette.

"It's good of you to see me," I say after declining the
cigarette.

"Seeing as how you've traveled all this way, I could hardly
leave you outside in the rain, now, could I?" he says with a
twinkle in his eye.

Like the journalists from England, Europe, and Japan
milling around outside? Maitland was right: their number
one propaganda target is the United States. "Do you mind?"

I put a tape recorder on the desk, next to my reporter's notebook.

"Fire ahead," Gallagher says expansively.

"Who planted the Cheltenham bomb?"

"Dead on the point. The truth of the matter is, at this stage, we don't know."

"You are prepared to state categorically that it wasn't you?"

"You must understand, Patrick, that Sinn Féin is not the IRA," says Gallagher, who served twelve years for being an IRA member, possessing an MI carbine, and for causing an explosion that killed two RUC officers. "However, Sinn Féin does accept the IRA denial of responsibility."

"Why?"

"Let me put it this way, Patrick. IRA units have carried out operations in the past without approval from the Army Council, but the Army Council accepted responsibility. This time they're saying that none of their units was involved."

"What about a splinter group?"

The twinkles and smiles vanish. "Whoever carried out this bombing was no member of the Provisional IRA and no member of Sinn Féin. It's counterproductive to the peace process we're committed to. We find it totally unacceptable for the British government to break off negotiations with us."

"Why should the US public believe you?"

"Because, Patrick, the British government, whatever its public statements, has always privately accepted the IRA's word in the past. The American public should be askin': why does it not accept it now?"

"You tell me."

"The only conclusion is that the Brits want an excuse to break off the peace negotiations because they're determined to keep their grip on the Six Counties."

"I'm going to quote you on that."

His voice takes on a hard edge. "You can quote me as saying that the British government breaking off peace talks with Sinn Féin will be the cause of any resumption of the armed struggle."

The man's anger is genuine. I return to the Europa, inclining to the view that the bombing was carried out by a hardline splinter group rather than ordered by the IRA leadership as a covert operation giving them plausible deniability—and which went horribly wrong.

The man with a thin face, dark receding hair, sideburns, and a ponytail, who is sitting at the Parisian café-like counter of the Morning Star, a Victorian pub in dark mahogany with frosted glass windows, has to be Martin Breslin. According to Todd Fraser's assets, Breslin is one of the few journalists with sources inside the Provos' Army Council; he is also heavily in debt to a bookmaker.

When the two people he's talking with get up and leave, I move next to him, by one of the mirrored wooden partitions between sections of the horseshoe counter. "Martin Breslin?" I give him my card. "Can I get you a drink?"

"Thanks." He finishes his whiskey. "I'll have another Bush."

"Two," I say to the barman.

The barman pours out two Bushmills while Breslin reads my card. "*Washington Post*, eh? What's a big man like you doin' talkin' to the likes of me?"

"I want to commission you."

"How did you know who I am?"

"We've got a file of your pieces for the *Sunday Tribune*. You're the only one here who looks like your photograph."

"Charmin'," he says with one eye on the television screen, which is showing a horse race. "What can I do fer you? Don't you have stringers to do your legwork here, or what?"

"That's news. I'm features. I want color and insight. Ulster on a knife edge. What prospects for peace now? What do the main players think? What do the communities here think? Who do they blame for Cheltenham?" I finish my whiskey and order two more. "Interested?"

He raises his eyebrows. "What's the goin' rate for a poor Irish hack?"

"Two hundred and fifty dollars a thousand words."

He snorts. "Big spender!"

"We could be talking more." I lean closer. "It's too crowded here."

He nods to a small room away from the bar. "The snug."

"No. Let's take a walk."

He shrugs, downs his drink, and follows me out of the door. The narrow alleyway leads up to the almost completely modern, characterless High Street, from which run dark Dickensian alleys leading to saloon bars. We head in the direction of the river.

"Serious money means a *Post* exclusive," I say, "but I need to know if you can deliver."

"Try me."

"We've heard rumors about rebel units in the IRA, groups who were opposed to the ceasefire in the first place."

He talks out of the side of his mouth. "Sure that's no rumor. Most of the South Armagh Brigade were against the ceasefire, and so were units in the northwest, from Derry, Tyrone, and Donegal." He turns to stare at me. "And you want to pay big money for that? Catch yerself on."

"Twenty thousand dollars if you name and source the group responsible for the Cheltenham bombing."

He stops. "Jesus! You're talkin' big now, Mr. Connor. And do ye think I'd live to spend it?"

"Nom de plume. Paid in cash, pounds sterling."

He gives me a quizzical look. We've reached the end of the High Street. In the center of the crossroads a clock tower, a smaller version of Big Ben at London's Houses of Parliament, leans to one side. A cold wind whips from across the river, where the shipyard's two giant yellow cranes, each shaped like the top three sides of a rectangle, stand idle like gallows awaiting their victims.

"Double that if you name and locate the one who gave the orders."

He purses his lips. "That would take a lot of research. Dangerous research. I'd need an advance. Fifty percent."

I shake my head. "Maximum advance of two thousand five hundred pounds sterling. Balance on delivery."

"You have the advance?"

"Not on me."

"When?"

"Tomorrow."

He nods. "Lunchtime tomorrow in Kelly's Cellars. You'll find it."

I might have been a British paratrooper in uniform from the stares I attract. Belying its name, Kelly's Cellars is at street level, but the brick walls and arches, low ceiling, black beams, and suspicious faces peering from the sepulchral gloom almost convince me that I've strayed into a private underworld. I walk through the poorly dressed drinkers, who talk in accents so strong I can barely tell if they're speaking English or Gaelic, to find Breslin sitting alone at a corner table with his back to the wall. "I'll have a pint of green," he says.

The barmaid sees that I'm with Breslin and serves a pint of Carlsberg and a Bushmills for me. I hand him the lager and sit down.

"Thanks. Do ye have anything else for me?"

I put a folded copy of the *Belfast Telegraph* on the table. He takes a drink, picks up the newspaper, slides out the brown envelope, and surreptitiously checks the used twenty-pound notes.

"When can you deliver?" I ask.

He leans forward across the table and whispers, "My advice to you is to leave the country within the next three hours."

I seize his wrist and apply pressure with my thumb.

"Are you fer real?" he says, and looks over my shoulder.

Three men lounge against the black bar. Two are dressed in denim jackets and one in a windbreaker. All three wear black woollen hats. All three stare at me.

"I checked with the *Washington Post*," Breslin says. "Not the 'direct number' on your card. The switchboard."

I release his wrist. "The envelope."

"That's my fee for the advice. I'd follow it if I were you." He stands up and walks out of the pub. The man in the windbreaker joins him. The other two remain, still staring at me.

ULSTER NEEDS JESUS flashes by on my left before the M2 expressway climbs past the steep, darkly wooded slopes of Cave Hill, its craggy peaks sharp against the cold sky, and leaves behind the vast sweep of Belfast Lough spoiled by the clutter of shipyard cranes at its mouth. After a quarter of an hour through rolling green fields the expressway dips toward the exit road for Belfast International Airport, but I press on. It was the brown-haired and bearded Patrick Connor who left Kelly's Cellars followed by two men in denim jackets and black woollen hats, checked out of the Europa, and went upstairs to pack, but it was a gray-haired and moustached John MacLaughlin wearing black hornrimmed spectacles who slipped out past the columns in the Europa lobby and collected the Ford Escort from Avis which now passes the airport exit road.

Shortly afterwards the expressway tapers into a two-lane undivided highway which runs through municipal housing with lampposts flying the Irish tricolour, followed immediately by the brick and green-painted steel fortress of an RUC barracks and observation bunker directly overlooking the road where it crosses a river flowing into a lough. After Toome Bridge the road gradually climbs northwest into cloud hugging a coarse moorland of heather, rocky bogs, patches of snow, clumps of pine, and a few sheep.

As the light fades, the road descends through a wooded valley to the city of Derry, whose pastel houses and stone spires terrace the hillsides rising from both banks of the River Foyle. Three hours after receiving the warning to leave the country I drive the Escort slowly past the Victorian three-story stuccoed row houses behind Derry's Magee University College to find an anonymous lodging house offering bed and breakfast, where I check in under my second cover as John MacLaughlin.

Chapter ✤ Thirteen

THE NEXT DAY is gray and miserable, full of drizzle and mist. After showering in the bathroom down the corridor, I return to my bedroom and use the small sink in the corner to rinse my hair with more gray dye. Dressed in turtleneck sweater, sport pants, and windbreaker, I refix the gray moustache, put on the black hornrimmed spectacles, and then replace the dye and adhesive next to the three passports, the Browning, and the spare magazine in the false bottom of my suitcase.

The landlady, Mrs. Nolan, a plump widow of uncertain age and inquisitive nature, is waiting in the downstairs dining room. It is not a room I'd choose to visit with a hangover. Discordant bright colors leap at me from the patterned carpet, florid wallpaper, and framed department store reproductions on the walls.

The students have disappeared for their winter recess—much longer than the recess in the States—leaving me the sole focus of Mrs. Nolan's solicitude. I struggle through a huge plateful of fried rashers of ham, eggs, sausages, tomatoes, mushrooms, potato cake, and soda bread, politely answering Mrs. Nolan's questions with probes of my own about the region from which hardline units of the IRA operate. Finally I escape to the hired car and head for the cemetery.

Two hours later my route takes me past the seventeenth century fortified stone walls of the old city, now reinforced by twentieth century corrugated steel sheeting, British Army observation towers protected by wire cages, and steel pylons bristling with antennae, microphones, and cameras that look down on the drab concrete three-story apartment houses, two-story row houses, and empty blacktop parking lots of the Bogside. A freestanding red gable wall flying the Irish tricolour proclaims in yellow YOU ARE NOW ENTERING FREE DERRY. The end wall of an apartment block commemorates the thirteen unarmed Catholic civil rights marchers killed by British troops on Bloody Sunday in 1972, and a new black and white mural of almost photographic quality shows a young boy in a gas mask about to throw a petrol bomb.

Just before the blue double-decker Craigavon Bridge a new bronze sculpture shows two men reaching out to each other across a divide. Will it be this civic statement or the black and white mural which proves prophetic? That depends on finding the Cheltenham bomber.

After crossing the bridge I make a right and follow the road along the bank of the wide gray Foyle, where it meanders through rich green pasture, large well-kept farms, and villages with gray Presbyterian chapels and curbstones painted in red, white, and blue: Protestant farming country.

A right fork signposted Lifford points toward two Buddhist pagodas: vertically stacked green boxes separated by smaller boxes and topped by a green pyramid. As I drive closer I see that each tower is protected from halfway up by an inverted pyramidal steel mesh cage. Closer still and the large green boxes of the first tower are made of corrugated steel, and the smaller boxes between them contain bullet-proof glass panels to observe me from different levels as I approach the narrow gap in a long two-story-high green steel fence. Behind the tower stands a 150-foot-high steel pylon bearing antennae, cameras, and microphones.

The gap in the fence is guarded by a red and white hooped pole barrier followed by a series of ramps to slow vehicles and a raisable steel barrier to trap them as the narrow route takes me past a bombproof brick bunker with blastproof one-way windows. I'm not directed to the vehicle search area behind a brick wall, but allowed to drive slowly round a second, larger observation bunker, over more ramps and another raisable steel barrier by a third observation bunker, until a raised hooped pole releases me onto the road, observed by the second pagoda.

This border post is far more formidable than the guard post protecting Britain's top secret GCHQ—more formidable, indeed, than any guard post I saw at the Soviet labor camps in Siberia.

Half a mile later the road crosses Lifford Bridge over the Foyle, passes an old prefabricated hut marked Customs Post from which no one emerges to check anything, and I see a blue sign FÁILTE GO DÚN NA NGALL, Welcome to Donegal—and the Irish Republic.

I had imagined the church would be traditional, but it is 1960s church-in-the-round made of pebbledash concrete, and the nearby parochial house is a matching bungalow. The door is opened by a middle aged woman whose gray hair is tied up in a bun. "May I see Father O'Boyle," I say.

"Come in," she says, leading me to a plastic chair in a waiting room adorned only by a crucifix and a photograph of the Pope. "Who shall I say is calling?"

"John MacLaughlin, from New York," I reply.

If Todd Fraser's asset is correct, the priest who enters the room has close connections with hardline IRA units operating in the northwest of the island, in the counties of Derry and Tyrone in "occupied" Ulster and the county of Donegal which was part of the original province of Ulster and is now in the Irish Republic. I hope he proves more productive than Martin Breslin.

Alert blue eyes shine from Father O'Boyle's narrow lined face below receding gray hair. "Would you take a cup of tea, Mr. MacLaughlin?" he asks.

"That would be very welcome, Father," I say. "And please call me John."

He goes to the door. "Brigid, tea and biscuits in the living room if you'd be so kind." He smiles at me and leads me out of the waiting room. "Come through now, we'll be far more comfortable here."

It's the type of room where you expect to see plaster flying ducks on the walls. We sit on brown velour easy chairs either side of a low glass-topped coffee table, in front of a gas fire with a tiled surround.

"Now what can I do for you, John?"

"I'm trying to trace my grandfather's grave."

"Did he come from this parish?"

"He was born in Derry."

The bright blue eyes examine my face. "Indeed. Then why do you come to me?"

The housekeeper brings in a tray of tea and biscuits and sets it down on the coffee table.

"He left Derry to join the Donegal Brigade of the IRA after the War of Independence in order to fight on against Partition. That's when we believe he was killed."

The quizzical expression remains on the priest's face.

"I was told you were something of an authority on the subject, Father."

"I would hardly describe myself as an authority," O'Boyle says. "What was his name?"

"Eamon MacLaughlin."

The priest sips his tea. "MacLaughlin," he says to himself. "Eamon MacLaughlin. The Donegal Brigade did have some young lads from Derry, and some of them were killed by the Free Staters. It would be usual, though, for them to be taken home to be buried. Did you not find him in Derry City cemetery?"

"No, Father," I lie.

"If he's buried in the South you might have a problem finding the grave. It's not a part of our history the Free State here wants to remember, and there are hundreds of MacLaughlins in these parts."

I try to look disappointed. "So there's no hope of finding him?"

"Not necessarily. There were Derry men among those killed at Drumboe, though I can't for the life of me recall their names. That's well worth while checking out."

"Where's Drumboe, Father?"

His eyes fade into the distance. "Sometimes I ask myself the same question." He focuses back on me and cheers up. "One thing's for sure, you'll never find it by yourself. Come on, drink up your tea and I'll take you. It's a slack day for saving souls."

In the half hour's drive the drizzle turns to rain which sweeps across farms as large and as Protestant as those in the North but without the painted curbstones. The wires between the wooden telegraph poles on the left are bowed with noisy black carrion crows, who also fill the trees and the fields behind the hedge bordering the road. I've never seen or heard so many crows.

We pass through the one-street town of Stranolar and Father O'Boyle directs me to the right, before the gray bulk of a church by a river crossing. The narrow lane turns into an avenue through tall Scots pines. "This once led to the big house at Drumboe," says the priest. "The British used it as a barracks in the War of Independence, and after the Treaty the Free State Army took it over."

We emerge into fields once more and he tells me to stop by a hedge. He points to the right. "Here's what we're looking for."

Three flagpoles stand forlorn guard over a small enclosure on the steep green hillside.

"What became of your grandmother?" he asks as we wait for the rain to ease.

"After Partition she took my father and his sister to relatives in New York for safety."

He nods, as though the tale were familiar.

When the downpour relents we clamber over a five-barred gate, jump across a stream, and squelch up a steep sodden field, scattering half a dozen sheep but leaving three bullocks standing their ground.

A rusting green gate creaks open in the low concrete wall that encloses the three flagpoles and a gray granite Celtic cross bearing the inscription

IN PROUD AND GLORIOUS MEMORY OF
THE DRUMBOE MARTYRS
COMDT-GEN CHARLES DALY,
BRIG-COMDT SÉAN LARKIN,
LIEUT DANIEL ENRIGHT AND
LIEUT TIMOTHY O'SULLIVAN
WHO GAVE THEIR LIVES IN DEFENSE OF
THE IRISH REPUBLIC
AT THIS SPOT ON THE 14TH MARCH 1923

GUID ÓRTA.

Father O'Boyle makes the sign of the cross. "For all their fancy titles they were nothin' but young boys, barely past twenty."

"What happened, Father?"

"They were prisoners in Drumboe House. The Free Staters took them out and shot them as a reprisal." He shakes his head sadly. "Partition was an evil thing, setting Irishman against Irishman."

"It still is an evil thing, Father."

O'Boyle looks over the republican plot. "'The fools, the fools, they have left us our Fenian dead, and while Ireland holds these graves Ireland unfree shall never be at peace.'"

"He was right," I say.

The priest's bright blue eyes stare at me. "Pádraig Pearse?"

"My father."

"Why do you say that?"

"He was Fergal MacLaughlin, the longshoreman who helped Michael Flannery and George Harrison smuggle guns to the IRA."

He looks up at me. "You didn't come here to find your grandfather's grave, did you, John?"

"I came here to find my grandfather's spirit. Before he died my father told me that his father would have been proud of what he did. I'd like them both to be proud of me."

"And how do you think I can help?"

"A few of us in New York were never happy with the ceasefire. It seemed a device by the British to disarm the IRA without offering any real concessions. We wonder if there are any here who maintain the cause that my grandfather gave his life for. Perhaps they can advise how we can best support the struggle."

The priest gazes thoughtfully at the Celtic cross. Finally

he looks up and says, "Perhaps you should give me a telephone number where you can be contacted."

Mrs. Nolan is waiting for me when I return to the lodging
house the following afternoon after visiting pubs in the Bogside. "There's been a telephone call for you, Mr. MacLaughlin. Someone called Kieran. He said he'd meet you in the
Cúchulainn at eight."

"The Cúchulainn?"

"It's a pub across the border, just before Buncrana."

Todd Fraser goes up in my estimation. Father O'Boyle
has led me to the hardline IRA units who opposed the ceasefire. I take out the Browning and check the firing mecha-
nism. There are routes across the border that avoid the
security checkpoints, but I'm not yet familiar with them. Besides, I should only need the gun when I'm certain which
individual ordered the Cheltenham bombing. I replace the
gun in the false bottom of the suitcase.

I needn't have worried about the security checkpoint. On
this Friday evening the long straight road out of Derry to
Buncrana is busy with cars, private buses, and hitchhikers
heading for the nightclubs dotted along the shores of the In-
ishowen Peninsula in the Republic. No one is stopped at the
border post, similar to the one before Lifford Bridge but less
sophisticated. A quarter of a mile later a change of road surface from a hard macadam to a softer, potholed asphalt is
the only indication that I've crossed into the Irish Republic.

After bumping across the sunken tracks of a disused
railroad, the unlit road narrows and runs between hedges
for most of the way until a dense blackness opens up below
on the left, bordered by tiny twinkling lights on the far side

of Lough Swilly. Half a mile past a village I slow and find the exit road to the left which drops down to the level of the lough. A narrow road to the right takes me beneath the Buncrana road and leads to the parking lot of the Cúchulainn pub.

I pull into the lot and turn off the ignition. The old familiar thrill runs down my spine. More powerful than any drug, the threat of danger is the best antidote to the male menopause.

I push open the door and enter a poorly lit low room with whitewashed walls, black beams, and a log fire. The babble of conversations ceases. The only sound comes from the pool table, the clack of ball against ball, where the two players continue their game with the intensity of the mute. No one looks at me straight, all observe me out of the corners of their eyes.

I go to the small bar and order a half pint of Guinness. The balding barman whose worry is fixed in wrinkles on his forehead serves me with the stout, the change, and a nod. The conversations resume as murmurs, no one table able to overhear any other. At the bar I overhear nothing.

"Where can I find Kieran?" I ask the barman.

The conversations cease.

The barman nods to a closed door.

"Thanks." I take the half pint of black liquid and cream froth with me.

The door opens into blackness broken by the shaft of light from the bar.

"Close the door behind you," says a hard voice to my right.

As soon as the door shuts out the light, a line of three table lamps dazzles me.

"Put down your glass. Stand facing the door with your arms stretched out," the hard voice orders.

The body search is not professional, but it would have found the Browning.

"Stay there."

Footsteps sound on the stone floor.

"Now come and sit on the chair."

The chair faces the table on which stand the three table lamps that shine into my eyes. I guess there's one man behind each, but I can't be certain.

"Welcome to Donegal," the hard voice says.

"Charmed, I'm sure," I reply.

"We've heard of your father, John," a softer voice behind the left light says, "but why are you here?"

I stare into the dark above the lamps. "We don't want the republican side to be defenseless if the armed struggle is being renewed."

"Who says it's being renewed?" a third voice asks.

"Cheltenham says," I reply.

The silence is broken only by the sound of my breathing.

Eventually the soft voice says, "The Army Council denied responsibility."

"We're offering assistance to whoever is taking the fight to the British, whether it's the Army Council or another part of the Army who remain loyal to the cause my grandfather died for."

"Who sent you, Mr. MacLaughlin?" the third voice asks.

"A group who feel that the leadership of the movement in the States has been fooled by the peace process."

"Specifically who?" the third voice persists.

"I'm sure you understand our precaution," I reply.

"What are you offering?" the soft voice asks.

"What do you want?"

"If it comes to all-out war," says the hard voice, "we'll need SAM-7 missiles and rocket grenade launchers."

"I think we can manage that. Let me have an inventory."

Muttered consultations take place behind the blinding

lamps. Finally the soft voice asks, "Where can we contact you, John?"

I give him one of the reserve telephone numbers which the company's New York office has been briefed to answer as John MacLaughlin's private office. "When I do get what you need," I add, "how do I contact you to arrange delivery?"

An ominous silence descends, like the pause between the guilty verdict and the judge's sentence.

"We'll find you, John," says the soft voice, "when you least expect it."

Chapter ❖ Fourteen

YOU DON'T EXPECT to find a Polish restaurant in the heart of the exclusive residential area just south of London's Kensington Gardens, nor do you expect an interior of modern minimalism. And Katarzyna Litynska didn't expect to be invited for dinner. As soon as she is seated in the small room she says, "Why dinner? Why here?"

In many ways she evokes memories of Jill. Not physically. Her shoulder-length hair is blonde, not red, and the wide eyes, high cheekbones, and full mouth remind me of beautiful Slav women I met in Warsaw and Moscow. But she transmits the same contradictions—shyness and directness, innocence and wantonness, vulnerability and danger, gentleness and strength—that I found irresistible in Jill.

I lean across the table and say huskily to the FBI's London representative, "Because I find you attractive."

She pouts. "Because you think I'll be flattered, because there's no danger that anyone from the embassy or from Five will see us here, because you've failed to trace the

Cheltenham bomber on your own, and because you don't want my deputy to know what you're about to ask me."

I'm rescued by the waitress who brings two ice-cold shots of vodka and the menu.

"I throw myself on the mercy of a very perceptive—and very attractive—woman."

She tosses her head. "What kind of Polish restaurant serves Irish stew?"

"Actually it's an Irish restaurant but tonight, just for you, they changed their name and put Polish dishes on the menu."

She downs the vodka, looks me straight in the eye, and parts her lips in a smile. "John Darcy, it's just possible your Irish charm may save you, but first I want to know why."

"Katarzyna, US intelligence people . . ."

"My friends call me Kate."

"Kate, our people have been killed or maimed. Those who recover from their physical injuries will never recover psychologically. They'll never get over losing their children, seeing their mangled bodies."

She nods, and then says, "I'm not sure my grandmother would recognize half these dishes. I'll start with the pierogi filled with sauerkraut and mushrooms, followed by venison with a mixed berry sauce. My grandmother certainly wouldn't recognize that. You may choose the wine."

While I study the menu and the wine list, she studies me. After I've ordered, she says, "There's something more. You must have seen people killed before. The Agency wants you to track down the bomber, but it doesn't want the Bureau involved and it won't give you written authorisation to go unilateral in Britain. If you find the bomber, terrific: it'll boost the Agency's case for retaining counterterrorism overseas. But if the British discover that you're running your own operation on their territory before you find the bomber, the Agency will disown you, even produce psychiatric reports

to prove you're way out of line. You know how they operate. So, what I want to know is: why do you want the bomber
so badly that you're putting your future at risk?"

"What future?"

She puts down her glass and her clear blue eyes look into
mine. "I see. Even so, that doesn't answer my question."

She's even more perceptive that I realized. I haven't
asked myself that question, and I'm not sure I know the answer. The words come out slowly. "I guess I needed to prove
I can still achieve something with my life."

"To CIA management?"

I shake my head. "To myself." My fork plays aimlessly
with the dish of herring fillets. "Then I went to Cheltenham."
I lay down the fork and stare at the mangled strips of fish.
"Sure, I've seen bodies before, but I've never seen the body
of a four-year-old girl with her legs blown off, never felt so
strongly that here was a crime crying out to heaven for justice. It gave me the chance to . . . to do something I could
be proud of, something with no hidden agenda, the kind of
thing I joined the company to do all those years ago." I look
up, fearing her response. "That must sound corny."

Her reply is surprisingly soft. "No, John, not from you."

"When people started blocking me off, because they
wanted to protect their turf or their careers or their pen-
sions, I just got madder inside."

"What did you do?"

"While the Brits were fighting among themselves for the
lead role, or making political capital out of the bombing, the
trail was going cold. I took a little direct action: a crash penetration in Northern Ireland."

She raises her eyebrows. "Risky?"

I shrug. "I suppose there was a risk the Brits would find
out."

Her laugh is like the tinkling of Waterford crystal. "What
did you find out?"

"My best guess is that Cheltenham's down to an IRA splinter group who are supported by Irish republicans in the States. I made contact with a hardline unit operating from across the border in the northwest of the island. I'm pretty sure they do have a link to the States, but their security at this end is tight. Without cooperation from MI5, MI6, and the garda I haven't the means to put them under full surveillance and establish that they were responsible for Cheltenham."

She starts her venison and we eat in silence. When she's finished she says, "What do you want me to do?"

"Has Five asked the Bureau to follow up a US connection for Cheltenham?"

"Not as far as I know."

"That is just typical of the Brits' inefficiency. Kate, ask your people to trace any Irish republican group in the States assisting a hardline IRA faction who oppose the ceasefire, discover how they are assisting, and who their contacts are in Ireland."

Large innocent eyes betray a knowing smile. "Consider it done."

"Can you avoid telling Washington I'm the consumer?"

"No problem. I'll say that Five have tasked me. They probably will when the studious Ms. Ackroyd finds the right forms to fill in."

I push away my plate. "Kate, you've just made an old man very happy."

"Old man! John Darcy, you're in your prime."

"Wisniowka to finish?"

She shakes her head. "Krupnik. But warm."

After the waiter has brought the honey-flavored vodka, she says, "What are you doing over Christmas when you manage to escape from the endless round of parties?"

"I'll be too busy for the parties." I daren't go to any of the British parties in case Jill Maitland is there. As for the embassy ones, there is no more lonely a place than a party where all the others are enjoying themselves.

She sips the krupnik and then puts down her glass. "You need to relax, John. Come over to my place at Christmas. I'll give you a real Polish Christmas dinner."

In her eyes I see the promise of a firm, young body. I would plunge into the fount of rejuvenation at any other time, in any other city. But not Christmas, not London. The memory of those last two Christmases I spent in London with Jill would drain away all pleasure. "You're very kind, Kate, but I'm afraid I'll be working through Christmas. Perhaps a theater, in the New Year."

She gives me a strange look. She's not used to being turned down. "Perhaps."

Shortly before Palmer is due to return, Lorna brings me a signal. "The DDO is making a routine visit to the station."

"When?"

"His plane lands at eight tomorrow morning."

Dave Sutton making a "routine" visit to London? At twenty four hours' notice? "Have Alfred pick me up at seven and take me to the airport."

Sutton wastes no time. As we are driven back from Heathrow he checks that the soundproofed window separating passengers from chauffeur is closed and then says, "The White House is leaning on us."

He half turns so that his small beady eyes can gauge my reaction. "What progress have you made on the Cheltenham bombing, John?"

"Not much. We're following up the only lead we have."

"Who does it point to?"

"Too early to say."

"What kind of lead?"

"A possible American connection."

"Christ Almighty." Sutton takes a large white handkerchief from his pants pocket and mops his brow. "Tell him to turn the goddamned heating down."

I put my finger on the communications console. "Alfred, lower the temperature, please."

"The media back home are making a big show of another foreign policy blunder," Sutton says, "and the White House needs answers. How does the President respond to Sinn Féin denials that the IRA was responsible for bombing American women and children? How does he respond to middle America demanding he break off relations with Sinn Féin and abandon his peace initiative for Ireland? He can't risk losing the Irish American vote, but he can't be seen as soft on terrorism."

Our Jaguar reaches the end of the expressway from the airport and becomes stuck in the commuter traffic crawling into central London.

"You don't appear very concerned, John," Sutton says.

I shrug. "I'm not a politician."

"Too goddamned right you're not. Don't you see the opportunity?"

What is this sallow-faced man with the thatch of blond hair talking about? The killing of fifteen people is an opportunity?

"The President can't afford to be labeled indecisive yet again," Sutton says. "He's got to do something, *anything*, to show he's in control. But he daren't act until he knows for sure precisely who ordered the bombing. Meantime, Congress is insisting on a radical restructuring of the Agency. Some are even backing Moynihan's demand that the President close us down."

He settles back in his seat. "Come to think of it, an Irish

American connection wouldn't be such a bad idea. We could use it to silence Moynihan."

The car stops. I stare out of the window at the group of enthusiastic retirees outside the ornate terracotta frontage of the Victoria and Albert Museum. Perhaps Stan Brooks has the right idea about quitting just as soon as he qualifies for the early retirement pension. The traffic lights change to green and we move on.

"It's all down to you, John."

I turn back to face him. "What is?"

"If you can deliver proof that the Cheltenham bombing was ordered either by the Sinn Féin/IRA leadership or else by some breakaway group which you can identify, you'll provide Jack with a winning hand to play for the company's future."

"Does that mean you'll give me written authorization for GOLD CUP?"

"I'd love to, John, you know that. But with Congress on our backs we simply daren't be seen breaking the rules—at least not unless the operation is acknowledged as a success. But I promise you one thing. Provide me with the names Jack needs, and I'll have you well positioned in whatever emerges from the restructuring."

The only position I want is as far away from Langley as possible. "Just keep Palmer out of London for another month."

I feel almost like an adolescent on his first date. I check the bottle of Chateau Talbot to make sure it's the right temperature, though I'm not sure what I'd do if it wasn't. I check the place settings on the polished antique oak table, the first time it's been laid for two, and then pick up the internal phone. "Imelda, don't forget to take the caviar out of the refrigerator at a quarter to eight, and don't put too much mustard on the steaks before you grill them."

"Mr. Darcy, I've told you before. Everything's under control."

I wonder whether I should put another log on the fire or whether that would block out the warm glow for too long. Perhaps I need some more ice in the ice bucket, but then I don't want the champagne to be too cold.

The doorbell sounds. I close the dining room door behind me, go into the study and check the monitor showing the front doorsteps, and then hurry to the door rather than use the entryphone.

"Welcome," I say as Kate walks in. I take off her black leather coat. Underneath she's wearing the dark blue suit she often wears at the embassy. Perhaps she hasn't had time to change.

"I hope you don't mind my suggesting I call round?" she asks.

"I'm pleased you did."

"I didn't want you to invite me for dinner."

"No problem," I say. "Imelda usually cooks enough for two anyway, so it's absolutely no trouble."

"Are you sure?"

This hesitancy is a side of Kate that I haven't seen before. "Sure I'm sure. There's a bathroom along the corridor, down three steps just past the study. The drawing room is upstairs. We'll see what Imelda produces in about half an hour."

She walks straight up the stairs.

Nobody—American or English—who sees the drawing room for the first time fails to comment on the cornices or the fireplace with its marble mantel or the view from the two french windows over Chester Square gardens. Kate sits down on one of the Chippendale chairs and says nothing.

"What would you like to drink?"

"Nothing, thanks, John. I wanted to see you before the GOLD CUP meeting tomorrow."

"Fire away, Kate," I say as I pour myself a bourbon.

"The Bureau has checked out all known districts where militant Irish republicanism survives in the States. It's come up with nothing in Boston, San Francisco, Chicago, Cleveland, Detroit, and Philadelphia."

I nod and sit down facing her. The tight skirt has ridden partway up her thighs.

She looks at me. "That leaves us with New York."

So Maitland has led us up a blind alley. "The Feebees won't find anything there. New York's Irish-Americans may support Sinn Féin and use political muscle to try and get a united Ireland, but they're far too integrated into society these days to get involved with terrorism."

She shuffles uncomfortably on her chair. "When were you last in New York, John?"

Kate Litynska may be very alluring, but I really don't need a Polack to lecture me about Irish New York. "If you really want to know, I spent a weekend with my folks in Woodside before I took up this assignment. Believe me, Woodside is one of the few Irish-American places left in New York."

"The Bronx?"

"For heaven's sake, Kate, the Bronx has been Black and Hispanic for years."

She avoids eye contact. "I mean the north Bronx."

Suddenly I suspect where she's leading.

"The hard men who fled Northern Ireland after the mid-eighties have reclaimed Bainbridge from the Latinos," she says. "Walk along Bainbridge Avenue today and you'll find those downrent places that used to serve tacos and enchiladas to the sound of mariachi music are now dark little pubs—pubs with names like The Volunteer that serve Jameson from behind bars decorated with republican paintings by prisoners in the Maze."

Now I know where she's leading, and I don't like it. "What have you found out?" I ask in a subdued voice.

"When your friend Maitland took over Five's Terrorism Directorate, he asked us to put these people under surveillance. We tapped the phones of the leading players and wired their meeting places. We had more bugs in the Phoenix bar than they had bottles of Guinness."

"And?"

"They're convinced the peace process won't lead to a united Ireland. They think the current IRA leadership have betrayed the cause. We got a wiretap of one saying that Michael Collins had the right idea when he wanted to machine gun movie queues in London; it's only when the war is brought to Britain that the republican movement achieves success. John, I have to tell you, ceasefire or not, we believe they are still buying guns for the Provos."

"What about bombs?" I say slowly. "Bombs with a Cheltenham address label on?"

"Before the ceasefire Maitland asked us to put the screws to them, and so we had half a dozen of their leaders indicted for gun running. Since then they don't talk to anyone they don't know and trust. The word from our assets is that the key meetings have moved upstate, to Pearl River in Rockland County, but beyond that we have no specific information." She looks me straight in the eye. "We need it, John."

After a pause I say, "I can't help you."

"Yes, you can, John. You set up this investigation. You're in a position to deliver."

"He's just a priest at St. Brendan's."

She shakes her head slowly. "Your brother is not only one of the Bainbridge parish priests, he also runs Tír na nOg, a community center which assists illegal Irish immigrants, including Provos who've fled Britain."

Chapter ✤ Fifteen

TÍR NA NOG. I guess my utopian kid brother hasn't changed. Before we were old enough to go to school, Mom would sit Joe on one side of her and me on the other and tell us stories from that emerald isle of St. Patrick and of leprechauns where she was born. Joe's favorite was about Oisin and Tír na nOg, the enchanted island off the Irish coast which was hidden from outsiders by mist. Those granted the privilege of discovering it found a land where the sun shone every day, where food grew aplenty for everyone, and where you stayed forever young.

Later, when she thought we were old enough and when Pop was working the four-to-twelve shift, she or Uncle Fergal would recount more recent Irish legends, of how our grandfather had volunteered for the Irish Republican Army in the War of Independence, how he had been forced to flee Derry for Donegal after opposing the treaty that accepted British sovereignty over six counties in the North, and how he had been killed by the treacherous so-called Irish Free State.

Pop was third generation American and, though he was an active member of the New York Police Department Emerald Society and the Woodside division of the Ancient Order of Hibernians, he was uncomfortable with gun running republicanism. "Has Fergal been round again, filling the heads of those boys with all that fighting talk?" he'd ask Mom. "Don't you think they see enough violence in Queens with all these Negroes moving in?"

Mom said nothing.

I then discovered a legend that both Mom and Pop could agree about. It changed both Joe's and my life.

At first Joe wasn't interested, but conscientious sixth grader that I was, I said, "Joe, Sister Teresa said every student at St. Sebastian's must watch *This Is Your Life* tonight," and so he stayed in to see the television program. In those days Joe looked up to me. He Brylcreemed his hair into an Elvis style like I did and dressed in my last year's clothes. Some people even mistook him for me.

Pop, still in his uniform pants and shirt, sprawled in the big armchair, Mom sat in the other armchair brushing little Kathleen's long black hair, while Joe fidgeted on the couch next to me. He stopped fidgeting shortly after the familiar image of Ralph Edwards began the story of Tom Dooley. After he qualified as a medical doctor, this Notre Dame alumnus volunteered for navy service aboard the USS *Montague* which transported Catholic refugees from North to South Vietnam following the Geneva Accords which split the country at the 17th parallel. Appalled by what he saw, Tom Dooley transferred to refugee camps in Haiphong where he treated "610,000 filthy, diseased, mutilated Asians fleeing the godless cruelty of communism." When the Viet Minh took over Haiphong, Dr. Dooley was one of the last Americans to leave.

Our whole family watched as this cleancut American

patriot—an Albert Schweitzer with the looks of Pat Boone—
asked in a high-pitched staccato delivery, "What can you do
for children who had chopsticks driven into their inner ears
to prevent them hearing the word of God? How do you
treat an old priest who had nails pressed into his skull to
mock Christ's crown of thorns?"

Ralph Edwards supplied the answer. "This young man,
still only twenty-nine years of age, left the Navy, took with
him three former Navy corpsmen, and entered Laos, the
ripest plum for communism, where he set up a hospital at
Nam Tha, a village five miles south of the China border.
Here he ministered to over a hundred patients a day, fund-
ing the enterprise from donations and the proceeds of his
book, *Deliver Us from Evil*. Now Dr. Dooley is launch-
ing MEDICO, the Medical International Cooperation
Organization, to provide hospitals throughout southeast
Asia."

Neither Joe nor I ever forgot the answer Tom Dooley
gave when Ralph Edwards asked why he was devoting his
life to this work. "Aw, hell, sir, we just want to do what we
can for people who ain't got it so good."

I studied hard, determined to become a jungle doctor
like Tom Dooley. Joe organized his class to collect Dooley
kits—cloth bags filled with soap, toothpaste, toothbrush, as-
pirin, a can of Coke, gum, rosary beads, and other essential
items—and sent them off to MEDICO.

By the time I was in seventh grade Tom Dooley had
been voted one of America's most admired living men,
alongside Albert Schweitzer, Winston Churchill, and Pope
John XXIII. In the sweltering August of that year our whole
family watched CBS Television relay the three-hour chest
surgery at New York's Memorial Hospital to try and remove
Dr. Dooley's cancer. Undeterred, the jungle doctor returned
to Laos. Seventeen months later, the day after his thirty-

fourth birthday when he was visited by Cardinal Spellman, he died.

"They gotta make that man a saint," said Pop as he put down the *Daily News*. Inspired, I redoubled my studying and won a place at Regis High School, the endowed Jesuit-run private school in mid-Manhattan which offered free places by competitive examination for top ranked Catholic boys throughout metropolitan New York.

Joe, as usual, followed me a year later. But, while I continued to study hard, Joe spent more and more time on the school's community action program, tutoring underprivileged children in Harlem.

"Where are you off to tonight?" demanded Pop after supper.

Joe shrugged. "A youth club."

"St. Sebastian's?"

"No."

"Where?"

"A new place near 127th and Fifth Avenue."

Pop shook his head. "Joe, I don't understand you. Wednesday afternoons you have the chance to play football in Central Park and you go teach Negro kids in Harlem. Now you go mixing with them at night. Why can't you be like your brother and make something of yourself? Look at John, he's home studying."

"Go easy, Pop," I said. "Joe always gets honor cards, and the youth club is the place he helped start for the kids he tutors. The fathers encourage it. Joe's just doing what he can for those who ain't got it so good."

"Harlem's not safe at night. Don't you think I know? Negroes don't have the same values we do."

"Joe'll be fine," I said, shepherding him to the door. "All the guys round there know him."

"Just you make sure you're back inside this house by eleven, that's all," Pop called after him.

In the lobby, out of sight of Pop, Joe punched my left biceps. "Thanks, man. I'll do the same for you one day."

I didn't make it to Notre Dame, but I did win an Air Force ROTC scholarship to major in science at Fordham University in the Bronx. A year later Joe followed, but he opted for philosophy and, with his natural ability, picked up a Fordham scholarship.

Like the Jesuits at Regis, the Jesuits at Fordham encouraged community service, and Joe became one of the driving forces in Fordham Sodality, where he built on and extended his program of academic and social support for the underprivileged in Harlem.

The split began in '67. Pop asked if we wanted to go with them as a family or were we going as part of the student body to the Loyalty Day parade in support of the Vietnam War.

"I'm not going, Pop," Joe said.

"Whaddya mean, Joe, you're not going? You got no pride in your country?"

"Pop, it's because I've got pride in my country that I'm not going."

"So, now you read some book by that . . . that degenerate . . ." He struggled for the name.

"Marcuse," I added helpfully.

"Yeah, that's him . . . you think you're a wise guy."

"Pop, if you listen to Dorothy Day, to Father Dan Berrigan . . ."

"These people know better than Cardinal Spellman? Joe, I don't know what's come over you. You play that Rolling Stones garbage on your phonograph, you dress like you come out of a soup kitchen, and you grow your hair like you're a girl or something." He shook his head.

"Jesus had long hair. I don't remember his father bawling him out for that."

"Joseph! I will not have blasphemy in this house! When I think that one time you were a member of the Junior Holy Name Society, I wonder what I did wrong. Why can't you be more like your brother?"

"Oh yeah? Join the Air Force, travel the world, meet lots of interesting people, and kill them." He stormed out and slammed the door behind him.

"I'll not have that boy . . ."

"It's OK, Pop," I said, "it's just a phase he's going through, he'll grow out of it."

He didn't.

USAF bombers at Da Nang exploded on our television screen; US troops in camouflage battledress retreated under fire in the Saigon suburb of Cholon; and, incredibly, US troops ran around in confusion in the gardens outside the white stuccoed walls of the United States embassy while Viet Cong fired at them from the inside.

"And General Westmoreland just told us the Viet Cong are beaten!" Joe said. "Jesus Christ! What happens when the Viet Cong start winning?"

"Joseph!" Pop yelled. "For the last time! I will not have blasphemy in this house."

The fight froze when Joe said, "Wait!"

We turned to watch the end of the program. White names on a black background rolled silently up the screen, like the credits at the end of a movie except these were the names of US soldiers who had died that week in Vietnam. I don't know how long the name check continued, but twice Joe said, "Oh my God," and I gestured to Pop not to say anything. At the end Joe just got up and walked out.

Mom looked at me and I said, "Two of those were kids that Joe tutored in Harlem."

The grinning Bobby Kennedy thanked his campaign volunteers for helping him win the California Democratic presidential primary, just as he'd thanked Joe and me after he'd won the New York Senate seat. A TV camera followed Bobby and his bodyguards as he left the ballroom and escaped from his enthusiastic supporters through a kitchen passage. We heard shots. We saw a distraught Asian kitchen worker kneel by the side of the prostrate body. Joe left the TV room.

I found him packing in his bedroom.

"I gotta move out, John."

"Why?"

"You know why. Mom gets upset when the old man and I fight, and now . . . now we've got nothing left to agree on. Don't you see, big brother, it's the end."

"Joe, I'm as cut up as you are."

He looked up from stuffing his clothes into a big holdall and pushed back his shoulder-length black hair. "It's more than that, can't you see? This is more significant than Jack Kennedy's assassination. For the Blacks it's more significant than Martin Luther King's assassination. It's the end of hope, the final proof that the powers that really run this country will not permit radical change through our so-called democratic process. You raise up a radical leader through the conventional system and he gets shot down. If you want to change things you got to take action."

Chapter ❖ Sixteen

IT'S IRONIC HOW my folks assumed that Joe was the activist in the family and I was the studious one who opted for a desk job in the Department of the Air Force to avoid combat duty in Vietnam. It was action which I relished in the Agency, using the Department of the Air Force and the State Department as covers while I fought our secret war. And the more I became addicted to clandestine action, the less I thought about what I was doing. But I need to think now.

I look at the expectant faces of the GOLD CUP team seated around the table in my office. "Well, Bruce?" I ask.

"Afraid my follow-up to your Northern Ireland mission has produced zilch." Bruce Davis seems reluctant to go further.

I try not to sound anxious. "Absolutely nothing?"

"Believe me, John, I had Menwith Hill intercept not just the phone at the Cúchulainn pub but all known IRA and Sinn Féin phones and faxes in Derry, Tyrone, and Donegal. Nothing incriminating."

"British intercepts?"

"We monitored all GCHQ intercepts commissioned by Five's T Branch. They drew a blank, at least on who was responsible for Cheltenham."

"But?"

He grimaces. "They showed loyalist paramilitaries sending people to buy arms and explosives in Russia. It seems they've had no problems raising the money."

Davis's enthusiasm for GOLD CUP is fading. He feels he's getting sucked into something much bigger. I guess he'll be prepared to continue NSA's unofficial surveillance, but only if I can hold out some hope that the risk will be rewarded. I turn to our MI5 liaison officer, who wants out of this operation as soon as possible. "Well, Stan?"

"According to Jennifer Ackroyd, Gloucestershire police have now completed their check of all people with known Irish connections in the area. They can't be certain about alibis because they don't know at what time the bomb was primed, but none of the names came up on Five's computer."

Terrific. Does he really imagine the IRA would use someone already known to Five or fail to arrange an alibi? "What about the bomb? Did any parts originate in the States?"

Stan Brooks looks down at his notebook. "The report from the Royal Armament Research and Defense Establishment at Fort Halstead showed that the explosive device was extremely efficient. The remnants were too disfigured for Five to trace where the parts came from."

"So Five has got absolutely nowhere?"

"Jennifer did mention a long shot, but I don't think it'll come to much." He says this reluctantly.

"Spit it out, Stan."

"It seems that one known IRA liaison officer is on the move."

"Who, when, where, why?" Todd Fraser is even more impatient than I am.

"I don't have her name," Brooks admits. "It seems it was all a stroke of luck. A week ago a team of Five watchers was looking out for drugs smugglers using the Boulogne to Dover ferry when one of them thought he recognized an IRA liaison officer in a blonde wig. Five followed her to Brighton."

"And?"

"They lost her."

"Heavens to Betsy!" This is the nearest our cleancut Mormon Fraser ever comes to swearing. After a year liaising with MI6, Fraser has adopted Six's contemptuous view of MI5.

"What did you find in Dublin, Todd?" I say to spare Brooks any further embarrassment.

"Six there arranged a meeting for me at a Redemptorist House with a member of the Provo Army Council."

It seems I was wrong to be skeptical about Fraser's inexperience and the quality of his contacts. Is my judgment clouded by resentment of his youth? "Well done, Todd. What did he say?"

"He denied that the IRA had anything to do with the Cheltenham bombing."

"Did you find his denial convincing?"

Fraser pauses. "I think I'd be convincing if I wanted to disown a foul up that killed US women and children." He looks uneasy. "There's something more. He wanted a message passed on to the US administration. He said the propaganda war being waged against the IRA would inevitably provoke a response."

"What kind of response?"

"He wouldn't say, but my guess is that the IRA is planning some kind of spectacular."

"But you say Five have come up with nothing, Stan?"

Brooks scratches his nose before replying. "Nothing on the Cheltenham bombing. One of Five's informers has reported that a Provo shooter in West Belfast has dropped out of circulation."

Christ Almighty. Protestant paramilitaries are buying arms and the IRA is planning a spectacular, with a gunman being primed and a liaison officer already in Britain. If somebody doesn't find out precisely who did order the Cheltenham bombing, it looks like another twenty-five years of terrorist war in Northern Ireland.

Davis looks at me. "What about the possible US connection you reported, John?" Before I reply, he adds, "What's the latest on that, Kate?"

Kate, who is wearing the same blue suit as last night, has not spoken a word so far and has focused on the legal pad in front of her. Now she stares straight at me.

When I say nothing she answers Davis. "The Bureau has eliminated all known hardline Irish republican groups in the States except one, in the north Bronx."

She pauses, and stares at me again.

"They're involved?" Davis asks.

Kate's voice is measured. "We don't know. They've gone to ground. We're having a problem following their trail."

I wait. When she says nothing more, I conclude the meeting. "We continue to pursue Operation GOLD CUP. We meet again a week from today unless there's a significant development."

The three men gather their papers, get up, and leave my office. Kate remains seated. When the others have departed she rises, goes to the door, and closes it. She walks over to where I'm sitting and stands with her hands on her hips. "I fell for that Irish-American blarney of yours. I really thought you were different. I thought you still had principles." Those large blue eyes bore into me and her voice is edged with scorn. "I admired you, I even . . ." She stops herself. "I also broke the rules and gave you twelve hours' warning. I was sure you'd act on the information."

"Kate, there's no action I can take . . ."

"Oh yes there is, John Darcy." She puts her hands flat on the table and leans forward so that her eyes are level with mine. "You go over and see your brother, find out from him what is really happening, where the players have moved to, and whether he has any lines into the Cheltenham bombing. He'll say things to you that he wouldn't say to us."

I shake my head. "Kate, you don't understand . . ."

"I understand that you're shafting yourself, John Darcy. You're laying yourself open to obstruction of justice."

I jump up with such vehemence that she recoils, scattering my notes over the floor. "Never say anything like that to me, ever again, understand! Have your people bug him, grill him, give him a harder time than anyone else if you really believe he's involved. Just don't ask me to do your dirty work for you."

Her eyes flash, and for a moment I think she'll hit me. Then she bends down, picks up my notes, and places them on the table. "I really don't think the National Theater on Saturday is such a good idea. Try your charm on someone more gullible, someone who admires your brotherly loyalty."

I watch Kate walk out of the door. How can I tell her that she's got it all wrong about loyalty?

Chapter ✧ Seventeen

"WHAT KINDA LOYALTY is Joe showing you?" Pop shook his large head.

Pop just didn't understand. He didn't understand why I helped Joe move out to a brownstone on 120th Street rented by some Catholic Worker friends from Columbia University, friends who shouted "pig" at Pop when he was called out of the 125th Precinct to go on crowd control duty at antiwar demonstrations. He didn't understand why I stayed loyal to Joe, even when Joe joined the Students for a Democratic Society. And now he was at a total loss. "You defend him, even when he's occupying the administration building at Fordham to protest the ROTC—who provide your scholarship?"

I gave up trying to explain to Pop that Joe was sincere in wanting to help those who ain't got it so good, that I might think he was misguided in what he was doing while still respecting his motives.

I thought it was because I stayed close to Joe that Father Paul, the dean for seniors, asked me to meet a friend of his. I crossed Rose Hill lawn, which was filled with chanting students, when a familiar voice rose above the slogans. "Come and join us, man!" Joe was fixing a placard to the out-stretched copper hand of Archbishop Hughes, the nine-teenth century founder of Fordham, who stared sternly at the banners flapping from the windows of the occupied ad-ministration building. I grinned and waved back, and went on through to Loyola Hall, the Jesuit faculty building.

Inside Loyola the thick stone walls of Father Paul's room deadened the noise. Father Paul, a genial gray-haired man in his late forties, got to his feet and offered me sherry from a cabinet next to the wood paneling that covered the lower half of the walls. Glass in hand he introduced me to Liam Walsh, a science alumnus from the class of '61. The broad-shouldered Walsh unfolded himself from an armchair. He was even taller than me, with an open, friendly face below tousled auburn hair styled in a shortened Beatles cut.

"It's a pleasure to meet with you, John."

"My privilege, sir."

"Liam, please."

"It seems to me," said Father Paul, "that we need to un-derstand these students better, to know what's troubling them. I've selected you, John, because you're close to them, and I hope you can help us. I've asked Liam to join us be-cause he may be able to supply answers to the questions they have."

I was flattered.

"Go right ahead, John," said Walsh, "you just tell us what's troubling these guys."

The armchairs in Father Paul's room were old, hard, and bumpy: no one could accuse the Jesuits of living in luxury. "Vietnam, of course," I said.

"Sure," said Walsh, "but what in terms of specifics?"

"They're concerned about the morality of the war," I said, "sending our young people halfway round the world to fight on behalf of a government that doesn't have the support of its own people."

Walsh nodded understandingly. "How do they figure that the democratic government of Nuyen Van Thieu hasn't got the support of the Vietnamese people?"

"They've seen it on TV, the Tet offensive. We had to defend Thieu's palace for him, the Viet Cong took over our embassy, and . . ." I shrugged at the self-evident case Joe and his friends had made.

Walsh glanced quickly at Father Paul. "I ought to have guessed," he said to me. "Do you want to know the real story behind those superficial, misleading images on the TV screen, John?"

I wasn't sure what he meant, but if he was a friend of Father Paul he deserved a hearing. "Try me."

"The South Vietnamese government agreed a truce with the communists to celebrate Tet, the Vietnamese New Year. So naturally the South Vietnamese army and we stood down. Then—wham!—they sneaked up on us. That is just typical of how the communists operate. They gave their word, broke it, and our own television people were dumb enough to show what appeared to be Viet Cong unopposed in the South, when our people were on an agreed R and R. I have to tell you, John, we lost a lot of good people that week, killed by communist duplicity."

"I think the lesson to be drawn," said Father Paul, "is that you can't always believe what you see on TV."

"Right," said Walsh, "but our TV allows the communists to score big propaganda victories. These student demonstrations are reinforcing that propaganda, building up a head of steam that could bring this nation of ours to a major crisis."

"Liam," I said, "you can't seriously be suggesting that what the students out there are doing puts America in danger?"

Walsh paused and put his glass down on the floor. "May I share a confidence with both of you?" he said in a low voice.

"You have my word," said Father Paul. "John?"

"Certainly," I said.

"We have grounds for believing that the Soviets are pulling the strings."

"I find that hard to swallow," I said.

"John," he said, "I've not the slightest doubt that the guys out there are one hundred and ten per cent genuine in what they say and believe. But they're being duped. They're being used without their knowledge as part of a propaganda war to demoralise the American people. That propaganda already forced Johnson not to run for another term. Now the Soviets want to foment such public outrage that we'll be forced to pull out and leave them with a walkover victory in southeast Asia."

Walsh could see that I wasn't convinced. Father Paul refilled our glasses.

"John," Walsh said, "I have to tell you that the student leaders at Columbia are drugged out of their minds. Do you know what happened when the SDS took over the administration building there? They broke open the president's filing cabinet and defecated over his files. Now tell me, is that the American way?"

"They're not doing that here," I said.

"John," Walsh said, "you don't have to tell me that. Fordham is different." He looked out of the leaded window to the gray stone tower of the university church. "Father Paul tells me that you're frequently at morning mass."

I blushed.

"There's no need to be embarrassed, John," Walsh said, "I was the same. And when I left, I always stopped in the porch and spent a quiet moment in front of the carving of the knight kneeling before an altar—you know the one—above the names of alumni who died in the service of their country, together with the inscription 'For Thee O God they have offered their Sacrifice.' Fordham instils values that are worth fighting for."

"That's what makes Fordham different," Father Paul said. "We believe in God, a God who so loves us that he has given us a unique gift: free will. In the spiritual world we have the freedom to accept God into our hearts or to deny him. In the secular world we have the freedom to choose how and by whom we are governed." His eyes twinkled. "And democracy also includes freedom of speech, as a few of our students are exercising on Rose Hill lawn."

"Can you imagine, John," Walsh asked, "what would happen in a communist country if their students took over a university administration building? You watched TV last year. You saw the Soviet tanks roll into Czechoslovakia and crush the Prague Spring. Do you think Brezhnev and his unelected cronies in the Politburo would allow the Czechs to introduce some democracy into their communist system? Of course not. So they did what they did in East Germany in 1953 and Hungary in 1956. They sent in the tanks and imposed hardline communist dictatorships which denied the people their God-given freedoms to worship God, to choose their government, and to speak freely. That's what communism is really about."

"Do you want to let them do that in southeast Asia, John?" asked Father Paul.

"Certainly not, Father," I said.

"It's all very well Dan and Phil Berrigan talking of liberation," said Father Paul, "but the Gospel says, 'the truth shall make you free.' Liam works for a part of the government that tries to separate the truth from the propaganda. He was recruited by Bobby Kennedy."

"Bobby Kennedy!"

"Right," said Walsh. "When Bobby was Attorney

General he invited a group of us from the National Students Association to his office and thanked us for countering communist propaganda aimed at the student movement. Can you imagine, John, what an impression that had on me? When the chance came to work full time combating communist propaganda, I jumped at it."

Wouldn't anyone in Liam's place? I thought.

"But I must also tell you, John, that our kind of work involves a life of self denial. We're pledged to secrecy, and so our mothers and fathers, brothers and sisters, friends and neighbors, indeed, the American people as a whole never know for whom we work, what work we do, what successes we achieve, what dangers we face abroad, and what sacrifices we make. Our only reward is the satisfaction of preserving our country and the free world from communist tyranny."

"In the final analysis," said Father Paul, "you either believe in God or you don't, and you either believe in God-given freedom or you believe in tyranny. You have to choose whose side you're on."

"I'd like for you to concentrate on your upcoming exams right now, John," Walsh said. "Afterwards, think about the work I've described. If it involves the idealism, commitment and loyalty to your country that I know you're seeking in a career, let Father Paul know and we can talk some more."

I didn't need to think. I knew where my loyalty lay. But loyalty is a jealous mistress. It's not because of loyalty that I won't go and question Joe. Quite the opposite. It's because of what loyalty demanded six months after my talk with Liam and Father Paul that I haven't had the courage to phone or meet Joe for twenty-six years.

Chapter ✣ Eighteen

You CAN NEVER completely eradicate guilt from your psyche, not if you've been born and raised a Catholic. You may no longer regard it as the stain of sin which remains on the soul until reparation has been made and the offense forgiven through the saving grace of Christ's death on the cross, but the knowledge that you are to blame, the shame which floods through you when you meet a victim who is unaware that you have wronged him, that stays with you for life.

The guilt is proportionate to the offense, and I've found the best way to handle major-league guilt is to avoid the victim. That's why I also avoided Maitland. But my guilt about what I did to Joe overcomes my guilt about Maitland, leaving a large residue of suspicion when Maitland phones to ask for a meeting. What has he got on Joe? "Do you want to come here?" I ask.

"No. Do you still use the rag trade?"

"Uh huh."

"I'll be there at ten."

The phone goes dead. Twenty years ago we'd talk freely

on the secure lines. But now that our technical people can monitor without trace almost all telecommunications, either directly or by reconstructing data from their radiation leaks, and then break most encryption systems, we're paranoid about using the phone in case the opposition are doing the same to us. So I understand why Maitland wants to meet rather than talk over the phone, but why doesn't he want to come to the office? It has to be personal. It has to be Joe. Surely Kate would warn me first? Or would she, after what she accused me of? I dial her number.

"The legal attaché's office," an unfamiliar voice answers.

"Is Kate there?"

"I'm afraid she's out. Who is that speaking?"

"John Darcy. Do you know where she is?"

"Yes, Mr. Darcy. Kate is at Thames House."

Sleeping with the enemy? I wonder if, at this moment, she's ensnaring Maitland with those large innocent eyes and that suggestive mouth. "What time will she be back?"

"She didn't say. Do you want to leave a message, Mr. Darcy?"

"No message."

The taxi drops me on Oxford Street, by a big department store just past Oxford Circus. I walk the short distance up Great Portland Street to the safe house. We're still using the same ones as twenty years ago; I make a note to change them. This one, admittedly, is ideally placed, less than ten minutes" drive from the embassy but right in the middle of London's rag trade district. Vans, cars, and people of all nationalities pass through the area at all hours of the day and night. Just off London's busiest shopping street, and near London's busiest subway station with six exits, it proved perfect for losing a tail and then going on to meet any foreigner without arousing suspicion.

The area hasn't changed much. Some of the establish-
ments have moved upmarket, with designer shopfronts and
names like Nina Louise International and Desiré of London,
and some shop windows display only a FOR RENT sign, but
most of the places are much as they were when I was last
here: fashion workshops and wholesalers with handwritten
notices stuck in the window reading "PATTERN CUTTER
REQUIRED—AT LEAST 3 YEARS EXPERIENCE—APPLY WITHIN."

I unlock the door next to the Cosmo Wholesale and
Stock House, and climb the three flights of stairs to our
apartment on the top floor.

It's as tacky as the apartment I had in Boydell Court all
those years ago. At least Susanne, who services our safe
houses, has left some coffee in the freezer compartment of
the refrigerator. While the coffee filters through I take out
two cups and saucers from the poorly painted yellow cupboard above the Formica kitchen top. But will we need
three? If the Bureau have got something on my brother, will
Kate accompany Maitland?

Or perhaps Maitland has discovered that I'm running an
unauthorized operation in Britain. That would be enough
for the Brits to have me sent back to Langley. But Maitland
wouldn't do that, it's not his style. He'd use the implicit
threat to exert leverage on me. But for what?

The buzzer sounds. The security television monitor
shows Maitland alone on the doorstep.

Inside the apartment Maitland takes off his cashmere overcoat and his trilby. I expect him to hand them to me as
though I were a hat-check girl, but he hangs them up himself on the hook behind the door. He seems strangely
subdued.

"Coffee?" I ask.

"No thank you." He takes a small leatherbound

notebook from the inside pocket of his pinstripe suit jacket, scribbles on it, and shows it to me: "Please turn off the sound system."

I go to the kitchen, pour myself a coffee, open a cupboard, and switch off the tape recorder which is fed by the bugs hidden in all the rooms.

"We're unwired," I say when I return to the living room. "Make yourself at home."

Maitland sits down on the pink velour settee. I've never seen him so ill at ease.

"What's the problem, Edward?"

He stares at me in a strange way. "You must promise to inform no one of what I'm about to tell you."

Just what game is Maitland playing?

"It's in your own interest," he says.

Then the bastard has got something on me—or Joe. If that's the case, I have no difficulty in lying to him. "OK, I promise."

The arrogance goes out of his voice. "The IRA has kidnapped Emma."

Jesus Christ! His only child.

He takes out a packet of cheroots. "May I?"

Under any other circumstances I'd take great pleasure in saying, ever so politely, no. "Sure," I say, "go right ahead. When did it happen? Where? How?"

"Yesterday afternoon, from her boarding school near Brighton."

"Have you got a description of the kidnappers?"

He shakes his head.

"Are you certain that no one at the school—student, teacher, doorman or whoever—can tell you what the kidnappers look like?"

"I haven't asked them."

"What! You're not going to rely on the statements they've made to the local police?"

"The school thinks it was the police who took Emma to a hospital where I was dangerously ill." He hands me a typed note. "A helmeted bike messenger delivered this to Jill around half past four yesterday afternoon."

> We have your daughter. Telephone her school. Say that, because of your husband's illness, Emma will be away for a few more days. If you do this before 5 P.M. today we will return Emma to you on payment of £200,000. If you fail to do this, or if you or your husband inform the police or anyone else, we will kill her.
> We will telephone instructions for payment. We will know if the police or any security organization is informed. We will also know if your telephone is being monitored. In either case we will kill Emma and bury her body where you will never find it.

"It doesn't mention the IRA," I say.

"Who else could it be? I'm no rich businessman."

He's right. "Is it a hardline splinter group?"

"No splinter group organized this," Maitland snorts. "We're up against the world's most efficient terrorist organization."

"What did you tell Jill to say to the school?"

"I didn't."

"Surely Jill phoned you as soon as she got the note?"

"She tried."

"And?"

"I was in an important meeting."

"You couldn't be disturbed for the kidnap of your own daughter?"

His thin lips tighten. "How the hell was I to know she wanted to talk about Emma being kidnapped?"

"OK, OK, I'm sorry. Go down to the school right now and get descriptions of these fake police."

He stubs out his cheroot. "The school is responsible for

Emma during term time. If I tell them that she's been kidnapped, they'd be legally obliged to inform the police. Read the note again. I can't risk it."

"But if you do it through the Security Service, surely that will avoid any publicity."

He lights another cheroot.

"What does your director general say?" I ask.

He doesn't answer.

I don't believe this.

He blows out a stream of smoke. "This is the propaganda spectacular that the Provo Army Council have been planning to follow up Cheltenham. It explains the sighting of that blonde-wigged IRA liaison officer in Brighton and the disappearance of one of their gunmen."

"Edward, you've no choice. You've to bring your office in on this."

"Really? Think it through. These people must know that I'm getting close to identifying the Cheltenham bomber, they know my home address, my ex-directory phone number, and the school that Emma attends. They've got an informer on the inside. It could be a secretary or a clerk in the Service, or possibly somebody in Special Branch. With so many different agencies involved in counterterrorism, it would be impossible for me to bring in the Service without that information getting back to the IRA."

"I need another coffee," I say. "Do you want one?"

He shakes his head.

I go and pour myself a second cup. Much as I can't stand Maitland, I don't wish this on the poor bastard. "What are you going to do?" I ask when I return to the living room.

"They telephoned last night. They want me to bring two hundred thousand pounds in low denomination untraceable notes. I stalled them by saying that I'd comply, but I can't raise so much money without selling the house. I said that I could raise ten thousand in cash by Monday, but first

I wanted proof that they have Emma and that she's still alive."

I hate to admit it, but I feel a sneaking respect for Maitland. This is not the patronizing fraud, but neither is this a distraught father who's come unglued. Perhaps it's that famous British sangfroid, but he's approaching the problem with a clinical coolness that I admire. "I'll get Menwith Hill to monitor your phone. The IRA will never know."

He shakes his head. "You promised to tell no one. I don't want either your or my people involved."

Then why has he come to see me? "Are you going to pay the ransom?"

His hazel eyes examine me. "You don't know the IRA. You Irish Americans seem to think that it's some idealistic liberation army. Understand this. They're the people who detonated a bomb next to the war memorial on Remembrance Day in Enniskillen, killing eleven and injuring sixtythree, all 'civilians.' They're the people who exploded two litter bin bombs in a shopping center in Warrington which killed a boy of three and a boy of twelve and injured fiftysix shoppers—and this while they were engaged in secret peace talks with an officer from Six acting on behalf of the government." He exhales a thin plume of smoke. "If I were to take the ransom to them, it would achieve nothing. They would carry out their plan to assassinate the man who's closing in on the Cheltenham bomber, and then they'd dispose of the bait."

"What on earth do you intend to do?"

He stubs out his second cheroot, sits back, and makes a steeple with his fingers. "Have your brother solve the problem."

"What the . . ."

"What I propose is this. You ask your brother to come over here and deliver the ransom. They won't kill an Irish-American priest, especially one who supports what they call the cause. Father Joe Darcy will tell them to hand over Emma unharmed, otherwise it will destroy what is left of their support in the States."

Suddenly I feel I'm playing poker with an opponent who knows all the cards in my hand. What *has* Maitland got on Joe? Is Joe involved in the Cheltenham bombing? Is this a device to lure Joe to Britain? Surely Maitland is not that devious? "It wouldn't work. Joe and I have been estranged for years."

"You'll just have to persuade him. Fly over and talk to him. I think I can stall them until the weekend."

If Langley found out that I was undertaking a private operation, they'd fire me without a pension—and then what would I do with the rest of my life? "Edward, I just can't do it. The DCI would be bent out of shape."

Maitland reaches into the inside breast pocket of his suit, takes out a photograph, and hands it to me.

The picture brings me up in goose bumps. If the long hair were red instead of black, you could mistake Emma for the Jill Maitland of twenty years ago. Her nose is more snubbed than Jill's, but she has the same elfin face. And those green eyes glinting like a wildcat's are identical to Jill's. "She's beautiful," I say. "I want to help, but what you propose is just impossible."

"You really don't know, do you?" It's the tone of voice I'm more familiar with.

"Don't know what, Edward?"

"You're looking at a photograph of your daughter."

Chapter ✣ Nineteen

THOSE GREEN EYES glint back from the photograph propped up on my desk in Chester Square. The phone rings yet again. The office can go hang.

That snub nose is a Darcy nose, just like Pop's. And the color of her hair comes from me through Mom. Their only grandchild. Kid sister Kathleen is into her legal career and is planning to have children some time in the future, though she's given up telling Pop that she and Michael use the rhythm method. Joe, I presume, is celibate, though with Catholic priests these days you can never be sure. And I? I am the great disappointment, neither priest nor provider of grandchildren bearing the Darcy name.

Emma is beautiful. Seventeen years old. Seventeen years in which I've been denied the opportunity to watch a wrinkled, red faced, tiny creature metamorphose into a beautiful young woman like this.

Not just watch, but nurture. Forty-eight years old and I've never changed a diaper, never held the nipple of a feeding bottle for a helpless mouth to suck, never cuddled a pained and frightened bundle in my arms and soothed it to sleep, never gained the trust of an uncertain infant while it takes its first faltering steps.

But Emma would have talked before that. All three of us talked before we could walk. Mom said that we were born with the gift of the gab. She encouraged us, but Pop was no role model. When I was frozen with anxiety on the first morning of grade school, he didn't see the problem. "You want me to take you in a baby walker?" I would have been much more understanding with Emma. What grade school did she go to? Probably a snooty English private school if it was Edward's choice, or maybe some progressive school if Jill had her way. The Sisters of Charity at St. Sebastian's were strict, and went over the top on the sixth commandment, but there's no denying they did give us a good education and taught us the difference between right and wrong.

With looks like Emma's and a personality even half that of her mother's, it would be difficult keeping the boys at bay. But I bet she's far too sensible to waste herself on some spotty adolescent. She's bright. That's clear from her photograph. What did Maitland say at the Garrick Club? She was going for interviews in December for Oxford University. I wonder if she's been accepted. I don't even know what she plans to major in.

On the back of the photograph there's a photographer's stamp, together with a handwritten inscription: "Roedean School. Emma Mary Maitland." Mary. That's my mother's name. Jill knew that. She even stole my mother's name. A wave of anger engulfs me. Jill Maitland has robbed me of seventeen of the most precious years of my daughter's life. What right had she? I gave that woman not only my body but also my soul. I would have worshiped her for the rest of my life. And what did she do in return? Play me along, take my seed, and then discard me when she's pregnant so she and Edward can bring up the child who is rightfully mine.

But who has betrayed whom? Was I not guilty of betraying Maitland while he was away in Northern Ireland? And what of the guilt that made me avoid all contact with Joe, whom I now need to rescue my daughter? Will he forgive me for what I did to him?

"It's for the sake of national security," said Lou Borelli, a kindly, balding man with a double chin who had introduced himself as a personnel officer. Six months after my talk at Fordham University with Liam Walsh and Father Paul, I raised my right hand and swore an oath never to disclose what I was about to learn of the Central Intelligence Agency during the selection process, and then signed the statement: my first experience of that drug which was soon to become addictive without my ever realizing it—secrecy.

"That applies especially if you don't pass the tests, John," said Borelli.

"Yes, sir," I said. I'd passed the security checks and I wasn't about to flunk these tests.

The medical tests presented no problems. The vocational, aptitude, intelligence, and personality questionnaires intrigued, bored, and then intimidated. On the third morning a psychiatrist probed my loyalty. By noon, exhausted, tense, and with my confidence shaken, I drove to downtown DC to seek some respite.

From the top of the Washington Monument I looked out over the long narrow rectangle of the Reflecting Pool to the giant seated white marble Abraham Lincoln. In my mind's eye I saw the black and white TV image of a quarter of a million people gathered around the Reflecting Pool, and Martin Luther King standing in front of the Lincoln Memorial intoning, each time on a higher note, the words "I have a dream." Opposite, across a wide expanse of lawn, sat the White House, which Jack Kennedy had transformed for me into a symbol of hope. And to my right, at the end of the long green sweep of the Mall, rose that guarantee of democracy, the Capitol, floating like a white mirage above the city, its dome topped by the statue of Freedom.

By the time I left the Monument through the circle of American flags, all thoughts of the Jesuit noviciate at St. Andrews on the Hudson had faded into oblivion. I was determined to join the priesthood of the secret arm of our government—if I passed the tests.

The irony of having to pass a lie detector test in order to qualify for a career in lying never struck me at the time. What did strike me, and the others in my recruitment pool, was fear. Rumors about the infamous polygraph had multiplied, fed by ignorance, since nobody who experienced it was permitted to talk about it. The poly was said to eliminate at least half the remaining applicants. It caused nervous breakdowns. It even resulted in suicide. The questions were directed at exposing drugs usage. They revealed homosexuality. My roommate and I spent a night figuring out how to avoid admitting that we'd once smoked a joint.

Twenty of us were in a classroom studying nonclassified briefings on the contradictions between the theory and the practice of communism when a secretary entered. "Mr. Darcy for the technical interview, please," she called aloud.

Muted conversations ceased. Nineteen pairs of eyes focused on me. I rose and followed her out of the room and down a long corridor. It was like going to confession after the first time I'd committed self-abuse.

She knocked on a door, entered, and passed me on to a man in his mid-thirties who was clean cut and clean shaven and who possessed an unblinking stare. The camaraderie shown by the other CIA officers whom we'd met was absent.

His every movement and gesture conveyed intensity under control.

The interrogator, who remained nameless, asked me to sign a statement acknowledging that I was submitting to the test of my own volition and that I would hold no claim against any person or organization afterwards whatever the outcome. My signature on this and on yet another secrecy agreement was smaller than usual.

The interrogator ushered me into a room lined with white acoustic tiles. A government-issue black leather chair faced away from a desk on which rested dials, tubes, electrodes, and three long narrow metal pens poised above three rolls of graph paper: a twentieth-century American version of a Spanish Inquisition chamber.

He seated me on the chair that faced a wall, moved a chair from behind the desk so that he sat opposite me, and handed me a list of questions. "These are designed to be answered 'yes' or 'no,' Mr. Darcy, so we'll review them now to remove any ambiguities."

I studied the list, which included:

Is your name John Patrick Darcy?
Have you ever been known by any other name?
Were you born on 21 January 1947?
Is your permanent address: 432 57th Street, Woodside, Queens, New York?
Have you ever engaged in homosexual activities?
Have you ever taken drugs?
Have you taken tranquillizers today?
Have you filled out your job application form honestly?
Have you ever known an official or an agent of a communist government?
Has anyone ever asked you to obtain employment with the CIA?
Have you ever been a communist or belonged to a communist organization?

Do you know anyone who has?
Have you ever been a member of any of the subver-
    sive organizations on the Attorney General's list?
Do you know anyone who has?

The pre-test interview lasted about an hour as the interrogator explored each question in depth, noting all names,
dates, and places. He rephrased certain questions to include "other than" so that I could answer a simple "yes" or
"no."

Then came the moment of truth. He asked me to remove my jacket and my wristwatch, and to roll up my left
sleeve. He wrapped a blood pressure cuff around my arm.
Next, he placed a corrugated rubber tube about two inches
in diameter around my chest and fastened it at the back so
that it fitted snugly. Last, he put a device with electrodes into
my right hand and clipped springs across the back of my
hand so that the electrodes maintained contact with my
palm.

He moved his chair behind the desk in order to ask the
questions to the back of my head while I stared at the
acoustic tiles in front.

I was convinced that if I kept telling myself that the answers were true—particularly the answers to which I'd given
half truths—I could beat the machine. The pressure cuff
around my arm inflated. I was unable to stop the pounding
in my chest and the sweating of my hands. I focused on the
tiny holes in the acoustic tiles and mentally repeated the
mantra "what I am saying is true."

The interrogator moved very slowly from one question
to the next, pausing before each question. I answered
promptly "Yes" or "No" as per plan. At the end he threw a
curve ball: "Have you answered all the questions truthfully?"

"Yes," I said.

The cuff deflated and I heard a shuffling of paper as he

reviewed the charts. He stayed in his chair, facing my back,
and asked what I was thinking about when I answered the
question as to whether I had ever taken drugs. "Nothing in
particular," I said. As we passed from question to question
he insisted with increasing intensity that I remember what
I was thinking about, and when he came to the question
about knowing anyone who was a member or supporter of
a subversive group, he added, "I must stress, Mr. Darcy, that
your cooperation is essential for a successful test."

"I wasn't thinking about anything, sir," I persisted. If
you stay consistent you can beat the machine, my roommate
and I had agreed, but doubt was beginning to gnaw away at
that conviction.

Up went the blood pressure cuff and we went through
the questions yet again. I strained my ears to catch changes
in the scratching of the pens as I told my half truths.

"We're having difficulty on some of the questions, Mr.
Darcy," my inquisitor stated. "Is there anything you wish to
say or clarify?"

It was bluff. Keep consistent. "No, sir."

He sighed. "There's no way for you to be hired without
successfully passing the test. Let's try this one more time."

I was racked with indecision. What if I told the truth
now? But I'd gotten in too deep. Would they accept me if I
admitted that I'd lied? I kept to my plan.

When the cuff deflated I heard nothing but the shuffling
of paper for at least five minutes. Then the interrogator said, "You're obviously having trouble, Mr. Darcy. I'll
leave you for five minutes to think about your loyalty to
your country."

As soon as the door closed behind him I was ready to
confess all to keep alive my chances of being accepted into
the brotherhood of clandestine guardians of our freedom.

Twenty minutes passed before he returned. I knew what
he wanted to hear. "Sir, I think I should clarify my answer

to one question. I was trying to protect my brother. Joe is basically a good man, he means well, but he's come under some bad influences. The Students for a Democratic Society, for example."

"I think you'd better tell me all about your brother, the people you identify as providing bad influences, and the activities he's been engaged in," the interrogator said.

A few weeks later Mom told me that Joe had been arrested and had been charged with a serious offense against the state. That was my first betrayal. My brother.

I look at Emma's photograph and steel myself to pick up the phone and dial Joe's number in New York.

"St. Brendan's," answers a middle aged female voice.

"May I speak with Father Joe Darcy?"

"I'll see if Father Flynn is available."

"I want to speak with Father Darcy," I insist.

"Father Joe is on retreat until a week Saturday, I'm afraid."

"Can you tell me where I can reach him? I'm his brother."

The voice cools. "Sir, I have to say that I've been receptionist at St. Brendan's for over fifteen years and I've neither met nor taken a phone call from any brother of Father Darcy."

"I haven't the time to go into our family history right now, this matter is urgent. Just tell me how to contact him."

"As I said, sir, Father Darcy is away on retreat. In case you are not a Catholic, let me explain that a retreat means a place where you can retreat from the pressures of the secular world in order to focus on the spiritual. Poor Father Darcy works such long hours at St. Brendan's that these days on retreat are precious to him."

"I do know what a retreat is. But what I have to talk to him about is a matter of life and death."

"Will you give me the details, please, sir?"

How can I tell this stranger on the phone over three thousand miles away that Joe is the only hope of rescuing my newly discovered daughter from the IRA? "I . . . I can't. It's a matter between us as brothers."

"If you give me your name and telephone number I'll pass on the message when he returns."

After a minute's silence the line goes dead.

Chapter ✣ Twenty

I SIT IN my car and watch a large attached house off Highbury Fields. But it's not this house I see, not this three-story late Victorian row with renovated white pilasters framing original paneled doors and sash windows in a redbrick frontage. What I see is a spartan bachelor apartment in an anonymous nine-story block in the St. John's Wood of twenty years ago. I see her waiting for me Friday evenings with two steaks ready to put under that antediluvian gas grill in the linoleum-floored kitchen, and a tossed salad and an opened bottle of French wine on that horrible Formica-topped table supplied by the managing agents. I see her asleep Saturday mornings with her hair fanned out over my black silk pillow case as the sun shafts through the gap where the drapes don't meet.

I'm always nervous before a major operation, but never anything like this. With company operations I know, more or less, what I'm facing. Now I don't. I don't know if this is Maitland's stratagem to lure Joe into British jurisdiction. Most of all I don't know how I can face Jill Maitland. My wristwatch says "Saturday 09.18." I promised I'd be there before nine.

I pick up a case and a brown paper carrier bag. With heavy legs I climb out of the car, approach the white paneled door, and press the brass bell. The spyhole set into the door peers at me. Two bolts draw back and a key turns in a lock. I can't stop my heart pounding.

The door opens. I never thought I'd be relieved to see the haughty features of Edward Maitland.

"You're late." He leads me through into a drawing room with white walls and corniced ceiling, black carpet, black wrought iron fireplace with black marble surround, and black leather sofa and easy chairs. It would have the austerity of a Trappist monastery were it not for the quality and simple elegance of the furnishings—and the presence of the woman sitting on one of the easy chairs.

Neither the tiny crow's feet at the corners of those gold-flecked green eyes, nor the pallor of the elfin face devoid of make up, nor the severity of the style in which her red hair is cut, nor the plainness of the black dress can prevent the longing which surges within me as fiercely as on that Christmas Day we first made love. But my head tells me that this is the woman who has used me and robbed me of my daughter.

She springs to her feet like a nervous animal, takes two steps toward me, and then freezes when she looks into my eyes.

In her eyes I see pain at the harshness in mine.

It's uncanny how we can still communicate without speaking. But twenty years ago our messages were simple and uncomplicated. Now I can't stop myself transmitting yearning mixed with bitterness, and she responds with what I foolishly used to interpret as love, mixed with fear and such despair that I have to avert my eyes.

"Now you two are reacquainted," Maitland's voice cuts through like ice, "do you want coffee?"

I nod.

"I suppose you'll be having your usual morning tipple," Maitland says to Jill. "When you've had your fix, make the coffee."

Glass clinks uncertainly as Jill pours herself a large gin and tonic. She takes a deep draft before leaving the room.

"I think we should concentrate on the job in hand," Maitland says as I watch her walk out of the drawing room. "They phoned on Thursday evening. No more than forty-five seconds. A man with an Irish accent said that I'd find what I wanted inside a Colonel Sanders Kentucky Fried Chicken box in the litter bin outside the tennis courts on Highbury Fields." He hands me the front page of Thursday's London *Times*, which has a message written across the top:

> Dearest Daddy,
>   I'm very frightened. Please do what they say.
>   All my love,
>   Emma

"Is it Emma's handwriting?"

He nods. "There was also a typed note."

> Here's your proof that Emma is alive today. If you re-quire further proof, we'll send her ears. We will accept £100,000 by tomorrow in used notes.
>   We repeat. If you want to see your daughter alive you will not tell anyone else. You must bring the money yourself.
>   We will telephone with instructions on how to de-liver the money.

"When did they phone?"

"Eleven that night. I pretended to be desperate, said that I was already collecting what cash I could lay my hands on, and that I could raise ten thousand pounds by Monday or one hundred thousand if I sold the house, but that would take at least a month."

From my time in El Salvador I know that these are good tactics. "Was it enough to pressure them?"

"They phoned back yesterday and said that they would take twenty thousand cash on Saturday delivered personally by me and that was their final demand."

"I guess it probably is."

"I agree."

"Have you got the money?"

He picks up a black Samsonite briefcase. "It's all in here. Jill's father supplied it, though he doesn't know what for."

Jill returns with a tray containing a flask and two cups. She pours out the coffee and gives me a sidelong glance as she hands me a cup. Surely she wouldn't use Emma to help trap Joe on British territory? Maitland takes a sip of coffee and then looks at his watch. "Where the devil's your brother?"

"He's here." I point to the brown paper carrier bag.

Jill opens the bag, takes out the contents, and turns to me in horror.

"From your Technical Services people?" Maitland asks.

He shows no disappointment that Joe won't be coming. So Emma really has been kidnapped. "No. Angels and Bermans, theatrical costumiers on Shaftesbury Avenue."

Jill takes out the clerical white collar and black suit. "You can't . . ."

"I can and I will," I say brusquely. "We're about the same height, age, and appearance."

"But if they check?" she asks.

"They'll find out that Father Joe Darcy is away on retreat." I turn to Maitland. "We need a cover story to explain how you know Joe and why he would come over and do this for you."

"Her department," Maitland says.

Jill sits down, smoothes her skirt, takes another long drink from her gin and tonic, puts her glass on a nearby small table, and stares down at her hands clasped together as in prayer. Slowly, almost reluctantly, she recites a story of how she met Father Joe Darcy, why she phoned him when she received the kidnap note, and what he said.

It sounds barely plausible, but she says her sister Elizabeth will confirm the story if the IRA check.

"It'll have to do," I say.

"You may be out of circulation beyond the weekend," Maitland says. "I suggest you tell your people that I've asked you to go undercover in an operation to trap the Cheltenham bombers. I'll corroborate if necessary."

He's right. For all his pretensions, Maitland is the consummate professional.

"Write out a note," he instructs, "and if you're not back by tomorrow night Jill will deliver it to the embassy first thing Monday morning."

She sits, pale faced, hands clasped together, and nods obediently.

Professional or not, he's not going to take over this operation. This is my daughter, and my plan to rescue her. "I've some work to do on your car," I say. "But first, fill it up and then park it at least a street away where it's not going to be observed."

"Why?"

I open the case I've brought and take out a ballpoint pen. "This is fitted with a voice-activated UHF transmitter. It's good for fifty hours, but its range is a thousand yards maximum. So we've got this." I remove a black box about three inches by three inches by one inch with a short stubby antenna projecting from the top. "The ballpoint pen transmits to this ultimate infinity receiver, which can be accessed by telephone from anywhere in the world. I'm going to fix it to the underside of your car. When I drive your car to the rendezvous, the ballpoint pen in my breast pocket will transmit everything I say to the black box. You will follow in my car with your mobile phone on an open line to the black box. That way you can hear what I say and be ready to back me up. Understood?" I hand him my car keys.

"Technology does have its uses," Maitland concedes. "The Jag's already full, but I'll circle around and park it out of sight."

He gets up, walks out of the room, and I hear the outside door close, leaving Jill and me together.

She stands up and walks toward me. Avoiding my eyes she goes past to the drinks cabinet and pours herself another large gin and tonic. She holds out a new bottle of Jim Beam.

I look at her and she puts down the bottle. At this rate she's not going to make lunchtime sober.

"Don't say anything, please, John."

Why should I remain silent? Is it British good manners? I hear Edward told you that Emma is your child, but it's not good form to talk about such things, so have a drink instead. Does she really think like that? When did she tell Edward that Emma was my child? Would she have told him if Emma hadn't been kidnapped? Would she ever have told me? What does she think I feel? Does she even care? Her eyes tell me that she does, but I know the price to pay for being ensnared by those haunting wildcat eyes. Has she nothing to say to me? Doesn't she feel the need to offer any explanation?

She pushes her hair back behind one ear, just as she used to when she was nervous, but her hair is now so short that the gesture has become meaningless.

Anger wells inside me, but she's gotten her own way once more. I'm confused by the sidelong glances and subliminal messages which are contradicted by her actions and her refusal to speak. I don't know how to handle the situation, I can't find the words. She's reduced me to the silence she wanted, but it's a silence too intense to bear. "I need to use the bathroom," I say.

Her voice is barely audible. "It's the door facing you at the top of the stairs."

I stay in there until I hear Maitland return.

The exhaust pipe on Maitland's Jaguar is secure and shows no signs of corrosion. It bends before entering the center muffler, leaving enough space for the ultimate infinity receiver. I wind adhesive tape round the exhaust pipe and under the black box four times. This practical job is uncomplicated and therapeutic. Do it properly and the communications system will perform faithfully: no confusing messages, no deceptions.

Back in the Maitlands' house I take the carrier bag and escape once more to the bathroom to change. Mom sent me a photograph of Joe just after he'd been ordained. I'd never seen him look so at peace with the world. The clerical collar feels tight round my neck. I examine the image in the bathroom mirror. Physically there's a strong resemblance, but the eyes appear harder and the mouth tighter. I try to smile, like Joe. The reflection grins back like a mask.

I enter the drawing room. Jill stares at me as though she's seen a ghost. I take a seat and stare at the telephone, willing the IRA to ring and curtail this torment.

Maitland lights a cigar. I have to admire his composure. To learn that your only daughter has been kidnapped is traumatic enough, but for your wife to compound the anguish by telling you that someone else fathered your seventeen-year-old child must drive you to the edge. What

mental torment must the poor wretch be suffering beneath
that controlled exterior?

The telephone's ring shatters the silence.

Maitland picks up the handset. "Hello." He turns to Jill.
"It's your father."

At noon Jill prepares some sandwiches. Edward eats his, occasionally casting a disdainful glance at me or Jill. I don't
blame him. I even feel sympathy for him. It can't be easy,
facing the man who's cuckolded you. But I've no sympathy
for Jill: she has betrayed Edward as much as she betrayed
me.

She clears away Edward's empty plate and the untouched sandwiches on my plate and on hers. Unspoken
words charge the room with an almost electrostatic tension.
I mustn't let it get to me. I need to focus on something practical. "Have you got a gun, Edward?"

"No."

"Fine back up you'll make." I open my case and take out
a blued steel Walther P-88 semiautomatic. "Used one of
these?"

He takes it and weighs it in his hand. "I've fired the
Walther PPK. This is a big bugger."

"It's more powerful and more accurate. It will only fire
when the trigger is pulled all the way through. The decock-
ing lever and the magazine release button operate from
either right or left side. The magazine holds fifteen nine-
millimeter parabellum shells."

"Christ," he says.

"It's got a windage adjustable rear sight for accuracy," I
add. I hand him two spare magazines. "I think these should
be enough. And you may need this." I take a silencer from
the case.

"What about you?" he asks.

"A priest can't carry a gun. I'm relying on you as my back up."

From the corner of my eye I see Jill's pale face turn white. She reaches for her glass.

The heavy silence returns. I can't take any more. "I need to be on my own," I say, "to try and get into the mindset of a priest."

Maitland gives me a quizzical look. "I'll show you to a room."

He leads me up two flights of stairs and opens a door. "Make yourself at home."

Posters and collages stare at me from around the white walls of a room poised between teenaged uncertainty and youthful elegance. The room has been tidied, but by somebody—perhaps a cleaner—who doesn't know where everything should be stored: a pair of jeans, a folded black T-shirt, and an Aran sweater hang over the back of a wicker chair on which are stacked books, compact discs, and a remote control for a music system, all of which, presumably, had been scattered over the gray carpet in the manner Jill used to strew things around my apartment.

A Macintosh computer sits on top of an antique desk, alongside a notebook that contains lines and ideas for poems, a bottle of prescription pills for migraine, a telephone, and a photograph of Edward Maitland in a cricketer's white shirt and pants. The poster above the desk is framed and shows the heads and shoulders of three couples in brocades and spaniel wigs advertising the National Theater's production of *Love for Love* at the Old Vic. Laurence Olivier is one of the men. More recent, unframed posters are spaced symmetrically on the other walls, interspersed with sports pennants in navy blue bearing the motif of what looks like a deer with a lead from its neck tied to a book. Above the bed are black and white collages compiled from magazines: a man and a woman in several dark, moody settings; adverts for

Calvin Klein's Eternity and Obsession perfumes; and photographs of two models in short dresses and waif-like poses.

One of the sliding doors of the white fitted wardrobe is open. I need to see and to touch the clothes that my daughter wears. Apart from one short dress in the same shade of green that Jill used to wear, the only colors are black, white, and gray: very short dresses in gray hopsack, white wool, black lace, black lycra; a black and white mini kilt, and black culottes; and two long dresses, a black strapless ball dress and a black silk dress. This is not the wardrobe of the schoolgirl of my imagining but that of a young woman who has developed her own style and tastes. Under whose influence?

The bottles of perfume, the body sprays, and the makeup on the dressing table confirm that Emma's childhood has passed without my ever having caught a glimpse of it. Strands of long black hair twist round the bristles of a silver-backed hairbrush which rests next to a silver-framed photograph of Edward Maitland.

Boxes of compact discs and cassettes fill the bookshelves next to the black stacked music system. Within the boxes labeled Pop, Classical, Folk, and Opera, all the CDs and cassettes are arranged in alphabetical order. Jill never had a system for anything.

Adult fiction lines the top row of the two other bookshelves, books for teenagers occupy the shelf beneath, and below that, titles for younger readers. The bottom shelf contains well-thumbed illustrated children's classics—the books I would have read to Emma in bed.

I sit down on the single bed, on top of a white bedspread decorated with batik black cats, beside a row of fluffy toy cats of all sizes and colors, and next to a pyjama case in the shape of a large black cat.

A silver cup inscribed "Emma Maitland. Morley Cup for Services to Drama Department" stands next to yet another photograph of Edward Maitland on top of the chest of drawers beside the bed. Like a thief I open the drawers. Earrings, bracelets, chokers, necklaces—all silver or stainless steel, nothing in gold—fill the top drawer. Bundles of envelopes containing letters to Emma pack the drawer below. Each bundle is from a different friend, and each envelope is in date order. Nothing could be further from the spontaneous, impulsive Jill I knew. The spy in me longs to read the letters, but the parent resists such intrusiveness. Photographs fill the bottom drawer. None is of Jill. They're mostly of Emma, from a baby through school portraits, both class and individual, to one about a year younger than the photograph I've had framed and put on my study desk in Chester Square.

Behind me the door opens. I smell Chanel Number 5, the perfume that I thought was the height of sophistication when I bought it for the first birthday of hers we shared as lovers. Guiltily I shut the drawer, but keep my back to the door.

The door closes. "John," she says softly.

I can barely trust myself to speak. "You knew when you were pregnant whose child she was, didn't you?"

"Yes."

I turn to face her. "Why didn't you tell me?"

She bows her head.

"That submissive wife routine doesn't wash. I never realized just how manipulative you are. You conveniently forget to tell me that I have a daughter. Seventeen years later, after she's been kidnapped by the IRA, you conveniently remember that I'm Irish American and my brother is a priest. You say to your dearly beloved husband that you know how to rescue Emma. Not only do you tell him that he's not Emma's father, you make the poor bastard admit it to me so that I'd ask Joe to get you out of trouble."

Tears glisten in her eyes, but her voice struggles to remain steady. "I never told Edward about us."

"Is that right? It took him seventeen years to figure it out? You must think I'm really dumb."

She looks me in the eye. "It was only after Emma was kidnapped that Edward told me he'd always known who her father was. He said he'd make you solve the problem for us."

I shake my head in disbelief.

"He asked if I thought he was stupid enough not to know that I'd been sleeping with you while he was in Northern Ireland. The baby couldn't be his. He'd had tests which showed he was infertile."

I don't know what to believe any more. I don't understand these people and how they behave. Maitland perhaps. His pride wouldn't let him admit he'd been cuckolded, and without Jill he wouldn't have her father's contacts and money to support the persona he's created for himself. But why did she stay with him?

"John," she says, "I once promised that I would never ask you to do anything for me ever again. I want to keep that promise. I'm not asking you to do this for me."

"I'm not doing it for you," I say bitterly, "I'm doing it for my daughter."

She takes three steps forward, reaches out, and touches my arm. "John, I've hurt you enough already. There must be some other way. I . . . I couldn't bear for you to be killed."

"I won't be."

"Tell Edward to take the ransom as they've instructed and you can act as back-up."

"It wouldn't work. The ransom demand is intended to increase the pressure on him, to distract him from focusing on their real purpose. The IRA want to lure your husband to where they can safely assassinate him. Right now, I'm in the mood to help them. The only thing that's stopping me is the knowledge that once they've done that they can't afford to let Emma survive as a witness."

"But what about the danger to you? How can you possibly maintain your cover as a priest?"

"No problem." I turn away from her and stare out of the window at the rusty yellow frame of an abandoned child's swing in the rear garden.

It was always I, not Joe, who carried the hopes for a vocation in the family. It was I, not Joe, who waited outside a locked St. Sebastian's Church on cold winter mornings, peering between the rusty yellow stanchions that support the elevated train track running above Roosevelt Avenue. Father Molloy was late, as usual.

One by one the faithful—mainly old women wearing headscarves and holding rosary beads—made their daily pilgrimage down Woodside Avenue, 57th and 58th Streets, and Roosevelt Avenue, which intersect at St. Sebastian's. Apart from the Rockline newsstand, where I collected the *Connaught Tribune* and the *United Irishman* shipped over from Ireland, the two-story brick buildings along the streets were shut. The Dennis J. Kennedy Funeral Home, Riordan's Fine Foods, Blarney Silver and Gold, Shamrock Travel Service, Finnegan's Bar, the Tower View Ballroom—advertising the Tommy Nolan Showband—and the black and white mock-timberframed Donovan's pub wouldn't open their doors for another two hours at least.

The pilgrims had to navigate the commuter traffic, which rapidly built up along the westward lanes of Roosevelt Avenue, while the El rumbled deafeningly overhead, taking workers from Queens across the East River to Manhattan.

At seven minutes to seven Father Molloy, the youngest of the priests at St Sebastian's, ignored the "Don't Walk" signal and hurried between the stanchions, said "Good morning, ladies" to the score or so of waiting parishioners, and threw me a bunch of keys.

While he went on down the side of the church to the vestry door, I unlocked the main door and the inner door, and turned on the lights, which we needed even in summer because our new parish church wasn't new: it had been converted from Loew's Woodside Movie Theater and had no windows. I led the parishioners down the sloping aisle of the 1920s baroque cavern, past the life-like figures of the Stations of the Cross on the Marian-blue walls, and toward the massive crucifix suspended below a crimson and gold canopy above the shining gilt tabernacle on the altar. But only I, after genuflecting toward the tabernacle, was permitted to pass the marble altar rail and go through the sanctuary to the vestry.

Father Molloy was combing his bushy hair and yawning between the robing prayers as he placed the stole around his neck and put a long green chasuble over his head. Quickly I put on my black cassock and the white surplice which Mom starched and pressed every Saturday. Palms joined together in reverence, I followed Father Molloy out of the vestry to the foot of the altar, genuflected with him, and kneeled at his right hand as he began the introductory rite of the holy sacrifice of the mass.

"Adjutorium nostrum in nomine Domini," he intoned.

"Qui fecit caelum et terram," my piping voice replied, while the congregation looked on silently or else murmured their rosaries.

I didn't need to read from the prayer card, I knew the Latin responses by heart. When I repeated the Confiteor my eyes looked up to the life-sized Christ hanging from the cross, the Son of God who was crucified for my salvation.

Joe became an altar boy a year after me, but he lacked my piety. "Do we get a cut of the collection money?" he asked when I was teaching him how to serve at the altar. And when he looked at the roster and saw that he was slated for the early morning mass that week, he'd say, "Hey, kid, swap you for the late show?" Nor did he attend the Miraculous Medal Novena on Mondays when he wasn't down to serve.

My parents' hopes crystallized on the Sunday after they received the letter saying that I had won a place at Regis High School. Our pastor, Father Curran, came back after the eleven o'clock high mass to join us in a celebratory lunch. Father Curran's roly poly appearance belied a man of uncompromising views, and I waited anxiously for one of his pronouncements when he pushed away his empty plates, lit a large cigar, and accepted a whiskey from Pop.

"Tell me, John," he said, "do you know the motto of Regis High School?"

"No, Father," I confessed.

"Deo et Patriae. For God and Country." He waved his cigar at me. "Keep faithful to those two precepts in thought, word, and deed, and you can rest assured that Christ and His Holy Mother will save you from eternal damnation."

"Yes, Father."

"What do you intend to do with this education the Jesuits are offering you?"

"I hope to study medicine, Father," I said, "and become a jungle doctor like Tom Dooley."

Father Curran nodded. "A shining example of service to God and country, a true Christian soldier in the fight against the communist Antichrist." He allowed Pop to refill his whiskey glass. "There are many ways of serving God in this life, John, but I think a fine upstanding young man like yourself will take the direct way. You know what I mean?"

I blushed.

"A vocation is the most wonderful gift God can give a

young man." He turned to my parents. "Pray that God may grant him the gift."

Both Mom and Pop smiled proudly.

"I'm not worthy," I said.

"John won't become a priest," said Joe, "unless they let him become a cardinal at the same time."

"Joseph! Go to your room at once!" Pop shouted.

A vocation was not something you chose, it was a calling from God, and the possibility that God might call me to the priesthood was never far from my mind at Regis. The more I prayed, I reasoned, the better chance I had of finding out how God wanted me to serve him in this life. Once a week each class participated in the holy sacrifice of the mass in the Regis Chapel, and on the first Friday of every month the whole student body attended a special sung mass at St. Ignatius Church on Park Avenue. Wednesday mornings also found me at ten to seven on the elevated platform of Woodside station, waiting to catch the Number 7 train to Grand Central and then the uptown Lexington Avenue Express to 86th Street so that I would be in time for the special 8 am voluntary mass at the Regis Chapel. Attending fifty of these voluntary masses qualified me to join the Regis Guard of Honor and wear a special Ichthus pin. Joe never did get his pin.

At Fordham my thoughts turned to joining the Jesuits, the élite of Christ's army on earth, but after my talk with Father Paul and Liam Walsh in my senior year it became clear what God was calling me to do.

"They've called." Edward Maitland's voice breaks through the reverie. "They've given instructions for the ransom."

Chapter ✤ Twenty-one

I'VE NO DOUBT that I can pass myself off as a priest when I meet the IRA, but they are expecting Edward Maitland. "You'd better wear my overcoat and my trilby," Maitland says, "plus my scarf to cover that dog collar, in case they're watching the house."

Disguised as a priest disguised as Edward Maitland, I look in the hall mirror to adjust the navy blue scarf. In the reflection I see Jill's distraught eyes watching me. Even after all she's done, a part of me wants to turn round and hold her tight. We both know I may not survive this attempt to rescue our daughter. Shall I go to the grave unforgiving and bitter?

Sentimentality has no place in an operation: I've no intention of going to the grave. Without a word of farewell I take Maitland's black Samsonite case and the spare keys for his Jaguar, open the door, and walk out into an afternoon sun shining from a cloudless sky. I must look odd wearing hat, overcoat, and scarf.

I turn into Highbury Terrace, a row of tall elegant

eighteenth-century houses, one of which has been sand-
blasted to reveal yellow brick beneath the grime. The terrace faces a large rectangle of grass which forms the upper
half of Highbury Fields. At the end of the terrace lies the
public telephone booth which the kidnappers specified.

Their note is wedged behind the coin box. Vulnerability sets my spine tingling. This glass-walled booth lies at the
intersection of three roads, one of which bisects Highbury
Fields and curves away and round to form a semicircle
which borders the lower half of the Fields. Almost any one
of the people strolling across or round this half of the Fields,
or sitting on the park benches, may be watching me. I turn
my back to them, unfold the note, and read it to the ballpoint pen in my breast pocket.

> Do not return home. Go immediately to a gray Volk-
> swagen Golf, registration number C264 DNW, parked
> outside the bottle bank at the other end of Highbury
> Fields. Keys in exhaust pipe. Instructions in glove
> compartment.

Shit! I'm not going to be able to use Maitland's car to deliver the ransom.

"We have a problem," I say calmly to the ballpoint pen.
"You've got to keep the ultimate infinity receiver within a
thousand yards of me or we lose contact. You can't follow in
the silver Jaguar: it's too conspicuous. Go straight to your car
and remove the black box from the underside. It's fitted next
to the center muffler of the exhaust system. Be careful not
to damage the antenna. Take it to my car and follow the Golf.
Not too closely, but don't let it get more than a thousand
yards ahead."

That, hopefully, will solve the problem. I leave the phone
booth and try to spot the IRA watcher while I walk past the
crescent of Italianate villas bordering the lower half of

Highbury Fields. A group of dog walkers congregates in the middle of the grassed expanse. Surely it can't be one of these? A young couple sitting on one of the park benches could be the watchers, but they're almost too obvious. More likely it's one of the many people crossing the Fields, going to and from the adventure playground at the far end or the public swimming pool next to it or the subway station beyond.

The gray VW Golf is parked near a line of large metal containers color coded for clear, green, and brown bottles. A bunch of keys lies in the exhaust pipe. It looks innocuous enough, but a car bomb is one of the IRA's favorite assassination methods. Maitland can afford the cleaning bill, I think, as I crawl in his cashmere overcoat beneath the car, looking for explosives taped to the underside.

When I'm helpless on my back an Irish voice says, "Can I help you at all?"

A pair of workman's boots and the bottom couple of inches of dark blue pants are visible next to the offside front wheel. I wish now that I had brought a gun. Slowly I edge my way out from under the car.

The dark blue pants belong to overalls worn by a ginger-haired street cleaner who is holding Maitland's trilby. "This blew off the bonnet of your car," he says. "That's a fine coat to be making a mess of."

"Thanks. I'm just trying to stop the exhaust pipe rattling."

"A brother of mine could sort that out for you." He reaches into his overalls pocket and produces a visiting card. He watches me while I read the name and address of a car repair workshop off the Holloway Road. Is he the watcher? Has he spotted that I'm not Maitland?

"Thanks," I say again.

"Not at all."

I wait until he walks away before opening the passenger

door rather than the driver's. Inside the glove compartment there's an envelope. The note inside says:

> Drive straight to Conways pub (see attached map). At 4:55 PM the barman will receive a telephone call for Jason. Take the call. We are monitoring you. If you telephone or contact anyone, the transaction will be terminated and the goods will perish.

Is this a bluff to put me off guard? There's nothing under the driver's seat or the other seats. I release the hood lock. No sign of any explosives in the engine compartment. This check can only eliminate the obvious. Semtex sheeting an eighth of an inch thick could be inside the driver's seat or the door lining or just about anywhere, and I've neither time nor opportunity to strip the bodywork to pieces. It worries me that the car is so near the public swimming pool, and families leaving the pool pass between the bottle bank and the car. I sit in the driver's seat with my fingers on the ignition key and wait until there's no one within range of a typical car bomb explosion. If there is a bomb, at least the end will be quick. But I will have failed in the attempt to rescue Emma—and I will have gone to my grave without forgiving Jill. A mother and young daughter leave the swimming pool and start walking in my direction. Before they come within range I turn the key.

A roar shatters the silence as the engine bursts into life. With the tension, my right foot was pressed too hard on the gas pedal.

My hands are shaking with aftershock. I take several deep breaths. If they had wanted to assassinate Maitland, surely they would have done it here with a car bomb. I must be safe, at least until the rendezvous.

They may be bluffing about the monitoring, but there's no point in taking risks. I drive the Golf out of Highbury

Fields, round the traffic circle at Highbury Corner, and follow the mapped route south before repeating the message out loud and giving the location of Conways pub. "I've got less than forty-five minutes to get there," I say. "Go there by another route if you can and park within a thousand yards of the pub." With this one-way communication system there's no guarantee that Maitland has heard me. There's even no guarantee that he's safely removed the ultimate infinity receiver from the underside of his Jaguar.

The route heads downtown, but then bears right to link up with the beltway heading west, past MI5's former headquarters, a featureless gray block above Euston Square subway station which looks as though it has been transplanted from eastern Europe. The traffic comes to a halt outside a church. Could Joe's passionate idealism turn to this? His unavailability troubles me. Maitland didn't seem surprised that Joe couldn't be contacted at St Brendan's. Does Maitland know something I don't? If Joe was involved in supplying arms to the Cheltenham bombers, has he now flown to Britain for the follow-up "spectacular?"

I leave the elevated expressway heading for Oxford at the exit marked Shepherd's Bush. Buses and cars streaming blue and white scarves partially block a large traffic circle. Thankfully they're heading in the opposite direction. I drive past Shepherd's Bush Common and, where the road splits three ways, follow the kidnappers' route straight ahead to a distinctly shabby area of west London. With ten minutes to spare I pull up by a blue-painted pub with large frosted glass windows displaying a handwritten notice, "Live Music Every Sunday." Above the windows gold letters on blue proclaim "Conways."

The pub is an ambush: a sea of white faces stare at me. Then I see that their eyes are focused above my head, on the television set mounted over the door. The pub is blue: except for the tables, every piece of woodwork—doors, window frames, and bar—is painted blue; blue and gold wallpaper patterned in leaves and peacocks adorns the walls; blue diamond-patterned carpet covers the floors; blue velour benches line the walls; and blue-gray cigarette smoke hovers like mist. The pub is Irish: soft brogues from the South compete with strident vowels from the North, and the only English voices come from the TV set; pint glasses of Guinness outnumber amber beer on the bar and tables; and in front of the mirror behind the bar, the upturned bottles for dispensing liquor display the labels of Jameson, Paddy, Bailey's Irish Cream, and Irish Mist.

The muddied cashmere overcoat plus scarf and trilby make me conspicuous among the denim jackets, windbreakers, and old tweed coats. I ease my way through to the bar, smile, and point to the pump handle for draft Guinness.

A seat at the opposite end from the door and the TV set, where I'll be out of view of most of the clientele, seems the safest place. It's perverse how perceptions change so quickly. Less than a week ago this Irish ambience would have provided a refuge from the alien British; now it's sheltering a member of the organization that has taken my daughter. Who is watching me, and does he have a photograph of Maitland? Who periodically takes his eyes from the television screen or his glass in order to observe me? It could be the dark-haired unshaven young man in denims following the game of pool; circling the pool table enables him to see everyone in the pub. It could be the older man with a shock of white hair who is smoking a cob pipe; across from the bar, his bench in the seating area raised two steps from the rest of the pub gives him a commanding view. It could be the barman. It could be any one of a dozen or more. But even if I did spot the IRA watcher, how would it help?

The babble of conversations erupts into cheering as the

face on the TV screen announces that Queen's Park Rangers have beaten Brighton and Hove Albion by two goals to one. The screen cuts to an interview with the manager of the victorious soccer club. The barman has to shout to be heard. "Telephone call for someone called Jason."

Half the people in the pub turn to watch as I shuffle past the pool table to the other end of the bar. "Doesn't he just look a Jason," someone quips. Others laugh.

"On top of the cistern in the left hand cubicle of the gents'," says an Irish voice on the telephone.

The blue door marked GENTS leads to toilets I would not choose to patronize. The old-fashioned water closet in the left of the two cubicles has a tank above head height, with a piece of string substituting for the chain. Standing on the seat I find an envelope on the tank lid. The message inside reads:

> Continue down Goldhawk Road and follow the signs for the M4 Motorway and Heathrow Airport. At the first service station on the motorway, after Junction 2, drive into the car park. You will find a blue Fiat Uno, registration number H261 XYU. Follow same procedure as for the Golf.

> YOU MUST COLLECT THIS CAR
> NO LATER THAN 5:30 P.M.

Kidnappers are always most vulnerable at the rendezvous. This paper trail, with timed legs which allow no opportunity to contact assistance, and the switching of cars point to a highly professional operation, as thorough as any of those carried out by experienced terrorist groups I encountered in El Salvador. The kidnappers are sure to search me. I can't risk their failing to detect that the ballpoint pen is a UHF radio transmitter. I'll have to dump it before any personal encounter. But when will that be? The smart ploy on their side would be to let Maitland think he's just collecting another message, and then surprise him. Except it's me, not Maitland, who'll be on the end of the surprise.

I wait until I'm driving down Goldhawk Road before relaying the kidnappers' message. They're taking me west out of London, but to where? Maitland would have a better idea of where they may be based, but I haven't a clue.

The traffic comes to a standstill, stalled by more buses and cars honking their horns and flying blue and white scarves from their windows. Time is running out. I swing across to the wrong side of the road and overtake a line of stationary vehicles. The sign on the side of one bus says Brighton and Hove Albion Supporters Club. Christ Almighty! When the kidnappers timed the legs of their paper trail, did they know that the roads would be blocked by traffic from a soccer match?

I reach the freeway with less than four minutes to go before the deadline for changing the car. By keeping the pedal pressed to the floor and overtaking illegally on the inside, I keep the speed of the Golf above 95 mph, risking both being stopped by the police and moving out of range of the black box.

I veer off into the rest stop and find the small blue Fiat. No time to worry if this car is primed to explode.

The message inside the glove compartment makes my stomach sink. Having taken me on a trail west out of London, the terrorists are now giving me a precise route to circle back and then head south. Any following car that undertakes the same maneuver will give itself away.

"Edward," I say to the ballpoint pen, "if you're still within range, they are directing me to a phone booth outside The Checkrs Inn in a village called Forest Row, three miles past East Grinstead on the A22. You'll need to switch cars to avoid being detected. Try a car hire company."

It's gone 5:30 P.M. on a Saturday. I don't know of a car hire company in England that will still be open.

The VW Golf performed as well as most American cars. This Fiat Uno, however, is powered—if that isn't too strong a word—by a one-liter engine. The heavy traffic and the poor acceleration of the Fiat scupper my plan to keep to the legal maximum all the way. Less than half an hour to the deadline remains when I join the three-lane M23 freeway south toward Brighton. I must make up time, despite the Brighton soccer supporters whose vehicles still swell the traffic. Even with my right foot pressed to the floor, however, this car manages only 80 mph on the flat. On the downhill stretches its speed creeps up to 90 mph, but the tiny engine roars so loudly that I half expect to see the hood burst open with an explosion of steam.

Leaving the freeway as directed leads to an undivided road, cutting down my speed to less than 30 mph. By the time this tin box on wheels has passed East Grinstead, darkness has set in. An undercover operations officer develops a sixth sense about his back-up team. I sense that I'm on my own.

British streetlamps cast their amber glow on the village of Forest Row, a hodge podge of old and new buildings either side of the A22 through road. The Checkrs Inn, a Tudor-style timber-framed building with red tiles cladding the gable and the top story, stands in front of a pull-off from the A22, after which a side road splits off from the main road. The pull-off is full of cars lined up neatly with their fenders pointing toward the curb. When I manage to find somewhere to park, my watch shows 6:38 P.M., seven minutes before the scheduled call to the public telephone in the booth indicated by the kidnappers.

A teenaged girl with long blonde hair just beats me to

the phone. Five minutes later she's still giggling into the mouthpiece. I point at my watch. When she finally sees me, she turns her back. She's probably Emma's age. I walk round to the other side of the glass booth, open the door, pull back my scarf to show the priest's collar, and say, "Excuse me, my dear, I have an urgent call to make."

She smiles and says, "There's another phone in the box next to this one." She turns away and I hear her explain, "It was nothing important."

The deadline for the kidnappers' phone call passes.

Ten minutes later the girl leaves the booth. I stand there, cursing, and praying that they'll make contact.

Just after seven the telephone rings. I snatch the receiver off the hook. "Jason," I say in my best English voice.

"The line has been engaged," a flat voice accuses.

"A girl's been using it for the last quarter of an hour. Why the hell didn't you use the other phone?"

"Just beyond The Checkrs Inn there's a shelter at the junction of the A22 and the side road. You'll find what you want inside a copy of *The Times* in the rubbish bin inside the shelter." The line goes dead.

The brick shelter is less than twenty yards away. I approach it with care, remembering the IRA trash can bombs in Warrington. The construction is divided into two, one half facing uphill toward the village hall and the other half facing back down the A22. On the side there's an inscription:

Erected to commemorate
the coronation of
HER MAJESTY
QUEEN ELIZABETH II
ON 2ND JUNE 1953

Is this the IRA's sick joke, to have Maitland follow a trail around southern England and then blow him up inside this royalist shelter?

Individuals and groups walk in and out of The Checkrs Inn; some glance in my direction. Across the main road there's a gas station, with two Caucasian adult males and one Afro-Caribbean adult female standing next to their cars by the gas pumps. All three cars have passengers. Who is watching me? And is that person holding the radio control for a detonator?

When does proper caution become paranoia? What the hell does it matter? There's only one purpose in my life now, and that's to rescue my daughter. And to do that I have to go into the shelter.

Neither section of the shelter is lit. In the dark I grope inside the first trash can, feeling greasy wrappers, cold french fries, a plastic bottle, and orange peel—but no news-paper. The can inside the other half of the shelter does yield a newspaper. In the amber streetlight I manage to decipher the typewritten sheet inside *The Times:*

> Proceed along A22. Approximately 2 miles after For-est Row you will reach a road junction, Wych Cross. Turn left, down the road marked "Hartfield." After 1 mile you will pass the Ashdown Forest Information Center. Stop at the third parking area on the left, 1 mile after the Information Center. It is marked with a wooden sign as "Townsend's."
> Park here, facing the picnic table, with only your side-lights on, and unlock the doors.

YOU MUST BE PARKED HERE
NO LATER THAN 15 MINUTES AFTER
RECEIVING THE TELEPHONE CALL.

Six minutes have passed since the call, leaving nine minutes to get there. No time to stop and phone anyone, even if I could risk using one of the public phones.

The A22 climbs uphill from Forest Row, and soon after leaving the village it enters a forest. Townsend's parking area has got to be the rendezvous: Ashdown Forest is almost on a line between London and Brighton, where Emma's school is. I repeat the directions into the ballpoint pen, with little confidence that Maitland will hear the message.

A senior citizen driving his sedan as cautiously as though the angel of death waits for him round the bend ignores my flashing headlights. I put my foot hard on the gas pedal. The car, roaring in protest, overtakes slowly and dangerously on the long bend.

At Wych Cross the unlit road to Hartfield plunges deeper into the forest, past a road sign warning of deer and then a floodlit hotel on the right.

In the dark I nearly miss the Forest Information Center, which is closed and marked only by an unlit wooden sign on the opposite side of the road. I ease my foot off the gas. About a mile further on the headlights illuminate a small wooden sign at road level. I stop and decipher the carved word "TOWNSEND'S." I turn into the narrow gap in the trees and the headlights sweep across a dirt clearing to shine on a solitary silver birch with a gorse bush to its left. To the left of that is a picnic table. I pull up in front of the table, turn off the brights, unlock the doors, and check my watch. I'm two minutes late.

Without the shrieking Fiat engine noise an eerie silence descends.

My eyes adjust to the dark. This pull-off is almost totally enclosed. Ahead, a lattice of fine, bare branches fanning out from slender trunks forms a black silhouette against a cloudless starry midnight-blue sky. The lattice extends to the right, where it merges into the solid black of the forest. To the left the foliage of what appear to be yews and spruces among the bare birches makes the screen impenetrable. I reposition the rearview and side mirrors to get the best line of sight to the pull-off entrance, but the narrow gap in the trees is lost amid the solid blackness of the forest below the night sky. Winking aircraft lights, like alien spacecraft, pass silently between fixed stars. I can't remember the last time I felt so vulnerable.

The infrequent car that passes along the road is heralded by a muffled drone that rises in pitch as a finger of light picks out the short stretch of road surface seen in the side mirror, followed by a brief burst of engine noise as headlights and red tail lights flash by the narrow gap in the trees.

It's more than twenty minutes past the deadline. Where is Emma? Have they found out that something's wrong and decided to abort the exchange? Calm down. It's all part of a psychological game to put me at a disadvantage.

Drained by the tension of the three-hour paper trail, my concentration lapses. I barely register that the muffled drone hasn't risen in pitch like that of a passing car before I'm blinded by a blaze in the rearview mirror. The approaching car swings round to my right and lights up a line of silver birch trunks rising ghostlike from a copper sea of dead ferns. The car kills its brights. White back-up lights burst into life as the car reverses almost into my door. I try to make out how many people are in the car to my right when the front passenger door to my left is wrenched open. I twist round to see the barrel of a gun six inches from my face. "Close yer eyes or I'll blow yer fuckin' head off," a voice rasps.

I've been suckered by one of the oldest tricks in the book. While I watched the car, the gunman emerged from behind the trees on my other side. I concentrate to try and etch into my memory that fleeting impression, but all I recall are two eye holes and a mouth hole in a black mask— and the stainless steel muzzle.

A flashlight shines into my face, forcing my eyelids to squeeze tighter still.

"It's not him. It's not Maitland," a woman says from my right.

"The orders are clear," the harsh West Belfast voice responds. "Maitland on his own. Any other fucker gets a head job. We'll dump his body in the woods. Nobody will find it before daylight."

The click of the gun being cocked chills the night. Slowly I draw the scarf away from my neck and say in my broadest New York accent, "Would you murder a Catholic priest?"

Chapter ✤ Twenty-two

THE ONLY PERSON I've ever seen in the trunk of a car was a priest. He was naked and his throat had been slit by an El Salvadoran death squad.

I recall that bare, bent torso as two kidnappers squash me into the trunk of the Ford sedan that has reversed up to the Fiat. But I must banish these and any other thoughts in order to memorise as much as possible about the journey from Townsend's parking lot.

The kidnappers have removed my watch, and so I visualise a clock starting at twelve and the finger of the second hand ticking round the clock face. It's an old trick for estimating elapsed time which a training officer at the Farm taught us. I hope it still works.

The car moves off and throws me to the right of the trunk as it turns left out of the pull-off. We're heading in the direction of Hartfield. The blacktop is bumpy. We're going in a straight line, down a slight gradient, and fairly fast in fourth gear. We overtake no other cars and no cars pass us on the other side of the road.

We swing right, then left, straighten, slow down, and make a sharp right. I slide toward the front of the trunk as we head down a winding road. The sound of the tires indicates that the surface is still blacktop, but there is a recurrent pattern, as though striations cross the road at right angles to the direction in which we're traveling. I'm pushed to the back of the trunk as the car changes down two gears to climb up a steep hill. The engine strain eases and the driver changes up through the gears as we cruise downhill for a shorter stretch, stop briefly—must be a road junction—and make a right, still slightly downhill. In all this time we've neither passed nor been passed by other vehicles.

This road follows a series of gentle curves downhill before making a sharp left. Still downhill we overtake two cars before coming to a halt. There's traffic noise here. We wait for a gap in the traffic before making a longer right onto a highway with a much smoother surface.

We come to a stretch where there's a whooshing sound and a buffeting as vehicles pass us on the other side. So, although it's a highway, this section is only one lane each way, and the air movements suggest we're in a tunnel, or perhaps a narrow road with no sidewalks and bordered by a windbreak of trees. The road winds through a series of Z-bends, and then the car slows before turning left onto a rough, bumpy track.

We travel slowly up this track for about five minutes and then stop. A car door slams. A gate creaks. The car moves forward and doesn't wait for the gate opener. We must have arrived.

They've made their first mistake. I'm confident that they've driven straight here; they certainly haven't retraced parts of the route to confuse me. I estimate we've been traveling for just over a quarter of an hour. If I'm right, and we've averaged 30 mph, their hideout is roughly eight miles by road from Townsend's parking lot, let's say six to ten miles.

And if we have arrived I can't afford to let them find this ball-point pen on me. I push it under sacking in the bottom of the trunk before the car stops.

I lie curled in the blackness of the trunk for another ten minutes before a handle clicks and the trunk lid opens to cold air, a faint light, and a rasping voice. "Don't ye fuckin' move."

A body partially blocks the dim light before the musty fabric of a hood is pulled over my head and eliminates the light entirely. "Out!"

My cramped legs probe the air until my feet touch dirt. All is silence. I can't hear the traffic on the highway.

A hand pushes my right shoulder round and a small, hard object is pressed into my back. "Straight on, you."

That's good. No one professionally trained would reveal precisely where his gun is by putting it in contact with his opponent's body.

After thirty-six paces over a dirt surface broken by patches of small stones, he pulls my left shoulder to wheel me into a turn. Another twelve paces and he pulls me to a stop, while other footsteps continue and a gate is unlatched. The gunman pushes me forward and then swivels me halfway to the right. Forty-eight paces over cobbles brings us to another gate, which leads onto an uneven grassy sur-face, probably a field.

My right hand is grasped and put round a leather han-dle. "Open it."

"Open what?"

"The briefcase."

The Samsonite case is locked. "How can I with this hood on? I'll give you the combination number when you release Emma to my custody."

"Either you open the case or we end this charade now,"

the woman's voice says from a distance. Her Irish accent is discernible, but much less pronounced than the man's.

"Turn round and I'll put a bullet in yer head," says the gunman, also from a distance.

Has Maitland booby trapped the briefcase? If the kidnappers are prepared to allow the sound of an explosion out here, we must be completely isolated. That's good news. I'd assumed they would keep Emma hidden in a city. An isolated base six to ten miles by road from Townsend's pull-off makes it much easier to locate their hideout. But that information will be no use if I'm on the receiving end of an explosion.

I raise the hood from my face and peer out. I'm in a field. Beyond there's only a black hill silhouetted against the night sky; no streetlights or house lights. The first digit of the combination lock clicks into place, followed by the other three. All I have to do now is open the case. Would that bastard Maitland have rigged it with a bomb without telling me?

"Do it," the gunman orders.

I turn my head away, flick back the catches, and pull on the case.

"Don't spill the fuckin' money!" the gunman shouts.

It's time to take the initiative. "You've seen the money," I say through the hood, "now I demand to see the child."

"You demand fuckin' nuthin'," the gunman replies.

"What kind of language is that to use to a priest!" I snap.

The gun presses into the small of my back. "I couldn't give a shite if you're the fuckin' Pope himself. Walk!"

The gunman has to open the gate back into the cobbled area, so the woman must have gone ahead and I'm guarded only by this amateur. I don't even know if Emma is here.

"I never said for ye to fuckin' stop," the gunman says.

"Emma!" I yell as loudly as I can.

"Daddy!" a faint voice replies. "Where are you?"

My daughter!

A hard metal object hits my temple. "Do that agin an' a'll stiff you!"

Footsteps scurry across the cobbles. "Get him inside!" pants the woman.

I lose count of the paces as I'm frogmarched across the cobbles.

We stop. Two scraping sounds, and then two doors creak open. I'm pushed forward one pace so that I'm standing on a metal grate. Another two scraping sounds and another two doors open, confusing me. I'm maneuverd to the left and then forward onto a hard floor.

After a pause the hood is pulled off my head. I'm facing a window shuttered on the outside and set in a white-washed wall peeling in places to reveal red bricks beneath. Anticipation shivers down my spine and slices through my stomach. What if Joe is in the room? Or one of the three IRA men at the Cúchulainn pub outside Buncrana, who saw me disguised only with gray hair dye, a moustache, and horn-rimmed spectacles?

I steel myself to turn and confront my captors.

No TV images and no CIA training courses can prepare you for the reality. The universal uniform of the terrorist, the black balaclava mask with holes for each eye and the mouth, menaces the beholder more than it shields the identity of the wearer. Especially when the wearer points a gun at you.

Joe isn't here, only the two terrorists who kidnapped me. The man is approximately five feet ten inches tall. He wears slimline Wrangler jeans and denim jacket over a red crewneck skinny sweater. He could be one of those who followed me out of Kelly's Cellars, or one of a hundred others I saw on the streets of West Belfast. His left hand directs the stainless steel barrel of a Smith & Wesson .38 revolver toward my chest. The woman is about five feet six and wears tight black jeans and a black leather jacket over a black cotton turtleneck. Her small hand holds a blued steel semiautomatic pistol with ease.

Behind them the lower half of a wide stable door is closed. Beyond is another stable double door. That explains the sounds of four doors opening. But this is no ordinary stable for horses or cattle. The solid brick walls, the stone floor, and a space too small for more than one animal are designed to imprison rather than shelter.

The woman takes aim at my head. "We said for Maitland to tell nobody else and bring the money himself."

It's essential to show that I'm not intimidated. Behind that dehumanising mask is somebody who shops in a supermarket, somebody who has a family, somebody who fears death as much as I do. "What does it matter?" I ask in a reasonable tone. "You have the ransom. Will you please release the girl."

She strides to within a pace of me. The balaclava is made of black wool. The eyeholes aren't cut evenly, giving the impression that one eye is higher than the other. They show thick black eyebrows above large, lambent brown irises so dark they almost merge with her pupils. "Don't try and be clever with me."

I maintain eye contact, attempting to convey that I have nothing to fear. "I'm a priest, a neutral intermediary. My only concern is to take that child safely back home."

"We'll see about that." She turns away. "Fetch him."

The gunman leaves and returns with a second man in a black balaclava mask. He's tall and gangly, and wears a green anorak over an argyle pullover and shapeless jeans with cuffs and a pair of cheap trainers. He's carrying what looks like a television remote control device, except that a slender antenna about nine inches long projects from the top. Thank God I dumped the ballpoint pen and decided not to carry a location trace.

"Sweep him," the woman says.

This second masked man presses a button on the radio frequency detector, points the antenna at the top of my head, and then brings it down, moving it from side to side. "He should be talking in case there's a voice-activated device," he says in an unsteady voice.

"Talk," the woman orders.

"I am an American priest on a mission of mercy. Unless you hand over the child unharmed, no one in the United States will believe your denials that the IRA was responsible for the Cheltenham bombing."

Underneath his balaclava mask this second man wears wire-framed spectacles. He avoids looking into my eyes. His own eyes go out of focus, as though he's trying not to see me, or else they look over my shoulder. I guess he's in his early twenties. I'll call him the Boy.

"The case?" asks the one I'll call the Woman.

"It's clean," the Boy says.

"On your way."

The Boy leaves.

"Off with your clothes," the Woman says.

I don't move.

The gunman swaggers up to me and presses the muzzle of his gun against my forehead. The mouth hole in his black mask shows an untrimmed black moustache straggling over his upper lip, from beneath which nicotine-stained teeth protrude. His eyes are gunmetal gray, almost dead.

"You heard," the gunman says.

"This is outrageous."

He cocks his gun. His pupils are dilated. This man has killed, and gets pleasure from it. I take off Maitland's overcoat, and then the clerical black jacket, followed by the priest's white collar, black shoes and socks.

"And the rest," says the Woman.

The collarless black shirt and pants join the pile on the floor.

"I said all your clothes."

I take off my underpants and kick them onto the pile. The Killer picks up my clothes, goes through the pockets, and removes my wallet. He puts the clothes into a plastic shopping bag on which the name Waitrose is printed in large letters.

"Well, well, what have we got here?" says the Woman. The wide mouth revealed by the mask hole opens into a smile of white, even teeth. She unzips her black leather jacket. The black cotton turtleneck stretches tightly over high, firm breasts. "You look very fit. Much too fit for a priest. More like SAS, I'd say." She moves up close and prods my stomach muscles with her gun. "In very good shape, except for this poor wee thing." She puts the cold barrel under my flaccid penis and lifts it up. "Don't you fancy me, soldier boy?"

"Maybe he *is* a priest," the Killer sniggers.

"Or maybe he's one of these big tough SAS posers who can only make it with little boys," she says. "Is that right?" she asks me.

I tell myself that this isn't personal, that these are just standard tactics to humiliate and demoralize a captive in order to establish dominance over him. I can't help feeling, though, that the Woman is enjoying it.

"Open your mouth," she says. She inserts the barrel of her gun between my lips. "Wider." She examines my mouth. "Not even a cyanide pill. What a disappointment you are."

I force myself to respond not as a seasoned CIA operative but as an Irish American priest. "I pray that God will forgive you."

"Before he does," she says, "face down on there." With the barrel of her gun she points to a six-foot-long cot covered by a gray blanket, the only thing in the room apart from a zinc bucket next to an old newspaper.

When I'm lying face down on the cot, she says, "Spread your legs."

I smell cheap scent. She murmurs into my ear. "Or would you prefer that my male friend here gives you an examination?"

The Killer sniggers again.

The Woman pulls apart my buttocks.

"Well, you're clean," she says. "Put the blanket on you."

I sit up on the cot. "I repeat. This is an outrage."

"Is that right?" Her eyes blaze through the holes in the balaclava. "Then why is it no outrage when you strip-search republican women visiting boys in the H-blocks?"

I must keep calm and avoid provoking her. After I've wrapped the gray blanket round me I say, "Now you've established that I'm only an intermediary bringing the ransom, may I please take custody of the child."

"We've established nothing," she retorts. She turns to the Killer. "Go and bring the Chief."

Chapter ✤ Twenty-three

THE CHIEF MAKES my blood run cold.

Like the others he wears a black balaclava mask, but there is an indefinable difference about him. Perhaps it's his stillness, perhaps it's the authority he conveys, or perhaps it's the way he stares at me. If Joe has supplied the IRA with arms, I'm dead.

From behind the holes in his mask the Chief's large eyes—bright whites surrounding small steely blue irises—move slowly as he inspects every inch of me, and then remain fixed on my eyes. He holds out his hand. The Killer gives him my wallet. Only then does he lower his eyes to look at the wallet. He searches through it, removes my driving license, and examines it.

He gazes at me before speaking, as if he were considering what to say. I'm certain he's already decided and the stare is intended to unnerve. There is a fine dividing line between danger that exhilarates and danger that paralyzes. The Chief is pushing me over the line. It's vital that I return his stare and sow seeds of doubt in his mind.

"Father Joseph Darcy," the Chief says at last in a flat nasal Ulster voice. He reads from the forged driving license. "St. Brendan's Rectory, 333 East 206th Street, Bronx, New York 10467."

The suppressed fear bursts out in humor. "My friends call me Joe."

The Chief doesn't alter his voice. He might still be reading from my driving license. "Our demand was clear. Maitland was to tell nobody. He was to bring the ransom himself."

Before the silence becomes unmanageable, I say, "His wife was desperate. She confided in me. She said that you'd kill him. She said you wouldn't harm an Irish-American priest."

"Is that a fact?" The Chief continues to stare at me. "My comrades here find it difficult to accept that an Irish-American priest even knows Edward Maitland, still less would be willing to help him."

"It's not Maitland I know, it's his wife."

"Is that so? I'd think you'd better tell me about it."

While I sit on the cot, the Chief stands in a relaxed, confident manner, feet astride, arms folded across his chest. He wears an old tweed jacket over an acrylic pullover and shirt and tie, and brown corduroy pants that are beginning to fray at the bottom. His hands are short and stubby, his fingernails severely clipped. A single band of gold on the third finger of his left hand is his only adornment.

"I first met Jill Maitland nearly twenty years ago," I say. "I was giving a retreat which she attended with her sister."

"Mrs. Maitland is a Catholic?" he asks.

"No."

"Then what was an English non-Catholic doing at a Catholic retreat house in America?" His questions are probing, but not aggressive.

"She was staying with her sister. She wanted to find

some space, to think through what she was doing with her life. Elizabeth, who's a convert, told her that she always found the retreats at the Passionist Center helpful for recharging her batteries. It so happened that during her stay I was leading a retreat with the subject of New Directions in Life."

"How did it so happen that you were giving the retreat?"

How would Joe respond? I give a wry smile. "I guess I'm well qualified to lead that particular retreat. Before I became a priest I'd served a year in jail."

"For what?"

"Destruction of government property and incitement to violence."

The Chief's fair eyebrows rise. "What did you do?"

"Pour chicken's blood over files at a draft board in Queens to protest the Vietnam War."

The Chief's eyes examine me again. That's his only reaction. No smile, no sign of approval or even disapproval. "Tell me about Mrs. Maitland."

"She'd majored in English at Oxford University, and we found that we shared a passion for Irish literature. We became friends, and whenever she came to visit her sister she would come to St. Brendan's or else she would invite me to supper at Elizabeth's house."

"Was it she who telephoned you about the ransom demand?"

"She was at her wit's end. I said that I would come over and that she was to tell her husband not to contact the police: they must do nothing until I arrived. I told the staff at St. Brendan's that I was going on a private retreat."

"Why did she think we would kill her husband but wouldn't harm an Irish-American priest?"

"Jill said she thought it was the IRA. Her husband's a civil servant. Something to do with the Ministry of Defense, I think."

I fear that those unblinking steely blue eyes are reading my mind. After what seems an interminable time he says, "The story is so improbable that it might even be true."

Mentally I breathe a sigh of relief.

"It's so improbable as to be a load of old gobshite," the Woman says. "What we've got here is an undercover SAS officer."

"With an accent like that?" the Chief asks her.

"Then whatever the American equivalent is. The FBI have been working hand in glove with the Brits against us in America." She moves to within one pace of me. "A few questions for you, Mr. Priest. Tell me about your church."

"It's in the north Bronx, just beyond the end of the D line. You can't miss it. It's a newish brick building designed in the shape of a currach."

For the first time the Chief's thin lips relax. "Do you believe St. Brendan really did reach America in a boat like that a thousand years before Columbus?"

"With God all things are possible."

"This retreat center?" the Woman snaps.

"The Cardinal Spellman Retreat House is about three miles from St. Brendan's, on Palisade Avenue overlooking the Hudson River. It's run by the Passionists."

"And Maitland's sister-in-law?"

"Elizabeth became a Catholic before marrying Glenn Stanton, an American banker she met in London. He was transferred back to New York. They live on Waldo Avenue in Riverdale."

"A well-rehearsed cover story," says the Woman.

"Sounds convincing to me," the Chief says. He lowers his eyes in thought.

A wave of euphoria sweeps over me. The interrogation has gone better than I'd hoped for. I've confused them and made them feel that I'm not afraid. More important, the cover story has held up.

Finally the Chief raises his eyes and stares at me. "I apologize for your treatment, Father."

Father! He addressed me as Father.

"But if you really are an Irish-American priest," he continues, "then you know what the Brits are capable of. Until we have positively established your identity, you'll appreciate that it's only prudent to assume the worst." He looks toward the Killer and then leaves the stable.

The Killer's grin shows nicotine-stained teeth. He takes a manacle which is chained to the wall, puts it round my right ankle, and locks it. "There's a bucket and newspaper in the corner if you shit yourself."

"Sweet dreams," the Woman says, and closes both halves of the stable door behind her. Beams slide over metal brackets to secure the door, a switch clicks, and the room plunges into darkness.

Chapter ✦ Twenty-four

THE WAVE OF euphoria ebbs as rapidly as it rose, dragging me into the depths of depression. The silence weighs as heavily as the blackness in this tomb of a cell.

I lie down, drained of energy. I've risked a car bomb on Highbury Fields, a trash can bomb in Forest Row, a shooting in a forest parking lot, and a booby trapped briefcase—and where has this got me? Naked on a cot beneath a rough blanket with one leg chained to a wall. Totally dependent on terrorists for my life. My cover is flimsy, and if they break it they'll have no hesitation in killing me. Maitland must have lost contact. His best opportunity to strike would have been to surprise them when they were taking delivery of the ransom. I don't know how many of them there are. I don't know where Emma is imprisoned. I do know that terrorists who think nothing of killing innocent children in Enniskillen, Warrington, and Cheltenham will have no hesitation in carrying out their threats to kill the girl they believe is the daughter of the man closing in on the Cheltenham bomber. And I'm powerless to stop them.

A tiny voice in my head warns me not to succumb. CIA training taught me to expect sudden swings of mood in a hostage situation. I must regain control. Analyze clinically. Think positively.

Emma is alive. She has heard my voice. She knows she is not abandoned. The kidnappers don't know my true identity. According to Maitland the IRA, unlike most other terrorist organizations, has rarely used kidnapping as a means of obtaining funds or exerting political pressure: they're inexperienced at this game. I, on the other hand, am no businessman or politician confused by sudden capture and isolation, traumatised by mortal danger, and emasculated by total dependence on captors. I've sufficient data to locate this hideout—if I can find some means of getting the information out. The IRA's normal method of operation through active service units suggests that this is a team of four, backed by support groups in Brighton and London who will have supplied and disposed of the cars and provided reconnaissance. Despite their black balaclava masks, I've memorised enough characteristics of the four terrorists to be confident of identifying them.

When it's light I'll explore the possibilities for breaking out. Afterwards I'll try negotiation. The hardest part will be to avoid showing hatred for these scumbags who bomb innocent children and now threaten to kill my daughter. Aggression will only provoke them. Instead I must work on each one in turn: draw out motives, probe weaknesses, sow doubts, secure respect, build a relationship, and win psychological dominance.

How?

The Killer. I've no doubt that he is. He's a soldier who obeys orders. If the Woman hadn't intervened he would have shot me—Irish-American priest or not—in Townsend's parking lot because those were the orders for dealing with anyone other than Maitland. His speech and demeanor suggest someone of low intelligence, violence prone, possibly pathological. Few possibilities with him.

The Woman, by contrast, is bright and takes decisions. Like the Killer she has no respect for the Church. She is close to someone who is, or has been, a prisoner in the Maze. She was hostile. Was this because she assumed I was SAS or was she playing the role of the hard interrogator? She's emotional, with a short fuse. When she's fully in control of herself she sounds almost English, but when she's angry she reverts to a Northern Irish accent. Interesting. I see ways of getting through to her.

The Chief showed no hostility toward me. Indeed, he showed no emotion whatsoever. He assessed my unexpected appearance rationally, took time over reaching his conclusion, and then was decisive. He would just as coolly order my execution if circumstances warrant it. He is, or has been, married, and is almost certainly a Catholic. Despite the IRA's £9 million illicit income, according to Maitland, the Chief's clothes suggest he's incorruptible. He's probably uncompromising and remorseless. He'll be difficult to crack.

The Boy is the one I've observed least. He's their electronics expert, the youngest and almost certainly the least experienced. He seemed the least self-assured, but that of itself is no guarantee he'll be susceptible to pressure: he could just as easily clam up.

Apart from their differences, the four have at least one thing in common. I thank my Irish republican mother for giving me the tools to work on that. A plan of action forms in my mind, and at long last I sink into sleep.

Daylight pierces the gaps in the shutters and wakes me. The chain is not long enough to let me reach the one window in this stable and peer through the gaps. Birdsong is all I can hear. No crowing of cockerels or lowing of cows. An occasional faint bleat suggests sheep some distance away. No smell of manure. This is not a working farm.

There is nothing with which to pick the lock securing the manacle. The links in the steel chain are firm, and the last one joins to a cast iron ring on the end of a bolt that is sunk deep into the wall. Although the white paint is peeling from the walls, the red bricks beneath are solid and the mortar is hard: nowhere can I get it to crumble with my fingernails. The stable doors, too, are solid. The most vulnerable part of the structure appears to be the red tiles that lie on top of exposed rafters which slope up from the top of the window wall and from the door wall to meet at a high roof ridge. I can't reach the window wall, and even standing on the cot I can't touch the top of the stable door wall. It's higher than the window wall. The roof must continue to slope down to an outer wall beyond the door wall. Of course. We passed through two sets of stable doors when I was brought to this place. This is a barred, secure pen inside a barred stable.

There's no hope of escape while I'm chained to the wall.

I slump onto the cot. I must resist this. If I slip so easily into depression, what must Emma be going through? I stand up, take ten deep breaths, and launch into a session of Canadian Air Force exercises. Afterwards I put the cot back in the position my captors left it, lie down, cover myself with the blanket, and prepare.

" 'It is not those who inflict the most who will win, but those who endure the most.' Who said that?" Mom asked.

I looked back blankly, but Joe, who was only in the fifth grade, piped up, "Terence McSwiney."

Uncle Fergal tousled his hair proudly. "Your granddad met Terence McSwiney when he was elected lord mayor of Cork, after the Black and Tans had murdered Tómas Mac-Curtain."

"When you next complain about wanting chocolates in Lent," said Mom as she collected the empty supper plates from the table, "just think about Terence McSwiney's hunger strike."

"The British thought they could beat us by brute force," said Uncle Fergal, "but every day of his hunger strike brought more and more Irishmen to the cause and broke the will of the British to impose their rule on Ireland. His martyrdom helped liberate the Twenty-six Counties."

"Isn't suicide a sin?" I asked.

" 'Greater love than this hath no man than that he lay down his life for others'," Mom said sharply.

"It's a noble tradition in Ireland," said Uncle Fergal. "St. Patrick himself went on hunger strike, and the Pope sent an apostolic blessing and a plenary indulgence to Terence Mc-Swiney. Eight bishops accompanied his coffin through the streets of Cork."

The bar grates back and the top half of the stable door opens. The masked Woman holds out a tray. "Your breakfast. Take it over to the camp bed and sit down. Go on you, do as I say."

I wrap the blanket round my waist, take the tray, and put it on the floor by the cot. She opens the lower half of the stable door and, legs apart, leans against the white-washed wall with her gun tucked in her belt and her hands on her hips. She's not wearing the leather jacket this morning. Does she get some perverse pleasure in flaunting herself while I'm naked? If it gives her a kick to taunt me with the rise and fall of her breasts, then I'm happy to play her game. I feel light headed with the anticipation of acting on my plan.

I take the mug of tea, look up from her breasts to the eyeholes in her black balaclava, and slowly push the tray toward her.

"Toast not good enough for you, then? Or is there something else you want?" She removes her gun and strokes the barrel with finger and thumb.

"It's not food that I want. I want to see Emma."

She says nothing.

"I've fulfilled your demand for a ransom," I say in a reasonable tone. "It's a justifiable demand on my part to see Emma. Until it's met I won't be taking food."

The Woman walks to within a foot of me and points the gun at my head. "How dare you!"

I fear she'll pull the trigger.

"So, you want to go on the blanket for real!" She turns on her heel, strides to the corner of the room, and kicks over the zinc bucket. Urine runs over the stone floor. She stalks back and kicks over the tray. "What the fuck do you know of hunger strikes?"

I sit on the cot and try to remain calm while her rage pours out in an unstoppable torrent.

"Forget all the sentimental crap you hear in the ballads. Let me tell you what it's really like. After the first few days you stop feeling the hunger gnawing at your belly. You just want to vomit the whole time. Tap water wrenches your gut in two. They give you bottled mineral water, but you can't keep it down. After a week you can't shit. Then you can't focus your eyes. You stagger round as though you've just downed fifteen pints. You're still puking, but nothing comes up except green bile. After six weeks you stop vomiting. You start talking clearly. They think you're recovering, or secretly taking vitamins, even though you look like one of those poor bastards in an Ethiopian famine—hollow cheeks, protruding eyes, and floppy skin that shows every bone in your body. And you know for why you stop vomiting? I'll tell you for why."

She leans forward and down so that she can look straight into my eyes. She's off balance. I could easily disarm her, but

I'm still manacled and I don't know where Emma is held. I return her stare and listen.

"It's because the brain cells that trigger the vomiting are too starved of vitamins to work. The nurses rub you down with olive oil to try and stop bedsores and gangrene. But they can't stop more of your brain cells closing down. You're rambling and incoherent. You go blind. You can smell the sickly nauseating stench of death on yourself. If you're lucky you slip into a coma. If you're not, they have to hold you down on the bed because agonising convulsions rack your body."

She stands up straight. "That's what you're making a mockery of."

I must do something to rescue what's left of my plan. "I didn't intend . . ."

"Oh no?" Anger flares again in her eyes. "Your good friend Maitland never tell you about it over a nice big dinner? About the fun he had in the Six Counties?"

"Maitland is no friend of mine," I protest. But she's not listening.

"Maitland and his friends let ten men suffer that barbaric death rather than let them wear their own clothes."

She slams the lower half of the stable door behind her. Before closing the top half she looks hard at me. "An' you want to go on hunger strike for your justifiable demand, do you? If I were you I'd start prayin' your story checks out."

Chapter ✤ Twenty-five

CHURCH BELLS RING in the distance, breaking the silence in this whitewashed cell. In another five hours the faithful will be walking along Bainbridge Avenue on their way to Sunday mass at St Brendan's. Pray that your story checks out. I dearly wish I could pray. But to whom? You can't pray to a God you don't believe in. I've never felt more like wanting to believe, to be certain that there's an all-loving all-powerful God who will reach down and rescue Emma from these terrorists. But it won't happen. Emma's life depends on me, and I've failed her.

How long will these terrorists take to contact their own people? How long will IRA headquarters take to set up a secret meeting with someone who is not under surveillance in Ireland and brief him to phone someone who is not under surveillance in New York? How long will that person take to pass on the message to the Provos in the Bronx? How long before someone from Tír na nOg goes to St. Brendan's rectory and asks the receptionist where Father Joe is? How long before the answer comes back to the Chief? How long have I got to rescue Emma? How, in God's name, can I do it?

I curl up on the cot and pull the blanket round me. Hopelessness brings on lethargy. Or is the lethargy caused by lack of food? I've gone beyond feeling hungry. Yesterday—was it only yesterday?—my total intake was two cups of coffee before going to the Maitlands' house, where I had another coffee, followed by a pint of Guinness at the Conways pub. Thirty six hours with alcohol but no food and it has only served to antagonize the Woman instead of winning her respect.

The warning voice in my head is fainter. I can't let depression drag me into torpor. I climb off the cot and force myself through a session of Canadian Air Force exercises.

Afterwards I feel better. I must decide whether to begin eating. The two pieces of breakfast toast lie on the floor, soggy from the urine spilt from the overturned bucket. I'm not that desperate.

The bar slides back on the stable door. If it's the Woman, I daren't provoke her further by continuing the hunger strike. I really don't know how I can get through to her.

"Your dinner," says the tall, gawky Boy in his black balaclava mask and green anorak.

Relief at not having to face the Woman again surges through me like adrenaline.

The Boy offers me a tray. I smell the roast meat and the gravy. They're tempting me with Sunday lunch. There's no knife or fork on the tray, but there is a spoon. How can I secrete it?

"May I have a mop, please?" I say as I look back over the stone floor of my cell. "There's been an accident with the bucket."

Still holding the tray, the Boy hesitates.

"I'm not asking for a broomstick," I say with a smile. "You can't fly away on a mop, and anyway, that's only for witches. Priests have to make do with prayer, and so far my prayers haven't managed to break this chain."

He puts down the tray, but on the far side of the stable door, out of reach. He leaves through the outer stable door and returns a few minutes later with a mop and a plastic bucket of water. Holding a gun in his right hand, he starts to mop the floor with his left hand. He sluices the floor, but can't manage to swab it dry.

"You don't have to do it," I say. "Let me."

The Boy hesitates.

"I promise not to hit you with the mop. My bishop would never forgive me."

He doesn't understand why I should be making a joke instead of showing fear. It undermines his own confidence.

"It's not a matter of life and death," I say. "If you insist on mopping my cell with one hand . . ."

The Boy hands over the mop and steps back out of the opened door, more than the chain's length away. He keeps his gun pointed at me.

I knot the blanket round my waist and mop the floor. The pen is three paces wide and four paces long, though the chain prevents my walking right up to the window wall. "The refectory floor at Dunwoodie Seminary is much bigger than this, so I became quite an expert at mopping."

When I've finished I hold out the mop for him.

Once more he hesitates.

"I'm afraid the fathers never taught us how to use mops as weapons, so I wouldn't be much good at fighting my way out of here."

The barrel of the gun wavers while he reaches for the proffered end of the mop. I hold onto the other end for a couple of seconds longer than necessary, grin, and then let him take the mop. I'm on a high, like an experienced lover anticipating a new conquest.

He tries to hold the tray with one hand, but needs to rest it on his gun hand to stop it tipping. I take the tray from him and put it on the floor by the cot. I pick up the mug of tea, sit on the cot, and nod toward the plate of roast potatoes, roast beef, gravy, and peas. "That was our treat for Sunday lunch at the seminary and I'd love to have it now, but I explained to the lady that I shan't be eating until I've seen Emma. I've brought the ransom you asked for. Don't you think it's reasonable that I see that she's alive and unharmed?"

He avoids my gaze. Apart from "Your dinner," the Boy hasn't spoken a word. Has the Chief instructed him not to talk to me? But the Chief doesn't know that his prisoner has twenty five years" practice of interrogation skills.

I crease my brow in a worried frown. "It's what I feared. She has been harmed."

"No she hasn't," he blurts out.

One vulnerability exposed. "Then why can't I see her?"

He stands with most of his weight on one leg and his shoulders hunched. He holds the gun in my direction, but he's never been taught proper balance for shooting. He looks past me. The bulbous lips revealed by the mouth hole in his black balaclava mask stay clamped together.

I need to play him like a trout: feed him more line before pulling him in. I shake my head sadly. "This can't be the IRA."

He makes no response.

I stare at him and say, " 'We place the cause of the Irish Republic under the protection of the Most High God, Whose blessing we invoke upon our arms, and we pray that no one who serves that cause will dishonour it by cowardice, inhumanity, or rapine.' "

The Boy's eyes, magnified by his spectacles, focus on me

for the first time. "You know the Declaration of the Republic?"

This is the line to feed him. "My grandfather fought in the War of Independence and then fought on against Partition. The old IRA would never have dishonored the cause by kidnapping an innocent girl, holding her to ransom, and then refusing to honor the ransom."

He shifts his weight from one foot to the other, but says nothing.

"Do you think it's honorable?" I stretch out my right leg, as if in cramp, and the chain rattles.

"That's not for me to say," he mumbles.

"Of course not. I understand that a volunteer has to obey orders. But in my grandfather's day the IRA was a democratic organization, the volunteers were consulted. 'I only obeyed orders' was the plea of Nazis at the Nuremberg trials."

"Have you finished with your tea?"

I cup my hand over the mug so that he can't see that it is empty. "Not yet. And since I have a sweet tooth, I'll be grateful if you put in three spoonfuls of sugar the next time."

He nods.

He's retreated into silence. I've got to find another means of drawing him out. First a distraction to put him off guard. "How long have you been interested in electronics?"

"Since I was ten," he replies, before stopping himself.

Followed by a provocation. "Was it a complicated job to time the detonator for the Cheltenham bomb?"

"The IRA didn't do that!" he protests.

"So you say. But you did set the electronics for other bombs, like Enniskillen, Warrington . . ."

"I did not!"

"You're an electronics expert."

"I didn't say I was a bomb maker," he mutters through his mask.

"Then I don't understand . . ."

"What I don't understand," the Boy says angrily, "is that if you come from a republican family, as you claim, then why are you helping the Brits?"

Good. He's opening up. "I'm not," I reply. "I support the cause of a united Ireland, but as a priest I cannot support the indiscriminate bombing of civilians and the kidnapping of an innocent girl. I'm sorry that you and the modern IRA do."

"It's easy to preach from across the Atlantic," he retorts, "but where I come from the choices aren't that simple."

"Moral choices always are," I say to provoke him further. "Where do you come from that's so special?"

"Coalisland."

I shrug.

"Suppose you've never heard of it, have you?" he accuses.

"No. And even if I had, it wouldn't alter the Church's teaching on what constitutes a just war."

"Just!" he exclaims. "Do you know what kind of justice we have in Coalisland?"

He's become agitated, but he needs more unsettling. "It can't be that different from towns in America."

"That shows how much you know about the Six Counties! It's a police state."

I smile. "The Irish always exaggerate."

"Exaggerate, eh? What town of four and a half thousand people in America has a police station built like Fort Knox smack in the center? With a huge pylon sticking up with cameras all over it? With microphones that can hear conversations for miles around?"

Like I saw in Belfast and Derry, I guess. "Perhaps there's a high crime rate."

"Too true. And the ones doing the crimes were the British paratroopers."

I give him a skeptical look. "Soldiers? What did they do?"

"They patroled the streets we went along to school, they were there when we came home from dinner, and they were waiting for us again when we left school. Every time they stopped us, called us Irish bastards, spread-eagled us against a wall, and searched us. You'd go round the corner and there'd be another patrol who'd do the same again. They were just looking for an excuse to stick the boot in."

It's beginning to spill out. A switch to sympathy now, so he won't identify me with the enemy. "Did they ever stick the boot into you?"

"Did they ever! Once I swore at a Brit and they took me to the detention center at Aughnacloy—that's nearly twenty miles away. The cell was a filthy hole. They only let me out an hour a day for exercise. I was scared stiff. They kept slapping me real hard, on the back of the head so it wouldn't show. They said they had to let me go after seven days, but if I caused any more trouble they'd lift me for another seven, and then they'd squeeze my balls until I'd never be able to fuck again. Those were the words they used. I was fifteen."

"That's terrible, my son. What did you do?"

He pauses. The gun hand drops to his side. "I'm no hero," he mutters. "I stayed in most nights doing homework. I wanted to get to university, out of the Six Counties altogether. I had an aunt who lived in . . . well, she lives in a town with a university in England. That was my aim, anyway, out of it all."

"You succeeded?"

"I did. But I knew plenty of fellas who weren't so lucky. Maybe they weren't as bright as me, but they were braver. They had nowhere to go and they knew it. All they could look forward to was a life on the dole, being harassed all the time. Or else fighting back."

"I guess you know some who did fight back."

He hesitates, but he's gone too far now to stop. "My

brother's best friend." Through the spectacle lenses behind the holes in his black balaclava mask, the Boy's eyes focus on a painful memory.

"Tell me. Help me to understand what it was like."

"It was one night in February," he says at last. "A group of us were at Clonoe Church car park, looking for a ride to a disco in Dungannon. We heard the rattle of gunfire. It didn't last long. It turned out that my brother's friend and three others had fired at the police station. It was like Don Quixote tilting at a windmill, so it was. There was no return of fire. Nothing. A lorry drove into the car park. My brother's friend was on the back, dismantling this big old machine gun. Then the Brits came."

He clams up again.

"I'd be scared," I say.

"I ran away," he admits.

"And then?"

"Then I heard loud gunfire. Continuous bursts. Submachine guns. It must have lasted more than five minutes. Then it stopped. In the silence I heard three distinct, separate shots." He looks down past his shapeless jeans to his cheap trainers. "After the funerals I left the Six Counties for good."

I've drawn it all out. He's a sensitive, idealistic boy, tormented by guilt. Now he feels exposed and vulnerable. Play him right and he's mine.

"Forgive me. I was making moral judgments about what you are doing without being aware of the situation you were in. I should have remembered that 'it is a sin against national faith to expect national freedom without accepting the necessary means to win and keep it'."

"You know Pádraig Pearse too?" He sounds incredulous.

Thank God for Mom and Uncle Fergal. "A little. Enough to understand why you joined the Provisional IRA."

"They asked me to help them, to try and get the peace process restarted."

I nod sympathetically. "We all want peace. But I fail to see how kidnapping an innocent girl like Emma can achieve that."

He averts his eyes, and then looks at his watch. "Will you eat now?"

Very tricky. "As a priest I cannot dishonor my word to the poor girl's mother. I must do everything in my power to bring Emma safely back to her. As I'm sure you understand, the fast is the only weapon available to the peacemaker."

He searches my eyes and I give him my sincere look.

"I understand, Father," he says at last.

"God bless you, my son. I'll pray for you."

Chapter ✤ Twenty-six

I HAVE TO fight back the urge to go ape. The Boy is their weak link, and I've got through to him! He believes my cover story. He's unhappy with the way Emma and I are being treated. He's inexperienced at handling a gun. He's someone the IRA has recruited in England within the last couple of months. He's guilty about running away from Coalisland, and he wants to restore the peace process. That gives a lot to work on.

What else can I deduce?

He's lived in England since he went to university; let's say he's been here four to six years. With his unfashionable clothes, ungainly manner, bulbous lips, and spectacles, he's hardly a raver. It's a good bet that he still lives with his aunt in a university town. The IRA would compartment this operation. The Woman—who must be the IRA liaison officer spotted in Brighton—will have drawn on support groups in London and Brighton, both of which have universities. She's unlikely to have used a third group. London is rarely described as a town, and so the Boy almost certainly lives in

Brighton. He's intelligent and sensitive. He knows the works of Pádraig Pearse, and probably shares Pearse's idealism. He has an expertise in electronics. But why did the IRA recruit him, rather than bring across one of their more experienced people? Does he really believe the IRA want to get the peace process restarted after the Cheltenham bombing? If so, how does he think kidnapping Emma will achieve that? Has he been fooled by IRA bombers planning a spectacular against Maitland to follow up Cheltenham?

Now I've got him to pour out his guilt, I need to build on the relationship. Electronics has too many associations with bombs, to which he reacted negatively. Irish nationalism seems the best bet to start him talking when he brings me supper.

Supper is a long time coming. The setting sun sends almost horizontal shafts through the gaps in the shutters. The light fades, the cell darkens, and supper still fails to arrive. The hunger strike gained the Boy's respect, if not the Woman's. Perhaps they've taken me literally and decided to stop offering meals, but I do need that tea with extra sugar if I'm to compensate for lack of solid food. I stop pacing the length of the chain through the shadows and sit on the cot to preserve energy.

The silence is broken by a vehicle approaching. It stops and a car door slams.

Still no supper.

I lie on the cot and pull the blanket round me. It's colder tonight. Or is it that two days without food make it feel colder? I try to sleep, but I'm still exhilarated, eager to work on the Boy.

A blazing light makes me squint. Through half closed eyes I see the glaring bulb which hangs from the rafters directly above the cot.

"Food," says the Killer's voice.

My heart drops. I'll just have to see how far I can get with him instead of the Boy.

I wrap the blanket round me, take the tray which he holds out through the opened upper half of the stable door, and return to the cot.

The Killer opens the lower half and his feet click on the stone floor. He's wearing scuffed pointed-toe cowboy boots with metal below the toecaps. He stands by the door, thumbs in the pockets of his slimline Wrangler jeans and his Smith & Wesson revolver stuck in a pearl-buckled broad leather belt. I'm tempted to ask why he's not wearing a Stetson over his black balaclava. "I thought you'd forgotten about me," I say.

"How could we forget such a charming man as yourself," says the Woman as she walks into the pen.

"You flatter me."

The Killer takes his thumbs from his jeans and hangs his hands by his sides. He really has seen too many Westerns. The Woman leans back against the white-washed wall on the other side of the opened door and folds her arms across the breast of her black leather jacket. "You spent such a long time with our comrade at dinner time," she says, "that we came to see what the attraction was." She's not angry. On the contrary, she's relaxed, almost amused.

"If I'd known, I'd have dressed for the occasion."

The Killer takes the gun from his belt, but the Woman shakes her head. She looks down at the tray containing cold sliced beef with bread and butter, plus an apple and a mug of tea.

"You cook a fine roast," I say.

"Not that you appreciate it. Are you still refusing food?"

"Only until I've seen Emma."

"I see you're determined to occupy the moral high ground."

"Join me. It's none too crowded up here."

"Who's the witty one, then?"

All is not lost with her. I glance at the Killer, who is spinning the barrel of his Smith & Wesson, and say to the Woman, "Don't you feel safe alone with me?"

Her masked head turns toward the Killer and nods in the direction of the door. He leaves. "I'm afraid you haven't impressed him," she says.

"I doubt if conversation is his strong point."

The lips of her wide mouth part in a smile of even white teeth. "It's true he's not so bright, but all liberation armies need people like him. He helps us keep discipline. Since the ceasefire he's been reduced to using an iron bar, but he really prefers his gun. He'd shoot his own mother if we ordered him to."

"Now why would a nice home-loving boy do a thing like that?"

"He wouldn't. His mother is faster on the draw than he is."

Her mood has changed entirely since breakfast time. Has the Boy convinced them that no British or American undercover agent would be able to quote Pádraig Pearse? I wonder how far she'll go. I hug my bare torso. "It's cold tonight. May I have my clothes back?"

"You'll be warmer if you eat your supper."

"You know why I'm not eating."

"Oh, I think you should eat tonight. You see," she says, "it'll be the last meal you have."

The large brown eyes revealed by the holes in her black balaclava flash with triumph. "When my comrade returns in the morning," she says, "the only thing he'll be bringing is his revolver."

I breathe in deeply to prevent my shoulders slumping. "Didn't he have the guts to do it tonight?"

"Oh, he won't like that, he won't like that at all. I

wonder," she pouts, "shall I tell him what you've just said? It might make him so angry that he'll need all six bullets before he manages to find one that'll kill you."

I can't let her see how shattered I am. "Does he have scruples about working on the sabbath?"

"Not him. It's our chief. He's a very religious man. He doesn't approve of executions on Sundays."

"But he does approve of shooting a Catholic priest in cold blood?"

The woman laughs and turns on her heels. Just before she closes the top stable door she says, "There's no danger of having that on his conscience. You see, we know who you are."

Chapter ✢ Twenty-seven

NAKED BENEATH A gray blanket I lie on the cot and wait for death tomorrow morning.

To have discovered after all these years that part of me lives on, that I have a child, that I have a daughter, to have heard her voice even, and yet to die without seeing her or holding her in my arms is a torment far exceeding any the IRA may inflict. I think of that photograph: long shiny black hair framing an elfin face lit by green eyes and a nervous smile. But when I try to bring that face alive, to see the lips part in laughter, the eyes glint with the lure of the wild, I see the face of Jill Maitland. The woman for whom I abandoned the love of God. The woman who abandoned me—without even telling me that I had a child.

Darkness grows. Deeper and quieter until it becomes a heavy silent blackness that disorients. When it encloses me I do not know whether my eyes are open or shut, whether I am looking up or down, whether I am alive or dead. Terror grips me. Terror at what I have done and, even more, terror at what I have failed to do with my life. Paths I could have followed, choices I might have made, actions I should have taken hover tantalizingly close, but when I reach out for them they vanish in the darkness of time past that can never be undone. But, however much these memories haunt me, I do not want the night to end. When this darkness retreats before the light of morning, another darkness, a far more terrible darkness, will claim me: the darkness from which no one returns.

I must cross this threshold alone, abandoned by all who once gave purpose to my existence. I try to pray, but the words, as though recognizing their own emptiness, die on my lips. Only one image stills the fear. The serenity on the face of Father Chávez, whose bare torso is squashed in the trunk of a Buick. The night before he was executed by an El Salvadoran death squad he, too, would have been imprisoned in a cell like this one, naked and chained to a wall as I am.

I know Inocencio Chávez almost better than the brother I'm impersonating. Although I never met him, I observed this Jesuit priest closely. He was about the same age as Joe and me, but shorter, darker, with an almost permanent five o'clock shadow. Unlike the Jesuits who taught at Regis and at Fordham, Chávez rarely wore clerical dress, preferring sweatshirt, jeans, and trainers. He attracted people like a magnet. During the Independence Day reception at the embassy I quizzed one of the American nuns who helped Chávez at the legal advice center he ran for peasants trying to form agricultural cooperatives. "Father Inocencio?" she giggled. "For him I'm tempted to drop the habit of a lifetime." His one other-worldly feature was his eyes. Hermit blue, they seemed to see through the poverty and degradation before him to some distant, better place. And, although I never spoke with him, I heard hundreds of hours of his voice on tape recordings.

Keeping Chávez under surveillance was my first

assignment in San Salvador back in 1984. The Salvadoran National Security Agency had told us that Chávez was a Soviet agent. The company officer I was replacing passed the case on to me. He introduced me to Alfonso García, an engineer at ANTEL, the National Telecommunications Agency. For a hundred US dollars a month García gave me copies of the intercepts ANTEL put on the phones used by Chávez at the Jesuit house and at the Central American University where he taught. I also had agents record Chávez's lectures. Finally, I placed a bug in his room at the Jesuit house. If Chávez was a leader of the FMLN terrorists and a Soviet agent, I was determined to produce the evidence.

One recording replays in my mind as powerfully as when I first heard it: Chávez's interrogation by the apostolic nuncio to El Salvador. Archbishop Bruno Meizinger had arrived only recently, sent by the Vatican to crack down on liberation theology. His Spanish was poor and Chávez had no German, and so they conversed in English.

You honor our house with your visit, Excellency. We are overjoyed that the Holy Father should have sent as his ambassador one who is eager to see at first hand the conditions of the Church in our poor country.

In contrast to Chávez's melodious phrasing, Meizinger spoke in a precise monotone, with equal stress on every syllable.

It has come to my attention, Father, that many of your students have joined the guerrillas.

How has this come to your attention, Excellency?

That is no concern of yours, Father. What should be your concern is why so many of them have taken the path of lawlessness. Could it be, perhaps, that they lacked proper spiritual guidance?

Excellency, I teach law, but in El Salvador there is no law. Every home is open to search without any kind of legal authorisation, every person—with the exception of the ruling élite and members of the security forces—is liable to extrajudicial execution. I cannot teach otherwise. This is something that we Salvadorans have to live with all our lives.

In the pause I heard the scraping of chairs and the rustle of papers before Archbishop Meizinger resumed.

I am informed that this so-called guerrilla war of liberation is a communist subversion directed by Cubans, who in turn are being instructed by the Soviet Union.

Right on the money, I thought at the time. But Chávez laughed. *Forgive me, Excellency, I mean no disrespect, but you must not believe such propaganda. We Salvadorans have been struggling for our human rights long, long before the Cubans began to fight for their freedom.*

Even if that were true, Father, there are legal and political means to fight injustice.

Excellency, the ruling élite in El Salvador imprisoned and tortured our political and labor union leaders. Little by little those who campaigned for the rights of ordinary people were driven to take up armed resistance against a dictatorship that denied them the rights that you in Germany take for granted. This is still the situation today. The wealthy landowners and their North American partners get richer while the mass of the Salvadoran people get poorer.

I fear that you exaggerate, Father.

Excellency, I beg you, come with me to La Fortaleza, to any rural area. See for yourself the stomachs of the children bloated by malnutrition, the faces swollen from parasites, and then go to see how the children of the rich live, guarded by thugs with Uzis in their villas in the northern suburbs of San Salvador, see what luxuries their money buys in the Beethoven Shopping Center. This is what decades of military dictatorship have reduced us to.

Meizinger paused before playing his trump card. *But now, Father, that excuse no longer applies. The election this* year produced a democratic government, one to which I am accredited by the Holy Father.

Chávez, too, paused before replying. Excellency, the election was a travesty. The main opposition groups were barred.

It was only the communists who were barred.

Communists! Communists! Excellency, every political activity is labeled "communist"—everything.

It is not the role of the priest to become involved in political activity, whatever it is labeled. The concerns of the priest are spiritual, not temporal.

But, Excellency, I am only doing what the Holy Father exhorted our brothers in Poland to do.

I heard a coughing and a nose-blowing, no doubt into the apostolic nuncial silk handkerchief, before Meizinger continued.

The Holy Father draws a sharp distinction between advocating social justice and taking up arms to break the fifth commandment.

Excellency, I have never taken up arms . . .

I am relieved to hear that.

But I understand those who have, and so would you, Excellency, if you lived in this country for as long as I have.

Never! God's commandment not to kill is a moral absolute; it is not, if I may borrow a phrase from the liberation theology which you appear to espouse, an option.

Surely, Excellency, the Church has always espoused the doctrine of the just war. Have not popes themselves led armies into battle?

That is different. Those were different times and different circumstances. A war is only ever justified in order to protect the lives of the faithful, and when no other alternative is available.

But, Excellency, what I am trying to say in my clumsy

way is that these are the circumstances in this country. Members of the Church in El Salvador can be taken at any time of the day or night and tortured and killed.

I accept, of course, that there are evil people in your country, Father, agents of the devil who have murdered nuns and assassinated an archbishop, but you must leave secular action on such outrages to the proper authorities. The Holy See has made strong representations to your government.

Excellency, when I speak of members of the Church in El Salvador, I do not mean only archbishops and priests and nuns. I mean the people of God, the countless thousands who are dragged off from their hovels in the city or in the countryside, whose mutilated bodies are found dumped at El Playón or floating in Lake Ilopango or, even worse for devout families wanting a Christian burial, who are never found at all, who simply disappear. These are the people of God who have no international advocates, no international television crews to film their wretched lives and even more wretched deaths.

I take your point, Father, but I trust that you take my point. It is not your role to encourage by your sermons or by your lectures those who take up arms against their government. If you send me a list of the people who have been abducted, I will myself, with the full authority of the Holy See, make representations to the government and demand that these death squads be apprehended and subjected to the full force of the law.

I thought the tape had stopped, for there was no sound for a minute or so. Then Chávez spoke, now matching Meizinger's precise tones.

Excellency, I lack your eloquence. I have not made myself clear. It is the government security forces who are undertaking these tortures and murders.

Father Chávez, I forbid you to repeat such slanders! This government is led by a Christian Democrat, a reformer whom I count as a friend.

Chávez's voice was tinged with sadness. *This reforming Duarte is the same Duarte who allowed himself to be used as the respectable civilian face of the military junta from 1980 to 1982, when over twenty five thousand of our people were murdered by the military.*

I think you mean armed terrorists killed by the army.

No, Excellency! I mean civilians. I mean women and children fleeing their villages who were fired on by helicopter gunships supplied by the Pentagon. I mean the survivors of such attacks who were rounded up by infantry, decapitated with machetes, and left piled up in a mound as a warning to others not to give food to the guerrillas. Come with me and I'll take you to empty villages where you will see the charred remains of peasant houses, where you will see tiny plots of land for vegetables now overgrown with weeds, where you will see a mound of human bones—and a separate mound of skulls. In this country, Excellency, you are forced to choose whose side you are on. Like Our Blessed Savior, my option is for the poor.

In the silent blackness of my death cell, I think of those same ideals that inspired Joe and me, of helping those who ain't got it so good. Chávez's God and his Church are ones I could have believed in, but I never got the chance to talk to him. Shortly after I submitted my field information report, which concluded that Chávez was neither Soviet agent nor terrorist, García brought me another tape.

I listened to this one at home. My Spanish was not fluent, and the man who telephoned Father Chávez spoke in that guttural, elided way of the Salvadoran uneducated, reducing a musical language to an ugly slur. I had to replay the tape several times to decipher the exact words, although the menace was unmistakable in any tongue.

Hello, Chávez here.

Is that the so-called priest, Inocencio Chávez?

I am Father Inocencio. What is it you want?

You, you fucking communist hypocrite. Out of the country in three days if you value your life.

My life has no value. It is dedicated to God, who has given me this vocation. I cannot abandon the flock entrusted to my care.

That evening I went to the home of Frederick Bowland, our deputy chief of station, to warn him that Father Chávez's life was in danger. Three days later one of my surveillance team reported that heavily armed men had forced Chávez into a van with tinted windows. A week later a Buick was found abandoned at La Puerta del Diablo.

Chávez faced not a single bullet, as I do, but a long, pain-racked death. How did he prepare himself for such a terrifying ordeal? How did he rise above fear and self-pity? How did he maintain the serenity that marked his face even as his tortured body lay in the trunk of the Buick?

With a terrible sinking feeling I realize that the Inocencio Chávez who inspires me with his life cannot inspire me with his death. Like all good martyrs Chávez would have feared dying, but not death. It is not the dying that I fear, but death itself. Unlike Chávez I cannot submit to the executioner secure in the knowledge that God is waiting to reward me with eternal bliss.

Terror seizes every atom of my body. I cannot, I dare not, I will not submit.

Chapter ❖ Twenty-eight

THE FLUTED SONG of a blackbird trilling up and down the scales breaks the silence of my vigil. As though cued by the maestro, an early morning chorus of other birds joins this soloist. I fail to identify them. Only the blackbird stands out by the beauty and virtuosity of his melody. If only one bird is allowed to sing in heaven, it will surely be the European blackbird. There won't be one in hell.

The serenade hasn't finished before the lightbulb blazes and banishes the shadows cast by the pale pre-dawn light. The bars on the stable door slide back, and three men and one woman, all wearing black balaclava masks, process into the cell. None carries a breakfast tray. The Woman carries a black hood. The Killer carries his Smith & Wesson revolver in what appears to be a ceremonial manner, holding the gun above his shoulder, finger resting on trigger, steel barrel pointing vertically upwards.

The Woman and the Killer stand either side of the Chief, facing me, while the Boy lurks behind this line.

Slowly I pull back the blanket, rise from the cot, and

stand naked before them. Like a gladiator before a contest, I'm resolved to battle for my life. And I've the plan and the combat training to win the battle.

"This tribunal, with the full authority of the Army Council," the Chief announces in his nasal Ulster voice, "has considered the following charges: one, that you are an enemy agent spying on the Irish Republican Army; and two, that you are attempting to sabotage an Army operation being carried out in Britain." He pauses. "It has found you guilty on both counts. With the power delegated to me I hereby sentence you to death, and direct that the sentence be carried out forthwith. Do you have anything to say before sentence is executed?"

"What tribunal?" I challenge. "When's the trial? When do I get the chance to answer your charges?"

"You presented your case on Saturday evening," says the Chief. "We investigated your claim. You're condemned by your own words."

"This is a travesty. You're acting as prosecutor, judge, and jury. I demand an appeal to higher authority."

"No appeal is possible."

"It's coldblooded murder."

"Do you have a last wish?"

I pause, and then say slowly and deliberately, "I wish to see Emma."

The Woman leans and whispers to the side of the Chief's black balaclava. His eyes focus down through the holes in his mask toward the floor. Finally he raises his eyes to stare at me. "Your activities have already put the girl in jeopardy. What you propose puts her at even greater risk. There can only be one reason for your request and that is to try and free her. Any rescue attempt is likely to render the hostage damaged or nonviable. That would be of no benefit to you, her, or us. Request refused."

What if I were to plead with him, tell him that I'm her

real father; would that change his mind? I look into his eyes
and know what his answer would be. But for my plan to work
I must be free from this manacle. "I demand to die with dig-
nity, not naked and chained like an animal. That was never
the way with the Irish Republican Army my grandfather was
proud to serve."

Again the Woman whispers to the Chief. My plan is slipping away. "You've searched me and found nothing," I say.
"Are four armed IRA officers frightend of one unarmed
priest?"

"Shut yer face," the Killer says.

The Chief stares at me, and then turns to the Boy. "Fetch
his clothes."

I doubt that the Boy is armed, and even if he is he won't
shoot me. I've never seen the Chief with a gun, and if he
has one it's probably for personal protection, carried in a secure rather than a quick release holster. I need to take out
the Killer first, the Woman second, and the Chief third.

The Boy returns with the plastic Waitrose shopping bag
which he gives to the Chief, who hands it to me.

I take my underpants. "I can hardly put these on while
my leg's chained to the wall."

The Chief hesitates. A good sign. He gives the Woman
a key. The Killer brings down the barrel of his revolver and
points it at my chest, while the Woman crouches down out
of his line of fire and unlocks the manacle. She moves side-
ways before straightening up.

I take my time dressing. The longer the Killer is holding the thirty-ounce Smith & Wesson in that position, the
more fatigued his arm and trigger finger will become.

In black socks, pants, and shirt I pick up the white clerical collar.

"Enough," the Chief says. "You don't need that, or the
shoes."

I look round the whitewashed cell at each of them, seeking their eyes through the holes in their black masks.

The Chief's eyes are fixed and unyielding. Next to him the Woman's large lambent brown eyes defiantly return my stare. The pupils of the Killer's expressionless gray eyes are dilated. I expect the Boy to show hostility or reproach for having been duped, but he averts his eyes.

"Kneel," says the Chief.

I obey.

"Hood him."

"I don't need a hood."

"Hood him," the Chief repeats.

"Are you afraid of looking into my eyes when you murder me?"

"Close your mouth, you, or I'll fill it with a gag," the Woman says as she takes three paces forward and puts the black hood over my head. The percentages swing against me.

I hear three steps; they almost certainly mean that she's returned to her position on the Chief's right.

The Killer's steel-tipped boots click on the stone floor. His gun presses against my right temple. Even through this hood the reek of his stale sweat invades my nostrils. I lean to my right and rest my shoulder against his leg. That will be his left leg; he's bending forward, with his left hand—his gun hand—above his left leg.

I don't know whether it's the nervous energy and the adrenaline pumping through my system, but time seems to move slowly, my perceptions heighten, and I feel totally focused and in control, as though my whole life has been a preparation for this moment.

My head returns the pressure of the gun muzzle, and the Killer responds by pushing even harder. Far too hard. Now all I have to do is quickly twist my head to the left and the gun will slide past, missing me even if it fires. My left hand

can grab and twist the wrist that holds the gun, and pull him
off balance across my right shoulder, shielding me from the
Woman, while my right hand slides up his leg and grabs his
testicles. My left hand can then pull off the hood and my
right take the Smith & Wesson as I roll to my left and fire
upwards at the Woman. Two shots for her, one into the
Killer on the floor, and then two at the Chief before he's undone his holster.

This gives me a thirty to forty percent chance of escape
against a one hundred per cent chance of death if I don't act.

"Although you and I are on opposite sides of this war,"
says the Chief, "I salute your bravery. Do you have any last
message to pass on to your family? Give me their names and
address and, as one officer to another, I give you my word
that your message will be delivered."

What message should I give? To whom should I send it?
Why is the Chief making this offer? *He hasn't used my name.*
Neither now nor when he pronounced sentence. Nobody
has. *He's asked me for the names and address of my family.*
Despite what the Woman said last night, do they really know
who I am? How certain are they that I'm not Father Joe
Darcy? Is that why the Boy couldn't look me in the eye?

The only purpose left in my life is to save my daughter.
*Any rescue attempt is likely to render the hostage damaged
or nonviable,* the Chief said, in that universal, deperson-
alised language of the professional killer. If my one-against-
four attempt doesn't succeed, the Chief will know for sure
that I'm no priest but an undercover operative. He'll conclude that Maitland has brought in not only the British Security Service but also the Americans to hunt them down.
He'll feel the net closing around them. He can't take Emma
to Ireland. Releasing her would be an admission of defeat.
Rather than that he will carry out his threat to Maitland and
kill Emma. The only certain way to keep her alive is to

convince him that I really am a priest. And that means I must respond as a priest faced with execution. I fix in my mind the photograph of Emma, bow my head, and await the death that will redeem something of my life.

"We haven't got all day," the Chief says.

"My only message is to God." A priest would say an act of contrition. But I can't remember how it begins! The only words I remember are the Latin words of the Confiteor, that confessional prayer I chanted so many times as an altar boy at St Sebastian's. *"Confiteor Deo omnipotenti, beatae Mariae semper Virgini, beato Michaeli Archangelo, beato Joanni Baptistae . . ."*

As the words flow automatically I recall what Father Curran told us: if you attend the holy sacrifice of the mass and receive Our Blessed Lord's Body and Blood on the first Friday of the month for nine consecutive months, the Sacred Heart of Jesus has promised that you will not be allowed to die without the opportunity of making a final act of contrition. Is this what he meant? That these words are now wiping away over twenty years of unbelief and mortal sin? I'm not saying the Confiteor as myself, but as my brother; I'm an impostor. Do the words still count?

"Finish, you," says the Killer, and I hear the hammer of his gun cock.

"Leave him," snaps the Chief.

". . . *omnes sanctos, et vos, fratres, orare pro me ad Dominum Deum nostrum.*"

"Have you finished now?" the Chief asks.

I ask God, if he exists, to take my life in exchange for Emma's freedom. "May the almighty and merciful Lord grant us pardon, absolution, and remission of our sins," I say, blindly making the sign of the cross in the air.

A bang on the temple, a deafening explosion, and the tension flows from my body like water from a burst dam. I collapse forward and my head hits the floor. A sharp pain, and then nothing. Only blackness.

A narrow band of light shines at the edge of blackness. It's below me. The band widens. It reveals the scuffed pointed toe of a cowboy boot.

I squint in the brightness as the Killer pulls the hood from my head. I raise my head from the stone floor and gingerly touch the painful swelling above my left eye. The Woman blows the end of her semiautomatic pistol. The eye holes in her mask turn toward me and her lips pull back from her teeth in a wide grin. The eye holes look up toward one of the wooden rafters. A splintered bullet hole marks the scene of this macabre game.

"I'm sorry, Father," the Chief says. "We had to make sure."

Only the Chief and the Boy are left in the cell.

I put on the white clerical collar and try to stop my hands shaking with aftershock as I fasten it behind my neck. I sit down on the cot to put on the black shoes, and remain seated.

The Chief hasn't moved. Like the first time I saw him, he stands confidently with feet astride and arms folded across his chest. I'm sorely tempted to spring at him, rip off that black balaclava mask, and smash his face into the stone floor.

"You'll understand, Father," he says, "that we have to take security measures."

I swallow back my instinctive response and reply in a calm voice. "Subjecting a priest to a mock execution is not what I call a civilized security measure."

"We had a problem. Our people did find that the

Elizabeth Stanton who lives in Riverdale has the same maiden name as Maitland's wife, and that she does know Father Joe Darcy."

Jill at least had the sense to brief her sister.

"St. Brendan's said that Father Darcy was away on retreat and couldn't be contacted."

"That's just what I told you. What was the problem?"

"The vote here wasn't unanimous in your favor. A strong view was expressed that you are not Father Darcy, but someone impersonating him."

"That's ridiculous. Do you believe that?"

Those thin lips curl in the nearest I've seen to a smile. "I've never known anyone, tout or undercover SAS officer, who hasn't admitted the truth when he's certain he's going to die, when he knows there's no point in keeping up the pretense."

I look at the holes in the black balaclava and try to recall if I've seen those small, steely blue irises in the middle of large whites, plus that thin-lipped mouth, in the face of someone wearing a Sinn Féin suit who appears on television insisting that his only concern is to bring peace to Northern Ireland. Is this the man who ordered the Cheltenham bombing?

"You have the ransom," I say. "Now I'd like to take Emma back to her mother."

"It's not as straightforward as that, I'm afraid. Our demand was for her father to bring the ransom personally."

"But . . ."

"It's been a bad ordeal for you, Father. Would you take a glass of whiskey?"

Is this a trick question? Does Joe still drink, or has he given up? I don't know him as a priest. "I'd appreciate a cup of sweet tea."

The Chief nods. "I don't have any use for alcohol myself, but I am partial to a mug of good tea." He turns to the Boy.

"When you bring Father's breakfast, make sure the tea's strong and sweet. Now go and fetch a washbowl for him, and don't forget some ice for that bruise on his forehead."

"I've already said that I'm not eating until I see Emma."

"Don't trouble yourself about that, Father. After you've washed and had breakfast, I'll take you to her."

My heart skips a beat. At last, I will see my my daughter, talk with her, hold her to me.

The Chief goes to the stable door, and then turns, as though struck by an afterthought. "Will you be needing to say mass, Father?"

Another trick? "I'd like a bible, but there's no obligation for us to say a daily mass."

"Not even on Sunday?"

"If we're able to, of course, but I haven't got the facilities here."

"Surely any bread and wine will do if nothing else is available?"

I have no alternative but to agree.

"If it looks as though you're still going to be here next Sunday, I'll see what I can arrange."

Joe returns from retreat next Saturday. If I'm still here on Sunday it won't be bread and wine that the Chief will arrange. "Let's hope that won't be necessary," I say.

Chapter ✢ Twenty-nine

IT'S TRUE WHAT they say about being on the point of death. Your whole life flashes before you. Everything was there—incidents that I'd forgotten about, incidents that I was proud of, incidents that I was deeply ashamed of—and yet it all occurred in the split second between my making the sign of the cross and the gunshot that accompanied the bang on the temple. It's given me a lot to think about. But later. The only thing that matters right now is that I'm going to see my daughter.

"I'm sorry about what happened," the Boy mumbles as he offers me a red plastic bowl and a towel.

I give him a reassuring smile. His guilt will be something to exploit when I figure out an escape plan. I splash my face with cold water, and dry face and hands before putting the clerical collar back round my neck. The high, hard collar rubs against prickly stubble on the upper neck and underside of my chin. The IRA's concession to hygiene stops short of a razor.

"I've brought this, Father," the Boy says, and offers me a wet dishtowel crumpled in the shape of a ball.

"What is it?"

"There's ice inside the towel, for the lump on your forehead."

"When will I see Emma?"

"Our chief said he'll take you after you've had breakfast."

"Then please go and get breakfast."

The Boy returns with a tray containing a bowl of cornflakes, a jug of milk, a plate of toast, and a mug of tea. After two days without food I wolf down the food and drink the sickly sweet tea.

"Can we go and see Emma now?"

"We have to wait for our chief."

I've read of adopted children meeting their natural parents after years of separation and instinctively sensing the bonds between them. Will Emma respond like that? But nobody will have told her that I'm her natural father. Do these emotional bonds operate by instinct? Will she recognize something in me?

If I've found it difficult to deal with swings of mood between elation and despair, how must a seventeen years old schoolgirl be coping after six days as a hostage?

A thought chills me. Will she have succumbed to the Stockholm Syndrome and identified with her captors? Will I find her mouthing IRA slogans and wielding a gun, like Patty Hearst with the Symbionese Liberation Army?

"How is Emma?" I ask the Boy.

He looks down at the floor. "All right."

"You've seen her recently?"

"Yesterday evening."

"What's her mood like?"

He hesitates. "I think you should see for yourself. It won't be long now."

⚬ ⚬ ⚬

Another hour passes before the Chief arrives.

"You said I could see Emma after breakfast," I accuse.

He stares at me through the holes in his black balaclava mask. "Your presence here has produced complications. I needed to consult about how best to proceed. In the meantime, for your security and ours, I'm afraid you'll have to stay here, fastened with the chain when nobody is with you."

"You promised I could see Emma!" If he reneges on this I really will tear that balaclava mask from his head and smash his face into the stone floor.

"I'll take you to her, but it's in your own interests not to be able to identify this place. I'll have to hood you."

From the pocket of his tweed jacket he takes the same black hood that the Woman put over my head a couple of hours ago.

Seeing nothing, and smelling only the mustiness of the thick cotton hood, I'm guided by the Chief through the stable door. One pace onto a metal grid, and a second pace takes me through the outer door and into the cold. Forty four paces in a straight line over cobbles lead to a gate, and through that onto rough grass, probably the field in which the Woman and the Killer made me open the Samsonite case.

The Chief guides me in a left turn after the gate, and twenty seven paces later a right turn. Six paces later we turn left onto some rough paving and proceed for eighteen paces, or is it twenty? In my anxiety I find it difficult to keep track. The last time I was hooded, when faced with execution, I was calm and in control; faced with seeing my daughter for the first time in my life, my stomach is knotted.

We turn left, over flat dirt ground, before the Chief tugs me to a halt.

He lets go of my arm. A sliding sound, like wood on wood, not on metal, is followed by the creaking of a door.

I step through onto a hard floor—concrete or stone—and wait while the Chief closes the door. "Be careful where you're walking, Father. The floor is full of rubbish." I'm guided four paces forward, a right turn, and then two paces. "We're going up some steep steps, so hold onto the rail on your right. There's no rail on your left."

Twenty wooden steps rise to a wooden floor or platform: this must be at least fifteen feet from the ground, higher than the floor above a normal room. I don't know how wide it is, and so I stand blindly, waiting for the Chief to pass. "Just stay there and hold the rail," he instructs.

I need to hold onto the rail because my legs have turned to jelly. Ever since Maitland showed me Emma's photograph and told me she was my daughter, I've imagined the moment when we first meet. I never imagined the apprehension that reduces me to a quaking mess. I never imagined the fear of rejection.

"What are you waiting for?" the Chief asks. "Walk straight ahead, I said."

He takes my arm and guides me through an opened door. Three paces past the door jamb and he brings me to a halt. A door closes behind us, but there is no sound of a bolt or a key being turned in a lock.

"You may take off the hood," the Chief says.

Sitting on floorboards, with her back against a low red-brick wall and her head bowed beneath rafters that slope up to a central ridge, the daughter I have never seen hugs her knees to her chest and doesn't move. Her face is covered by long black hair which cascades over her knees and bare legs, almost reaching the manacle around her left ankle sock.

"You have a visitor," says the Chief.

She doesn't move.

The words choke in my throat. I force them out. "Emma, don't be afraid."

Still she doesn't move.

"What have you done to her?" I snap.

"Nothing," he says defensively. "It's a priest to see you," he calls out to her. "Father Joe Darcy."

She raises her head, and her hair falls back to disclose an elfin face so like Jill's. Her eyes move from me to the Chief and back to me.

"I'm a friend of your mother's and your Aunt Elizabeth's from the States," I manage to say.

I look into her gold-flecked green eyes and will her not to give me away, but all I see is fear. "I've brought the ransom money."

The fear doesn't leave her eyes. The Chief is bound to sense that she doesn't believe me. I turn on him. "Can't you see the child's in a state of shock. I need to be alone with her."

He stares at Emma and then at me.

"What harm can it do?" I demand.

"Half an hour." He turns and opens the door. The wooden platform outside projects into a barn. The Chief bolts the door from the outside.

I long to take Emma in my arms and hold her tight, but when I step toward her she clambers to her feet, forced by the sloping low rafters of the barn loft away from the wall to which she's chained. "Emma," I say. She shrinks back, as far as the chain will allow toward the gable wall of horizontal clapboard, opposite the door through which I entered.

She's the most beautiful girl I've ever seen. Her long black hair falls unkempt past the shoulders of a white Aertex sports shirt to the top of her breasts. A short, pleated, navy blue skirt reveals bare legs bent at the knees as she cowers away from me.

"Emma," I say softly, "don't be afraid. Are you OK? Are you hurt?"

Her voice trembles. "Who are you?"

"I've brought the ransom money. What have they done to you?"

"What's happened to Daddy?"

"Nothing."

"What was that gunshot this morning?"

"It was nothing. They were just trying to scare me."

Her eyes dart warily, like a trapped animal's. "First they told me Daddy had been in an accident. Then they said he was bringing a ransom. Then I heard my name shouted. Then they threatened me and said there was a problem. Then I heard a gunshot this morning."

"I called out your name on Saturday evening. Edward is safe with your mother in Highbury."

"Why should I believe you?"

I try to keep the desperation out of my voice. "You must believe me, Emma. Edward and your mother are safe. They're waiting for you at home." I play the only cards I can use within earshot of the Chief. "All the fluffy cats on your bed are waiting for you, including the big black one you keep your pajamas in."

Her brow furrows.

"The one on top of the bedspread with batik black cats."

Slowly she straightens and looks at me as though for the first time. "Who are you?" The fear has receded from her voice.

I swallow back the words that fight to come out, and say instead, "A friend of your mother's."

Nervously she pushes her hair behind one ear, just like Jill did. "I've never met you."

I put my finger to my lips, glance toward the door, look into her eyes, and raise my voice. "I met your mother in the States, when she stayed at your Aunt Elizabeth's."

She returns my look. Then she nods slowly and looks toward the door. "Mum did say she met an American priest when she went to Aunt Elizabeth's," she says out loud.

Just like her mother and me: we can communicate without speaking!

She scrutinizes my face. "What's that swelling over your eye?"

"At first they didn't believe me either."

"Why did you bring the ransom instead of Daddy?"

"I decided that it would be too dangerous for him. The IRA was less likely to harm a Catholic priest."

She takes three tentative steps toward me, and then reaches out and gently touches the swelling on my forehead. "Have they hurt you?"

I want that cool hand to remain there forever. "No. It's nothing."

She removes her hand. "You're very brave to help us."

"Nonsense. I come from a long line of cowards; I maintain the tradition magnificently."

It doesn't bring even the glimmer of a smile to those lips. "You must respect Daddy a lot."

What can I say? Your precious "Daddy" is a two-faced scheming selfish fraud who isn't even your father? I glance at the door and wonder if the Chief is straining to listen. "Your mother was frantic."

"She has her own way of coping." She stops, as though regretting what she's just said. She stares down at the grimy wooden floor next to the zinc bucket and the pile of old newspapers. She grits her teeth but fails to stop her lips trembling. Her fingers bunch into tight little fists and her shoulders begin to shake.

I must get her talking to stop her relapsing into depression. I sit down on the bare boards and pat the space next to me. "Tell me what happened, Emma," I coax softly.

She lowers herself to the floor, hugs her knees, and stares into space.

When she starts to speak it is in a flat voice, as though it were somebody else's story.

"I was playing hockey in the period after lunch on Tuesday. Mrs. Williams came. She said there was a police inspector with an urgent message. I ran to the office. This policewoman told me that Daddy had been in an accident. He was dangerously ill. The police had sent a car to take me to the hospital straight away." She glances at me. "I was worried sick."

"I'm sure you were," I soothe. I lower my voice. "Would you recognize this woman?"

She nods slowly. "She had short blonde hair and wore a lot of make up," she whispers. "I think it's the woman here who wears a mask, but I can't be sure."

The Woman has thick black eyebrows, but she's almost certainly the IRA woman spotted in a blonde wig going to Brighton. "Go on."

"I got into the back of a car with the policewoman. After the car left the school she opened a bag." The words now come faster. "I smelled chloroform. It all happened so quickly. Before I could say anything she put a pad over my face. I struggled but she held it against my mouth and nose. I couldn't breathe."

"It must have been terrifying."

"The next thing I remember I was in the back of a van. I had tape over my mouth and round my wrists."

"May I have a look at your arms?"

I take each slender arm in turn. On the left one I find a small puncture hole above a vein. As I thought; they injected Emma after the chloroform. I wonder if the Woman is a nurse.

"And then they brought you here?" I prompt.

She nods, clamps her mouth tight, and stares down at the floor.

"Go on."

"The man and the woman who took me from the back of the van wore black masks over their heads." She is now speaking slowly again; each word has to be dragged protesting from the depths of her memory. "They brought me up here. It . . . It was horrible."

"Tell me," I say gently.

She hugs herself protectively. "The woman made me take off all my clothes. She searched me." Tears well in her eyes. "In front of that man with the moustache. It was horrible the way he kept looking at me."

I wrap my arms round her and hold her tight. Her pent-up emotion bursts out in tears.

"I'm sorry," she sobs.

"There, there." I stroke her back. "It's good to cry." I'm torn between wanting to comfort my daughter and wanting to strangle that sadistic bitch.

When the sobs finish the words come out normally. "They didn't give me back the watch that Daddy gave me for Christmas. Then the man who brought you here came. He gave me paper and a pencil. He asked me to write as much as I could about Daddy."

"What did you do?"

She sniffs. "I tore up the paper."

That's my girl.

"After I called back to you the other night, they said that if I shouted again they'd gag me and give me only bread and water."

Suddenly she pulls away and puts a hand to her mouth. "I'm sorry."

"Don't be. It's much better to let it out." I open my arms for her.

She shrinks back. "I mean I'm sorry because . . ."

"Because what?"

"Because . . . Because I feel awful. I haven't had a shower for a week. Since before I played hockey."

I hug her and nuzzle her hair. "You're fine, just fine. Don't let these people think they're winning. We'll show them that we don't care."

I feel her warmth down my left side. Time stands still. My left arm is cramped, but I don't want to remove it from round her shoulder. Ever.

She breaks the silence. "I try and be brave, like Daddy, but when they come in here with those black masks on, it terrifies me."

"They only wear those balaclava masks because they're frightened of you," I say. "Remember that."

"Frightened of me?"

"Take the woman. She's lost her make up and she's frightened you'll see her without it. You and I will call her Mrs. Messy."

Emma starts to giggle.

"And the man who came here with me," I say, "is frightened that you'll see the bald patch on top of his head. We'll call him Mr. Baldy."

"What about the tall young man?" she asks.

"He's frightened you'll see his pimples."

"We'll call him Master Spotty."

"Right!"

"And the horrible man with a moustache?"

"He's so ugly that he's frightened you'll laugh if you see his face."

"Mr. Ugly!" she says, and laughs.

She can have no idea how that tinkling laughter fills me with joy.

She wipes the tears from her cheeks with the back of her hand. "I haven't even got a handkerchief."

"Take mine."

"Thanks." She stands up, blows her nose, and holds out the handkerchief.

I too get to my feet. "Keep it, please."

She smiles her thanks. "Will they let me go now that you've brought the ransom?"

I can't raise her hopes. "I think they want some more money. But don't worry, I'll do all within my power to get you released as soon as possible."

"If I'm not free, will you come and see me tomorrow?"

"I'm kept chained to a wall, like you, but I'll try and persuade them to let me see you."

"Oh, please come." She looks at me in the way Jill used to when she twisted me round her little finger.

"I'll come even if I have to break the chain with my bare hands."

Her snub Darcy nose wrinkles with pleasure. "I think I'm going to like you."

Oh Emma, when we're free I'm going to make up for all these lost years, I promise you. I'll devote my life to you. I just know that we'll have so much fun together.

She comes close and whispers. "Who exactly are you?"

How I long to tell her, but these aren't the right circumstances. Not just yet. I bite my lip. "Father Joe Darcy."

She screws up her face in exasperation. "Who are you really?"

How the devil does she know that I'm not Joe?

"You look a bit like him," Emma says, "but I've met the real Father Joe."

My heart sinks. I put my finger to my lips. "Where?"

"New York," she says in a low voice. "Mum used to take me on holiday to see Aunt Elizabeth and Uncle Glenn."

The words are knife thrusts to the solar plexus. How

much of the cover story that Jill "invented" for me is actually true?

She puts a hand over her mouth to stifle a giggle.

"What's so funny?" I demand.

"You look as though you've seen a ghost."

"I didn't know you knew him," I say lamely.

"Father Joe lives only five minutes' drive away from Waldo Avenue. Sometimes we went to St. Brendan's, sometimes he came over to Aunt Elizabeth's. We often went for walks along the river. Mum usually took me." She gives me a conspiratorial look. "I think she hoped I'd become a Catholic as well."

"As well?"

"As well as her. She's a Catholic."

The knife twists and drains all strength from me. "Since when?"

"As long as I can remember, though I know she wasn't one when she married Daddy. Daddy won't let her take me to her church in London." She peers at me. "Is it important?"

I shake my head. No, I think bitterly, it's not important. It's not important that the woman I gave up the faith for has become a Catholic herself. "When did she first meet Father Joe?"

"I'm not sure. No, wait. Father Joe once joked that he'd met me before I was born, when Mum first came to see him."

When Mum first came to see him! Jill knew that she was pregnant, by me, when she left for that fateful trip to stay with her sister—the convert who is more Catholic than the Pope, Jill said—in order "to find some space, to try and sort out my life." And I had told her that Joe's parish was only three miles from Riverdale. The good priest Father Darcy must have counseled her that what God hath put together let no man, not even his brother, put asunder. He must have made a big impression for her to continue to visit him, for her to become a Catholic. This is worse than if Joe had betrayed me to the IRA. Then he would have robbed me only of the last twenty years or so of life. Instead he's stolen seventeen years of my prime, of living with the woman I loved and fathering this beautiful child with the Darcy black hair and the Darcy snub nose.

"As you're not Father Joe," Emma whispers, "who are you?"

Chapter ✛ Thirty

The whitewashed walls of the cell close in on me, reflecting and redoubling my anger. I take off the priest's collar and fling it to the stone floor.

Who am I? I would be Emma's father, and she would be free. If Joe hadn't betrayed me. If Jill hadn't swallowed all that Catholic morality. If she hadn't gone back to Maitland.

I stalk the length of chain three paces up and down my prison. The same fraudulent Maitland who failed to provide back up when I put my life on the line with these terrorists. These sadistic bombers who are using my daughter to fight their war with the British. And I've got five days before Joe returns to St. Brendan's. Five days to rescue Emma.

I'm not going to figure out how to do it in a rage like this. I sit down on the cot and take long deep breaths until I calm down.

One possibility can be eliminated: I'm not going to escape with Emma while I'm chained here. When the Chief brought me back, he called it the bullpen. That explains its solid construction. And if a bull can't wrench the chain from its bolt deep in the brick wall, there's no point in my trying.

Where Emma is held, however, the prospects are different. Those twenty wooden steps lead up to a loft covering half the floor area of an ancient barn. The loft is divided into two. The front part is an open wooden platform stretching the width of the barn. The rear part is closed off by a wall made of vertical tongue and grooved planks, with a door of similar construction in its center. This wall doesn't match the rest of the building; it appears to be a later addition, but old and warped enough to suggest that the planks can be prized apart. The door is locked only by a metal bolt from the outside. The wall opposite the brick wall, and the gable wall facing the plank wall, are made of old weathered horizontal clapboard in an even worse state of repair than the tongue and grooved wall. Removing boards should present no problem. In the gable wall is a padlocked door also made of old clapboard—presumably the door through which hay was taken in to or out of the loft—and this also offers a means of escape. The roof is similar to mine, but easily reached from the loft floor: taking out the exposed roof tiles above the rafters should be easy.

Then there's the floor of the barn itself. The Chief warned me to be careful where I stepped because it was cluttered with rubbish. The rubbish is farming debris, a source of potential tools and weapons.

The escape strategy becomes clear: I must persuade these people to transfer me to the loft in which Emma is held, and then I must find a means of releasing Emma from her manacle.

"Your post execution lunch," says the masked Woman handing me a tray over the lower half of the stable door.

I mustn't think of her as a sadistic bitch. I've got to try and establish a relationship with her, find where she's vulnerable, and work on that. "It doesn't look as appetizing as the pre-execution supper," I say as I take the sandwiches of white bread and the mug of sickly sweet tea. Her hands are neither soft nor calloused, fingernails neither long nor painted. Could she be a nurse?

"You haven't lost your sense of humor, then?" she says.

"I was convinced I was going to lose my head."

She comes into the bullpen and lounges with her back against the peeling white-painted brickwork. She wears the same tight black jeans and black leather boots as yesterday, but a blue woollen sweater has replaced the black cotton turtleneck beneath her leather jacket. She's holding a gun, but loosely and not in a threatening manner. "You didn't grovel for mercy, I'll say that for you."

"A priest has to accept the will of God."

"Then it's a good job we're not all priests."

I smile. "Perhaps you're right." I take a bite from a sandwich. "What will you do when the struggle is over?" I ask after I've swallowed the tasteless stuff.

She shrugs. "I haven't given it a thought."

"Will you go back to what you did before?"

"I doubt it. The war changes you." Her voice is calm, matter-of-fact.

I nod sympathetically. "How long did you live over here?"

"Why do you ask?"

"If I shut my eyes I'd think it was an Englishwoman talking to me."

"It comes in useful at times."

"I'm sure it does." Although she's relaxed, she's been careful to tell me nothing. She's been well trained. How can I pierce the guard? "Don't think of me as an enemy. I come from an Irish republican family."

She says nothing. The black balaclava hides any expression.

"What about you?" I prompt.

"What about me?"

"Is your family republican, or was it the hunger strikes that converted you to the cause?"

"Let's just say they reminded me whose side I'm on."

"I suppose it's the same with your friend, the one you said helps you keep discipline."

She laughs. "The Brits recruited him."

"Excuse me?"

"The Brits interned his father in '71. His da wasn't IRA, but they thought every Catholic was a terrorist back then. When my comrade protested the Brits beat him to pulp. He's been stiffing them ever since."

I shake my head. "So many innocent people have suffered. The sooner the British leave Ireland the better for everyone."

She tucks the gun into her jacket pocket and comes and sits on the end of the cot. No body odor mingles with the smell of cheap perfume. She's been able to shower and change her clothes.

Her large brown eyes give me a quizzical look, as though she's undecided. "Are they still saying that in America?"

She's responding well. Now's the chance to steer the conversation. "The vast majority of Americans—not just Irish Americans—were with us before the Cheltenham bombing. But when innocent people suffer support turns against us."

"It's the Irish people who've suffered," she says defiantly.

"You don't have to tell me that. But innocent people on both sides suffer. Like the girl you've kidnapped. I'm very worried about her."

"What's the problem?"

"I'm not sure you realize how stressed the poor girl is. As a woman . . ."

"Don't tell me how stressed the poor wee pet is," she sneers. "If she'd been born on Derry's east bank; if she'd seen the marchers in their bowler hats, white gloves, and orange sashes; if she'd heard the wailing of the pipes, the battle call of the flutes, and the frenzied rattling thunder of the lambeg drum; if she'd been threatened every day she went to school by boys shouting 'Kill a Taig a day and keep the Pope away'; if she'd seen petrol bombs thrown through the windows of her home in the middle of the night, forcing her ma and da to flee—even though da was English—then your pampered Miss High and Mighty would know what stress is all about."

She's slipping from me. "I sympathize with you, you know that. But Emma wasn't responsible for what happened to you. Surely you, as a woman, have some sympathy for the child?"

"I've no sympathy to spare for the children of our oppressors."

"Two wrongs can never make a right. Emma is an innocent in all this."

She stands up in front of me, legs astride, hands on hips. "Listen, you, I get sick up to here with all this sympathy talk. Why should a girl from England have greater value than a girl from Derry, or West Belfast, or Armagh?"

"As a priest I appeal to you . . ."

"You appeal to me neither as soldier nor priest."

"It's in your own interests," I insist.

"What is?"

"Emma has bottled up her fear, but if it bursts out you'll have a terrible problem with her."

"What's your game?"

I try to adopt the kindly but firm tone of a parish priest. "If you were to lock me in the same cell as the child, I could reassure her, prevent her from becoming hysterical and uncontrollable."

She laughs. "So that's it. And I thought you fancied young boys. If you really are a priest, then I'm sure our chief wouldn't want to encourage a Bishop of Galway situation, would he, now?" She picks up the lunch tray and takes it out of the bullpen. Before closing the upper stable door she says, "Look upon staying in here as a penance for your sins. I take it you have committed sin some time in your life?"

Chapter ✢ Thirty-one

ONCE WE ACCEPT that the purpose of human existence is to know, love, and serve God in this life and to be happy with him forever in the next, the real meaning of sin becomes clear. It is not just a breach of the laws of God governing and directing human beings. It is an offense against God himself, a rejection of our Creator's infinite love in favor of some created finite satisfaction. If the sinner is truly sorry for the offense, resolves to avoid not only the sin but also the occasions of that sin, and makes atonement for the offense, then, through the grace of Christ's sacrifice on the cross for our salvation, the repentant sinner is reunited with God. If, however, he dies unrepentant, the sinner remains separated from the love of God for all eternity. That is the pain of hell.

I need reminding about sin and penance like I need a hole in the head. But this is only a role I'm playing. I pick up the priest's collar from the floor where I threw it this morning and put it round my neck. Father Joe Darcy must see the Chief. He's my only hope of getting transferred to Emma's loft.

* * *

"You wanted to see me, Father," says the Chief after the Boy has cleared away the remains of the supper and passed on my message. Rain beats against the shutters of the bullpen window and the Chief's tweed jacket and brown cord pants are wet. The black balaclava mask is dry.

"It's about the girl," I begin.

"If it's to ask to move in with her, then that's out of the question."

The corners of his thin-lipped mouth are turned down. He'll be implacable on this. I've got to find a way through to him. What kind of man lies behind that black balaclava mask? His voice carries an unnerving assurance; it's the voice of a man used to being obeyed, the voice of a man with the power over life and death, the voice of a man who would order the bombing of innocent civilians in Warrington and Cheltenham while talking about peace with the Brits. Yet almost certainly he's a Catholic who goes to mass every Sunday, goes to confession and communion, is accepted by the Church, despite his refusal to renounce violence—the same Church that excluded me because I refused to renounce love. I focus on his wedding ring. "In the name of God, she's an innocent child. Don't let the woman humiliate her by making her strip in front of that man with the moustache."

The small steely blue irises set in large whites stare at me through the eyeholes of his mask. He says nothing. The silence is unnerving.

"Let the child have a shower or a proper wash," I say. "Give her a change of underclothes and something decent to wear, like a tracksuit, to cover herself, instead of being leered at by that man."

His short stubby hands clench. "If he lays a finger on her he'll be courtmartialled and shot. You have my word on that, Father."

"Let's try and avoid that situation. It would be better if he didn't go near her. He frightens her."

"I'll think about it."

"If you won't permit me to stay in the same cell to look after the girl, then at least let me join her at mealtimes to persuade her to eat. She hadn't touched her breakfast this morning."

He lowers his eyes in thought.

"Have you no compassion? On my grandfather's grave it's not much to ask."

He raises his eyes slowly and examines me. "You may see her tomorrow."

Thank God for that.

"Our people in the Bronx spoke well of Father Joe, of help given to volunteers who escaped to the United States."

How would Joe respond? "I do my best to keep up the family tradition."

"Your father?"

I give what I hope appears as a rueful smile. "Only in sentiment. He's a law-abiding cop in the NYPD. If he knew what we do at Tír na nOg I don't think he'd approve. It's sad, because his father was active in the Clann na Gael."

"You said your grandfather fought in the Civil War."

The Chief doesn't miss a trick. He must have debriefed the Boy after I'd talked to him Sunday lunchtime. "That was my grandfather on my mother's side."

"Did you know him well?"

"No. He was killed by the Free Staters."

He nods. "We lost good men that way. Collins was a fool to accept Partition and split the movement."

"My grandmother said Collins got what he deserved."

The corners of his mouth curl in what passes for a smile. "The bit about winning national freedom you quoted from Pádraig Pearse continues, 'And I know of no other way than the way of the sword: history records no other, reason and experience suggest no other.' Was it your grandmother who introduced you to Pearse?"

"It was mainly my mother and my uncle who taught me Irish history and literature."

He leans back against the stable door. "Long Kesh was my university. That's the one thing I thank the Brits for, the three years I spent in detention." His eyes look through the holes in the mask to some distant time; his voice is relaxed. "When the unionists smashed the civil rights marches back in '69, and the Brits sent in their troops to protect us Catholics, I knew instinctively what to do. But on the street you just react to what you see and hear, there's no opportunity to think. In the cages I had time to read a lot, to debate with the older republicans, to go into things much deeper, to look at what was happening in the context of a political problem, to question the morality of various tactics and directions."

I seize the opening. "Do you, as a Catholic, believe that kidnapping this innocent girl is moral?"

He doesn't hesitate. "If I believed what I am doing was wrong from the point of view of being a Catholic, I wouldn't be part of it. I believe God understands that in order to free Ireland from British tyranny we're forced to use the only means available to us."

He might be my CIA instructor at the Farm convincing me that the end justifies the means. "How do you reconcile that with what the Church teaches about killing and kidnapping?" the priest I'm impersonating asks.

He pauses before saying, "Do you, Father, accept everything the Church says?"

It's my turn to pause. At least I had the honesty to give up the faith because I couldn't accept what the Church said about loving a woman who is married to someone else. "Now that you have the ransom, you must let the girl go. You gave your word."

"Our condition was that Edward Maitland brought the ransom."

"To put his daughter through the torment of a kidnap like this is a cruel way to go about killing him."

The Chief stands up straight and folds his arms across his chest. "If we'd wanted to eliminate him we could have had him shot or blown up in London. We want to talk to him, on his own."

This negates all the assumptions I've made about an assassination trap for Maitland. "Why?"

Those penetrating eyes stare at me from the holes in the black balaclava. He comes to a decision. "We want to talk with him about what scuppered the peace process. We want to explore ways in which it can be restored."

"I'm relieved to hear it, but I don't understand what it has to do with Edward Maitland."

"Because of his job."

"Why him?"

"Edward Maitland is MI5's top man working against us."

"You're kidding." It pains me to refer to him as Emma's father, but I need to tease out as much of their plan as possible. "Even if he is, I don't understand why you kidnapped his daughter."

"Since the Cheltenham bombing the Brits have broken off all contact with us, even the unofficial contacts we had before the ceasefire. We need to speak to Maitland, face to face. We relied on him bringing the ransom personally, as we instructed, if he believed his daughter was at risk."

So much for relying on Edward Maitland. "Why Maitland, even if he is MI5? Why not a government minister?"

The thin lips revealed by the mask's mouth hole turn down in disdain. "Government ministers don't know the half of what goes on in the Six Counties, nor do they want to know."

My mind flashes back to the meeting of the Joint

Intelligence Committee before Christmas, and the file marked "Not for Ministers' Eyes".

"If we can persuade Maitland that the IRA wasn't responsible for the Cheltenham bomb," the Chief says, "then I believe that we can get the peace process restarted."

"Was it a hardline splinter group?"

"We've accounted for the movements of all our units. None was responsible for the Cheltenham bomb. We need to convince Maitland."

So it really was the Iraqis or another foreign intelligence agency targeting Clarence Thomson or the NSA unit at GCHQ. But Maitland was scathing about my theories. "How can you convince him?"

The Chief pauses once more. "The Cheltenham bomb has loyalist fingerprints all over it."

"Loyalist?"

"Just like the Dublin and Monaghan bombings." He stares at me. "Don't tell me you don't know about them."

I shake my head.

"That's just typical. The British and American media publicize Enniskillen, Warrington, and all the other IRA bombings, but ignore the biggest loss of life in a single operation since the Troubles began."

I really don't know what he's talking about.

"Three bombs exploded without warning in the middle of the rush hour in Dublin, killing twenty-six and injuring over two hundred and fifty."

His eyes harden. "Now catch this. After the bombs went off the Garda sealed the border with the North. Then another bomb exploded at Monaghan, killing seven and injuring fifty. When the Garda rushed from their border patrols to help the injured, the Dublin bombers escaped back to the North. To this day no group has admitted responsibility and no one has been convicted. But we all know who did it."

"Who?"

"The four organizers were identified as members of the Ulster Volunteer Force."

"I never knew the Protestant paramilitaries went in for bombings."

The Chief snorts. "At the time they were using Double Diamond beer kegs filled with explosives and primed with a black powder fuse. But the Dublin bombing was extremely sophisticated: three car bombs with timing devices that exploded within ninety seconds of each other; explosives mixed with such consistency and detonated so efficiently that no trace remained. Neither the UVF nor the UFF has carried out a bombing like that before or since. So who do you think put the bombs together? Who do you think planned the whole operation?"

"You tell me."

"The UVF killers were run by Four Field Survey Troop, the cover name for an SAS-trained special duties team located at Castledillon."

"Why bomb civilians in Dublin?"

"You have to understand the political situation in 1974, Father. Harold Wilson had just been elected prime minister in Britain. His Labor Party pushed the Sunningdale Agreement, which made unionists share power with republicans in the Six Counties and gave Dublin a role in the North for the first time. The Wilson government planned to phase out internment and transfer the British Army's role to the police. There was even talk of withdrawing British troops altogether." He looks at me. "Now do you see it?"

I play dumb.

"It's simple, Father. Hardliners in the British security forces thought Wilson was handing us victory on a plate. They instigated a loyalist general strike in the North and loyalist bombings in the South. A week later the Sunningdale Agreement collapsed."

The Chief unfolds his arms. "Now they fear this peace process will lead to a united Ireland and so they plant an 'IRA' bomb in Cheltenham to end it."

"I find it difficult to believe that members of the British security forces operate against their own government." But even as I say these words I know them to be untrue. Not only had members of MI5 worked to undermine British government policy in the past, they had tried to bring the government down. And I had helped them.

Chapter ✣ Thirty-two

IT ALL BEGAN with James Jesus Angleton.

After I'd completed training for the clandestine service at the Farm in 1972, the company assigned me to the United Kingdom Branch of Western European Division. I guess I'd been rewarded with this plum because of the high grades I'd scored and, in particular, the aptitude I'd shown for the latest electronic surveillance techniques. A year after joining the branch I received a phone call. "This is Mr. Angleton's secretary. Mr. Angleton would like to see you."

For the first time since the polygraph test I was plagued by anxiety. None of my year's intake had ever set eyes on him, but we were all in awe of the legendary James Jesus Angleton, who had headed CIA Counter Intelligence Staff for the past nineteen years. It was said that he was convinced there was a Soviet mole within the Agency. But how could he suspect me?

"Did you hear me, Mr. Darcy?"

"Yes," I stammered. "I don't know where to go."

"Second floor. Room 43 in C corridor. I'll expect you in five minutes."

My first impression was of this massive desk, cluttered high with files and papers, and behind it, with his back to the wall, a gaunt, almost consumptive figure dressed in a gray vested suit and enveloped in a miasma of cigarette smoke. He peered out at me over the top of large spectacles perched on a long nose below slicked-back graying hair parted just to the left of center.

"Sit down, Mr. Darcy."

"Yes, sir."

He looked up from a file, exhaled cigarette smoke, and said, "Are you anti-British?"

"No, sir," I said, which wasn't strictly true.

He took another draw on his cigarette and read the file. "Is your brother still involved in subversive activities?"

"No, sir," I replied. "After he was released from jail he went to work in the social action department of New York Diocesan Catholic Charities. He found he had a vocation for the priesthood. He's at Dunwoodie Seminary now."

He peered over the rim of his spectacles. "That didn't stop the Berrigan brothers, or the Melville brothers. Strange that subversive priests have subversive brothers. Is it something in the genes, perhaps?"

The interview was going badly. "I haven't seen Joe since I joined the company, sir. And with respect, I don't think genetics has anything to do with political attitudes. I'm happy for you to judge me on my record."

He picked up another file. "What's your cryptonym?"

I hesitated.

"Look, son, I'm on the bigot list, so don't make my life any more difficult than it already is."

"I took an oath not to disclose that cryptonym, sir, and so I'll be grateful if you look it up."

For a moment I thought he was going to hit me. Then his cadaverous features creased into a smile. "I do believe you're as good as the reports say you are." He slid across a packet of Virginia Slims. "I've found the man I'm looking for."

"No thank you, sir."

He raised his eyebrows.

"I mean I don't smoke, sir."

He smiled, pushed the files away, and leaned back in his chair. "I take it you've been briefed on procedures for liaising with friendly intelligence services?"

"Yes, sir," I said. "We learned all that at the Farm."

He looked me in the eyes. "Forget it. There are two things you must remember. First, there is no such thing as a friendly intelligence service. Second, all liaison services are penetrated by the Soviets, and thus all bilateral operations are compromised from the start." He stubbed out his cigarette. "That goes double for the British."

He took another cigarette from the pack and lit it. "I need someone in London, someone the British don't know is CIA, someone who can handle our latest electronics, someone who can stay calm under pressure. I take it you have no objections to being posted to London?"

"No, sir."

"You can call me Jim."

"Yes, sir."

This intense man placed his elbows on his desk, put his fingers to his chin while smoke from his cigarette curled up to wreath his face, and lowered his voice to draw me closer. "What I'm about to tell you, you won't find in the related missions directive for London."

I leaned forward to catch his words.

"Just over ten years ago a KGB major crossed over to us

from Finland. What he told me corroborated information supplied by a defector from the Polish intelligence service two years before: Britain's new prime minister, Harold Wilson, was a Soviet agent."

His hands moved away from his face while his fingers—except those clenching his cigarette—opened out and spun a web of conspiracy. "I offered a copy of my file to MI5 if they kept the information to themselves. Roger Hollis, Five's director general, refused, saying that he would be duty bound to show it to the prime minister—the very person under suspicion!"

I was well and truly ensnared.

"When we crosschecked our files," Angleton continued, "the reason that MI5 refused to take action became clear. All the evidence pointed toward Hollis himself being a Soviet agent."

None of these mindboggling disclosures was in the top secret files I'd seen at UK Branch. They explained why Wilson's Labor government had refused to send even a token force to support us in Vietnam.

"At the end of the sixties," Angleton said, "two Czech intelligence officers came over in unrelated defections. They named several Labor members of parliament and labor union bosses as successful recruits." His bright, intelligent eyes observed me closely. "You see where this is leading, John?"

"I'm not sure, sir."

"Go back over the reports from London station for this year. You'll find a series of industrial actions are bringing the Conservative government in Britain to its knees. Then," he said with a triumphant flourish of his smoking cigarette, "correlate the bosses of those unions with the names Frolik and August gave us, and you see that all this is a carefully coordinated conspiracy to bring down the Conservative government and replace it once more with Labor, led by none other than Harold Wilson."

The implications were hitting so hard I was reeling.

"What you have to understand, John, is that while we play poker, the Soviets play chess. We must expose them before they control the board."

"Surely we can take this information to MI5 now?" I asked.

Angleton's thin lips curled. "Goleniewski supplied us with an extremely detailed profile of a mole within MI5. Five's new director general is the perfect fit. The point is, John, we simply daren't risk another Hollis fiasco."

"What's the solution?"

He smiled. "You are." He lit yet another cigarette. By now my sinuses were aching with the smoke, but I didn't care. "If we're to prevent the Soviets bringing down the British government and replacing it with their stooges, we must have more than the allegations of defectors. We must have proof. I work closely with MI5's counterespionage branch, K Directorate. The people I've found most reliable are in K5, which operates against Soviet Bloc recruitment in Britain. They know what the Soviets are up to and they see MI5 management as, at best, too complacent and too squeamish: not prepared to do what needs to be done."

He pulled a new file from the stack. "I want you to go to London under deep cover. It'll be risky, so you need diplomatic protection, but out of the political liaison department where the Brits know our people are placed. They don't know you, and you'll go undeclared as an assistant labor attaché. Once there you'll liaise unofficially with K5 and show them this file on Wilson. Any questions?"

"Yes, sir. When do I start?"

"Within twenty-four hours of landing in London, telephone K5's Edward Maitland at his home and say, 'Our mutual friend, Jim, has given me some flies to help you catch a big trout.' "

It was more than a week after that phone call before I found an opportunity to show Maitland the file. I resented the way he swept me off to a cricket match at Lord's and back to his apartment for dinner, and then had the stupidity to insist I visit MI5's registry and inspect the women who worked there.

"Edward," I said, "I haven't been declared. The authorities here think I'm a regular diplomat, remember?"

A sardonic smile flickered across his lean, superior British face. "My dear John, if you were an unofficial CIA operative with whom I was working without sanction from MI5 management, the last place I would bring you to would be the office. Double bluff, old boy. Fear not, it will simply confirm your cover as an assistant labor attaché who's receiving a briefing from us on the British labor movement." He smirked. "With the bonus of showing you the stable where the Jills of this world are quartered."

Only later did I realize that his flamboyance was a façade. He was using that week to expose me to several of his colleagues and check me out. I must have come through the test, because he did call round to my Boydell Court apartment one evening dressed anonymously rather than in that lurid striped blazer he'd sported at the cricket match or the bright pink shirt and flowered tie he wore at the office.

He closed the file Angleton had given me and nodded to himself. "This confirms our own sources. We had a defector-in-place, Oleg Lyalin, who told us that his friend, a Lithuanian called Richardas Vaygauskas, was also KGB. Vaygauskas told Lyalin that he was in regular contact with a Lithuanian émigré, Joseph Kagan, who is a close friend of

Harold Wilson. We believe that Kagan is an illegal running a communist cell at the heart of the Labor Party. He liaises with Marcia Williams, Wilson's political secretary."

"Isn't this all circumstantial?" I asked.

"And I suppose it's a complete coincidence that the Wilson gang have made regular trips to Iron Curtain countries for years under the guise of promoting East-West trade, and that Wilson himself criticized the government for expelling Vaygauskas and one hundred and four of his fellow spies we'd identified—one of our greatest triumphs since the War. Believe me, Jim Angleton isn't wrong. Wilson is a bloody menace, but those lickspittles on the fifth floor don't have the balls to act."

"We need harder evidence."

"That's the problem," he said gloomily. "Without management's agreement we can't get it. Every microphone we use is recorded in the A Branch Index."

I relished the opportunity of being topside for once. "Not this box of tricks." I pulled out a suitcase from under my bed and opened it on the living room floor. Maitland's eyes devoured the equipment.

"What on earth are the two umbrellas for?" he asked.

"Unfold them," I said as casually as I was able, "and you have a receiver and a transmitter dish. These other little beauties are cavity microphones operated from outside by microwaves, and so no cables are needed."

"John Darcy," he said, "I think I'm beginning to like you. We're going to have some fun together."

"Can you install the microphones? I can't use our Staff D."

"No problem. We have a list of professional burglars we use when we want an extra cut out for plausible deniability."

"What's your leak probability assessment?"

"My what?"

"What is the percentage probability of someone finding out?"

"In plain English, fuck all. You see, my dear John, no one knows about our work because it is secret, and the reason that it is secret is that no one knows about it."

What I saw in London corroborated the allegations of Angleton's defectors and the opinion of Maitland and his friends in K Branch. By February 1974 industrial action had brought Britain to a standstill. Prime Minister Heath was forced to call a general election on the question of who runs Britain: the elected government or the undemocratic (and, I believed, Soviet-controlled) unions.

The bugging devices I'd supplied, however, produced nothing incriminating, and so Edward arranged for me to give unattributable background to selected journalists from *The Times* and the *Daily Telegraph*. But to no avail. The Labor Party gained a plurality of seats in the House of Commons, and Harold Wilson returned to power in March as prime minister with the support of the Liberal Party.

"Jesus Christ," said Edward, over dinner at his apartment. "Have you seen what the bastard's done? Paid off the miners, and put Michael Foot in charge of employment and Wedgwood Benn in charge of industry. No doubt they'd prefer the title 'commissar' instead of 'minister'."

"He's suspended arms sales to Chile and given asylum to Marxists fleeing the country after Allende's overthrow," I added grimly.

"Wilson's no fool," Maitland said. "He knows his minority government can't last long. I'll wager he'll call a snap election to gain an overall majority. We've got to stop him."

It was no longer just fun and games. We were in deadly earnest.

*   *   *

We took risks. In the early hours of one Sunday morning, when the Wilsons were away on an overseas visit, I became an eccentric American tourist who approached the policeman on duty outside the Wilson home in Lord North Street and asked the way to Westminster Abbey which, friends had assured me, I must see in moonlight. The kindly bobby took me to the corner of the street. "Down here, sir. No more than five minutes' walk, right opposite the Houses of Parliament."

It gave enough time for Edward's burglar to enter Wilson's house.

This break-in, and subsequent ones at the office in Buckingham Palace Road where Wilson stored personal papers, and at the offices of Wilson's personal legal advisor, failed to produce the evidence we were seeking.

The campaign widened. Edward told me that his group could count on the support of at least thirty serving and retired MI5 officers. Half a dozen of the most active met for dinner at Edward's apartment. After Jill cleared away the plates and Edward brought out the brandy, he said, "We are agreed that a Soviet agent must not be allowed to continue as prime minister?"

Amid the murmurs of assent I said, "But we don't have enough evidence to nail Wilson."

"If we are agreed on the ends," Maitland said, "we must seek other means."

All eyes turned to him. After offering round cigars, he said, "The break-in at Marcia Williams's place in Great Missenden reminded me that she has two bastards of which the Great British Public know nothing."

"What are you getting at, Edward?" asked one of the retired officers, a huge man whose face was ruddied by alcohol.

Maitland lit his cigar, inhaled, and blew out a long stream of gray smoke. "The age of one of them is consistent with conception having taken place while Wilson and his political secretary were in Moscow together. Rather appropriate, don't you think?"

"Edward," said Jill, "you told me that the father was a political journalist."

"True," said Maitland, "but how many people know that? Dear Marcia has guarded the secrets of her sordid little life even more closely than our director general guards his drinks cabinet. We can turn that to our advantage."

"No newspaper will run a story about Wilson having an affair with his political secretary if it isn't true," said a pinch-faced colleague.

"No British newspaper will run that particular story," Maitland corrected him. "And that is where John comes in."

He poured out more brandy, and said to me, "I'll give you enough details to plant a story in newspapers in the States. Let them know that the British prime minister and his associates are under investigation by MI5. Once the story breaks in the States, our newspapers will report that the American press are publishing disclosures about Wilson and an alleged affair with his political secretary who is suspected of being at the center of a Soviet spy ring. It'll be enough to bring this government down."

For the first time my conscience began to prick. I put down my glass. "Edward, do you ever have doubts about what we're doing? I mean, here you are, a civil servant, trying to overthrow the government you're supposed to serve?"

Despite the drink we'd consumed, he was stone-cold sober. "No, my dear John, I am not a civil servant, I am a crown servant. And to serve my monarch and my country, I am prepared to fight subversion with subversion. Do you not approve?"

I approved wholeheartedly.

The one thing that assuages my guilt is that the smear campaign against Wilson failed. But as I lie on an uncomfortable cot in this bullpen, I'm troubled by other memories awakened by allegations the Chief made last night. I watch pre-dawn slivers of gray form against the black of the shutter boards and try to remember where I'd heard the name Castledillon before. But it's inconceivable. The idea that the British Security Service was responsible for terrorist bombings is just as much conspiracy theory as the notion that Harold Wilson was controlled by the Soviets. The Chief is as paranoid about the Brits as I was about the communists.

Chapter ✤ Thirty-three

THE SLIVERS OF gray pale and diffuse to fill the bullpen with the half-light that indicates daytime in this permanently shuttered prison. My third day in captivity: four days left before Joe returns to St. Brendan's and blows my cover.

I stretch stiff limbs and begin planning for my visit to Emma. First release her from the manacle, and then organize the best method and time to break out of the loft and escape from here.

The stable doors creak open and both halves of the bullpen door swing back.

A tray is thrust through. "Take yer breakfast."

"Your chief said that I could see the girl today," I protest.

"Do what I say, or else."

It's easy to see how the Killer frightens Emma. It's not just his language or his appearance—the black balaclava mask, Wrangler jacket and jeans, and pointed-toe cowboy boots—rather it is the empty gray eyes behind the holes in the mask and the dilation of his pupils when angry or excited which convey an eagerness to carry out the threats he utters.

I take the breakfast tray from him. I mustn't show my own anger at being denied the visit to Emma. After putting down the tray by the cot I stand facing him, look into his eyes, and say in a relaxed voice, "I don't think you'd be such a big man without your gun."

He just stops his left hand before it reaches instinctively for the Smith & Wesson stuck in his pearl-buckled belt. "And I don't think you'd be such a big fella without that dog collar," is his imitative rejoinder.

I smile and remove the clerical collar. "Does a priest need a uniform to prove he is a man of God?"

"Don't come the clever fucker with me. And don't think I don't know you been tellin' tales to the Chief. I'll get me own back on you, so I will."

Good. My complaints about his behavior with Emma have created dissension in their ranks. "Before you bring me hot water and a towel for washing, I'll be obliged if you empty the slop bucket."

"I might just empty it over yer fuckin' head."

I stare at him, daring him to do it, knowing that he'll get into further trouble with the Chief if he abuses a priest. He backs down. A small victory.

No small victory over the Killer can compensate for not seeing Emma. Why has the Chief gone back on his word? I sit on the cot and hope that this is just a glitch, that I will be allowed to see her later.

At my age it's not often I want time to pass quickly. Now that I do it mocks me by standing still. No sunlight marks the passing hours: dullness seeps through the gaps in the shutter to suspend the bullpen in a gray limbo.

I count forty three rows of bricks from the base of the window wall to the top. If the height of each brick plus mortar is three inches, then the height of this wall is 129 inches, or ten feet nine inches. The apex of the gable wall is seventy rows, which is 210 inches or seventeen feet six inches, high. The apex of the roof is therefore six feet nine inches higher than the height of the wall. The distance along the gable wall from its end point to the midpoint beneath the apex is nine bricks in length. If the length of a brick plus mortar is nine inches, then this is eighty one inches or six feet nine inches. So the height of the gable is equal to half its length, which means the angle of the roof is forty five degrees.

I wonder how much time this calculation has taken. It contributes nothing to an escape plan, but I must try to keep mentally alert. What other mind games can I play? I could estimate the height of the wall in which the bullpen door is set and use trigonometry to estimate the distance between the bullpen door and the outer stable door, or I could count the total number of bricks in each wall. I prefer to visualize what will happen if I meet the Killer in single combat.

At long last hinges creak, and then the top half of the bullpen door opens.

"Take the tray."

The Killer thrusts a tray of sandwiches at me.

"I demand to see the Chief."

"You do what yer fuckin' told. Take the fuckin' tray."

"Not before I see the Chief."

"Suit yerself." He withdraws the tray and slams the bullpen door shut behind him.

I slump on the cot and stare at the whitewashed wall. So much for my escape strategy. The tiny voice in my head warns against depression. But each setback makes it more difficult to resist. I hold my head in my hands and feel the prickles of three days' growth of beard. What must I look like? Lawrence Palmer? God forbid. I go through a session of Canadian Air Force exercises. My back feels the strain of the sit-up-and-twists, and the damned manacle makes the stationary run plus spreadeagle jumps difficult, but by visualising the Killer's eyes I'm just able to manage the number of repetitions graded for flying crew under thirty years old.

The room darkens. Rain begins to fall. Individual drops build up to a tattoo which is whipped into gusts that pound the shutters like the frenzied rattling thunder of the lambeg drum.

> Out of Ireland have we come.
> Great hatred, little room,
> Maimed us at the start.

Yeats had the measure of that cursed emerald isle.

After what seems an eternity the bar on the top half of the bullpen door slides back. The door opens and a semi-automatic pistol peers across the threshold. The lower half opens and the masked Boy follows the pistol into the bullpen. "I'm taking you to have supper with the girl," he says.

I *am* going to see Emma! I fasten on the priest's collar to reinforce the Boy's image of me.

"Put this on your head, please, Father." He holds out the black hood.

Although I can't see him, I sense the Boy crouching down in front of me. He turns a key in the lock and releases the manacle. How easy it would be to disarm him. But not until I know that Emma can be freed.

He guides me through the rain to the barn. The number of steps is the same as when the Chief took me, and so they haven't taken the precaution of using a circuitous route to disorient me.

After the Boy has opened the barn door and leaves me in order to close it behind him, I turn my back on him, quickly lift the hood, stumble forward, and fall on top of what I've spotted. I tuck the length of pipe inside my jacket, under my left armpit, and struggle to my feet before the Boy reaches me.

"I told you to wait for me, Father," the Boy says. "Give me your arm or you'll trip again."

I give him my right arm and he guides me up the wooden stairs to the loft.

He removes the hood. Emma's long black hair is shining and she's wearing a green nylon tracksuit with red and blue panels across the shoulders and chest and upper arms, but her face is white and tense.

"I hope you approve," the Boy says.

"Thanks," I reply, and turn to my lovely daughter. "I hope you like the color of the tracksuit. Harrods said I could take it back if you want to change it."

The tension in her face relaxes. She steps forward and gives me a hug. "Thank you . . . Father."

"Will you free Emma from her manacle for supper?" I ask the Boy.

"The Chief keeps that key."

That eliminates one possibility. "Will you let us eat alone, then? With Emma chained to the wall you're in no danger of losing your prisoner."

The Boy hesitates.

"For pity's sake," I say. "What's the problem? Bolt the door if you're so worried."

"Your supper's on the floor," he says. He backs out, closes the door behind him, and the bolt slides home.

"Are you OK, Emma?"

"It's so good to see you. I thought you were never coming."

I wink. "Didn't I say that I'd break the chain with my bare hands?"

A smile lights up her face.

White Aertex shirt, underpants, and bra hang over one of the collar beams between the rafters. "You look wonderful," I say. "Have you had a shower?"

"No. But Mrs. Messy brought a bowl of hot water, soap, shampoo, a flannel, and a towel."

"I told you these people are just ordinary human beings behind their masks. I'm sure you charmed her."

Emma giggles. "I don't think Mrs. Messy was very thrilled. When I asked her for a hairbrush she told me not to push my luck."

"And she failed to provide a bottle of champagne. I'll have to complain to the management of this hotel." Then, in a low voice, I say, "Keep talking." I kneel down and check the manacle round her ankle. It's too tight to maneuver off, and I still have nothing with which to pick locks.

"Let's start supper," I say out loud. "Bless us, O Lord, and these thy gifts which we are about to receive from thy bounty, through Christ our Lord. Amen."

I take a sandwich over to where the chain from Emma's manacle is fixed. "What happened when you went to Oxford for an interview?"

"How do you know about that?"

The chain is secured, not by a bolt fixed deep into a solid wall as with mine, but by a wrought iron bracket screwed into a low wall made of bricks that show signs of erosion, with loose and missing mortar between. "You'll be surprised." I remove the piece of steel pipe from inside my jacket. "How did you get on?"

She stares, fascinated. "Brilliant!"

I glance toward the door.

"St. Hilda's offered me a place if I get two As and a B at A-levels," she says out loud.

"That's your mother's old college, isn't it?" I say, trying to keep the level of my voice constant, despite straining to lever the bracket from the wall.

"How do you know that?"

"Keep talking," I mouth.

"I see," she says. "You're going to surprise me with what you know."

I stuff the rest of the sandwich into my mouth before trying to get a better purchase on the bracket. "What do you major in?"

"Pardon?"

"What's your main subject? English, like your mother?"

"No. Chemistry, physics, and maths."

A science major, as I was. If only she knew from whom she inherited her aptitude for science.

"Daddy was keen I went into science, like he did."

The hell he did. Maitland's only science was whatever basic math they taught at Sandhurst military academy.

"Daddy says a science background gives you so many more career options. Scientists can do all kinds of things. Look at Daddy. He's a very senior civil servant, whereas Mum, well, she hasn't done much with her English degree."

Emma gives me one of the mugs of tea. After a few sips, I hand it back to her and renew pressure on the bracket.

"Daddy's so clever. I wish I saw more of him. But when you've got such an important job like his I suppose you have to spend a lot of time at work."

In frustration I press down even harder. The pipe slips from the bracket, pitching me forward onto the floorboards.

"Hide the pipe," I whisper to Emma as I scramble to my knees before the bolt slides back from the door.

The Boy is holding his semiautomatic nervously. "What was that noise?"

"It's nothing," I say. "I'm afraid I fell over again. I've been getting these dizzy spells since the mock execution."

"Mock execution!" Emma gasps. "Was that the shot I heard yesterday?"

"It was nothing. I'll be OK if I just sit down a while."

"What mock execution?" Emma demands of the Boy.

"It was a kind of test," the Boy mumbles.

"It was nothing," I repeat to Emma. To the Boy I say, "Just give me another five minutes or so to recover."

Reluctantly he leaves and bolts the door behind him.

"Gosh, that was brilliant!" Emma whispers. "You almost convinced me."

"Would that performance have been a contender for the Morley Cup?"

"How do you know about the Morley Cup? Don't tell me. I'll be surprised at what you know about me. When this is over I'm going to find out about you."

And I'll be overjoyed to tell her. "What did you win the cup for?"

"I was Titania in the school play last year, *A Midsummer Night's Dream.*"

I test the clapboard of the gable wall, opposite the door I came through. "Your mother used to act, didn't she?"

"Only amateur, at Oxford. Nan—her mother—was a professional actress."

I prize one board up to make a gap. "Wasn't she a member of the National Theater?"

"How on earth do you know that? Nan was brilliant. She played with Laurence Olivier."

"In *Love for Love* at the Old Vic." There's a drop of

fifteen feet and the farmhouse is on this side of the barn. Damn.

"Now I really will have to find out how you know so much about me."

I hold Emma by the shoulders and whisper. "We haven't long, so listen carefully. I'm going to need a lot more time to free the bracket that fixes your chain to the wall. You've got to do some more acting."

"What do you want me to do?"

"When they bring your breakfast tomorrow, act hysterical. Scream that you want to see me. Can you do that?"

She nods eagerly.

"Good girl."

I move Emma's cot so that it covers the marks on the wall I've made near the bracket.

She stretches up and kisses me on the cheek—for the first time in my life! "Thank you ever so much," she whispers. "When we're free I'll tell Daddy everything you've done for me. He'll be ever so grateful."

Chapter ✣ Thirty-four

A HEAVY DOWNPOUR drenches the hood and a chill wind sticks the soaked material to my face, partly blocking nostrils and mouth and making it difficult to breathe. The Boy directs me from the barn through to the wet grass of the field.

Escape is going to be much more difficult than I first thought. It's vital I have every meal with Emma in order to prize the bracket free before Saturday, when Joe returns. We'll have to break out during supper and use the cover of darkness to escape the farm. More specifically, I must overpower whoever brings me for supper—probably the Boy—as early as possible, and secure and gag him to give us a half hour start before he's missed. If Emma's towel doesn't prove adequate for restraining him, I'll have to hit him hard enough to knock him out for at least half an hour.

"Be careful, Father," the Boy says as I bump into a gatepost. "Here, take my arm."

The only other way would be to break out of the bullpen in the middle of the night, and then break into the barn loft. Which is only possible if they leave me unmanacled.

We reach the shelter of the bullpen and I remove the dripping hood. The masked face of the Chief stares up at me. He is sitting on the cot with a foolscap notepad on the knee of his brown corduroy pants.

"Good evening, Father," he says.

The Boy looks at the Chief, who says to me, "I hope it won't be long now, Father, but, for your own good, you must remain secured."

I wonder how often he's said "it's for your own good" as he's given the order for a beating or a shooting. The Boy bends down, locks the manacle around my left ankle, and seals his fate for Friday suppertime.

The Chief nods for him to leave and pats the cot next to him.

All my instincts revolt against intimacy with this terrorist who is prepared to kill my daughter if he deems it necessary to achieve his goal. But my goal is best served by acting as a priest with Irish republican sympathies. I sit down and turn to face his black balaclava mask.

"Now, Father," he says, "you undertook this mission in order to obtain the girl's freedom."

"Right." And that is precisely what I will do at suppertime on Friday if I can unchain her.

"You also want to see a permanent peace in Ireland?"

"Of course I do." And the best way to achieve that is by putting terrorists like you behind bars and throwing away the key.

"Well, Father, I'm going to give you the opportunity to achieve both." The black wool of the balaclava accentuates the whites of the eyes that gaze at me through the mask holes. "I want you to write to Edward Maitland. Assure him that we only want to talk with him, without the politicians and the bureaucrats, about how we can restore the peace process. If he comes, I will guarantee his safe conduct and release you and his daughter."

If this proposal is genuine, then securing Emma's release by agreement puts her at much less risk than my escape plan. I return his gaze. "No harm will come to him or the girl?"

"You have my word."

How far can I trust this terrorist? "What can I say that will persuade him that it isn't a trap?"

"Why should we kill him? Like the Cheltenham bomb, it would defeat our whole strategy of giving up armed conflict in return for negotiating Ireland's freedom." The Chief's small irises gleam like polished steel. "Don't you see, Father? We've reached an historic turning point in the struggle for liberation. The will of colonial powers to enforce their rule has collapsed all round the world. The Russians have surrendered their empire in eastern Europe. The Brits have negotiated the transfer of Hong Kong to China. The Israelis have restored Palestinian lands to the PLO. Even the white supremacists in South Africa have handed over power to the ANC." His short stubby fingers grip my arm. "The tide of anticolonialism is unstoppable. We're determined to ride on the tide. We believe we can persuade the Irish and American governments that there'll only be a permanent end to violence in Ireland when there's a permanent demilitarisation, when the IRA and the loyalist paramilitaries are disbanded *and* the British army is withdrawn to Britain."

His words do have some logic, but there's a flaw. "From all I've heard, the loyalist paramilitaries will never disband unless they're certain that Northern Ireland will remain part of the United Kingdom."

The Chief relaxes his grip on my arm. "Some won't disarm, but they'll be marginalised, like the Afrikaner paramilitaries. The majority of Ulster unionists feel betrayed because the Brits have already talked to us. Once the message gets home that there will no longer be a British army to keep them in power, and that the United States will offer economic help to a united Ireland, they'll soon see where their best interests lie, just as the majority of white South African businessmen and politicians did. Mark my words, Father, provided we can keep Dublin and the Irish American lobby with us, we'll achieve our goal of a united and independent Ireland by negotiation, not by killing Maitland."

He leans back. "He trusts you, doesn't he?"

"I hope so." But do I trust Maitland? "What if he doesn't come?"

The Chief doesn't hesitate. "Then we won't be able to convince the British that we weren't responsible for the Cheltenham bombing. They won't resume negotiations with us, and we'll have no alternative but to resume the war in order to increase the pressure on them."

"But it's a war you can never win."

The Chief's thin lips clamp in determination. "We can't win in the sense that we don't have the military capacity to drive the British army into the sea, but we do have the capacity to bring the Six Counties situation to crisis point at any time of our choosing. If the Brits don't take the opportunity we're offering them now for an honorable withdrawal, they'll find themselves in an untenable position. We'll take the war back to the streets of Britain and scare away foreign banks and foreign investment. We'll hit the Protestant communities in the Six Counties and the loyalist paramilitaries will strike back. The security forces will be forced to act against them, and the Brits will find they're being shot at by loyalists. After that, do you think the British voters will still want to pour away four and a half billion pounds a year to maintain a 'disloyalist' colony in Ireland?"

This scenario of calculated slaughter is made all the more chilling by the calm, measured way in which the Chief spells it out. The wet priest's collar is tight round my neck. I run my finger along the inside to try and ease it. "You said that you want peace. If you pursue that strategy, you'll never have peace. Northern Ireland will become another Bosnia."

The Chief leans close enough for me to see the individual strands of wool in his mask, but it is the steeliness of his eyes which rivets my attention. "We want peace, Father, but not peace at any price. Remember the struggles: from the 1916 Rising, the War of Independence, the Anti-Treaty War against the Free State, the bombing campaigns in England in the late thirties, the resistance campaign in the fifties and sixties, through the liberation war we've fought in the Six Counties since 1969. Remember the sacrifices: in battle, by execution, and through hunger strike. And remember the volunteers who languish this very day in British prisons. We can't betray all these for a peace that leaves the Six Counties maintained as a British colony by a massive British military presence. Surely you understand that?"

What was it that Pádraig Pearse wrote? Patriotism is in large part a memory of heroic dead men and a striving to accomplish some task left unfinished by them. "But as a priest, a man of peace, I shrink from the violence, the deaths of so many innocent people."

"I understand that, Father. I'm a pacifist myself by inclination, but there are times when you have to fight for your principles. Would America be a republic today if George Washington hadn't fought for freedom?" His voice is persuasive. If he'd been born in Manhattan he would probably have become seriously rich. Instead he was born in Ulster with the cause coursing through his mother's milk, reaching him undiluted from generations past. And now he wears the black balaclava mask.

"That was a war of liberation, army against army," I say. "You're planning terrorist acts against civilians."

He speaks with great patience, as though to a slow-witted pupil who should know better. "Menachem Begin was branded a terrorist by the British under their Palestinian mandate before he became Israeli prime minister and was awarded the Nobel Peace Prize. So was Kenya's Jomo

Kenyatta, and Zimbabwe's Robert Mugabe, in the days before the Queen invited them to Buckingham Palace. Thatcher condemned Nelson Mandela as a terrorist, and now he is fêted by her successor as Nobel Peace Prize winner and President of South Africa. It's not just that one man's terrorist is another man's freedom fighter; today's terrorist is tomorrow's international statesman."

He leans back, and that grim smile shows again. "We've seen it all before in Ireland. The British sentenced Eamon de Valera to death for terrorism, reprieved him after American intervention, and later treated him as the respected Irish head of state. The 1921 British government said it would never sit down with terrorists and murderers. Within months it invited Michael Collins, the man it labeled the chief terrorist and murderer, to Downing Street and agreed a peace treaty that conceded independence to all but six counties in Ireland."

"But these men renounced violence."

"Of course they did, Father." His voice carries the merest hint of menace. "But only after they'd achieved their objective: liberation from British colonial rule."

The ends justify the means, the principle of the terrorist and the CIA operations officer. "No matter how noble the goal, the Church cannot approve of terrorism."

He peers at me suspiciously. His tone alters, not yet angry but less relaxed. "That word 'terrorism' again. The Church should pay more attention to St. Augustine. He writes of a pirate captured by Alexander the Great. 'How dare you molest the sea!' " says Alexander. 'How dare you molest the whole world,' " the pirate replies. 'Because I do it with my little ship I am called a thief; because you do it with a great navy you are called an emperor.' " The powerful states of the world have hijacked the word 'terrorism' to mean acts of terror carried out against them, but never by them."

"Any terrorism that takes the lives of innocent civilians is morally wrong." In the guise of a priest I find myself acting like a priest. If I keep this up long enough, will I come to believe in God again?

"Let me tell you, Father, our kind of terrorism takes very few lives. The vast majority of civilian deaths are caused by state terrorism. It's governments that have given us the holocaust and the gulags. All the people killed in the cause of Irish liberation since Wolfe Tone began the armed struggle in 1798 to the present day do not equal the number of civilians killed in a single night in Dresden by the British Royal Air Force during the Second World War."

"But that was war," I protest, "when no democratic options were available." The look in his eyes warns me that it would be self-defeating to remind him that Ireland has democratic options, and that only ten per cent in the North and three per cent in the South voted for Sinn Féin and the armed struggle. "Terrorist bombings of innocent civilians will destroy your support in the United States," I say instead.

All patience vanishes, along with the reassuring voice of the public speaker. "Is that right? Then tell me, Father, how many innocent civilians have been killed in Latin America by state terrorists who were armed and trained by the United States military? How many innocent civilians have been killed directly by United States terrorism in Vietnam and in Grenada? We don't take kindly to being lectured on terrorism by the United States."

He leans close and stares at me. "It's time to decide whose side you're on."

He stands up, walks to the door, and turns round. "Think about that while you think about what to say in your letter to Maitland."

When he has gone I stare at the blank sheet of paper before me, wishing that he had never mentioned Grenada.

Chapter ❖ Thirty-five

THERE IS NO more beautiful island in the Caribbean than Grenada, and back in 1983 it all seemed like a noble adventure, spiced with high politics, danger, and that even more addictive drug, secrecy.

The summons came in a phone call that roused me from a restless sleep.

"Yeah?"

"We'd like you in the office for a meeting at five. Dress casually, like a student—jeans, trainers, that kind of thing—and bring an overnight bag."

"Sure." I groped in the dark to put the phone back on the hook. Five? The luminous hands of the alarm clock showed a quarter after four. This was Sunday morning. Had World War Three started and no one told me?

Within twenty minutes I was driving through a strange, lifeless Washington and searching for a news bulletin on the car radio.

. . . at least forty-six marines were killed when a truck packed with explosives drove through barriers and into the

*lobby of the four-story marines headquarters in Beirut. The
dawn suicide mission by fanatical Shia terrorists wrecked
the building in which members of the American peacekeep-
ing force lay asleep. Troops are searching through the rubble for survivors . . .*

I came in off Route 123 and took the Dolley Madison
entrance, parked in the staff lot, hurried up the front steps
and through the double row of glass doors. The white and
gray marble walls and columns of the gigantic foyer never
failed to give a sense of importance and exclusivity, and
never more so when the guard at the front desk said, "Mr.
Darcy, sir, will you go straight to the conference room in C
corridor on the third floor."

At first I thought I'd burst in on the wrong meeting. No one
from Soviet Bloc was there. I recognized only one person
in the off-white characterless conference room. The chief
of Latin American Division, Frank "Flashy" Burridge, was
wearing a white suit with a large blue handkerchief spilling
from his breast pocket. He introduced me to the others,
mainly honchos from Latin American and the National Security Council.

"Since Maurice Bishop was killed on Thursday," Burridge said to me, "our feet haven't touched the ground. Yesterday the Vice President chaired a special meeting of the
National Security Council. Rod?"

"On Friday," said Rodney Mendez, a scholarly looking
man with a voice that carried the assurance of a national
radio announcer, "we were presented with an opportunity
to turn things our way. The Organization of East Caribbean
States asked us to intervene and restore democracy and
human rights in Grenada." Mendez put his elbows on the
table, made a steeple with his fingers, and continued, "What

I'm about to say is strictly top secret, you understand, Mr. Darcy."

"Right," I said.

"The President has ordered a naval task force bound for Lebanon to divert to Grenada, just in case. Colonel Oliver North and I have drafted a National Security Directive for armed intervention in Grenada. As yet the President hasn't signed it."

A secretary came in and gave Burridge a note. "The death toll of US marines in Beirut has risen to two hundred and forty one," he read aloud.

Mendez gave a satisfied nod.

"You got a problem, John?" Burridge asked.

"No. I just assumed this five A.M. meeting was called in response to the Beirut terrorist bombing."

"It was," said Mendez. "Two hundred and forty one marines killed by Soviet stooges should convince the President to sign that draft National Security Directive. The United States of America must show the Soviets that we will no longer tolerate terrorism by their proxies, whether it's in the Middle East or Latin America."

"There's just one problem," said Burridge. "The request by the OECS does not justify US military intervention under international law. To protect the President we need a request from the one internationally recognized legitimate authority in Grenada."

"That's where you come in, John," Mendez said.

"Me?" I said. "I'm Soviet Bloc."

"The problem we have is with the British," said Mendez, stroking his chin. "We naturally assumed we could count on them, particularly after we'd supplied them with intelligence for their Falklands campaign. They owe us, and Mrs. Thatcher is a good friend of the President. But we've run into a problem. It's their Queen. It seems she's technically head of state of Grenada, and doesn't like the idea of US troops invading her domain. Thatcher won't go with us on this one."

Typical British imperialist arrogance, I thought to myself.

"There is one way round this, however," said Mendez. "If the Queen's representative, the governor general, asked for our help, that would legitimise the operation."

"I still don't see what I can do."

"Rosina's been there under deep cover as a medical student," said Burridge. "Rosina?"

The woman with shoulder-length black hair, whose white T-shirt emphasized her ebony skin, had said nothing so far. I sensed that her large almond eyes had been glinting with amusement, though I could see nothing funny in the problem we faced. "There's only one person who can persuade Sir Paul Scoon to ask for US help," she said, "and that's his security adviser. His name is Maitland."

My heart sank. Edward Maitland was the last person I wanted to see. Correction, the next last after Jill Maitland. But it couldn't be him, could it? "The Maitland I knew was domestic security."

"He was," said Burridge. "It seems he was involved in a covert operation, setting up some terrorists to get shot when they went to an arms dump in Northern Ireland. The Royal Ulster Constabulary felt they hadn't been cut in on the deal or something, and they leaked. All hell broke loose, with demands for an inquiry into a shoot-to-kill policy."

"What do those dumbos think you shoot for, for Chrissakes?" someone muttered.

"They decided to move Maitland out of the firing line, so to speak." Burridge waited for an appreciation of his joke.

"What's he doing in Grenada?" I asked.

"His cover is legal adviser to the governor general," Rosina Harris replied. "In practice he's advising Scoon on security and checking out foreign involvement in the Grenadian security forces."

"Well, John," said Mendez, "do you want to protect the President against charges that, technically at least, he violated international law when dealing with this Soviet-backed terrorist regime?"

Within forty minutes of leaving Langley I followed the jeans stretched across Rosina's mobile ass up the short flight of steps to the twelve-seater special mission aircraft waiting for us at Andrews Air Force Base. I helped her off with her denim jacket. She wasn't wearing a bra beneath her tight white T-shirt.

"What are you thinking?" she asked as she settled into the seat next to me.

"I'm impressed," I said, "with everything that's been organized at such short notice. I never knew we were so efficient."

The glint of amusement changed to a cynical grin. "Where've you been for the last three years?"

"Warsaw, and before that, Moscow."

"Casey began setting this up as soon as Reagan appointed him DCI. Two years back he tried for a double whammy with Grenada and Suriname, but the Senate Intelligence Committee fixers thought it was off the wall."

I looked out of the scratched Plexiglas window. The beaded grid of streetlights radiating from the dome of the Capitol shrank and faded as we headed away from Washington and into a brightening pre-dawn gray wash smeared with pink-tinged white clouds. "Well, they've certainly moved their butts since Thursday."

"You're not hearing me, John. The plan simply went back to the drawing board. Why do you think the Second Battalion of the Seventy-fifth Rangers began practicing parachute jumps to take over Ephrata Municipal Airport and liberate hostages a month ago?"

"A month ago?"

"Right."

"But that was way before Bishop was shot."

"Now you are hearing me."

"And the Organization of East Caribbean States?"

She showed me a row of brilliant white teeth. "We helped set that up two years back. On Friday they accepted our advice to call for US intervention."

I frowned.

"Hey," she said to encourage me, "you heard what the Red Menace said."

"Who?"

"Rod Mendez. Grenada is a small island. A manageable operation. A golden opportunity to fuck the Soviets."

The pilot's laid-back Oklahoma voice crackled over the intercom. "Right now we have 'round twenty thousand feet. Weather's looking good and I anticipate a flight time to the Grenadines of five and a half hours, giving us touchdown round twenty after one local time."

Her almond eyes examined me. "You getting scruples, John?"

I thought of the brutal Soviet-controlled regimes in eastern Europe and southeast Asia. And now they were exporting their terrorism to our own backyard. "Why do you think I joined the company?"

"Hang in here, John," she said. "Latin America is where the action is right now. Believe me, Casey knows what this President wants. Unlike the wimps at State, Casey will deliver. Flashy Burridge has a direct line to Casey, so pull this one off and you're on the fast track." She handed me coffee in a polystyrene cup. "Sit back while I brief you on the case you put to Maitland."

° ° °

With the sun high in the sky, the shallows off the Atlantic coast of Union Island showed as yellow streaks in an azure sea. Shortly after landing at this nearest point of foreign soil to Grenada, Rosina and I were aboard a forty-foot motorised yacht and heading south through rough waters, under cover of shark fishing.

Silvery flying fish darted out of the waves and skimmed for yards near our hull as though expecting to be fed. Above, large black-headed laughing gulls chortled for attention while we ate the sandwiches Logan, the skipper, provided. When we passed the smaller Grenadine islands to our left, we were joined by larger, dark brown frigate birds. Seemingly without moving their long narrow crooked wings or their forked tails, these graceful creatures glided abreast of our mast before striking with their hooked bills to rob the gulls of their prey or scoop up flying fish.

Logan shouted from behind the wheel. "Want to try your hand?" He pointed toward the fin of a shark. "I have rods and bait in the hold."

I shook my head. I was content just to stand with Rosina on the heaving deck and watch the azure sea turn crimson as the red sun sank rapidly below the horizon.

"He probably has booze, guns, drugs, and illegal immigrants below deck as well," Rosina said. She indicated the darkening outline of an island ahead. "Grenada. Let's go."

I strapped on my shoulder holster, put on my windbreaker, and climbed down into the inflatable powerboat. I reached up and Rosina slid down to join me.

Logan had anchored the yacht three quarters of the way down the western coast of Grenada. I untied the inflatable, started the modified outboard motor, and Rosina pointed me toward Grand Mal Bay.

The crimson sea had turned silver. I had never seen a moon so big or stars so bright. The Grand Mal beach was a white landmark below a dark mass that rose to mountain peaks. Behind and to our right, black shapes dotted the silver mirror: Admiral Metcalf's flagship, the helicopter carrier *Guam*, supported by the huge aircraft carrier *Independence* and thirteen other navy vessels.

"You're sure the beach will be safe in this moonlight?" I said above the muffled engine drone.

"The PRA will have their eyes glued to the fleet off St. George's," she said. "Don't worry."

The powerboat plowed through the sea, sending back waves of spray to drench us. When Rosina turned round from the front of the boat, her T-shirt was soaked. "Enjoying it?"

"Better than servicing dead-letter drops in Gorky Park," I yelled back. "And it sure beats the hell out of a training course at Blue U."

We dragged the boat up the beach, and I hid it in dense undergrowth behind a large Texaco storage tank while Rosina brushed away our tracks with palm leaves.

"This will be the trickiest part," she said, "because of the curfew. We need to avoid the roads."

She led me up off the beach, waited in the undergrowth to check that no members of the People's Revolutionary Army were patroling the potholed road, crossed, and headed into a plantation of tall, thick sugar canes. "Careful of the fronds," she whispered. "They're sharp."

On the far side of the plantation I followed her into a dense forest whose overarching foliage hid the moon. The sweet scent of jasmine hung heavily in the warm velvety darkness. My stumbling disturbed monkeys who rustled unseen branches and chattered in annoyance, drowning an unfamiliar background of pipings, chirpings, and hissings. Rosina stopped and I bumped into her. "Don't worry about the bats," she said. "And the snakes aren't dangerous. Well, most of them aren't." She grinned. "If you're frightened, you can hold my hand."

I don't know how she navigated the route but, after scrambling uphill and bearing right through the forest, she led me out into the open. "It's up this road. I can't see or hear any patrols, but it'll be safer if we keep to the shadows until we reach the Maitlands' residence."

Her words were cold water thrown in the face of a drunk. High on the mission, I'd forgotten about Jill Maitland. "It's best if I go on my own," I said soberly.

She shrugged. "OK. It's the largest of those white villas over there. Here's the map showing you how to get to the Grand Anse campus."

"What about you?"

"Don't worry about me."

I checked my bearings. When I turned round she'd disappeared.

I made it to the Maitlands' villa without any problems. I was far more anxious about facing Jill Maitland than meeting a PRA patrol. The wrought iron gate opened onto a paved path which cut through a lawn bordered by bougainvillaea shrubs and climbed three steps to a porch. I knocked on the oak door.

"Who is it?" a voice called from behind the door.

"It's John Darcy."

Edward Maitland had changed little in the eight years since we'd worked together in London on the Wilson mission. His chestnut hair was still neatly parted, though a little longer

and showing streaks of gray at the temples. His face was
leaner, but still conveyed an amused superiority. "You look
as though you need a drink," he said. "Do sit down, and don't
be afraid of dirtying the sofa. The maid will clean it tomorrow."

The potted plants, the watercolours on the white walls,
the Afghan rugs on the parquet, the wicker bowls of dried
flowers placed discreetly on small cane tables were Jill. I sat,
tensed, waiting for her to appear, quietly panicking at how
I would handle the situation.

"I don't have bourbon," Maitland said as he handed me
a glass, "but I trust this single malt will do."

Should I ask after Jill? It would seem impolite not to. But
then he might summon her if I did.

He sat down in a kapok-cushioned rattan armchair opposite, stretched out his legs, and said, "Now tell me, to what
do I owe the honor of this unannounced visit?"

I flunked the question about Jill and launched into the
case I'd rehearsed mentally many times since Rosina had
briefed me.

"Bishop was never a communist," Maitland replied. "A
Marxist, I grant you, but also . . ." He gave a supercilious
smile. ". . . a Catholic, who believed in what you Catholics
call 'social justice', if I have the theology correct. Of course,
what really infuriated you people is that Castro was the only
one prepared to help him. Take a look out of the window.
You'll see four fishing boats in the harbor. Castro's gift to
help Grenada start a fishing industry."

"Edward," I said, "don't tell me that this General Austin
who shot Bishop and formed a Revolutionary Military
Council isn't a hardline Leninist."

Maitland sipped his malt whiskey. "That was a bad business. Coldblooded butchery. But as for Hudson Austin, we
trained him as a prison guard in Jamaica, and that's about
his barrow. No, the man who's really behind this is Bernard

Coard, and it wasn't political, it was personal. Bishop and Coard were rivals since their schooldays."

"I'm not interested in the finer details of Caribbean politics. The fact is the Soviets and the Cubans have set up a Marxist military dictatorship in our backyard."

"Dear oh dear. From where do you obtain your intelligence? Most of the Politburo think Grenada is a province of southern Spain."

"Now tell me the Cubans aren't building an airport at Point Salines with a nine-thousand-foot runway for Soviet bombers."

Maitland sighed. "I've always thought you people relied too heavily on technology. What your aerial photographs can't tell you is that this airport is being built for the tourist trade."

"Horseshit."

"My dear John, don't you think I checked this out? A British electronics firm is in charge of equipping the airport. A military air base requires radar, hardened aircraft shelters capable of withstanding bomb blasts, a secure set of underground fuel tanks, underground weapons storage, antiaircraft defense, perimeter security, et cetera, et cetera. None of these exists or is contracted for at Point Salines."

"If these arguments don't convince you we should intervene, please accept that we have a legitimate concern for the safety of a thousand US citizens on this island."

He went to the mahogany bar in the corner of the whitewashed room, returned with the bottle of malt whiskey, and refilled our glasses. "Sir Paul and I had a meeting yesterday with Austin about the safety of the two hundred UK citizens here. Austin said that all foreign nationals—including the Americans—are free to leave, and he will personally guarantee safe conduct to the airport at Pearls. Your good friends, the government in Barbados, won't allow the regional airline to resume its scheduled services here, and so four planes have been chartered. They'll fly into Pearls tomorrow and take out anyone who wants to leave."

He walked to the large window that overlooked St. George's Bay. Out to sea, beyond the two promontories that curve round to embrace the harbor, tiny lights twinkled among the dark shapes of the US fleet. "How many people do you have out there?"

"If you include the Rangers ready to board Hercules transporters at Barbados airport and the Eighty Second Airborne Division on standby at Fort Bragg, Admiral Metcalf can call on fifteen thousand men."

Maitland turned from the window. "Shall I tell you what former prison guard Hudson Austin can call on? One thousand members of the Cuban-trained People's Revolutionary Army; forty three Cuban military instructors plus about seven hundred and fifty Cuban construction workers, but Castro has condemned the Bishop killing and ordered his people to do nothing but defend themselves; and a few thousand members of the People's Militia, whom Hudson has disarmed because he fears they'll turn on him. Grenadians are outraged over Bishop's slaughter. Tell your troops to hold back three months and the people here will have rid themselves of Austin and his so-called Revolutionary Military Council."

I couldn't understand why Maitland was being so unhelpful. After all (or so I thought at the time), he didn't know of my affair with his wife. It was I who should feel guilty. Instead, I was angry.

"Where are you based?" he asked.

"The Grand Anse campus of St. George's Medical School."

He raised his eyebrows. "You can't go back there now because of the curfew. You'll have to stay here for the night. You can sleep in Emma's room."

"I don't want to inconvenience anyone."

"Oh, but you won't. She's back at school now. It's a shame you didn't come a couple of months ago, when Emma was here."

I was conscious of his eyes scrutinising me.

"You look puzzled," he said.

"I'm sorry. I don't know who Emma is."

"Didn't we tell you? No, of course not. You left London so suddenly and we lost contact." He took a Cuban cigar from a wooden box and guillotined one end. He held a lighter flame to the other end and sucked on the cigar. "I imagine you were whisked off to some top secret location, and we didn't know where to send the card." He exhaled slowly through lips curled in what I then interpreted as triumph. "Jill and I have a daughter."

I put my glass down on the parquet. I didn't know which was worse: finding out that Jill had cemented her marriage to this . . . this supercilious Brit, or failing in my mission to get the governor general's signature. I couldn't bear to lose at both. "We can't wait three months. We've been asked by the Organization of East Caribbean States to help restore democracy and human rights in this region."

"I see," he said. "Just as in El Salvador, and Guatemala, and Pinochet's Chile, and . . . But I needn't continue. What I don't understand is why you need me." His eyes seemed full of hatred, though I didn't understand why. "If you want to do something, you go straight ahead without asking. You always do."

I struggled to contain my anger. "It would assist Anglo-American relations in the intelligence community if the governor general were to add his name to the OECS request for outside help."

He puffed on his cigar and poured himself more whiskey without offering me any. "I see," he said after he'd taken a drink. "Langley have more brains than I credited them with. They sent you as a reminder that they know I was up to my

eyes in the plot to get rid of Wilson as prime minister. If that
leaked out now it would not exactly help my position in a
certain police inquiry being conducted in Northern Ireland." He took a sip of whiskey. "The price for their silence
is Scoon's signature."

"Nobody mentioned the Wilson plot, believe me,
Edward."

"Of course not. They merely plucked you out of Soviet
Bloc and sent you for a holiday to Grenada."

I stood up and vented my anger. "Hell, Edward, it isn't
like that. We're talking state terrorism here. The bottom line
is: whose side are you on?"

Chapter ✛ Thirty-six

THE SHEET OF paper the Chief left for me to write to Maitland on stares back blankly. I put down the pen. I no longer know whose side I'm on.

"You are soldiers of Christ," boomed Father Curran from the stage of St. Sebastian's school assembly hall, "waging war with the devil for the souls of mankind."

"The Soviet Union," said Father O'Halloran from the dais in my classroom at Regis High School, "by declaring itself an atheist state and persecuting the Church, has shown itself to be the principal agent of Satan on this earth."

"In the final analysis," argued Father Paul, sipping sherry in his room at Fordham, "you either believe in God or you don't, and you either believe in God-given freedom or you believe in tyranny. You have to choose whose side you're on."

The white walls surrounding me are oppressively close. Opposite, one section between two and four feet from the stone floor is pitted and cratered. The indentations are all fragments of the same shape. The shape of a hoof. Where,

in frustrated rage, a bull tried to kick its way out of this pen.
These tight enclosing walls soar up three times the height
of a bull to a lofty ridged roof. They are impenetrable. But,
while they imprison, these white walls also protect against
the dark and the cold outside.

Everyone chooses the side of good rather than evil. The
only problem is to decide what is good. A Catholic in the sixties accepted that the Church defined what is good. If that
simple answer now seems barely credible, at the time it carried with it the reassurance of certainty—a certainty shared
by hundreds of millions in a Church preserved from error
by God through his vicar on earth, the Pope. It was this certainty, I suppose, which appealed to my uncompromising
nature. Or was it this certainty which molded my uncompromising nature?

"If you enter the boxing ring," said Tony Petillo, one of
our instructors at the Farm, "and your opponent drugs the
water you drink between rounds, if he has a switchblade in
one glove and repeatedly stabs you with it, do you continue
to fight according to the rules?" He moved away from the
podium and strode back and forth across the front of the
classroom. "Let me tell you, the opponent who labels America *glavny vrag*, the main enemy, obeys no rules. In its quest
for world domination, the Soviet Communist Party uses
every dirty trick in the book—and some not in the book—
to try and destroy our religions, our allies, and our way of
life." He paused, and seemed to look each one of us in the
eye. "You here in this room are not going to let that happen."

A patriot throughout the seventies and eighties had no
doubt what constituted good and evil—and equally no doubt
that we had to fight the evil empire with its own weapons if
we were to preserve freedom and democracy.

Just as Russian patriots doubtless took the same view
And Irish patriots too.

Do these banners of faith—in God or country—shelter

us from the consequences of our actions? Or blind us from distinguishing good from evil? And what happens when the banners conflict?

I stand and walk three paces up and down the cell. I've always been more comfortable with doing rather than thinking. The only certainty now is that I'm on the side of nailing the Cheltenham bomber who massacred innocent Americans, I'm on the side of achieving a peaceful and united Ireland and, above all, I'm on the side of saving my daughter.

If persuading Maitland to come here and talk with the IRA will achieve all these things, why do I hesitate?

The bullpen door opens and the Chief enters. "You're ready, Father?" he asks.

"One question," I say.

His eyes stare hard through the holes in the black balaclava.

"What do you have to hide?" I ask.

The eyes search my face for some sign, but I remain impassive. "Nothing," he says finally.

"Then why do you need a mask?"

"I don't know how all this will end. It's better you don't see me."

"You're asking me to trust you."

He lowers his eyes in thought. When he raises them he says, "We've been down the path of negotiation with them before. It nearly finished the movement. Now we give them as little information as possible in case anything goes wrong. That's our policy until their withdrawal from Ireland is written in tablets of stone." He pauses, and then adds, "Have you written the letter?"

I hand him the page of writing. He studies it in silence. "Well," he says at last, "that's very persuasive." His lips curl in amusement. "If ever you decide to give up the priest-hood, there'll be an opening for you in our propaganda department."

"What do we do now?"

"I'll have this letter delivered overnight."

"And then?"

"We wait to see what Maitland's reply is."

Chapter ✣ Thirty-seven

MAITLAND'S REPLY TO the question I had confronted him with the night before in Grenada came late in the morning, as I was standing at the large window in his villa watching the US fleet beyond St. George's Bay. The telephone rang. "The Maitland residence," I said.

"I've just been in conference with the governor general," said Maitland. "You can have what you came to Grenada for."

Flushed with triumph I hurried from the villa. I had gone less than a quarter of a mile when a Japanese pickup truck of the Central Water Commission overtook me and screeched to a halt. Two PRA soldiers wearing East German helmets and Cuban army leather belts jumped out. One pointed an old British SMLE bolt action .303 rifle at me, the other held an AK-47 assault rifle.

Nobody was going to stop me from delivering the message that would enable us to restore freedom and democracy to Grenada. As the two armed revolutionaries approached, I pretended to blow my nose so that my right hand was nearer the shoulder holster.

"What you doin'?" asked the elder of the two, who held the AK-47 loosely in one hand. He must have been in his early twenties.

At close quarters I'd take out both of them. Looking over my shoulder to distract them, I said, "Visiting a lady, but please don't tell anybody."

"You been havin' married tail?" the teenager chortled.

The other grinned. "Papers, please."

I put my hand inside my windbreaker and felt the gun. The younger one needed to be closer to his companion to give me the best chance. I withdrew my identification documents and held them out between the two soldiers in an attempt to draw them together.

The elder one took the false papers. He read them slowly, silently mouthing the words, and then handed them back. "Me brother, he student too. He bright. He go Barbados." He looked across the russet-roofed white buildings cascading down green hillsides to the multicoloured rowing boats, launches, Castro's trawlers, and a shabby steamer at peace in the still, reflective waters of the harbor, and beyond to a sapphire sea where the gray *Independence* and its armored accomplices lay waiting. "You American," he said. "You tell me. What little Grenada do Reagan?"

I was spared answering by the teenager. "Where you goin'?"

"Back to Grand Anse campus."

"Jump in. We take you. You don' want husband find out what you bin doin'."

Rosina led me to an office off a student dorm, opened the door, put up her thumbs, and said, "Didn't I tell you John would deliver?"

A thin, moustached man of about my age rose from

behind a desk and grasped me by the hand. "Congratulations, John! All systems go from now on in. Want a drink?"

"Hey, you guys," Rosina said, "we got work to do."

"Yes, sir," the field station chief said with a smirk at me. He went to a filing cabinet and took out a short-wave radio transceiver. "Your scalp, John. Do the honors."

"Gabriel calling Heaven," I said into the transceiver. "The cousin has agreed. Do you read? Over."

A voice came through the static. "Heaven to Gabriel. Whoopee! Tell him to pack his toothbrush. We lift him three thirty tomorrow morning. Over and out."

"Well, John Darcy," said Rosina, "that's your brownie point in the bag. Time for you to go before the boys start letting off their fireworks. Four charter planes are leaving from Pearls today between noon and three."

"I know." Having got us to the starting line I wasn't about to back away now. "I'll see you safely off, but I'll stick around. Make sure this Scoon guy comes through."

"John," she said quietly, "you may be male and white, and I may never be promoted to your rank, but this is my operation."

I checked the luminous dial of my watch. It was past four in the morning, but nothing stirred among the shadows cast on the Government House lawns by the graying pre-dawn sky. I left my observation post and went down the grand staircase to the first-floor reception room where Rosina waited with Maitland and two suitcases.

"How's he taking it?" I asked.

"His Excellency the Lord High Governor Bloody General requires that soldiers avoid walking across his tennis court," said Maitland. "I trust your marines will carry his bloody suitcases—if they ever get here."

"What I mean is, do you think he'll hold?"

"Sir Paul can always be relied upon to remain loyal to the winning side."

It was nearly five before moving dark shapes materialized as a detachment of Seals in camouflage helmets and battledress. I opened the main door. "We were expecting you earlier."

"We lost four men when their landing craft overturned," said a fresh-faced officer. "Now, sir, my name is Lieutenant Steve Johnson and my orders are to secure the safety of the target. The main force will land at dawn by helicopter and parachute. Once they've taken St. George's they'll collect the target and 'copter him to the *Guam.* That will be accomplished noon at the latest. In the meantime, sir, you are to reassure the target that all is under control."

The flush of dawn behind jungle-clothed mountains brought the drone of aircraft, followed swiftly by the pounding of antiaircraft guns. A buzzing plague of locusts grew into a clattering squadron of thirty or so Apache and Cobra helicopters, passed above, and headed into the orange sky between the mountain peaks. Ten stubby turboprop Hercules transporters flew in the opposite direction from Barbados before releasing blossoming white flowers which fell to earth in the southwest.

Lieutenant Johnson checked his watch and then tuned in a transistor radio.

This is Radio 1580, an American voice announced, *assuring you of our friendly intentions. This joint Caribbean-American exercise is being undertaken to restore democracy and human rights in Grenada. We ask all loyal Grenadians to support this action. We ask the People's Revolutionary Army to cooperate with our troops. We assure the Cuban military that no harm will come to them if they lay down their weapons. Please stay tuned to this station for further instructions.*

This sounded uncomfortably like the recordings I'd heard of broadcasts made by the Soviet troops invading Czechoslovakia.

Maitland walked over, said, "May I?" and returned the transistor radio.

. . . we will fight them on the beaches, we will bury them in the sea. Radio Free Grenada calls on all patriots to defend Grenada against the imperialist Yankee invaders . . .

The SEAL lieutenant snatched back the radio.

The door burst open. "Lieutenant!" a young private said. "They're coming!"

I followed the Seals outside to see an armored personnel carrier pass through the gates of Government House and head up the gravel drive.

"Fire!" yelled the lieutenant.

Three SEALs dropped to the crouch position and discharged their automatic rifles at the APC. It stopped, its hatch opened, and a black hand reached out and waved a white handkerchief.

"That's called burying us in the sea," Lieutenant Johnson said. The SEALs laughed.

The head of a Grenadian soldier emerged from the hatch and shouted, "Don't fire! We come protect de governor general."

"He's under the protection of the United States of America," Lieutenant Johnson yelled. "Come out with your hands up."

"Fuck you, man!" The Grenadian soldier's head dropped back down and the barrel of the APC's machine gun swung toward us.

"Shit!" said Johnson.

The clatter of the machine gun gouged chunks of masonry from the stuccoed façade of Government House as we scrambled for safety inside.

"Dave," Johnson said, "have we got comms?" Another fusillade hit the wall. "Call in a Cobra to zap the bastard."

The corporal called Dave radioed to field command. "Oscar Four Bravo, this is Lima Zero Tango, do you read? We need Cobra strikes at an enemy position on the drive outside Government House."

Minutes later the whap-whap-whap of a helicopter swooping low was followed by the tattoo of a Gatling gun. A burst of fire exploded the window, hit the marble floor and ricocheted to crater the plastered wall above the stone fireplace, smashing a daguerreotype of Queen Victoria.

"Jesus Christ!" said Johnson. "Call those mothers off!"

Radio 1580 continued to assure the population of Grenada that the Caribbean force had secured St. George's and the airports at Pearls and Point Salines. The screaming of jets, the pounding of bombs, and the cacophony of machine gun, mortar, and rifle fire told a different story. Other PRA armored vehicles moved up to pin us down in Government House. Four hours after we were scheduled to be lifted out, Lieutenant Colonel Smith, commander of the 22nd Marine Amphibious Unit, spoke to Johnson over Dave's short-wave radio.

"Steve, we're running into more opposition than we expected. Can you guys hang in there? I'm going to try a landing before dawn tomorrow."

Soon afterwards we lost electricity and water supplies. The PRA unit tried to storm Government House. The SEALs fought them off.

Dusk brought a lull in the fighting. No one knew for how long. Rosina had been missing since the failed PRA attack, which left the bodies of two Grenadian soldiers sprawled on

the gravel drive. I found her in one of the second-floor bed-
rooms, leaning against the jamb of an opened french window and staring out across the balcony.

She didn't hear my approach. The curves of her body
were outlined against the moon-silvered water of the bay.
No lights shone down in St. George's, but the flames from
a large blazing government office on one of the promontories cast an orange glow over the subdued city.

Tonight I needed her. Hurt and humiliated by Jill having borne Maitland a child, I needed to restore my pride between Rosina's thighs. "Rosina," I began.

"They're Black," she said.

I was within touching distance of her.

Still with her back to me she said, "The people out there.
That rag bag of a People's Revolutionary Army. The other
poor bastards scared out of their wits."

She, too, needed comfort tonight.

Her voice was low and husky. "That's why the company
is afraid of them. Black people who call each other 'comrade', within fifteen hundred miles of the US coastline."

She lit a cigarette and turned round. "When I was fourteen I had a poster of Malcolm X on my bedroom wall. I
wanted to join the Panthers." She blew out a stream of
smoke. "My folks insisted I go to college. That was the way
Blacks would fulfill Martin Luther King's dream, not by terrorism." The cigarette end glowed. "I bought it all, and
ended up joining CIA." She turned back to watch the flames.

I put my hands on her shoulders and murmured in her
ear. "You're under stress, Rosina."

"You don't hear me, do you?" She flung the cigarette
over the balcony and walked past me out of the bedroom.

A dawn chorus of howling jets, thundering bombs, whirring
helicopters, booming artillery, and crackling automatic

weapons broke the tense silence of the night. After three hours the noise died. Armored personnel carriers lumbered up the gravel drive; they were American and unopposed. They took us to a cricket ground by the sea just north of the city. Colonel Smith climbed down from his amtrack command vehicle to greet Sir Paul Scoon and usher him into one of several helicopters waiting on the gouged green lawn. Maitland and I were directed into another helicopter.

The blades whirled and we rose from the flat oval field now strewn with amphibious tracked vehicles, M-60 tanks, and Jeeps in addition to the choppers. St. George's lay quiet in the early morning sun. Not a soul was to be seen on the narrow streets which meandered up from the water's edge through the tin-roofed quayside buildings to the russet-roofed white villas planted among a profusion of vegetation on high ground on one side, and past the stone and pink stucco of the Anglican church and the gray tower of the Catholic cathedral to a cemetery on the other side.

Across the harbor mouth lay the smouldering ruins of the government building we'd seen burning the previous night, while on the promontory below a hole gaped in the green roof of Fort Rupert, the eighteenth century limestone citadel where Maurice Bishop had been executed by his comrades just seven days before.

The helicopter circled as it gained height. The sun spangled a waterfall cascading down a jungled mountainside toward a tropical forest. It glinted in the windows of a gray bastioned building flanked by a barracks and the wreck of a stone building.

"Precision bombing," boasted the marine sergeant who accompanied us. "We sure flattened Fort Frederick."

"I wouldn't let Sir Paul hear you," Maitland shouted above the noise of the helicopter.

"How come?"

"Fort Frederick is that rather ugly but perfectly intact gray edifice flying a flag."

The marine stared at him.

"The smoking pile of rubble nearby is what the locals call the Crazy House," said Maitland. "It's a mental hospital. Or, rather, it was."

Rosina wrote me later to say why she'd quit the company: the bodies of forty seven inmates had been found beneath the ruins of the Crazy House.

In my dream I step through the rubble. Past policemen. Blue overalls, blue safety helmets, white masks. Searching. Concrete slabs, timber spars, glass splinters, unattached legs. An acrid smell clings to me, a spirit unwilling to depart the scene of death. "In all my twenty-five years," a broad Scots voice resonates. "String him up from a lamppost outside Belfast City Hall," the policemen chorus. "Outside CIA headquarters," Grenadian voices echo. I retreat. Into a shiny green room, neon lights, tall white cabinets. "Body number forty-seven," say the clipped tones of small, sharp-faced men with pencil moustaches. Frantically I unzip white plastic bags. "Black female aged between three and six with Downs syndrome and both legs missing." A sea of accusing ghoul-like faces advances on me. Escape! Escape! Down the blackened remains of a long red carpet. The crash of bombs punctuates the rattle of machine gun fire. The crash of thunder punctuates the rattle of hailstones against the shutters.

Cold sweat streams from my body as the bullpen materializes in the first, dull light of a storm-battered English morning. I pull the blanket round me. The nightmare has ended, but the questions won't go away. How did the PRA soldiers killed by our invasion of Grenada balance the two hundred and forty one marines killed by Shia terrorists in Beirut? As for the forty-seven mental patients, whose side were they on?

Chapter ✣ Thirty-eight

I THOUGHT SLEEP was worst: the domain of the subconscious where I'm helpless to prevent long-suppressed memories from springing free and replaying vivid images which intercut and merge to create grotesque nightmares. But the empty hours immediately after sleep are far worse. The unwanted, newly liberated memories of the night before invade the conscious mind and confront me with questions I shrink from answering.

I thought I knew what loneliness was. To go to a movie theater and have no one to exchange opinions with afterwards. To spend time buying the right ingredients, employ skill cooking them to perfection, and have no one to share the meal with. To come home after a day at the office and have no one to bitch to or share triumphs with. To lie in bed at night and have no warmth to snuggle up to.

But none of these can compare with being assailed by self-doubt and having no one to comfort you. To be overwhelmed by the fear that your only achievements in life are measured in damage to others, and be deprived of the one person who means most to you, the only one who can reassure you that your life has some worth. This loneliness is a physical ache, a craving for human contact to displace the ghosts from the past which possess me. Please let me see Emma. Soon.

The welcome grate of the bars on the bullpen doors ends the torment of the waking hours. Emma acting hysterical must have persuaded the Chief to let me join her at mealtimes.

"Your breakfast," says the Boy.

"Emma," I almost shout. "I want to see her."

The Boy avoids my eyes. "Please eat up, Father."

The day stretches ahead, with nothing to do but wait for Maitland's reply to my letter asking him to come. I daren't rely on him. The only certain way to free Emma is to prize free the bracket that fixes her manacle to the wall. What will move the Chief to let me spend enough time with Emma in the loft? And if I fail, what will become of Emma when Joe returns in three days and I'm exposed as an impostor?

How do I stop these demons conspiring to drive me out of my mind?

"I need to see the Chief," I say when the Boy comes at lunchtime.

He hesitates. "Before or after you've seen the girl? The Chief says you can have your meals with her if you want."

"How are you?" we say together.

"Fine."

"Fine, now you're here, Father."

But she's not. That innocent face is whiter than before, and dark shadows circle her eyes. "It's so good to see you," I say after the Boy has left and bolted the loft door behind him.

She holds me tight. "When are they going to let me out?"

"I . . . I don't know."

"I shouted and screamed," she whispers. "I threw the breakfast tray on the floor." She chokes back the tears. "It wasn't all acting. I thought they were never going to let you come and see me again."

"I'm here now."

"Don't leave me."

Never! But I have to drag myself away. "I must work on the bracket," I whisper, "and you must eat your lunch so they'll let me come again at suppertime."

Raising my voice I say grace before meals, tell Emma in a whisper to keep talking loudly enough to cover the sound of my work, and take the pipe to the bracket.

Rainwater drips through gaps in the red tiling of the loft's low roof and runs down the brick wall to which the bracket is secured. I kneel down in a large damp patch on the floor and use the pipe to scrape the brickwork behind the bracket.

"Have some tea, Father," Emma calls out as she peers at what I'm doing. "How long before you break it?" she whispers.

"I hope to have levered the bracket from the wall by the end of suppertime today," I whisper back.

"Then we escape?"

I shake my head. "During supper on Friday, but I hope it won't be necessary."

"Why not?"

"I've written to Edward, asking him to talk with them. They've promised to release you if he comes."

She puts her hand to her mouth. "How could you?"

I lay down the piece of pipe. "To free you, of course."

"It's a trap. I couldn't bear for Daddy to be harmed! Let's break out tonight."

"Shush!" I raise my index finger to my lips. "The last thing I want is to put you at risk. If we do have to break out of here, it'll be very dangerous. You'll have to carry the chain and run with that manacle round your ankle. It will be much better if they agree to let you go. Their chief has promised that no harm will come to Edward."

Her green eyes flash suspiciously. "Why do they want to talk to Daddy?"

"They say they want to restore the peace process in Northern Ireland, and Edward will be able to convince the British government that they really have called a halt to violence."

"There's only one way to put an end to violence in Northern Ireland and that's to put people like them in jail."

"Right now we're in no position to do that, so let's hope Edward agrees to meet them."

"Daddy will come if it means I'll be released, you can bet your life on that."

That's not something I am prepared to bet my life on. "We'll review the situation Friday lunchtime."

She grimaces and holds her head.

"Emma, you're not OK, are you? Is it your migraine?"

"How do you know about my migraine? OK. You know everything about me, I should have guessed."

Only a fraction of what I want to know.

"I'm better when you're here, but when I'm on my own I feel lonely and frightened, and then I get a migraine. I told Mrs. Messy about the migraine last week, but she just said, 'Tough.' ".

"When Master Spotty collects me," I whisper, "we'll tell him what tablets you need. I'm sure he'll get them for you."

I raise my voice again. "The important thing is to have something to do when I'm not here. What would you be doing at school now?"

"Right now?"

"First lesson after lunch on Wednesday."

"Physics."

"Who's your teacher?"

"Dr. Randall."

"Sit down on the floor," I instruct, "with your back against the wall—that's right. Now, after I've gone, close your eyes, breathe deeply, and relax. Slowly count to ten, still taking deep breaths. Tell yourself that after the count of ten you are in your classroom and Dr. Randall is about to begin your physics lesson. Visualise what he looks like . . ."

"Dr. Randall's a she."

"Right. Visualise what she looks like, what she's wearing, what she's writing on the blackboard, where you're sitting, and who is sitting near you. What can you smell? Maybe the chalk dust, maybe the polish on the desk. What can you taste? Maybe the end of the pencil you're biting on without even thinking. What can you feel? Maybe the chair is hard. Now you are there in the classroom. Listen to what Dr. Randall is saying and visualise writing down notes in your notebook. Go through the whole lesson."

"Can it be something other than physics?"

"It can be anything you want, like the game of hockey you most enjoyed. The important thing when you're locked away on your own like this is to follow a routine. This should include periods when you're mentally out of your cell: that way the confinement becomes less depressing."

She tilts her head to one side, just like Jill. "I don't know what I'd do without you."

With those words she banishes my loneliness.

"Do you play these mind games when you're on your own?" she asks.

"Sure."

"What do *you* imagine?"

How can I tell Emma that, to keep away the demons, I spent all morning visualising her, using the memory of those photographs in the bottom drawer of her bedside cabinet to see her as a baby, as a young child listening to those illustrated children's classics that I read to her in bed, and as a schoolgirl whom I help with homework? "It's a secret."

"That's not fair," she pouts.

"I promise I'll tell you when we're both safe, away from here. Think of it as a surprise to come."

"I bet it'll be a nice surprise."

"It will be, I promise you."

I resume gouging out a channel in the masonry so that the steel pipe can slip down between the bracket and the wall. "Tell me about this school you attend," I say to cover the scraping noise. "Do you like living away from home?"

"Daddy chose the school, though I think Grandpa and Nan pay the fees. Daddy said it was best for me to go to a boarding school because he wasn't home much during the week."

"But your mother is."

"That's not the same."

I would never have sent Emma away to an all-girls school. "Don't you miss boys in your class?"

She screws up her face. "Boys of my own age are immature and boring."

"You must miss home."

"I'm not away from home all the time. Apart from the long vac in summer, and Christmas and Easter vacs, we also have long leaves in the middle of each term. I was due home for the Lent term long leave the day after I was kidnapped. Daddy will be worried sick about me."

"What about your mother? Just think what she's going through right now."

She shrugs. "Mum will just get plastered. She always does whenever she can't cope, which is most of the time."

I stop work on the bracket. "Emma! You shouldn't say such things about your mother."

She tucks her knees up underneath her chin and hugs her legs, just as when I first saw her. "I know I shouldn't. But it's true. I've overheard Daddy telling her that he doesn't know why he keeps on working, most of his salary goes on keeping Gordon's gin company in business."

"Perhaps there's a reason your mother drinks. Have you ever thought of that?"

She nods.

"Well?"

"I don't think I should say."

"You can if you want to. Your secret will be safe with me."

"Promise?"

"Promise."

"Cross your heart and hope to die?"

I look pointedly at the manacle on her ankle and at the door being guarded on the other side by a member of the IRA. "In these circumstances," I whisper in mock conspiratorial tones, "I think I prefer just to promise."

She giggles.

It's wonderful to see her laugh, to distract her from this Damoclean sword hanging over her head.

"Well," she says, aping my tone, "once in the long vac I came home from playing tennis with this boy. He was spending his summer holidays in England with friends of ours up the road, and I invited him for tea. He was three years older than me and rather hunky. Mum knew how I felt about him, and I warned her that I might be bringing him back. She got tea and biscuits ready for us, but she didn't have any tea herself, she kept going back into the kitchen. When she tried to pour John a second cup, her hand was shaking and she poured it all over the carpet. I went into the kitchen to get a cloth and saw a bottle of gin. It was half empty. Mum was in the drawing room apologizing to John, but she couldn't pronounce her words properly. She was well and truly wrecked. It was so embarrassing, you couldn't believe it. I just burst into tears, ran upstairs, and locked myself in my room."

This isn't the Jill that I knew. "And?"

"And when I finally unlocked the door, she was sobbing her heart out. She said she was every so sorry, but seeing me with such a nice boy and so happy brought back memories. I think it was the gin, but once she started she couldn't stop talking. She said John reminded her of the only boy she'd ever really loved."

I swallow. "Did she say any more?"

"Did she ever! I said that John didn't look a bit like Daddy, and she said she didn't mean Daddy. So I said, if that was the case, why hadn't she married him instead of Daddy."

I can hardly bring myself to ask the question. "What did she say to that?"

"You'll never believe it. She said that she'd met this man *after* she was married to Daddy. Don't you think that's a terrible thing to say?"

How do I answer? "No, Emma, it need not be a terrible thing to say."

She screws up her face. "She said it was because of what Jesus taught that she hadn't left Daddy."

My voice has gone hoarse. "She'd become a Catholic?"

Emma looks at me in a strange way. "She said the worst thing was she couldn't tell this other man. It would hurt him too much, and she'd already hurt him enough by pretending she'd stopped loving him."

Chapter ✤ Thirty-nine

A WROUGHT IRON bracket measuring four inches by two inches, with four Phillips screws at each corner, stands between the two of us and Jill. Jesus taught that love was the greatest of all virtues. It was only a Church led by unmarried men—men who regard women as saints or whores—which prescribed denial as the expression of love. Only an uncaring pitiless institution would condemn a woman to live with a man who hates her, and set a barrier between her and the man she truly loves, the man who fathered her child. Strengthened by anger I push down hard on the steel pipe to try and dislodge the bracket.

"Don't you want any supper?" whispers Emma as she holds out a plate of baked beans. "You hardly had any lunch."

I shake my head. "I want to make sure you can be freed before I'm taken back to the bullpen tonight."

At last the protesting pipe inches down the channel gouged out of the red brickwork. I wipe the sweat from my brow and drink some tea. "We're almost there."

I lean on the pipe to lever the bracket from the wall. It won't budge.

"What's wrong?" Emma whispers.

"Nothing. Talk loudly to drown any noise." I sit on the floor, hold the pipe with both hands, brace my legs against the wall, and pull. Emma chatters on about what she wants to do at college. The bracket begins to move. I pause, grasp the pipe tightly, and strain with arms and legs. The pipe trembles. Suddenly I'm on my back. Emma falls silent. The pipe is bent in two, the bracket is still fixed to the wall.

"Are you hurt?" Emma asks.

In a rage I grab the bracket and wrench at it.

"Brilliant!" Emma says.

The stubborn bracket lies in my hand. "Right. Back to work." I tear off bits of toast, dunk them in the tea, squeeze them into the screw holes, replace the bracket, and push the screws back in until they're flush with the bracket and appear secure. With the handkerchief we share I wipe away the masonry dust, and then pull Emma's cot back to where it blocks the view of the bracket from the door. "Whenever Master Spotty or any of the others come in here, stand as far away as possible from the bracket, but always leave the chain slack."

"Right! Will you have some supper now?"

"We haven't finished. Hold your hands together." I take the small fluffy towel from the beam, wrap it round her wrists, and attempt to tie a secure knot. "See if you can get out of that."

Within minutes she's free. We have nothing that will bind the Boy's hands and feet and gag him.

"What will you do?" Emma asks.

"Don't worry. I'll think of something." I already have.

•   •   •

The Boy knocks before opening the loft door, apologizes for asking me to put the hood back on, and leads me back to the bullpen.

"Do your people come from Leinster, Father?" he asks after closing the bullpen door behind him and removing my hood. He now trusts me to the extent that he keeps his gun in his anorak pocket. It will be easy to overpower him and obtain that gun.

"No."

"Then they're from Galway," he says.

"Right. How do you know?"

"If you're not one of the Norman Darcys who settled in Leinster, then it's a fair bet you're from one of the fourteen tribes of Galway. Your Irish name is Ó Dorchaide, you know."

He kneels to lock my manacle. As the top of the black woollen balaclava leans forward, I pick out the spot where a good hard blow with the butt of the gun should knock him out for half an hour. "Is that right? What does the name mean?"

"It's from the Irish *dorcha* which means dark," he says proudly. "So you must be a dark one then, Father."

I try not to smile. "Do you know Galway?"

"The one holiday we had was a week in Clifden."

I need to keep him talking, to build on the relationship I've established and increase his trust in me. "What did you like best?"

"The Sky road. It was magic."

I feign interest. "Tell me all about it."

The eyes behind the spectacles focus on a happy memory. "Clifden's in a narrow bay. The Sky road climbs up from Clifden and out along the coast."

"What can you see?"

"Inland there's the Beanna Beola—Twelve Pins in English—a ring of granite peaks rising like dark blue sentinels from the brown moors. And on the left the turf and the gorse fall away into inlets where fishermen use currachs. Peat is piled outside their wee white cottages. I tried to speak to two women, but they only had Irish. It was just like the Ireland I'd always been told of. When we reached the furthest point we looked out across the sea to the islands. Ma said that if we looked hard enough we could see America. That's where she always dreamed of going, far away from the Troubles."

The Boy was born after the Troubles began; the poor bastard's never experienced anything else in Ireland but soldiers patroling the streets and daily body searches, except for one week in the South.

"Have you ever been to Galway, Father?"

"I sure have."

"What did you think of it?"

"It was the friendliest place I ever visited."

The bullpen doors open and the Chief walks through. A cold draft sends the light bulb swinging on its flex.

The Chief stares at the Boy.

"I was just coming," the Boy says.

The Chief nods and the Boy leaves.

"Maitland has replied to your letter," the Chief says.

I can't tell from his tone or his eyes whether this is good or bad news.

"He's insisting on conditions." The small blue irises in the large white eyes scrutinise my reactions. I remain impassive, sitting on the cot while he stands, legs astride and hands in the pockets of his brown cord pants.

"The first condition," the Chief says, "is that the meeting takes place on neutral ground in the open. The second is that, if he is to be alone, then so must the IRA man. The third condition is that you and his daughter are released before the

talks begin. Now," he says, folding his arms across the chest
of his tweed jacket, "what do you think we should do?"

"It seems to me," I say cautiously, "that his terms are not
unreasonable."

He lowers his eyes in thought, and then slowly raises
them. The corners of his thin-lipped mouth relax their expression of grim determination. "I agree," he says. "Congratulations, Father. You've done well. You've earned your
freedom."

He leaves the bullpen, closes the lower stable door behind him, and slides the bar across.

"When will you meet him?" I call out.

"As soon as we've made arrangements for the rendezvous. Sleep well." He closes the top half of the stable
door and switches off the light.

I take off my priest's collar and lie down on the cot, hardly
daring to believe my good fortune. Tonight death no longer
casts its shadow over me. Tonight I will sleep soundly for the
first time since my capture.

I close my eyes and see the blackness of the Boy's balaclava. I see the point where I'm about to strike him. And I
know that I was deluding myself. No blow like that with a
gun butt can be precise enough to knock him unconscious
for half an hour: it is just as likely to kill him. The realisa-
tion that I was prepared to murder the Boy in cold blood as
a means of freeing Emma burrows into my peace.

Thank God I've been spared having to choose between
killing the Boy and putting Emma's escape in jeopardy. It's
as though my prayers have been answered after I offered my
life in exchange for Emma's freedom. But what sort of life
have I offered? A life in which I conducted a smear campaign to try and oust an elected British prime minister, in
which I helped engineer the United States' invasion of

Grenada, a tiny island which posed no security threat to us, in which . . . but the list is endless.

Why should I torment myself with these memories of the past? It's nothing more than a Catholic guilt complex. Give me a child at the age of seven, the Jesuits say, and we'll make him God's for life. Between them the Sisters of Charity, Father Curran, and the Jesuits had me from the ages of six to twenty two. Little wonder that the need to atone for sin still lurks in my subconscious.

But what did I do that was so very wrong? Was it not these selfsame priests who encouraged me to fight evil? Whatever means I used, I did so for the greater good.

I turn over and breathe slowly, relaxing each muscle group in turn to induce sleep. Springs in the cot which I have never felt before press into my body. Sleep will not come. I get up and inch my way in the dark as far as the chain will allow toward the window. If I concentrate I should be able to detect the gaps in the shutters by slithers of less intense black, narrow slits into a night softened by starlight. But all is an unrelieved black. Have I lost my bearings even in this tiny cell?

What happened to my ambition to help those who ain't got it so good? My desire to help my country preserve the free world from tyranny? I can't just blame individual station chiefs, or even the whole of Latin American Division. Moral corruption permeated the organization from top to bottom. And that included me. CIA wasn't interested in genuine intelligence if it contradicted our policies, and I needed no coercion to collect and disseminate "intelligence" designed to support our clandestine operations. By ignoring genuine intelligence, I contributed to the greatest of a whole string of CIA failures: the failure to identify the terminal weakness of the Soviet economy which caused the inevitable collapse of the Soviet empire. Covert action, not intelligence gathering, is the engine that drives CIA: what began as a means of countering Soviet subversion has become an end in itself. How can the overthrow of governments, the conducting of secret wars, the directing of terror programs, the burglarising and discrediting of US citizens who expose us, and the repeated lying to Congress advance the cause of human rights, freedom, and democracy which I set out to defend?

I can't even hear the whisper of the wind in the trees. In this cell I see nothing, hear nothing, smell nothing, taste nothing, and feel only the manacle round my ankle. But I am not alone. The ghosts of the last twenty five years silently ask how I could fail to see then what is patently clear now. They don't understand what it was to be part of CIA. So trapped in its clandestine mindset, so arrogant in its unaccountability, so convinced by its certainties, I failed to recognize when noble ideals distorted into brutal fantasies.

I try to retrace my steps, but the chain pulls me up sharp. I have to follow the chain back to its bolt in the wall and then grope from the wall before I find the cot.

It is always the certainties which breed the lies. In an Orwellian way those awful certainties transform reality and paralyze any ability to distinguish fact from fantasy. And this fantasy has become so powerful that it demands new enemies to feed on now the Soviet Union is no more.

In its certainties, too, the IRA's noble cause of liberating Ireland from colonial rule is no different from CIA's noble cause of protecting liberal democracy, its anti-British fanaticism no different from our anti-communist fanaticism, its terrorism no different from ours. But I can thank the IRA for two things. This isolation under threat of death has forced me to see clearly what I have been stumbling toward, and it has brought me close to the daughter I never knew I had. This reprieve gives me a second chance, an opportunity to walk away from the lying and the killing and the cover ups.

I lie down and pull the rough blanket over me. At forty-eight years of age it's not too late to make a fresh start, now that I know Jill has never stopped loving me. When Emma and I are released from here the three of us will plan a new life. I'll quit the company and we'll move far away from Washington and London and all places associated with the past. By summer Emma will have finished school and by the fall she'll probably be at Oxford University, so maybe we'll live in Oxford. No. I mustn't be possessive. She's now a young adult, with her own life to lead. Jill and I could move to California or Mexico or Canada. No. That would be too far for Emma. The west of Ireland? Yes! Where I encountered nothing but friendliness. There are two theaters in Galway city, and Dublin is less than two hours' drive away. What would I do? The Irish government doesn't tax an author's income from royalties. I've always wanted to write. Perhaps I'll write a novel. Not the kind of glamorised myth of how we patriotic white hats beat the dastardly black hats which the Agency's public relations people promote. I'll tell it how it really is.

Emma will stay with us during her Christmas and spring recesses and her summer vacations. There'll be so much to do and say. Not only will she get to know me, she'll get to know and appreciate the person Jill really is. It will take time, and it won't always be easy. Emma will come to see Jill in a new light. She'll see that the one thing that will stop Jill drinking is for her to stop living a lie. Once she's separated from Edward and living with me, Jill will be totally different from the person Emma despises. There will be big adjustments to make. It won't be easy for Emma—I've seen how she idolizes Edward. But Emma is a sensible, mature girl. We'll support her if she wants to spend the occasional weekend with Edward—if, indeed, he invites her—but I'm certain she'll soon come to appreciate what a real, loving family is.

Emma. Emma Darcy. It sounds good. The name flows much better than Emma Maitland. It could be the name of a romantic heroine, or an actress. I drift off into sleep, comforted by these plans for a new life. Plans or fantasies? Whatever, they're infinitely preferable to the fantasies I've been acting out over the past twenty-five years.

Chapter ✦ Forty

BRIGHT SUNLIGHT STREAMS through the gaps in the shutters, replacing the storm-laden gloom of recent days. At times like this God seems tantalisingly close, filling everything with a presence that is indefinable. It is not a spirit of omnipotence, or judgment, or even love. It is just there, waiting for me to open myself to it. But I hold back, in part fearing the demands it will make, in part dismissing the whole thing as a figment of my imagination, a projection by my subconscious of a need for certainty and reassurance.

The one thing in my life which is real and tangible is Emma.

"Have you heard the news?" I ask the Boy when he unlocks my manacle.

He nods.

"Isn't it terrific?"

"We should go for your breakfast now."

It's even warm enough this morning for him to have

discarded the anorak he's worn every time I've seen him. I put on the hood and let him guide me to the loft.

"It's been agreed!" I say to Emma as soon as we're on our own. "No need to risk breaking out," I whisper. "The Chief will free you when Edward arrives."

We hug each other. She leans back and looks into my eyes—just like Jill did—and laughs with joy.

"Didn't I tell you that Daddy would come and set us free?"

Nothing's perfect.

"And you promised that you'd tell me all these secrets about yourself," she adds.

"I always keep my promises."

"When?"

"When we're released."

"When will that be?"

My mind has been so focused on reforming my life, ridding it of all the delusions of the past, that I've omitted to deal with the immediate future. I won't survive to enjoy the fruits of this new start unless the rendezvous has been arranged before Saturday. "Let's find out." I knock on the loft door.

The bolt slides back and the door opens to disclose the Boy gripping his gun.

I put up my hands. "OK, sheriff, you caught me fair and square, I did it."

Emma giggles, but no smile softens the Boy's grim stare. "Come in," I say. "I only wanted to ask when your chief has arranged the meeting with Edward Maitland."

The Boy hesitates in the doorway before coming inside and closing the door behind him. He stands there in an argyle sweater and shapeless jeans, not knowing where to put his semiautomatic now that he can't stick it in his anorak pocket. "Tomorrow afternoon," he mumbles through his balaclava mask.

I could almost hug him.

Although he's speaking to me he's staring at Emma. I can't blame any boy of his age; she is beautiful.

Emma is also conscious of his stare. "What are you looking at?" she asks, her green eyes glinting flirtatiously like Jill's.

He turns away to face me. It's not longing I see in his eyes but fear. "Father, was Maitland responsible for the Cheltenham bombing?"

Emma's eyes blaze like a wild animal's. "How dare you! Get out! GET OUT!"

The Boy backs away and seeks the safety of the door, but I get there first and push it closed again. "Why do you ask?"

"Because he's an Irish . . ." Emma begins.

"Quiet, Emma!" I order. The Boy and I stand next to the door. The eyes behind his spectacle lenses seem close to tears and his lower lip trembles. "I think you'd better sit down, my son, and tell me what's troubling you," I say gently.

He lowers his gangling frame onto the cot. He seems all arms and legs. He puts the gun on the cot beside him and stares at the floor. "Last night they told me that the Cheltenham bombing was ordered by the same MI5 officer who leaked British security files on IRA members to loyalist death squads during his last tour of the Six Counties. The name of the officer was Edward Maitland."

"That's a lie!"

"Quiet, Emma!" I repeat. "Go on," I say to the Boy.

He says nothing, but continues to stare down at the floor.

I sit down on the cot next to him. "You trust me, don't you?"

He nods.

"Then tell me how you became involved in all this."

When he does speak, it is with his head bowed, as though

he is admitting his sins in a confessional. "The woman came before Christmas, Father. She said they needed to talk with MI5's counterterrorism chief, to prove to him that they hadn't been responsible for Cheltenham. Because the Brits had cut off all contact, the only way was to lure him to a meeting using his daughter as bait." He pauses and looks up for a response.

I nod encouragingly.

"She asked my aunt to find out what she could about the school where his daughter was. She asked me to find a safe house between Brighton and London. Later she asked me to check Maitland for hidden microphones or any other electronics." He glances toward Emma. "I agreed to help, Father, because the Provos said this meeting would get the peace process restarted."

"There's nothing to be ashamed of in that," I say. I glare at Emma, willing her to silence. She doesn't understand, but she complies.

"What do you need to tell me?" I coax.

He stares down at the floor again. "They're not going to release you."

"I told you it was a trap!" Emma accuses me.

"Your chief gave me his word. Did the woman talk him out of it?"

He shakes his head. "From what he said last night, he's never had any intention of letting Emma go, either when he first sent the ransom demand or when he had your letter delivered. It seems he's done it before with touts who've gone into hiding. He's given his word to their families that no harm will come to the suspects if they come back and answer a few questions. When they arrive for the meeting they get taken off and shot."

Emma is sitting on the floor, hugging her legs. Her face is white. The defiant glint of the wildcat green eyes has changed to the nervous flicker of a trapped animal.

"How does he square that with his conscience?" I ask.

The Boy shakes his head. "He says the ends justify the means, Father. Touts cause the deaths of volunteers by informing on them. They must be eliminated to protect our volunteers and to show potential touts that there's no hiding place if they do inform on us."

"Edward Maitland is no informer."

"The Chief says he's worse. He's wrecked our whole strategy. Unless we can get back to the peace process, the war will start again and hundreds more volunteers will go to their deaths. Maitland will have their blood on his hands."

"But he told me that if he wanted to have Maitland killed he could have had him shot or bombed in London."

The Boy bites his lip. "He's got a video camera. He intends to film Maitland giving all the details of how he set up the Cheltenham bombing. He says it'll turn the tables on the Brits. When people in America see the confession on television, admitting what the Brits are doing to prevent a peaceful solution for the Six Counties, there'll be such an outcry that the Brits will be forced to withdraw from Ireland for good."

Suddenly I'm struck by the thought that this is a trap, a stratagem to lull us into implicating Maitland in the Cheltenham bombing. "That's absurd. Maitland isn't going to read your script into a video camera unless you torture him, and that will be obvious on film."

The Boy glances at Emma again. "The woman says that if the Brits can get the Guildford Four and the Birmingham Six to confess to crimes they didn't commit, then she can get Maitland to confess to one he did—if he's got a drop of father's blood in him."

I get up from the cot and go to sit down on the floor next to Emma. I put my arm round her shoulders. Her whole body is shaking, but she refuses to cry. I wish she would, but she's determined not to show her fear. We must break out of this place today. But dare I confide in the Boy? It would be so much easier with his cooperation. I think he's genuine, but all the instincts cultivated during a quarter century of deception scream out never to trust anyone. The Chief's duplicity reinforces these instincts. We need the cover of darkness. I can delay telling the Boy about the loosened bracket until he has proved beyond all doubt that he's on our side.

"What do you intend to do?" I ask him.

He shakes his head helplessly. "I don't know, Father. I'm scared stiff. If they find out that I've told you this, they'll kill me, sure they will. They frightened me even before they told me they weren't going to let you go. The one with the moustache, he boasted about how many people he's shot. Not just Brits. Catholics. People who refused to pay the war tax."

"You mean protection money."

"They're no different than the Brits. I didn't join to be part of . . . of this."

"How do they plan to meet Maitland's conditions?"

He hesitates. I hold Emma close and say, "Don't worry. He won't let them harm you."

"After I take you back to the bullpen," he says, "I'm to find a place in Ashdown Forest, a clearing overlooked by trees where a second volunteer can hide, check that Maitland is on his own, and then surprise him while the one with the moustache pretends to release you and begin talks with Maitland."

"The Chief isn't going to meet Maitland?"

"It was decided it would be too risky to expose him, in case Maitland comes with a back up. The one with a moustache volunteered to bring Maitland in."

"What transport do you have?"

"A car and a van."

"Will you help us escape?"

He looks up mournfully. "How can I?"

"You could release Emma."

"I can't. I've told you. I've only got the key for your manacle, the Chief keeps the key for Emma's."

"Supposing I were to say that we don't need the key. Will
you help us then?"

He shakes his head. "I wish to God I'd never got involved
in this."

"But you are involved, my son. And if you don't help
Emma escape, you will be just as guilty as they are for whatever happens to this innocent girl."

He sits there, hunched, staring at the floor. His hands
are clasped together, his knuckles white, his breathing fast
and erratic. "They'll kill me, so they will."

"No," I say firmly. "We all three can escape."

After what seems an age, he says, "What is it you want
me to do, Father?"

"Which vehicle are you using to find a meeting place?"

"The car."

"When you return, leave the car parked as near as possible to the barn, but out of sight of the house. Before you
bring us supper tonight, disable the van. That's not critical,
so if it places you in danger don't do it. But if you can do it
without arousing suspicion, put the van out of action. Bring
the car keys with you to supper. I'll have Emma released
from her chain. The three of us will take the car and drive
to safety."

Emma has stopped shuddering. She too is staring at the
Boy, willing him to agree, but his eyes are still searching the
gaps between the floorboards for some magical means of escape. Slowly he raises his balaclavaed head and looks straight
at me. "Can you promise me, Father, that Maitland didn't
plant the Cheltenham bomb?"

It all fits into a pattern: Maitland leaking security files
to loyalist paramilitaries on his last assignment to Northern
Ireland; Maitland being removed to Grenada to avoid a
shoot-to-kill inquiry on his previous assignment; and

Maitland spending most of his time on his first assignment at Castledillon—the top-secret intelligence base from where, the Chief alleged, the Dublin and Monaghan bombings had been planned. It would explain why Maitland assigned the inexperienced Jennifer Ackroyd as Cheltenham case officer and why he keeps personal control of all reports to the Joint Intelligence Committee on the bombing. But I banish these thoughts. There is only one thing I want in this world and that is to save Emma. I look him in the eye and say, "I promise you that Emma's father is innocent."

He nods. "Will you promise me one other thing, Father?"

I look into the frightened eyes of a young man who desperately seeks the courage not to compromise his ideals. "What is it, my son?"

"If I help you, the IRA will pass a death sentence on me. Will you promise to protect me?"

I promise him, just as I promised Alfonso García.

Chapter ✣ Forty-one

WHEN I MADE my promise to Alfonso García I fully intended to keep it. I was, after all, a senior case officer in our San Salvador station, transferred there with a promotion after the success of my mission in Grenada.

At the time I was haunted by the image of Father Inocencio Chávez's naked body in the trunk of a Buick. My failure to prevent his murder made me determined to track down his killers. García hinted that he might have information for sale and so I left a message with his wife for him to meet me away from ANTEL headquarters and the embassy.

As I sat near the open-air pool in the Sheraton Hotel and the time for the assignation passed, I realized I'd made a mistake. The place was too public and out of García's class: if he had any sense he wouldn't turn up.

I stood up to leave and saw García's face, pitted like a pineapple, emerge from the dark interior into the sunshine. He ambled over and, dressed in red nylon shirt and jeans, sat down at my table and surveyed with satisfaction the disdainful Salvadoran families whose clothes had been bought in New York or Paris. A waiter came from the thatched bar. I ordered a Jim Beam and club soda. García pointed toward the nearest table and said that he would have one of those drinks with pieces of fruit and tropical flowers attached to the rim.

I asked what he knew about the White Warriors Union, which had made the death threat to Chávez.

"Señor," he said, adopting the nonchalant posture of the man at the nearest table, "you employ me to give you copies of telephone taps. Do you wish to employ me to provide you with other information?"

I placed ten ten-dollar bills on the glass-topped table.

His natural demeanor reasserted itself: he scooped up the notes, took off one boot, put the notes inside, and replaced the boot. "Did you see how they tied him up?"

"His hands were tied behind his back."

García looked round and lowered his voice. "No, no, señor. Not his hands. His thumbs. And no signs of torture. And his throat was slit."

"Is that a sign of the White Warriors Union?"

A knowing smile creased his pockmarked face. "The Treasury Police." He gulped down the cocktail.

I called for more drinks. After the waiter left I said, "Are you seriously trying to tell me that rogue officers from the Treasury Police killed Chávez and pinned the blame on the White Warriors Union?"

"There are no rogue officers in the Treasury Police, señor."

"Then who did kill Father Chávez? The Treasury Police or the White Warriors Union?"

"What I am telling you, señor," he confided, "is that the White Warriors Union, the Maximiliano Hernández Martínez Brigade, the White Hand, the Secret Anticommunist Army, and the rest of the death squads are phantoms." He leaned back in his wicker chair, once more a aspiring member of the Salvadoran élite, and studied my reaction. "I must leave soon, señor. I am a busy man, you understand."

It was a crude ploy, but I was determined to find out who was really responsible. Father Chávez had alleged that the death squads were paper covers for the government security forces, but when I put this to Frederick Bowland, our deputy chief of station, he confirmed what my contacts in the security forces had told me: the death squads were right-wing mavericks. "I'll make sure your time is compensated, but I want to know who murdered Chávez."

"I cannot give you names, señor, but I can tell you this. The death squads are made up of the Treasury Police or the National Guard or the Army, acting under orders from their superiors."

It's always difficult with paid informers to know when they're telling you the truth and when they're telling you what they think you will pay to hear. "That's absurd. I don't pay for rumors."

"Señor, I tell you truth, not rumors."

"How do I know?"

"Because, señor," he said grandly, "I have a friend in the Treasury Police, and he tells me about his special missions. But I cannot say more. You will understand that, as a businessman, I have obligations to my other clients."

"Two hundred dollars if you can prove what you say."

He looked at the wallet I put on the table. "What proof do you want? My friend, he will not tell to you what he tells to me when we drink together."

"What does your friend tell you?"

"That his commander says who to take to Treasury Police Headquarters, how to persuade them to talk, how to kill them, and where to dump their bodies so that they are blamed on death squads."

"How to kill them?"

"Sure. He says they must not use bullets, because their bullets can be traced back to the security services. This is what the American told them. This is why they slit Chávez's throat."

I tried to sound skeptical. "What American?"

"The one who gave them the machine that looks like a radio with wires coming out of it, the wires that you fix to a prisoner's feet or his prick. The American told them that electric shocks were the best way to persuade subversives to talk. Electric shocks don't make bruises or broken ribs, and so no one can prove they've been tortured."

"I don't believe this story of an American."

"Would I tell you a lie, señor?"

"What is the name of this American?"

"Señor, I do not know."

"If I'm to believe you, I must have his name."

Uncertainty and fear colored his voice. "It will cost much money."

"Another two hundred dollars."

He hesitated. "We are talking here of Americans, señor. They are worth more than Salvadorans. At least five times more."

"Five hundred dollars. And if it's not genuine the Treasury Police will find out that you've been talking to me."

His eyes darted round the tables in the open-air bar. "Señor," he pleaded in a whisper, "these things I tell you as business confidence. You cannot . . . you must not . . . betray me to the Treasury Police. I have a wife and seven children."

"You've nothing to fear if your information is true."

"You promise to protect me if I get this information for you?"

"I promise."

"On your mother's grave?"

"On my mother's grave."

•   °   °

Half a dozen unshaven Treasury Police, wearing mirrored sunglasses, dark green sweat-stained uniforms of shiny artificial fiber, holstered revolvers, and cartridge belts with many cartridges missing lounged in the shade of the graffiti-daubed gray walls of the cathedral. I walked past them, crossed the main square where urban peasants bustled between fly-buzzing market stalls and makeshift awnings, and headed for the protective concrete outer walls of the embassy compound.

For once I paid no heed to the blood-red slogans denouncing American imperialism and supporting the FMLN which appeared overnight beneath the marine guard's tinted glass sentry box set high in the bombproof wall. I was exhilarated. I had been in San Salvador less than three months but, if García proved reliable, I was about to find out who really did organize the death squads.

I spent the afternoon in my air-conditioned open plan office preparing a field project outline. Three days later Frederick Bowland invited me for a meeting. Bowland had his own office, with his own Stars and Stripes behind his desk and his own picture of President Reagan on the wall, his own iced water machine, and his own view over the swimming pool. With his neatly combed hair, hornrimmed spectacles, constant smile, and portraits of a loving wife and healthy children on his desk, he might have been the successful vice president of a Florida property development company.

"John, make yourself at home," he said, indicating a comfortable chair on the other side of his desk. "I'd like to say how pleased we all are with the progress you've made in so short a time." He looked down at a file on his desk. "But that's not surprising for an officer who's been awarded the Agency's Medal of Merit."

I shrugged modestly. "I was lucky to know someone in Grenada who helped swing things our way."

"Let me assure you, John, that the company never awards medals for luck. I can see why Flashy was so eager to have you on board. Because, make no mistake, John, this is where the cold war will be won or lost. But with your background in countersubversion and Soviet Bloc I don't have to tell you that."

His confident, confiding manner, his way of treating you as one of the select, was irresistible. He picked up another file. "I've given great consideration to your field project outline—and may I say, John, how well you've set out your proposal. It does, however, throw up a few problems. Take the agent you suggest. I fear that García is not reliable."

"The station has used him regularly for taps when we didn't want to go through ANTEL."

"And he's proved competent there. But it seems to me that he's overreaching himself if he claims he can inform on the Treasury Police. Besides, why pay the monkey when we control the organ grinder?"

"I don't understand."

"John, I see you as a comer here, one of the people destined for the top. May I share with you some strictly confidential information?"

I was flattered. "Of course."

"I knew I could rely on you, John." He smiled. "Colonel Nicholas Carranza is on our payroll."

"The head of the Treasury Police!"

"Even in the short time you've been with us, John, I'm sure you've seen how this is a totally different ball game from what you've been used to. In Soviet Bloc you were fighting them hand to hand, so to speak. Here it's done through proxies. The Soviets are using the Cubans and Nicaraguans and we have to use what's available."

"The death squads?"

He took off his hornrimmed spectacles and pondered the question before he answered. "No doubt some of Carranza's people take the view that you have to fight terror with terror."

"What about Father Chávez? I had him under surveillance for two months. There was no evidence that he was a member of the FMLN, still less a Soviet agent."

Bowland appeared pained. "I guess it's always difficult to distinguish between paid up members of a terrorist organization and those who give them support and encouragement."

"Are you justifying the torture and murder of priests and nuns?"

"Certainly not, John. When Director Casey paid us a secret visit last summer, he met with Carranza and told him straight: the publicity generated by death squads killing US citizens is counterproductive; it just makes Congress block the administration's military assistance to El Salvador."

"Congress has got it right for once."

A frown crossed his brow. "John, you and I may have doubts about a particular operation, about some things that may go wrong. But, unlike certain people on the Hill, you and I can see the big picture." He stood up and examined the world map on the wall opposite his window overlooking the pool. "In the forties and fifties the Soviets went for Europe and took half of it. In the sixties they and the Chinese wrapped up most of Asia. In the seventies, while the administration was running around like a headless chicken over Vietnam and Watergate, the Soviets made big gains in Africa. Now they're making their biggest play of all: they're spreading their evil empire to the Americas. You helped kick them out of Grenada, but they've still got Cuba and Nicaragua, and I tell you, John, on a strictly confidential basis, our assessment is that Honduras, Guatemala, and El Salvador are in grave danger right now. If we lose here, the

Soviets control the strategic waist of the American conti-
nent. And after that? My guess is they'll go south first,
weaken us economically by cutting off our sources of raw
materials and our markets for manufctured goods in South
America. Then it's up to Mexico, southern California, use
the Blacks to destabilise our inner cities and . . ." He returned to his desk and looked at the photographs of his children. ". . . And I can't bear to think any further."

I heard no more about my proposed operation to identify death squad members. When I next met Alfonso García to arrange some telephone taps, he told me his wife had
just had another baby and he wanted to earn more money
as an informer. As proof of his usefulness, he said, he would
give me the name of the American I'd asked for. It was
Frederick Bowland.

After García's body was found at La Puerta del Diablo, the
lava outcrop where we had discovered Father Chávez's
body, I asked for a transfer back to Soviet Bloc. Before I left
I sought out García's widow and gave her what was left in
my bank account in San Salvador. I told her it was for a
promise that I failed to keep.

This time I will keep my promise. I won't resign from the
company until I've arranged for the Boy to be given a new
identity and a new life in the United States, out of reach of
any IRA executioner.

Darkness has already fallen. Supper can't be far away.

The bars grate on the outer stable door, the light is
switched on, and the upper half of the bullpen door
opens. I stand up to greet the Boy and finalise details of our
escape.

A tray is thrust through. "Your supper," says the Woman

Chapter ✣ Forty-two

SUNLIGHT STREAMS THROUGH the gaps in the shutters again this Friday morning, but I no longer feel the presence of God, only a sense of abandonment. Why didn't the Boy come last night and help Emma escape from these fanatics? Did they catch him trying to disable the van? Or was he a plant? Was it a deliberate ruse by the Chief to have the Boy befriend us and gain our confidence in order to find out what I know of the Cheltenham bombing? I have a horrible feeling that breakfast will provide the answer.

"Take your breakfast," says the Woman, holding a tray through the opened upper half of the bullpen door.

"The Chief promised I could have my meals with the girl," I protest.

"I haven't got all day. If you want to eat, take the tray."

I carry the tray back to the cot. She doesn't come into the bullpen. "Where's the tall young man?" I ask.

"So, it's the cozy chats with himself that you're really

missing, is it?" She leans over the lower half of the door and nods toward the slop bucket. "I'll empty that after lunch."

Lunch also fails to provide the answer. Afterwards I lie down on the cot. Panic rises. Slowly at first, and then it grips me completely. What's happened to Emma? Thank God I didn't confide in the Boy that I'd already freed Emma's chain from the wall. Will they discover the loosened bracket when they unmanacle Emma this afternoon in order to use her to trap Maitland? What will they do with me now?

The bars slide back from the door. Both halves open. The masked Killer comes into the bullpen and throws me a black woollen scarf. "Tie this round yer eyes."

"Why?"

"Yer goin' out."

"Where?"

"Didn't we promise to set you free?"

Why a scarf instead of the hood? I wrap it round my head and tie it at the back.

"On the floor with ye."

I sit on the floor with my legs straight out in front. The Killer tightens the knot and spreads the scarf wider over my face, cutting out the narrow gap that I left in order to peer down. The key turns in the lock and the manacle falls from my ankle.

"On yer feet."

I stand up. He presses what feels like the muzzle of his gun into the small of my back and pushes my right shoulder. I grope for the jamb of the bullpen door, take two steps and feel the jamb of the stable door. As I begin to head forward across the cobbles, my right shoulder is pulled round. "Straight on," says the hard clipped West Belfast voice.

After twenty-one paces his arm brings me to a halt. He brushes past and I hear a gate open. "Come on, you."

I feel my way through the opened gate and he turns me roughly to the right. I tread blindly over a dirt surface, he wheels me to the right again, and I stumble forward until my head bangs into a metal wall.

"Mind you don't walk into the van," he sniggers.

"Where's Emma?" I ask.

"Get in the fuckin' van." He pushes me and I feel my way round to the opened door at the back of the van.

I step up into the van, reach out, and touch a knee.

"No!" a frightened voice cries.

"It's only me," I say to Emma.

"Sorry, I'm blindfolded."

"So am I." What is the hood being used for?

I grope for the bench along the wall of the van and sit down next to Emma. Instinctively we fumble until we touch hands. She grips mine tightly. "It'll be all right," I soothe.

"Touch those blindfolds an' ye'll wish ye'd never bin born," the Killer says. The doors clang shut. I haven't heard him climb into the van. If he were here I'd smell his body odor. I pull the blindfold down just far enough to see. No one else is in the back of the van. There are no windows to look out of. Two doors—presumably the driver and passenger doors—slam shut.

"Why didn't Master Spotty . . ."

"Shush," I say to Emma.

A diesel engine turns over and splutters into life. The van lurches forward. I visualize a clock starting at twelve and the second finger ticking round the large white clock face. The van stops, a gate creaks, and then we bump down a dirt track for about five minutes before stopping again. Drones rise to roars and then fade away as cars and trucks speed past us. When the sounds cease the van swings right onto a smooth surface. This road winds uphill through a series of

Z-bends and reaches a stretch where there's a whooshing sound and a buffeting as vehicles pass us on the other side. After this we stop, wait for a gap in the traffic, and make a long left onto a blacktop that's bumpier than the road we've left. The van is using the same route into Ashdown Forest that the car took leaving it six long days ago.

The van runs easily, but only for about fifteen seconds before the gears are changed down as it begins to pull up-hill.

Emma is shaking. I put my arm round her. "I don't know what happened to Master Spotty," I whisper. "Did they notice the bracket had been loosened?"

"No. I stood on the other side of the camp bed and kept the chain slack, just like you told me."

"Well done, Emma."

"I couldn't sleep last night. I've been scared stiff all day."

"Don't worry, I'll see that no harm comes to you."

She holds onto me tightly. "I feel safe with you."

Emma is the one thing these bastards will never take from me while there's breath left in my body, no matter what's needed to stop them.

The van takes a left instead of a right. We're not following the route back to Townsend's parking lot.

"What will happen to Daddy?" Emma whispers.

"Edward's trained to look after himself," I say. I hope I'm right. I'd almost believed Maitland was responsible for Cheltenham. My loathing for him was enough to turn circumstantial evidence into a conviction of guilt. Though I hate to admit it, Maitland was correct in his analysis. The peace talks on the future of Northern Ireland hadn't been going well for the IRA, and the Cheltenham bombing had backfired on them. The planned propaganda spectacular that Todd Fraser had learned of in Dublin was a brilliant ploy to turn the tables. A videoed confession from the head of MI5's Terrorism Directorate that he had organized the Cheltenham bombing to destroy the peace process would provoke an international outcry and force a British withdrawal from Ireland.

The protesting engine labors up a long climb until it reaches the relief of a level road. A couple of minutes later the van swings right onto a rough surface and stops. Gears grind as the van maneuvers back and round before straightening up and coming to a halt.

I estimate that we're roughly four miles from the farm.

The door handle turns. I put back the blindfold.

Someone climbs in. The confined space reeks of the Killer's odor.

"Turn to your right and take off your blindfolds," he says. "But I warn youse not to look back."

Emma's fingernails bite into the palm of my left hand. The opened doors of the van reveal the gravel surface of a pull-off. Beyond, a grass path cuts a swath about a hundred yards long through gorse in yellow bloom, leading up to the crest of a hill where a clump of evergreen trees is outlined against a clear blue sky.

"Get down and walk toward those trees. Don't look back. Remember, I'm behind youse with a gun in me pocket."

I clamber down first. As I help Emma I sneak a look. An anorak hood covers the Killer's head and a black scarf hides the lower half of his face. I can't see the second IRA member.

Emma and I walk hand in hand toward the trees. I strain to hear who is behind us, but the worn grass path betrays no telltale sounds. When it reaches the pine trees, the path skirts round the right edge of the clump.

"Follow the path past the trees," the Killer instructs from behind.

I think I hear feet swishing through long grass, but I can't be sure.

The path circles halfway round the clump of trees and then leads down a slope to a clearing, in the middle of which is a bench facing away from us.

"Sit down on the bench and look straight ahead," the Killer calls out.

I glance back. The Killer is waiting by the side of the clump. The Boy has chosen this deserted spot well. From the Killer's vantage point at the crest of the hill he can see down one side to the road and the path leading up from the pull-off, and down this side to the bench where Emma and I are seated. The clump of trees shields us from the road and the pull-off. It is also ideal for hiding the second IRA member.

My first instinct is to make a break for it now. But the only path through the gorse away from the Killer leads straight down the hill. The Killer would only need to shoot down the path and he couldn't fail to hit us. We've no alternative but to wait for Maitland. Any back up he brings by road will be spotted by the Killer well in advance. The only hope is a surprise attack from the air by helicopter.

Like lovers, Emma and I sit on the bench, hold hands, and gaze at the view. The path continues downhill, past the gorse and on through long coarse yellow grass to a valley floor hidden by dense pine and birch. The other side of the valley is covered by yellow grassland mottled with coppery remnants of dead fern and purple-brown patches of heather, softened by a golden glow from the sun behind our backs. The straight line of the horizon occasionally emits flashes of silver as the sun picks out the windows of a car passing down the road on the opposite ridge.

If green sward replaced the heath I could be back in the rolling valleys and ridges of the Sussex downs to which we escaped on a sunny March weekend shortly after CBS had reported President Ford warning senators that further investigations into CIA might uncover assassination attempts on foreign leaders.

"How come they're called downs?" I said after we'd walked up the steep path from Eastbourne to the clifftop at Beachy Head, and climbed the seven turf-covered chalk promontories she called the Seven Sisters. "They seem all ups to me."

A breeze from the sea blew Jill's long red hair across her face. She pushed her hair back behind her ears and pouted. "Your problem is that you're a simple city boy from New York who prefers to travel by car."

"And your problem is that you're a randy country maid who prefers to make love in walking boots."

"John Darcy, how dare you!"

"Have you ever made love in walking boots?"

"I refuse to answer that question."

"Well, you're about to now."

The wildcat green eyes glinted with challenge. She turned and fled inland, along the valley toward a copse. I chased after the swirling red hair, the billowing anorak, and the flailing jeans. I caught her when she reached a hollow sheltered by bushes, and pulled her down to the soft springy turf. We tumbled into the hollow and I rolled on top of her.

"They can see us from the South Downs Way!" she panted as my hand slid up underneath her Aran sweater.

My mouth stifled further protest. Her body stopped struggling when my hand moved down to the zipper of her jeans. The panting increased, turned to gasps, and finally into cries that mingled with those of the gulls circling overhead.

"What are you thinking?" Emma asks.

I look at those same glinting green eyes, the same tilt of the head when she asks a question, and the same habit of running her fingers through her long hair when she's nervous. "Of a time before you were born."

A shadow steals across the valley. Above, a sparrow hawk glides across the sun, searching for its prey.

"He's coming," the Killer calls.

The Killer comes down the path to the clearing. He stands with one cowboy boot on the bench, facing back up the path.

"Emma?" It's Maitland's voice.

She turns round and shrieks, "Daddy!"

Maitland, dressed in an olive-green Barbour field jacket and brown cavalry twill pants, walks down the path into the trap the IRA have set for him.

I grasp Emma's hand but she struggles free and runs toward him. They meet halfway between the bench and the clump of pines, and she flings her arms around him. He holds her protectively and looks at me. Is it my imagination or is there a gleam of triumph in his eyes? I don't like the way he's holding Emma. She's in the Killer's line of fire.

"I'm alone, as you see," Maitland says to the Killer. "As good as my word. Now I want Emma safely out of your way in my car before we begin talking. Father Darcy will remain as an impartial witness."

What's Maitland's game? Is he relying on me to help overpower someone he thinks is a lone IRA delegate, or does he genuinely want to talk about restoring the peace process?

"It's not you givin' the orders round here, Maitland," the Killer says. "Take a look behind youse."

Maitland looks over his shoulder. The Boy emerges from the pine clump. I was wrong about the pimples. The face below his cropped hair is unmarked and tense. The eyes behind the wire-framed spectacles are focused in a way I've not seen before. The right arm is held out straight. The right hand grips a semiautomatic pistol.

"No!" Emma cries.

"Quiet, you!" the Killer says, and unzips his anorak to reach for his Smith & Wesson.

"Throw away your gun."

The Boy has reached Maitland. His pistol points past him at the Killer.

"What the fuck!" the Killer exclaims.

Maitland disentangles himself from Emma, glances at the way the Boy is holding his gun, reaches across, takes it from him, swiftly redirects the barrel at the Killer, flicks off the safety catch, and pulls back the charging lever. "I think I'd better handle this," he says with that icy smile of his. "Now do what your young friend asked," he says to the Killer, "but make sure you are holding the barrel when you remove your gun or else . . . well, I'm sure you're familiar with the rest of the saying."

With a volley of curses directed at the Boy, the Killer complies.

"I suggest you pick up his gun," Maitland says to me, "check that it's in good working order, and then keep these two amused while I take Emma back to the car."

I too comply. The Killer turns to me, but stops when he hears the click of the safety catch release and sees the way I hold the Smith & Wesson. "I'm afraid I have used one of these before," I say.

"Some fuckin' priest you are," he says.

Maitland laughs. "Come on, old thing," he says to Emma. "Let's take you away from all these nasty men."

The Killer's anorak hood has dropped back and the scarf has fallen away from his face. Without his terrorist's black balaclava mask he is far less intimidating. He even seems smaller. The straggly black moustache and protruding teeth sit on a weasel face below unkempt hair. He looks like one of life's losers, the one who left school without qualifications, the one who is permanently unemployed, the one whom girls laugh at behind his back, the one whose lack of articulacy manifests in violent outbursts. I suppose that being a volunteer in the Irish Republican Army has given him some element of self-respect, has even legitimised in his own eyes his natural aggression. "As for you," he snarls at the Boy, "you know what happens to touts. Yer a walkin' corpse, so ye are."

"It's not like that," the Boy's ashen face protests. "We agreed to release Maitland's daughter and Father Darcy. Maitland agreed to come here to talk about how the peace process could be restarted. We can still do that." He appeals to me. "Isn't that right, Father?"

"That's right," I say. "For God's sake, take this opportunity to end the violence once and for all."

"Ye wouldn't be sayin' that if the SAS had dragged you back from over the border and hammered ye stupid."

"But can't you see," the Boy pleads, "someone's got to stop the violence. Let's give peace a chance."

"Splendid sentiments, though not entirely original. I believe it's the title of a song by John Lennon." Maitland stands, hands in the pockets of his Barbour field jacket, at the edge of the clearing.

"Edward," I say, "Emma's safe. You've got the upper hand. Use it. Get them back to the negotiating table."

"I've no authority to negotiate nuthin'," the Killer mutters.

"I'll take the van and find a phone box," the Boy says. "I'll ask the Chief to come here, tell him the Brits are prepared to talk."

"How far away is he?" Maitland asks.

"Ten minutes' drive . . ."

"Tell him nuthin', ye stupid fucker," the Killer cuts in.

"There's no need to go to the trouble of finding a phone

box," Maitland says. He takes what looks like a mobile phone from his left pocket.

"How do you know the number?" the Boy asks.

That icy smile again. "Oh, I have his number." He presses a button. The uneasy stillness is broken by a muffled rumble. The Boy peers to his right and I follow his gaze. On a distant green hillside, roughly in the direction of the road from the pull-off, a puff of white smoke forms.

"What the fuck was that?" the Killer exclaims.

"Twenty thousand pounds well spent," Maitland replies.

It takes a moment for the Killer to grasp that the Samsonite case containing the ransom money was booby trapped. His face contorts in fury. "You said you checked that case, ye stupid fucker!"

All color has drained from the Boy's face. He looks as though he is about to vomit. "I swept it."

"Your sweeper wouldn't detect the Semtex which lined the outer casing," Maitland says, "nor the detonator. Officially, part of an IRA active service unit have just blown themselves up while preparing another bomb."

"Ye fuckin' dickhead! I told you we couldn't trust the Brits, so I did. Now you really are a walkin' corpse."

It's difficult to appreciate that the mangled bodies of the Chief and the Woman are now lying beneath the wreckage of the farmhouse: that puff of white smoke is so small, so distant. "Maitland, for God's sake, I gave my word . . ."

From the right hand pocket of his field jacket Maitland takes the Walther P-88 semiautomatic that I lent him, and attaches the silencer. "Did they intend to keep their word?" With his gloved hand he points the gun at the Boy. "You, over there, next to your friend."

"No!" I shout.

Maitland stares at me.

"I promised to protect the Boy if he helped us."

"That boy is dead meat, so he is," the Killer says.

"The boy, ah yes, an unexpected bonus," Maitland says. "I agree. He's in mortal danger and we must protect him." He swings the gun round toward the Killer, aims, and squeezes the trigger.

The phut seems innocuous. The Killer's head jerks back and a red-gray spray shoots out from the rear. His head rocks forward and his hands grope up, but fail to reach the small dark hole in the center of his forehead. His legs crumple and he collapses on the grass with a whimper.

"Another member of the Cheltenham bomb team has just experienced a hard arrest," says Maitland with satisfaction.

"Oh my God!" the Boy cries. "It *was* you. You did Cheltenham." He turns on me. "You promised me that Maitland didn't plant the bomb!"

"He was quite right. I didn't plant the bomb, nor did any member of the British Security Service," Maitland says with a supercilious smile. "It was a couple of reliable chaps who know a chap who used to work with me in Northern Ireland before he retired from the Army's Intelligence and Security Group."

The Boy puts his hands to his mouth. "And I thought I was helping to bring peace."

"Oh, but you are," Maitland says. "There's only one way to bring peace to Northern Ireland."

"The peace process . . ." the Boy begins.

"Bollocks. For twenty-five years I've been trying to counter an IRA terrorist campaign to achieve by violence what they've failed to achieve by the ballot box. I've seen that campaign take three thousand lives because the politicians haven't had the balls to do what's necessary. Now the IRA promise to stop killing innocent people, do you think we should reward them by overriding the views of the democratic majority?"

"But it's you, not the IRA, who killed fifteen innocent people in Cheltenham!" the Boy shrieks.

"Those coffins draped in the Stars and Stripes brought home to America just what Sinn Féin/IRA has been doing in Ulster for twenty-five years. That bomb is destroying Sinn Féin support where it matters. As soon as the White House pushes Dublin into a joint security operation with us, we'll go in on both sides of the border and finish off the IRA once and for all. Then, and only then, will there be peace in Northern Ireland. Fifteen deaths is a small price to pay."

"You murdering bastard," says the Boy.

"On the contrary," Maitland says, "think of how many lives I'm saving. Without Cheltenham, American pressure would lead to a united Ireland, and then loyalist paramilitaries would declare all-out war. I'm saving Ireland from turning into a Bosnia, don't you understand?"

"It's you and people like you who are the real terrorists!" the Boy screams.

"Oh dear," Maitland says. "I'm so sorry you don't see it my way. We'll have to decide what to do with you."

The car park at Coalisland is written all over the Boy's face. He looks round frantically, but there is no escape. He drops to his knees in front of me. "Oh my God! Do something! Help me, Father! You gave me your word!"

"Maitland!" I shout as he aims his gun. "I promised to protect the Boy. Without him, you and Emma would be dead."

"I very much doubt that. But you're right. I should be grateful that he helped." He lowers his gun.

I pull the Boy to his feet.

"I propose a suitable reward," Maitland says. "How would you like a quarter of a million pounds, a new identity, and a new life in Australia or Canada?"

The Boy looks from Maitland to me. "Take it," I say. "Get out of this mess. You're young. You've got your whole life ahead of you."

The Boy's eyes dart frantically between Maitland and me.

"All you have to do," Maitland says, "is testify that your late companions carried out the Cheltenham bombing."

"You fucking bastard!" The Boy launches himself at Maitland.

Maitland's first silenced shot stops him. The second smashes his spectacles.

I take three steps to where the Boy has fallen, drop the Smith & Wesson, and kneel to examine the crumpled body. Blood trickles from the dark hole where his left eye used to be. I don't even know his name.

"Father," he croaks. "P . . . pray . . . for me."

"Shush," I say. "Save your strength." But he's beyond saving.

"I . . . I've committed . . ."

He has no need of an apostate's prayers. He acted out of the highest motives and he's paid with his life. That is atonement enough for whatever sins he's committed.

He grips my hand. "Please, Father."

I release his grip and make the sign of the cross over him, saying the words he desperately wants to hear. "I absolve you from your sins, in the name of the Father and of the Son and of the Holy Spirit. Amen."

The right eye shows a flicker of recognition before dulling into unseeingness. Blood no longer trickles from the left eye socket.

"Very impressive," Maitland says. "I hope he went to hell a happy man."

I cradle the Boy's head in my arms. A sticky mess of brain, muscle, and blood smears my priest's black jacket. "Does your director general know about Cheltenham?"

"No one in the Service does. As for the DG, she thinks you can defeat the IRA with a computer. She doesn't know what it's really like out there in the field."

That's why Maitland used me and not the Security Service to try and rescue Emma. Not because he feared the IRA would find out he'd brought in the Security Service, but because he feared the Security Service would find out why the IRA had kidnapped Emma. I look up from where I'm kneeling. "Very neat. You'll provide the names the White House has demanded by identifying the IRA kidnap team as the Cheltenham bombers. Even if it does mean shooting an innocent boy like this in cold blood."

"It's a dirty war we're fighting. They don't obey any rules, so neither can we. You know that."

"He saved Emma's life. All he wanted was an end to violence."

Maitland puts the Walther back in his pocket. "Take off that priest's collar. Remember what you said in Grenada? The bottom line is: whose side are you on?"

Slowly I shake my head. "I was wrong. Something, someone, has to break the spiral of violence. This boy tried in his way."

Maitland raises his eyebrows. "This doesn't sound like the fearless anticommunist John Darcy that I knew."

I lay the Boy's head on the grass, next to the Smith & Wesson. "You're not going to get away with this. Or with the Cheltenham massacre."

Maitland stands there, legs astride, arms folded across his chest, looking down at me. He might almost be the Chief. "What, pray, do you intend to do? Write one of your bureaucratic field information reports?"

"I'll make sure this one gets to the very highest level, even if I have to break in the DCI's office to do it."

"Oh dear," he says with a sigh. "You never were much good at playing office politics, were you? Do you seriously imagine the CIA are going to jeopardize all the investments they've made in Britain since the Second World War? Especially," he says with one of his supercilious smiles, "when it boils down to your word against mine? Do they really value you so highly?"

"I'll find a way. I'll go public."

"Who's going to believe you rather than me? Will Emma support you?"

I feel sick to the stomach. We both know the answer to that question.

"Do you suppose the CIA will even let you try to go public? You wrote a note telling your station that you were going undercover to help me trap the Cheltenham bombers. It was your gun that killed these two terrorists. Undercover operatives cracking up under stress is very common."

The bastard has thought it all through. "They won't get a chance to stop me."

He removes a gun from his pocket. It's not the Walther, but the gun he took from the Boy. He'll kill me with an IRA gun after my gun has shot two of them. He really does think of everything.

"There is absolutely nothing you can do to prevent me from pinning responsibility for Cheltenham on this IRA unit, you know that. So why make a futile gesture? You'll either be treated as a psychiatric case courtesy of the CIA or I could shoot you now. Far more sensible for you to endorse my report and pick up another medal."

Still on my knees, I snatch the Smith & Wesson from the grass by the Boy's head and stare up at that expression of effortless superiority. I will him to make one move, just one tiny gesture so I can convince myself that I shot him in self-defense.

His hazel eyes examine me. "Let's not be foolish, John I meant what I said about your being under a great deal of stress. You've been through a lot this past week. What you need is a break, a holiday. You and Emma together. It's time she learned who her real father is. After you've helped me wrap up this business, I'll break it to her gently. I'm sure that's the only way, aren't you? Then you can spend time away from all this, father and daughter, getting to know each other."

I lower the Smith & Wesson. He smiles. "Good man. I knew you'd see reason."

He turns and walks up the path toward Emma. All I need do is follow him. What other choice do I have? One final cover up and then I really can quit the company and make a fresh start with Jill and Emma in the west of Ireland.

Maitland passes out of the shade of the pines. The sun, low in the sky, casts his long shadow over the smashed spectacles and crumpled body of the Boy who placed his trust in me.

"Maitland!" I call out, barely recognizing the despairing voice that echoes round the peaceful valley.

He turns, still holding the Boy's gun.

The Smith & Wesson almost explodes in my hand. It kicks back like a mule. Maitland staggers. His left hand grasps his side as he crumples and falls. Slowly I rise from my knees and walk toward him. His mouth gapes wide, his eyes stare blankly. There's no need to check for a pulse.

I didn't hear her running down the grass path. Emma thrusts me aside and drops on her knees to hug him. Her body convulses in sobs.

I stand there impotently, the Killer's gun in my hand. Finally I say, "Emma . . ."

She looks up at me, the front of her green tracksuit smeared red. The cry that emanates from my daughter's white contorted face is not human. It will stay with me to the grave. "You killed Daddy. You killed my Daddy! I HATE YOU!"

AUTHOR'S NOTE

Many of those who helped in the preparation of this novel wished to remain anonymous. It seems invidious to name some and not others, and so I shall simply express my gratitude to them all: they know who they are.

Responsibility for any errors and the use or interpretation of facts is entirely mine.

J. H.
London

JOHN HANDS has written two other novels, *Perestroika Christi* and *Darkness at Dawn*.

He has been published in eight countries, from the United States to Russia, and was shortlisted for the Deo Gloria Prize.

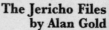